NW15

Bernardine Evaristo has written three novels which fuse poetry and fiction, *Lara*, *The Emperor's Babe* and *Soul Tourists*. Her forthcoming prose novel, *Blonde Roots* will be published by Penguin Books in 2008. She has held many international writing fellowships, was chair of the Poetry Society of Great Britain (2003) and has judged several literary prizes including the National Poetry Competition (2005). The recipient of several awards, she is a Fellow of the Royal Society of Literature and the Royal Society of Arts. www.bevaristo.net.

Maggie Gee has published ten acclaimed novels, including *The Burning Book*, *Light Years*, *Where Are the Snows*, *The Ice People*, *The White Family* (shortlisted for the Orange Prize and the International Impac Prize), *The Flood* and *My Cleaner* (Telegram Books). Her latest book, *The Blue*, is a collection of short stories. She is the first female chair of the Royal Society of Literature and a Visiting Professor at Sheffield Hallam University. Her work has been translated into eleven languages.

NW15

THE ANTHOLOGY OF NEW WRITING
VOLUME 15

Edited by **Bernardine Evaristo** and **Maggie Gee**

Granta Books
London

Granta Publications, 2/3 Hanover Yard, Noel Road, London N1 8BE

First published in Great Britain by Granta Books 2007

A CIP catalogue record for this book is available
from the British Library.

1 3 5 7 9 10 8 6 4 2

ISBN 978-1-86207-932-8

Typeset by M Rules

Printed in the UK by CPI Bookmarque, Croydon, CR0 4TD

Contents

Introduction

Welcome to *NW15*, a vivid, surprising and political collection of some of the best new prose and poetry written in English this year. Get ready to fasten your seat-belts, because you will soon be at Heathrow airport, where so many people begin their knowledge of Britain. We will take you to Israel and Iraq, and after that to many other parts of the globe where English is sometimes spoken: China, Ethiopia, Ghana, Israel, Japan, South Africa. To safari lodges and gay clubs, to the gentle world of British bookshops and the violent world of war, to factory floors and haunted landings. You will find characters you don't meet every day, such as Andrew Crumey's blind cosmologist and Kerri Sakimoto's Japanese priest, and you will see new sides of people you might have taken for granted. Rahat Kurd elegantly subverts received ideas about why women wear veils, and Doris Lessing asks disconcerting questions about two men and a schoolgirl looking at paintings in London's National Gallery. Selma Dabbagh, a British Palestinian, tells her controversial story of a brutal Israeli raid on a Palestinian settlement through the eyes of a disaffected Jewish teenager, while Fiona Sampson and Pam Zimmerman-Hope reinhabit the terror and the snatched pleasures of Jews in the 1930s. In the last section of the book you will find out, from Julian Barnes, how a writer imagines himself inside two very different fictional beings, Ma Jian tells us what it is like to write when you are torn between two cultures, and Ursula Holden describes how, after a lifetime's work, writers may be 'punished by the gods.' And then there's dying, of course: poems by Rob Mackenzie and Robin Robertson flash forward to the chill and thrill of those 'Last Few Seconds'.

Around 700 pieces came in, though what we editors actually saw had been pre-sifted by Helen Gordon at Granta. Much of the best writing came from names unknown to us and perhaps to you also, which was a surprise and a delight. Choosing independently from the same pile of manuscripts, we two editors came up with many overlapping choices, though naturally we did not always agree. And the writing defied generalisation. This year's women wrote with panache about war, politics and the bigger world: this year's men wrote tenderly about the heart and home life, love and dancing. There were good young writers and good old writers, good white writers and good black writers. We would have liked more comedy, but Tod Hartman's wild humour and Alasdair Gray's spoof 'Introduction' made up for a general dearth, while Gerard Woodward gently satirised the northern arts scene in his story about the Small World puppet company. Poets were witty too: Karen McCarthy gives a satisfyingly Gothic edge to warfare with neighbours in 'If I was a Buddhist I'd chant for your happiness'. We did not think about where writers came from until we had decided what we liked most, and then we found our selection was extremely diverse. As a rule of thumb, when our views did not coincide, either an absolute passion for a piece or an absolute dislike were respected.

We say 'passion' and 'dislike', which are emotional words, deliberately, because there is nothing like reading a piece several times, on different days and in different moods, for making you realise how much literary judgement is affected by emotion, and how fixed opinions can shift (though of course technical carelessness is always going to grate.) Going away to read each other's favourites, we quite often changed our minds about pieces we had firmly rejected, and vice versa. Writers who were in the end turned down should remember that what you have here is the result, not just of individual tastes, but of a degree of tough but good-tempered horse-trading in the last stages. In some cases, the rejected material was undoubtedly as good, but either we could not agree about it or we were not impassioned enough for it to survive that final jostling for room.

The world of writing in English is rich, multiple, energetic and challenging. A lot of it is urban, but you will find bindweed and blackberries pushing up against the breeze-blocks. It is coming to meet you now, head on. You are through security, ready for takeoff.

Maggie Gee and Bernardine Evaristo

Selma Dabbagh

Down the Market

It takes us ages to get to their house from the airport. First thing he says to me is that it's a bad time for me to be coming. Not, 'Welcome,' or, 'Have a nice trip?' or anything like that. Just that it was a bad time and the way he looks at me is like I should know what he's on about. So I just nod my head and think that as far as I'm concerned I'm going to have a damn good time because I'm the one who got here over that smart-arse David Levenstein and I'm the one with the two hundred quid travel money in my pocket, not him.

Uncle Abe – well, Ben at the Aliyah Society told me to call him 'Uncle', but he's nothing like my uncles, I can tell you – has got this long beard and a massive great gun across his back. Ben had shown me a photo of him before I left, but because he was smiling in that one and didn't have the glasses he looked different, sort of Father Christmassy. I am well impressed by the gun and ask if I can look at it and he says not now because it's loaded but when we get to their place I can try some out on their range. Wicked, I think. Wait till I tell them that when I get back. Then I ask him whether he's in the army and he bites my head off, telling me that they are a bunch of sell-outs who don't defend anyone and that you can only trust yourself and your own kind. I decide not to ask so many questions after that, but it is hard as everything is new and I've never been out of London on a plane before.

Ben had told me hardly anything about Abe's family. He'd been planning for me to go to some kibbutz farm until it fell through and Abe's group had come forward saying they'd have me instead. Ben had looked kind of nervous when he told me, like he was doing something he shouldn't do, and kept saying, 'These people are very loyal to their country, do you understand?' and at first I'd thought Union Jacks and National Front and freaked a bit until I realized they didn't exist there anyway and they wouldn't be asking to have a Jewish kid staying with them. I was a bit relieved not to be going to a farm. I don't do pigs and all that muck.

I wanted to sit in the front, but Abe tells me to get in the back and sticks the gun on the front seat. He's got this real American-TV-type accent, like the guys in the programme my Nan finds so funny, *Taxi*, and I want to ask him if he's from the same place but don't know that he'd like that question either.

It's all motorway and not so different from home, just hotter and yellower. There are lots of big adverts with smiling girls eating yoghurt with Hebrew writing. There's no one about because it's six in the morning. It gets different when we get to the hills, which are more deserty, like in *Indiana Jones*, but it's still all early morning wishy-washy with only the lines of the hills showing. Then we come to this place where there are all these men just standing in lines by the side of the road with cabins with police in, like you get in the City, except they have short Uzi guns and a small star of David on their uniforms. There are also these big concrete cubes in the road, like the ones I saw on the beaches with my Nan, which she says were built during the war to stop the Germans coming in and, like I said, all these men are just standing there and there is a big long line of traffic behind them. They are the first people I have seen since we left the airport. No one's talking to them and they're not talking to each other. They look like the Turks down on Green Lanes with droopy moustaches and belted suit trousers. They are a bit dusty and sad-looking. I ask, 'What's that?' and he just says, 'Checkpoint. Arabs.'

So sure, cool, he doesn't like talking.

Then he catches me off guard by asking about my bar mitzvah and I try to move on because I am still scared someone is going to find me out because there's some stuff I wrote on my hand and cheated off when I did the Aliyah reading and there's no way I could do it again. He says it's a great idea, this two Aliyahs, so we connect becoming a full Jew with bar mitzvah, getting older and coming to Israel, meeting Jews who've done the second type of Aliyah by emigrating to Israel, and I say, 'Sure,' because I am still well chuffed about the money in my pocket and the plane ride. I liked take-off more than landing. Brilliant the way the plane tips after you go up, like a motorbike taking a sharp corner. Then he says that so many Jews in the West end up marrying goyim, almost half, and then they forget what being a Jew is about, so it's a good thing I am coming here and seeing what being a Jew is all about. I agree, then say, 'What's a goyim?' and he turns round and stares at me like I am stupid, then shouts, 'You don't know what a goy is? A non-Jew like these filthy Arabs.' Then he says, 'You're not going to marry a goy, are you, boy?'

I think about the dusty men on the side of the road and say, 'No.' Then I start wondering about the girls in my class and think the only one who's Jewish is that Ruth The Tooth Weissmann and I wouldn't want to marry her either. She wears these really naff socks with lace turn-overs. I wonder if Susie Black is a goyim. That bastard Adam Blandford saying I shouldn't even look at her as she's out of my league. Should've punched him. He won't say that when he hears about me doing rifle shooting.

I see this old woman walking down the side of the road carrying a pot on her head. She's wearing a long black dress with red flowers stitched around the hem. I say, 'What's that on her head?' and he says, 'Water,' and I think that's quite cool too because it's like going to Africa or something, like Adam Blandford's brother who went to Mexico for his year out and lived with a peasant family in the hills eating worms and stuff, and I wonder whether I'll have to carry water at Abe's place.

We have to slow down when we go through a town where the houses are close to the road and the road gets narrower. Some shops are starting to open and men are sloshing water out on to the pavements and wiping them down. I see some women who must be Muslims because their heads are covered like the ones you see around the Whitechapel mosque. One of them has little toddlers but when she sees our car she pushes them behind her, so we can't see them any more. I am going to ask Abe whether he saw her do that when there's a *ping* as a stone hits the windscreen, like when you are driving too fast on gravel, and he says, 'Bastard Arabs!' and something else in Hebrew that I don't get and leans over to the passenger seat. The windscreen looks OK to me but Abe's going really slow, looking up at the houses, but everyone's gone, even the woman with the toddlers. All just vanished like when characters get zapped in cartoons. Then he speeds up and we're out of there in seconds.

'These fucking politicians!' he says, and I laugh because it's kind of cool to have an adult say that when they are talking to you. Ben at the Society went ape when I just said, 'Shit' in front of him and the only other adult I know who swears when talking to me is the wino near the school, who just rants, '*Ya fackin', fackin', fackin'*,' every time anyone goes near his bench. 'They were meant to build us a road around that village but they keep changing their minds. They're going to sacrifice us like lambs with their stupidity. Should bulldoze the lot of them.' When he says that I can see him going at the Houses of Parliament in a giant yellow Caterpillar and somehow, with him looking all angry like that, you could really see him doing it.

We don't talk for the rest of the way. It's hot in the car with the sun shining through the windscreen on to us and I start wishing I hadn't worn my new Tommy Hilfiger top because it's going to get all spoilt if I sweat and stuff.

The entry to where they live is really wild. The road goes on and on up a hill and the hill is completely circled with a fence higher than the walls around Holloway Prison and there's barbed wire wrapped around the top. There are sentry posts with searchlights every so often all around it with ladders going up to them. Like tree houses for grown-ups. We have to stop for the guards, but get waved in as soon as they see that it's Abe. It makes me think of the film *The Great Escape*. I ask if I can go up into a watch tower and Abe says, 'No' and looks at me like I am starting to piss him off.

When you come in, though, it's different – like another world. There are lots of red-roofed toy-town houses sitting far apart from each other and they have big lawns and sprinklers and pools! It's like everyone has their own pool. It's the kind of place where people carry brown bags full of 'groceries' and say, 'Honey, I'm home,' and kids play in the streets all day. Wicked, I think.

Abe tells me that of his five kids the boys around my age are at Yeshuva summer school and really I should go too but they couldn't get a place in time, so only his daughter, Tamara, who's a bit older than me, and the baby are in the house. This is kind of a bummer because Ben had told me there were boys my age, but I'm glad that there were no places at the Yeshuva. No way was I going back to school in the holidays.

There are a bunch of men at Abe's house waiting for him when we arrive. They look like Abe but some are skinnier and nerdy-looking. They are all wearing guns like he did at the airport, across the back. They look through me as we go to the door, although I can see Abe talking about me and chucking his thumb in my direction. One of them pulls my bag as I go past him into the house and says, 'Hey, when you go back, you tell your government to give us some support. Yeah. Stop being such Arab lovers,' and they all laugh because the way he pulled my bag made me wobble a bit.

Abe's wife, Ada, sounds just like him. She's shiny fat and wears a scarf on her head kind of like a Muslim woman and a big T-shirt saying, 'You Talking to Me?' It's the biggest house I have ever stayed in. It's so big it even has double things, like there are two dishwashers, two ovens, two sinks in the kitchen and two bedrooms for Abe and his wife. Then I meet Tamara and I think, Eat your heart out, Adam Blandford! because she is really, I mean *really*, fit. Sort of like the teeny pop stars my sister pins to her wall. And she says, 'Yeah, hi, limey,' and I don't know what this means, but I am really glad I did wear my Tommy Hilfiger T-shirt after all.

Abe's wife says they are going to pray and do I want to join in? so I pretend that I am really tired and lie in my room for a while. There are no cool posters in the boys' room that I am staying in, just a huge one of a big old building saying 'Returning Soon – King Solomon's Temple' and I think maybe it's a film like *Atlantis*. I sit on the bed and check my logbook from the plane that the pilot signed for me and figure I have to come here and go back another eight and a half times to get a flying badge, which is a bit of a downer. I take off my T-shirt and sleep for a bit in the rest of my clothes on top of the sheets.

At lunch Abe says again that I've come at a bad time and Ada agrees. I don't think I can ask why, so I say, 'How long have you lived here?'

Tamara silently mimics me across the table, and Ada says, 'We were called here five years ago to perform our duty to God and our fellow Jews,' then Ada looks at me and says, 'I bet your mom is happy you are here.' She squeezes her head into her chin when she says this and I just say, 'Yes.' Then Abe and Ada start talking to each other like I'm not there.

'It's the army's fault for taking his gun. It was pure murder – they knew the Arabs would recognize him and he'd be attacked,' Abe is saying, and I say, 'Why did they take his gun?', which makes me feel like someone in a gangster movie, and Abe looks pissed off again when he replies, 'They had no reason. No reason.' He prods his fingers into the table when he speaks. 'He was just defending his people and our land. They were saying he was causing trouble and going on too many sprees around here, but it's bullshit.' I giggle at that but Tamara doesn't even look up. She's sucking spaghetti from her plate. I don't understand what Abe said but pretend that I do. Abe's ignoring me again and talking to Ada.

'I said to the guys that we should suspect the Arabs who drove him to hospital first but they told me that they were clean. So I says, "About as likely to find a clean Arab as to find a kosher pig!"' They both laugh a lot and I do a bit too, because I know pigs aren't kosher. 'But it looks like this new army commander is going to make some changes round here. He's already told us that the curfew's been on again since the attack and will carry on until four, then will start again at six, so if we want to go down there we need to get moving by three-thirty.' Then he says to Tamara, who's now looking up at him, 'Wanna go down the market, honey?' and she gives this big grin and says, 'Yeah, cool.'

'Do you want to take your new friend from London with you and show him what it's all about?'

I think of the two hundred quid folded in the envelope in my pocket and think maybe the market will have PlayStation 2 and a mobile like Adam Blandford's or maybe, I think as I look at Tamara, some cool clothes.

'Sure, Daddy,' she says, 'we'll go with Aaron too.'

'I've only got English money,' I say.

'Hey, don't worry about money,' says Abe, and I figure I'm about to be given a treat.

Before we go Ada takes ages covering Tamara's face and arms with sunscreen lotion and then hands me the tube, but I just rub a bit on my hands and give it back.

The town's just down the hill but we all go in convoy with lots of cars and the guys who were standing outside the door talking to Abe when I came and some of their kids. There are lots of flags and it feels like a celebration, a street festival or something. Except everyone has a gun, even some of the kids my age.

In the car I try to make a joke about Aaron, Abe and Ada's names sounding like something from Dr Seuss's children's books (I say, 'Like you got a fox in your socks too?') and Aaron gets really nasty, shows me all his tracky metal teeth and says to Tamara, 'I think your English friend is a Mussy,' and I ask, 'What's a Mussy?'

So Tamara says, 'A Mussy is a Jew who can't stand up for himself. A Mussy can't defend the Jews. Jews who died in the Holocaust died because they were Mussies.'

I've never hit a girl, like ever, but the idea that she is saying my Nan losing all her family in Poland was my Nan's fault or my fault makes me so wild I can't really speak. My chest is banging too much. But like that wasn't enough, then she says, 'A Mussy is a pussy,' and I know that Abe's heard her because I can see him smiling in the rear-view mirror.

I'm even more gutted when we get to the town. It's poor-looking, like the town we have driven through with the woman carrying water. Everything is closed too. All I can see are metal shutters and lots of spray-paint graffiti and black and white pictures of men, women and children plastered all over the walls with writing in what I figure is Arabic under them. One of them says 'Martyr' in English and I want to ask Abe about this word but he's looking really serious so I don't. I see some red spray-paint graffiti saying 'FUCK ISRAEL' and I want to show someone but don't do that either. There are some flags too, painted on walls; not like the ones we've got, these are green, white, red and black with stripes and a triangle, not a star. It's really quiet. I can just hear some birds chirping in the trees and the sound of the air conditioning in Abe's car whirring away.

Then there's a sound of shutters going up all at once and, really fast, people start coming out of the houses. Some stalls get set up so quickly you could blink and miss it. Makes the guys on our market look like a bunch of dossers. Men, women and children come out of houses and alleys and open-topped trucks come in with food – vegetables and things – and everyone is crammed into this space buying, selling and shouting but like they are all on play and fast forward pressed down together.

Our jeeps are down a bit from where the market is. It's sort of a stage platform up there, but the shoppers don't seem to see us, or just look over at us quickly and move away. We all seem to be waiting. I keep thinking, If we just want to go through, why didn't we do it when it was all clear and if we need to buy stuff, why don't we go now? I can see the army over on the far side, about six soldiers standing in front of some jeeps with stars on, and they have Uzis too, like the ones at the checkpoint. Near them there's an odd bunch of people by some white jeeps. They are some women wearing black, a couple of nuns and some young men and women in T-shirts and jeans. They are all holding banners and some of them have got expensive-looking cameras around their necks. Everyone is watching the people shopping.

Then Abe says, 'Go' and there are some horns honked and everyone starts piling out of the cars. Aaron and Tamara scream, 'Come on, move it,' at me and I just follow.

When the people see us coming, they try to do in reverse what they have just done when putting out the stalls: they try to fold them all up again, but they can't do it as fast. There are some people at the back of the crowd who are screaming as they still haven't bought anything, but it's too late. The shutters are all coming down, the truck engines are back on and stuff is being hurled on to the backs of them.

Tamara and Aaron, her metal-mouthed friend, go ahead of me and run up to one of the stalls that hasn't quite folded away yet and yank everything on to the floor. For a second I think that they've maybe just slammed into it by mistake, then I see them grab some bags from a woman who's shopping and throw everything in them on to the ground and jump on it – all these cucumbers and tomatoes. They pick up some of the tomatoes and start pelting them at the shoppers like it's a game of paintball. The grown-ups with us start doing the same thing but they are also using their guns to knock food on to the ground and smash up stalls with the butts. There's lots of pushing and grabbing and I can see a kid down on the ground in a bright green tracksuit trying to pick up some cucumbers and I don't know how he can stay there because I feel sure they're going to stamp on his fingers. The men and women with the banners start taking pictures and the army comes forward and stops them from getting any closer. I hear one soldier shouting something in Hebrew, then he grabs the camera and smashes it on the ground.

The square is emptying pretty quickly but Tamara and Aaron move so fast I don't know where they are. Then I see her leaning back with this rock in her hand and there's like a *whoo-whack* sound as it flies, then hits the head of an old man in a long white robe with a white headscarf and blood gloops out of his head all over his clothes. This old nun starts going crazy when she sees that and screams at Abe, 'How can you do this? How can you let your children grow up as murderers? You think this is what God commands?' and he goes over to her, and *shit*, this I couldn't believe. He just smacks her right across the face and says, 'Shut up, you Nazi.' I mean this woman is older than my Nan. It's so hard to remember what happened next because there was so much going on. The group with the nun are trying to look after her and shouting at the army in Hebrew, then the kid, and I recognize him, the one in green who was on the ground, gets up and pelts Abe in the head with a stone. Man, that took some guts. He's a skinny little bugger too and younger than me and Abe's holding his gun and all.

It is then that the army really move, their guns doing *kerchunk, kerchunk* and I am thinking, well, just thinking, Shit! Shit! I mean you don't think straight really. I know I thought, 'I need to get out of the way,' and there was this voice in my head just going, '*RUUUN!! RUUUN!!*' So I run across the square because I think there is somewhere I can hide and the kid runs down there too and overtakes me. He's as fast as a ferret and I don't know why I follow him but he seems to know where he's going and it's like the mazes in *Tomb Raider* back there, really narrow alleys and the walls of houses with closed-up windows on either side. The soldiers come out behind me and they're like in *Terminator*, with these big heavy legs that swing out from the hip. They're scary all right but it seems this kid thinks he can outwit them. He's hopping around and really taking the piss, sticking his head out from behind corners, lobbing cucumbers at them and calling out insults, taunting them. He treats it like some game. I tell you, I ain't no sissy but I wouldn't be treating it like some game if I had these guys after me down some alley. No way. I'd be out there with the white hanky, me.

I find some steps round the side of a shop and I go up on to a low roof. When I get up there the kid's gone but the soldiers are still pointing their guns down the alley. I can hear some children screaming in one of the houses and I see a door open and a kid just run out into the alley. He's a little boy, younger than the other one, and you can hear his mother screaming for him to come in but he's out in the alley in his pyjamas and has seen the soldiers pointing their guns at him and he just can't move. One of the soldiers goes up to him, picks him up by the scruff of his neck and sticks his gun in his stomach. I guess they were really riled after all that teasing with the other kid but there's just no way they could've thought it was the same one. And the boy, he just pisses himself. I mean, *really* pisses himself. You can see his pyjama bottoms go dark and it starts dripping down off his feet. His eyes are really big and he's saying, 'Mama, mama.' It kills me.

I keep thinking they're going to let him go, that it's all some kind of joke. Then all the doors in the alley open at the same time and all these women come out screaming, '*Ibni, ibni.*' Well, that's what it sounded like anyway, and some of them are also saying in English, 'My son, my son.' So I guess that's what it meant. This confuses the soldiers a bit. They just stand there with the boy dangling and dripping and crying for one of his mothers and they don't know what to do. I kind of guess they're thinking it is better to go out with any boy rather than go out empty-handed. They're not even looking at the women, though, and I get the feeling that the kid being covered in piss is bothering them more than the women but you can't really tell.

I look up for a second and see the kid in the green tracksuit on the other side of the alley on a roof. He sees me too and gives me this big grin, winks and puts his finger to his mouth. He's like Peter Pan the way he bounces around. He waves his hand down, showing me to get below the wall, so I do and then he must have stuck his head over the top because I hear him shouting, '*Ay, ya shlomo*,' at the soldiers and shots being fired up into the air. It's not funny being on a roof with guns being fired up right next to you, I tell you. I shat myself.

When it stops I move across the roof on my tummy and there is all this crap up there, cartridge cases, drink cans, crisp packets and in one corner, I don't want to look, but I think it's real crap. I mean human, not dog or anything. Someone must've been up there for a long time.

From the other side of the roof I put my head up again and can see the elf boy hopping across the roofs among the Eiffel Tower TV aerials and satellite dishes like he hasn't a care in the world. There's the heavy sound of the soldiers running further down the alley and I can hear a boy sobbing, so I reckon they must've dumped the other one.

The roof is a whole separate layer of town. I can see the hills and the place where Abe and Ada live, which is really quite near but looks unreal, like a painting by numbers compared with everything else. A wind is getting up and there are heavy dark clouds moving low and close from the hills. They are so low there are splodges of shadow following right under them. I start going from roof to roof. I can see Abe's car parked over to the right and the kid's going the other way and I head in his general direction. Nothing else is moving except for this big white luxury coach which is driving in. BIBLE TOURS OF THE HOLY LAND, it says in loopy writing. From where I am I can still see the kid popping along and now I have a clear view of the wider alley that the soldiers are going down. The kid runs away from me, making sure they see him. Then he goes down low and moves back towards me bent double. When he gets close he dips down some steps and runs into the alley.

I think he is trying to shake them off by getting on to the other side, but when he gets down there he turns. There can't have been any steps on the other side, so he stays on the alley going the opposite way to the soldiers, but the coach is there, slap bang in his face, at the end, blocking his way. I can see him and the coach, In the alley I see a door opening a bit and a woman try to get the boy to come in but he can't have seen her or heard her because he doesn't react and it's like he's having to think twice, but he doesn't really get the chance because one of the soldiers swivels and sees him and they're all shouting to each other. So the kid just leaps on to his belly and starts scraping his way under the coach like a dog.

They start firing at him. There are still some old fogies in sloppy clothes and baseball hats getting off the coach and they all start screaming. Yanks, I think, because I hear one screeching, '*Dear Gawd! Oh, dear Gawd!*'

But the soldiers are already there almost. It's not a long alley, two hundred yards or so, and they are shooting at the boy like maniacs and I think, Shit, this kid's got the lives of a cat, as I see his feet pushing him forward. But one of the soldiers must've hit a tyre because there's this *bam! bam!* Then a lurch as the coach leans over to one side, like a horse sitting back. Dust and sand blow up against the wall. When it stops the feet are still scraping but the soldiers are there and now I feel my whole neck tighten and my chest heave. Now he's really stuck.

When his feet stop I let my insides go. I spew Ada's lunch on the roof and I keep on puking even when there's nothing left inside, when it's just green bubbles and fluffy spit. I am shaking like I did when I got hit by a car that one time outside school. I can't stop the shakes so I stop trying to stop them as it makes it worse to try.

The wind's really got up when I go over to the jeeps. It's an angry wind with glass grains in it that cut. There are two ambulances by the cars we came in. Medics are with Abe, who's got a butterfly plaster on his forehead. Abe's also got Tamara, a rabbi and some of his friends around him. Otherwise the ambulances are empty. I can't see the old man or the nun. An army officer is explaining something to a guy from Bible Tours. Soldiers are trying to jack up the coach to change the tyre and get the kid out. I see the body as they pull it out – red all over the green with the hair a black smudge.

Abe calls me a schmuck and says the Arabs could've killed me with me going in there. I don't say anything. He calls over one of the other guys and tells him to arrange for Bible Tours to come over to their place for a talk to understand the problems that the community faces. The other guy says, 'Great idea,' and slaps Abe on the back and Abe gives this 'all in a day's work' type shrug.

It's really pelting down when we're in the car and Abe's swearing at the road and the weather. I don't talk on the way back. I think they can smell the sick on me. When we get to their house I lie on the bed and try to get the boy winking out of my head and the taste of spew out of my mouth. I sit up and take from my pocket the envelope with the two hundred pounds in no longer slippery twenty-pound notes. I go in to see Abe and I look straight at him and tell him I shouldn't be here. I tell him I faked the Aliyah reading and that I cheated. I tell him that David Levenstein should've won. I tell him that we should arrange for me to go back because it's not right. He kind of laughs and I wonder whether he's about to say, 'Schmuck' again but he says he'll phone the travel agents.

'It'll cost you,' he says, so I say, 'I've got money,' and I like saying that. He gets out his phone, has a conversation in Hebrew and then turns back to me and gives me a figure in shekels. He takes out a calculator. One hundred and ninety-eight pounds and forty-three pence.

'I've got money,' I say again but like saying it a bit less this time.

I know this'll sound funny but what I hear when I think back on when we returned up the hill that day is this warbling, wailing sound coming from the town. It was like lots of women, but I don't know how they would've done it. It was a beating, fluttery sound like birds going up into a stormy sky and it was kind of spooky. Spooky but joyful and triumphant. I know it doesn't make much sense; you had to have heard it. To me, it sounded like a warning, but I don't think anyone else was listening.

Richard Beard

Hearing Myself Think

Heathrow Airport is one of the few places in England you can be sure of seeing a gun. These guns are carried by policemen in short-sleeved shirts and black flak jackets, alert for terrorists about to blow up Tie Rack. They are unlikely to confront me directly, but if they do I shall tell them the truth. I shall state my business. I'm planning to stop at Heathrow Airport until I see someone I know.

In the busiest airport in the world this shouldn't take long, and I expect to be home before Ally leaves for work. It is 6.43 a.m. My gaze slides between so many faces that I instantly forget everyone I don't recognize, except for a young girl, eleven or twelve, looking Lebanese and wearing a wedding dress. She has red cotton flowers dotting her black hairband, a tight curve over her wild, swept-back hair. She is someone I do not know.

Go to the busiest place and stay there. I'm always telling Victor and Clemmy that we have to do what makes sense, and I'm now leaning expectantly against the barrier at Terminal 1 Arrivals.

Astonishingly, I wait for thirty-nine minutes and don't see a single person I know. Not one, and no one knows me. I'm as anonymous as the drivers with their universal name cards (some surnames I know), except the drivers are better dressed. Since the kids, whatever I wear looks like pyjamas. Coats, shirts, T-shirts, jeans, suits; like slept-in pyjamas.

The first call comes at about 7.15. Feeling detached and powerful, I let the phone vibrate jauntily in my pocket. There's a second call ten minutes later. I check it's Ally, as if expecting someone else, and then turn off the phone.

Most of the passengers arriving from Glasgow (BA1473 0700), Manchester (AA6614 0710) and Aberdeen (BD671 0720) are men, including Celtic football fans in green and white hooped jerseys, and tartan hats with a fluorescent shock of hair at the back. The orange hair is attached to the hat. I would normally explain this to Victor, who is five, to see him marvel at the kind of serious stuff I know. Also, he shouldn't assume every Scot has orange hair. Not all Scottish people are the same, just like not all Daddies are the same.

Early-morning arrivals can look like new-born babies, pinched, querulous. Their first instinct is to look for someone they know, even when they're not being met. There is a man with a feather in his cap, and a man telephoning threats of violence. There is a small boy with his mother, hyped up on sugar drinks and true-life air travel, who shouts 'Telephone!' every time he hears a ring tone. He is very busy. He is very noisy.

As I say to the children, think it through. I'm standing at Terminal 1 Arrivals when I live less than eight miles away. Few of the people I know will be arriving at this time of the morning. Of course not. They'll be leaving, and from one of the other terminals.

Terminal 1 is not a serious terminal. It has mostly domestic flights, and therefore lacks emotional distinction. Between Leeds/Bradford and London there isn't the difference for long-distance passion. Back from Newcastle, couples climb in the car and go where they're going.

'Good trip?'

'Rainy. You?'

'Yup.'

Along the white and yellow walkways, air-conditioned, temperature-controlled, my eye catches on pale-blue turbans, and fat people. Without shading, in this bright permanent daylight, all fat faces look similar, and therefore like the fat people I know. The features are diminished, hard to make out, scrunched up by unmeant flesh. I stare hard, because I wouldn't want to miss anybody.

At a corner table of Costa Coffee, at the entrance to Terminal 2, a posh lady in a dark skirt and sky-blue cardigan is wiping off a table with the heel of her leather glove. I knew this would happen. I finally see someone I know, and it's not someone I want to see.

It's Ally's mother.

I stop dead, about twenty feet away, hoping she doesn't notice me. I should be at home in the house she helped us buy inside Heathrow's sixty-three-decibel noise contour. In return for not being able to hear ourselves think, we get a discounted semi and a small garden where we can play name-that-airline. Garuda, Iberia, JAL. We put on a brave face.

The lady looks up sharply and reaches for her bag. She adjusts to focus on me, neutral at first, then frowning. She is not Ally's mother, though they do look alike.

I hurry on to Terminal 2 Departures, where men my age are leaving the country in confident cutting-edge trousers. I check the screens and the first city I see is Zagreb, making me think of Serbia and therefore Iana, and that is not good.

08.10 OK653 PRAGUE GATE CLOSED
08.20 LH4791 HAMBURG BOARDING
08.30 AF2671 PARIS CDG GATE OPEN

And so on. Here in Terminal 2 Departures I can expect to see, if not anyone I know now, some go-ahead contemporary from my college days. Mine was a serious university, and if I hadn't caught glandular fever I'd have left from this very gate for the third year of my Modern Languages degree. I had a job as a classroom assistant in Zaragoza, but it wasn't to be. I stayed in bed in my childhood bedroom for two and half months, then went back to college, where I met Ally, who was studying Zoology.

Five or six years ago, more like seven, eight in fact, we used to know a lot of people. They won't have changed much, as we haven't. An outer shell of success, perhaps, fluent in several languages and modishly bored with travel. Here in Heathrow Terminal 2 at 8.20 on a Tuesday morning, we can both be proud of turning out more or less as we'd hoped.

'Where to?'

'Zagreb.'

'Wonderful city, Zagreb.'

We'll compare jobs and children, look at our watches and promise to keep in touch. Finally, as my like-minded friend turns towards Passport Control, I'll touch his sleeve (or her sleeve, it could be a her, though I'm thinking it's a him), I'll touch the sleeve of his suit jacket and ask whether I should sleep with Iana the Serbian teenager. Whatever the answer, I'll then go back to the car, be home in twenty minutes no one the wiser, and Ally will still make it to the office by ten. If she hurries.

The only flaw in this plan is that I still haven't seen anyone I know.

It turns out that the people I falsely think I recognize are very like acquaintances I rarely see. The anxious, calculating face of Mrs Roberts, but with her it's not so much the face I recognize as the large square glasses. There's a jolt of indecision about a pony-tailed cousin, and then Mr Browning, who marks out the soccer pitches, though it can't be him because he's in hospital. The team had a whip-round. They call me Mum, and when I tackle more fiercely than strictly necessary, Psycho-Mum.

I linger at Terminal 2 Departures like someone saying goodbye, having said goodbye to someone I love. This is where Iana would wave off her fat and physically unfit husband, if she loved him. When they moved in, we spied on them from an upstairs window. He was so much fatter and older than her that we made them a married man with his recent au pair. Which is in fact exactly what they are.

Perhaps I'm more likely to recognize women. I more often look twice, because women at airports are an ideal type. They have no fear of leaving, or being left. I look closely for a woman I might know among the Pontypridd Ladies' Hockey Club, European Tour 2007. This is both absurd and not impossible.

Hours pass by. I'm tired out by thinking, and when I should be looking at faces I'm looking at legs. The way her baggy cargo pants grab and release her buttocks, a recent arrival from Milan but also Iana when, singing to her Walkman, she swings along our street to the shops.

I turn on my phone and don't open any of Ally's text messages. It rings immediately, and forgetting I'm powerful I answer.

'Where are you?'

'Heathrow.'

'Where?'

She isn't shocked, or challenging me to say something more credible. There's a plane going over our house and she can't hear what I'm saying. I wait for it to pass, and in the foreground of the background, Victor and Clemmy playing, or fighting.

'I'm at the airport.'

'You're supposed to be here.'

Nag, nag, nag.

I disconnect and worry about the car in the Terminal 1 car park at two pounds for half an hour. Now that I can hear myself think, I'm thinking that the Short Stay car park is not a serious car park, not if you want to hide a body in the boot. Long Stay would be a better bet. In Long Stay you'd get a month before anyone took an interest.

Short Stay is rubbish for dead bodies, but better for sex. At every hour of the day there are people having sex in the Short Stay car parks at Heathrow Airport. With so many couples reunited, and true love as urgent as it is, it must be happening all the time. Though not to me, even when I met Ally off the plane from Jakarta. I was trying to fit the trolley between a concrete pillar and the side of the car when she confessed to sleeping with a guy called Tim. Tim was not Indonesian. He was from Aldershot.

I've never knowingly seen Tim, so Tim from five years ago isn't one of the people I'm likely to bump into beneath the bright lights at Terminal 2 Departures. Besides, he'd be at Terminal 3, a serious international traveller like Tim. Terminal 2 is Europe only. It is not a serious terminal.

Inside Heathrow Airport I can't hear the planes. It is the only place in the Heathrow corridor where this is true, as if everyone has arrived or will leave soundlessly, like angels. I hear myself thinking about all the people I know who have let me down by not leaving early on a Tuesday morning for glamorous European destinations. My former colleagues from the insurance office must still be stuck at their desks, like I always said they would be, when I was stuck there too, wasting my time and unable to settle while Ally moved steadily onward, getting her PhD and her first research fellowship at Reading University, her first promotion.

Our more recent grown-up friends, who have serious jobs and whom therefore I half expect to be seeing any moment now, tell me that home-making is a perfectly decent occupation for a man, courageous even, yes, manly to stay at home with the kids. These friends of ours are primarily Ally's friends. I don't seem to know anyone any more, and away from the children and the overhead planes, hearing myself think, I hear the thoughts of a whinger. This is not what I had been hoping to hear.

I start crying, not grimacing or sobbing, just big silent tears rolling down my cheeks. I don't want anyone I know to see me crying, because I'm not the kind of person who cracks up at Heathrow Airport some nothing Tuesday morning. I manage our house impeccably, like a business. It's a serious job. I have spreadsheets to monitor the hoover-bag situation and colour-coded printouts about the ethical consequences of nappies. I am not myself this morning. I don't know who I am.

The phone rings. I connect and push it to my ear.

'When can we expect you back?'

I won't sob for her. I'd rather not speak.

'I have to be somewhere. You know that.'

I press the button and put her back in my pocket. We haven't been getting on well, Ally and I, though usually we try to talk it through. I say I sometimes feel tired and listless, and she says join the club. We make appointments with the doctor and blame the flight path, with heavy aviation fuel dropping down upon us in a constant invisible drizzle, blighting our little garden, poisoning what's left of our brains.

So then. It must have been jettisoned aviation fuel that made me sit next to Iana on Iana's rented sofa and place my hand on her thigh, on the cotton of her khaki cargo pants, midway above the knee.

Deep breath. After a brisk walk, I have found the one place in Heathrow where no one I know will see me crying, or feeling sorry for myself. Churches are traditionally useful for this kind of thing, and the church in the middle of Heathrow is called St George's Chapel. I sit in a chair at the back, my hands flat between my knees, rocking backwards and forwards. This would be a good place to hide. It would also be a good place to come if you believed in a God who was able to help.

Mrs Roberts is about sixty years old and lives two doors along from us with her disabled husband. She rents out her self-contained basement to Iana and Iana's absent, negligent, fat, middle-aged lover. One day Iana went upstairs to tell Mrs Roberts that the washing machine had stopped working, except her English wasn't so good. Mrs Roberts then called me because everyone knows I have nothing better to do.

I left the kids with Mrs Roberts and went downstairs with Iana, just about making sense in a German she partly understood. I proudly showed her how to use the trip switches in the fusebox. She offered me a cup of tea. She was young and lonely and I, I sometimes think I'm not where I'm supposed to be. I went round to Iana's flat more than once, always during the day while Ally was at work. I pretended to help, and then we sat side by side listening to the planes, not daring to hear ourselves think.

Ach. I stand up sharply and double-handed slap my forehead.

Telephone.

'Ally.'

'Look, I'm not angry.' She has to pause while a plane comes in. 'I just have to know when you'll be back.'

'I can't say.'

'Why not?'

'It's taking longer than I expected.'

'I thought we'd agreed about everything. You said you were happy to do it.'

'I won't be long. Promise.'

I'd set myself a target. I will get married and have children and live happily ever after. I will be a sensitive human being who supports his successful wife. I understand and can visualize this story, its beginning and middle, and this is the story I want other people to see me living, the man I want them to know. Then one Tuesday morning I seem to have mislaid the ending.

Could have been braver, I suddenly realize. Could have aimed higher. In fact, I should have gone straight to Terminal 3.

I get moving, stumbling, almost running, because if you start something you have to finish it. I say this to the kids. It's one of my lines, part of my play-acting as a dad that gets us through the days until Mummy comes home.

Terminal 3 is a serious terminal. In the same hall you get incoming from Washington and Jeddah mingling with frequent flyers on Iran Air. My daytime television knowledge of Islam is enough to warn me I'm in the presence of desperate fanatics who hold life cheap, and within a ten-mile radius of Slough, Heathrow Terminal 3 is where history is most likely to happen.

I stand there, waiting.

When she finished her PhD, but before starting her first job, Ally went travelling for three months in Indonesia, where she met Tim from Aldershot. It was here at Terminal 3 that I saw her off, and met her when she arrived back home in a sarong. Did not have sex with her, as I'd been hoping to do, in the back of the car in the Short Stay car park.

At Terminal 3, single men who are not limousine drivers or terrorists are sex tourists. In shorts and faded polo shirts they're on their way to Manila and Bangkok, where dark, humid bars heave with numbered girls. If I was doing it, it would be different. It wouldn't be so bad. I'd pick one girl and stick with her. If she was value for money, I would.

What am I thinking? I would, but I don't. I'm not a sex tourist, I haven't even had sex in a Heathrow car park. There is not a body in the boot of my car. I didn't even make it to my gap-year job in Spain. I have a wife and two children and live eight miles from Heathrow Airport and I'm failing to see anyone I know.

I should wait at the entrance, or near the shops. At the bus rank, or the exit from the Piccadilly Line. So many choices, and by making the wrong one I end up stuck for ever in this simple unflinching daylight. There are people I know in the airport. There must be. We just haven't been in the right place at the right time.

Staying where I am, I think that when I graduated I imagined a few years of exotic travel before a glorious homecoming, rich and famous and beyond reproach. I applied to teach English in Tokyo. Ally didn't want me to go, so Dad drove me to the airport, but at the last minute, clutching my ticket, I found I couldn't leave. I wanted Ally. I'd cried and Dad hadn't understood, and we'd got back in the car and driven home.

No one seems to notice that I'm not right. Sixty-three decibels sixteen hours a day, the invisible pestilence of drifting fuel, can't hear myself think. I have the motivation to blow this airport to kingdom come, and after five hours of wandering aimlessly, thinking, going nowhere, in this of all places I should have been arrested. To make the arrest more serious, by a policeman with a big black gun. And then when I'm cleared, everyone will know I'm innocent.

It gets harder to see individual faces. The most I see now of Heathrow's daylight people are obvious external markers. A goatee, dark glasses, a rolling walk, a short skirt, a sombrero. A purple shirt and tie set. Flip-flops and cracked yellow toenails. A waistcoat, a hairpiece. I will be stuck here for ever, living on coffee dregs and apple cores, and when I do eventually see someone I know, they don't at first realize it's me. I see someone I recognize, her long nose casting a shadow over her lips. As an unexpected stranger, making eye contact, she is surprisingly attractive.

My wife Ally is pale-haired, pale-skinned, moon-faced, her hair tied back. She is seven months pregnant and she has a small child clutching each hand, tugging her arms straight like heavy luggage. These two children are my children. My wife has her head on one side. She lets go of the kids and they run towards me, as if I'd recently arrived from a great distance. Ally holds out her arms. I recognize that gesture, her glistening eyes, her attempted grin which she bites off before it disintegrates. She is livid, but with my children clutching my legs I have at last seen someone I know.

I can therefore go home.

Robin Robertson

Unfound

I remember playing tag
with my daughters:
they never caught me then
and never would;

or that last game
of hide and seek,
when night fell
and they went to sleep

and woke the next day,
while I remained here
hiding: unfound
for years and years.

Jacqueline Crooks

Moose

(novel extract)

I am a different person now, with a different name, for reasons you will come to understand. Even back then our identities were shifting, like the latest dub versions, as we sought the strongest positions in the dancehall, flexing, bucking and cotching, driving ourselves backwards and forwards, until that grinding exhalation when the magic in us was ignited.

I no longer live inside the concrete mass of that urban estate. But the characters of that world are still in my thoughts. Here, in this hideaway that I cannot name, it is Moose who is always in my thoughts. I remember the night we met.

'Come on,' Asase called. She was in front as usual, pushing her way down the stairs; her head held high, aloof, as if she had disowned everyone – even herself. Asase was more than beautiful, she had a proud and cunning mind, an incongruous mix of urban grit and rural sensibility. Men wanted her for her lips: curled and red like a fuse.

We were three inner-city girls – two Caribbean and one Irish. No one expected better. We went down into the Crypt like all the other twenty-year-olds. Deep into the dub-hard dancehalls in St Anselm's Church – an underworld dance in a church named for a saint and an exile.

'I'm behind you,' I called. I had my hand on her back, and she was leading the way down. Rumer was above us, at the top of the stairs, joking with a group of rastas. Rumer was an Irish gypsy who wore African head wraps around her frizzy red hair, and long African-print skirts. I turned back to see her laughing, mopping her eyes, gasping, 'Oh stop, no more, pleeeze,' as she made her way down. She had asthma, and the damp basement and smoky atmosphere of the club made her wheeze for days afterwards. Despite this she was always joking and giggling. She was the one who could make us laugh at a funeral.

When we got downstairs Asase pointed out a small gap against the wall, at the side of two bulky speaker boxes. We followed her into the low-lit basement and sealed ourselves in a corner of the Crypt, mummified by sweat, ganja and the hypnotic bass-line thud of dub and its echoing instrumentals. Within minutes Rumer and Asase disappeared into the crowd, pulled by invisible hands to dance. I was alone with the coffin-sized speaker boxes, their vibrations shaking the life out of me. Nobody walked into the Crypt without someone to watch their back. Not even a rude-bwoy, decked out in sovereigns and gold duckets, would go in without someone he could nod to across the floor. You had to learn how to rock-down-steady. Then make it back up again.

I made it up again and again, dancing with various anonymous men, damp with dancehall sweat and stale Paco Rabanne cologne. Then I was on my own. It was three o'clock in the morning. The lights were lowered and the crowd had become a grinding mass of slip-eyed dub devotees. The Dub Master had arrived and had control of the decks. He was spinning drum-and-bass versions that were rocking the dancehall. No one really knew much about the Dub Master, but some people said he used to be a preacher in Port Antonio, preaching all the way from the bamboo foothills down to the little shanty settlements near the Rio Grande. Now he wore a pin-striped suit and his dreadlocks were bundled under a red woollen hat.

The music was irie. I was dipping, vibing and rising against the wall, smudging the charcoal of the grey streets off my back. The drum beat channelled through me until I was beyond the point of sweetness, outside my body, skimming the creamy darkness. I was moving beyond the night-time sky into the ritual of rhythm that had created the universe. The Dub Master was toasting into the microphone as he changed records: slack-jawed, slicking up words from his tongue. Dancers surfaced from lock-tight dancing, patting scrunched-up clothes and flattened hair. Spirals of ganja smoke were twisting through the resin darkness, creating a landscape of half-recognized tropical shapes and silences. I thought I saw a body rise into the air; thought I felt fingertips brushing the top of my head. The room began to spin, but I pressed myself into the dub beat, skanking on the tips of my toes.

Something powerful was coming alive in the Crypt.

I half-turned when I felt elbows jabbing into my ribs. It was a broad-based woman, snappy and cut-eyed, hair wrenched into tight cane rows. She was decked out in a crisp pair of Farrah trousers and a suede Gabicci top, gold-tipped shoes: a Stix-Girl, and she was smirking at my cheap A-line skirt and my plastic-patent shoes. I looked away, wishing myself into another place, but Stix-Girl pushed harder, knocking into me as she danced. Maybe I could slink forward, like there was suede on my shoes, but she would only follow. I don't know if it was the sound of the dub – the echoing instrumentals stretching my imagination to bursting point – but I thought I heard Millie-Ma, Asase's mother, her voice swirling among the smoke, saying, 'Yuh not to fight in church, not in front of a saint. It would turn out bad for yuh – for anyone.'

The speaker boxes were shaking as if they were about to explode. I had to act quickly, so I dipped beneath Stix-Girl's angry face and stepped as deep as I could into the dub bass line. I threaded a row of steps away from her and to the side. Then I saw Asase dancing towards me. Asase skanked as if she were treading water, her hands scooping the air in front of her, then arcing out to her sides. She came closer and closer to Stix-Girl, shouted something at her and shoved her aside.

There was a snapshot moment – that was all you had time for in a place where everything moved with dub-dread speed – and Stix-Girl made her critical assessment of Asase. She realized the trap she was in: aggressor turned prey. Now it was Stix-Girl who, like myself a moment ago, was longing for the shelter of her mother's womb. I watched as she tried to style it out, sweeping away, tossing her tight scalp as if she did not care. Fronting it to the end.

'All right?' Asase asked.

I nodded. I felt relieved and ashamed.

'Now watch this,' Asase said, and she nodded to the far corner, where a tall man in an Italian suit had just walked in. He had the two-timing red-brown skin of her father, Hezekiah, and the same shoelace moustache. I watched as Asase disappeared towards him. Asase came from hard-grained country stock. Her mother, Millie-Ma, came from the fishing village of Alligator Pond and could gut fish from head to tail with one flick of her wrist. Asase both adored and despised her mother for her country ways: walking down the street with a bandana askew on her head, slippers on her feet and her socks straddled around her ankles. And, whether she liked it or not, Asase was as dextrous as her mother when it came to handling slippery fish and sharp knives.

It was four-thirty. Lovers'-rock time. The lights went off. Men moved with a mute biological urgency, loading their bodies with the worn-out weight of the women. I was dancing with a man who called himself Moose, who kept his crotch a polite distance away from my pubic bone, while smiling out from some secret shade, as if he had a hat pulled halfway down his face.

'Just cruising, checking out the raves west of the river,' Moose said, when I asked what he was doing this side.

'The Dub Master always mashes it up,' I said, 'but nothing else happens around here.'

He pulled away from me and looked down at my face. 'I think there's plenty happening here – enough for me anyway.'

Moose came to the Crypt that night with his moose shoulders straining at his Italian silk shirt. He had a small head and a long, wide jaw. Bronze-brown skin, dark-rimmed eyes and an elegant wide-bridged nose. He was older than me, twenty-eight. He would have been handsome, except his mouth was scrunched up as if he were chewing on something inedible. As he danced with me, he pressed his face into my hair. We danced for the next few hours. His soft, subtle scent drew me in, and I rested my face against his chest, on the raft of his ribs, and felt bittersweet pain, like a home-coming that was years too late.

Towards the end of the dance Asase and Rumer regrouped and came back.

'These are my co-pees,' I said to Moose. He nodded to them without saying anything, but I saw the way he looked at Asase.

The Dub Master was calling, 'Last dance, last dance, tek your partners.' It happened quickly: Moose took Asase's hand and they began dancing.

The lights flashed on and off, then on again.

The dance was over.

It was six-thirty in the morning when we came out of the dance-hall to an ash-buffed sky, littered streets and dotted birdsong. The friction of light and air burned our red eyes. It seemed as if some great destruction had removed everyone from the face of the earth, and we, the dub dancers, emerging from the Crypt, were all that was left.

'Moose, you don't have to chip, do you?' Asase asked. 'Come with us. Muma always leaves a pot of chicken out.' She ran the tip of her tongue across her top lip. 'Once you taste my Muma's hand, you'll be back every week.'

Moose looked past me, at Asase, and said, 'My car's round the corner. I'll drive.'

There were still groups of people milling around the church, exchanging numbers on empty cigarette boxes. We walked past them, around the corner and piled into Moose's butter-coloured Rover. Asase slid into the passenger seat. Everyone was quiet in their dub-dreaming, so I laid my head against the leather headrest. I could smell pine-scented air freshener, and Moose's aftershave, which smelt like blue river water skimmed with musk. The cassette was playing the Valentine Brothers singing 'These Lonely Nights'. The roads were empty and beautiful; just the four of us, and the yellow streetlights reflecting on the canal as we drove across the bridge towards the estate.

We pulled up outside Asase's block and everyone got out the car.

'You know what,' I said, 'I think I'll go straight home.'

Rumer came and took my arm. 'You bleached, girl?' Her voice was tight and wheezy.

'I'm just, you know . . .'

Moose offered to take me home, but he was looking at Asase, waiting for her response. I wanted to walk across to him, tilt and moor his gaze to my face.

'No need,' I said. 'My block is just across the Green.' I pointed vaguely to the row of tombstone tower blocks that backed on to the railway.

'Call me tomorrow,' Asase said. She smiled at me, and her smile was a prism that distorted everything. I did not know what she was thinking.

'Laters,' I said, and I walked away.

Asase, Rumer and I lived on the same estate. Rubbish bins overflowed with Valium boxes and crumpled Tennent's cans. Those who were able-bodied worked in the sausage factory in New Town, piping rag-bone meat into rancid casing. Maybe that kind of work held people together. Our estate was not as bad as some of the others; people had not turned on each other – yet. Sometimes old people's bodies were found in the winters – frozen to death. But summers were good: children played happily in the scrag-end play area of stubbly grass, on the rusty swings and in the sparse sand pit.

Yes, but summers came and went so quickly.

The sun was forcing itself higher in the sky when I let myself into the flat. I lived with Pops, a dark-skinned, soft-spirited man who wore natty cardigans, trilby hats and turned-up trousers. Hard to believe that he was once a bomber pilot, cupped inside the cockpit of a Lancaster, 11,500 feet up in the sky, carpet-bombing cities and igniting firestorms in the Second World War. He had arrived in London from Lluidas Vale, Jamaica, in 1940 with three pounds in his pocket and a suitcase with one good suit, three pairs of long johns and a razor. Twelve weeks of training, then he joined the RAF. He wanted only peace now.

His size-eight tartan slippers were outside his bedroom, precision-placed. There was a circuit of light around the door and I could smell his cigar, which smelt like the mush of damp tropical earth mixed with oriental seeds.

'That you, Tutus?' He always called me Tutus, a Jamaican term of endearment.

I went through the lounge, which was monochrome, like the set of an old black-and-white film: a grey, grizzled picture of Pops in his RAF uniform, an old gramophone cabinet cluttered with china, crocheted doilies on the backrest of the sofa. Everything was the way Muma had left it. I knocked and went into his room. Pops was sitting in his armchair, bundled in his plaid dressing gown, reading with his glasses slipping down his nose. His face was as round as a banjo, scrubbed and shiny, and he had pods of curly hair, neat as if they had been planted.

'You all right, Pops?' I knew that he had slept for no more than five hours, without sound or movement, waking at dawn. Daytime was his blind spot; he couldn't navigate himself through daylight, when nightmares of the past tormented him. He only ventured outside the flat late at night, when it was completely dark.

'You g'lang to bed. Ol' man like me don't need no fussing.'

I kissed the top of his head. 'I'll do rice and peas later.'

I went to my room and climbed into bed. I wondered what it must have been like for him when he lost Muma. She had died of a stroke while giving birth to me. There was a picture of them on the wall in my room, arm in arm, Muma in a taffeta dress and Pops in a white tropical dress suit. I wondered how she had suffered the pain, the oxygen failing to reach her lungs, her brain. The heart. I started to cry for everyone: Pops and Muma. I cried when I thought of Moose, Asase and Rumer sitting in Millie-Ma's kitchen, eating and laughing. I imagined Asase folding the Rizla into knife-edge creases; blowing smoke into Moose's eyes. I knew Moose would come back, week after week, purring across the river in his Rover, smelling sweet and smiling. I knew he would take us to the Crypt, to blues parties on the estates – wherever we wanted to go – because he had fallen under Asase's spell.

I fell asleep crying, trying to pluck the comfort of my Muma's voice from the darkness. But it wasn't her voice I heard in my dreams, it was the flip-flap of muddy heels, the yik-yakking of spirits that had not yet given up on life. I felt fingertips brushing the top of my head, and I knew they were not Muma's hands. Muma had come only two or three times, with tales of the afterlife. No, these were not her fingers, because these fingers were hot, raging with an indomitable life force.

Rob A. Mackenzie

In the Last Few Seconds

In a smudge of tail-lights you watch your soul go,
then you spin round corners you would have taken
slow before you gulped back the rum. The bottle
    rocks on the backseat.

When a soul slips off, does it shed its body
and the drink that drives it? Or keep guard over
falling debris? Nights like this drop like voices,
    warning that all roads

end in vapour; nothing turns blank so gently
as a hairpin bend on a high cliff. Headlights
catch the grassy verge where you lose control, rouse
    breakers like sparklers

from the wind-scrubbed inlet. The impact crushes
bones to powder, slows up the sinking. Husks of
crumpled metal, covered in rust and seaweed,
    smear at the bottom.

You expect a flashback, a potted bio
of divorce and automobile replacement –
how one breakage led to another – film noir
    bleaching the blackness,

but instead stars blister across the sunroof.
Cracks appear. You wait for the tunnel sponged in
light from some new world. But the car splits water,
    floats in its shadow.

Alasdair Gray

Men in Love: The Posthumous Papers of John Tunnock

Introduction by Lady Sim Jaegar (novel extract)

We Sim Jaegars are a widely scattered clan. Though born and educated in England I am now resident in Los Angeles with all the
rights of a United States citizen. The Edinburgh Festival has twice
drawn me to Scotland, yet I never dreamed I had a distant cousin
there until a solicitor's letter last year arrived 'out of the blue', as
they say. It told me that John Tunnock had died intestate and I was
his next of kin, and asked how I wished to dispose of his estate –
some thousands of pounds in a savings account with a terraced
house in Glasgow's Hillhead district. The current sale price of such
houses was anything between half a million and a million.
Furnishings, domestic appliances, ornaments, pictures and books
had not yet been professionally valued, but a Glasgow agent of
Christie's had written expressing interest in a stained-glass panel
representing Faith, Hope and Charity in the stairwell window,
since records of the William Morris workshop indicated that it was
designed by Burne-Jones. If I wished to view my cousin's former
property without residing in it (which was perhaps likely, given the
circumstances of his death) I would easily find accommodation in
a neighbourhood Hilton.

   This letter had clipped to it a cutting from the *Glasgow Herald*
dated three weeks earlier. It said that John Tunnock, retired school-
teacher, aged sixty-four, had been found dead of head injuries at his
home in the city's West End and the police were holding an investi-
gation. Attached to the clipping was a further note from the lawyer

saying the police had taken all evidence the house could yield, no arrests would be made and he had ordered the removal of blood-stains. The place was now thoroughly tidied and cleaned, all locks on doors were changed and a new up-to-date burglar alarm installed.

Well! God knows I have all the money I need but a business-woman can always use more. My investments are safe because I work closely with my brokers and lawyers – not that I suspect them of corrupt practices, but when professional men's judgement is at fault (and no financial speculation is ever flawless) they sometimes automatically ensure that the cost is borne by inattentive clients. My canny attitude brought me to Glasgow against the advice of American and English friends who said I would be in danger of criminal violence, and pointed to my cousin's fate as a warning. My omniscient insurance adviser disagreed. Glasgow, he said, certainly had the greatest density of European poverty, ill health and crime west of the former Communist empire – in one district life expectancy was seventeen years less than that of those living in the Gaza Strip before the recent Israeli–Lebanese war – but the murder rate was still three-quarters of that in most US cities. Statistics showed that in Glasgow's Hillhead area a woman was marginally safer than in Beverly Hills, especially if she did not wear bright blues or greens while watching television football in crowded pubs. These colours, that sport, such pubs do not tempt me. To Glasgow I came.

Next morning at the Hilton hotel I had a business breakfast with the solicitor, Alasdair Gillies. He could tell me nothing directly about my cousin, never having seen him. Legal documents in the possession of his firm, letters in the Tunnock family home, had enabled him to trace me through a distant relation who had emi-grated in Victoria's reign. They had also revealed a family secret. John's mother, Griselda, was eldest daughter of Murdo Henderland Tunnock, for many years minister of Hillhead Parish Church. Like her two sisters she never married. Unlike them she had left the family home, first becoming a typist in a local tax office. In 1936 she was promoted to a superior post in London, where, five years later at the age of forty-two, she gave birth to John, her only son. The birth certificate gives a line of unpronounceable consonants as the father's name and gives his occupation as Polish naval officer, which seems improbable. Griselda brought her baby to Glasgow a few days later, deposited him with her sisters (their parents being dead) and returned to London. Soon after she too died, crushed by a falling wall while cycling to work after a night of heavy bombing by the Luftwaffe.

John's subsequent life with his aunts seems to have been unusually cloistered. He attended Kelvinside Academy and then the University of Glasgow, both less than ten minutes' walk from the family home. He trained as a teacher at Jordanhill College, a ten-minute bus ride to the west, later becoming Headmaster of Molindiner Primary School in Robroyston, a half-hour journey in the other direction. He never owned a car. Mr Gillies suggested that his aunts 'kept him on a very short leash'. They were his housekeepers until 1977, when he took early retirement in order to look after them, helped by visiting nurses and a firm of cleaners. Before then he had taken short summer vacations in Millport or Rothesay, Firth of Clyde resorts. Afterwards, he seems never to have slept outside the family home, though the last aunt died in 1998.

'Had he no sex life?' I asked. Mr Gillies said apparently none before 1998, but afterwards some diary notes suggested he had 'lashed out a bit'. I asked what that meant. He said I should read the diary to find out. I said his silence on the matter suggested dealings with prostitutes, or homosexuality, or paedophilia – now so notorious that one fears to show kindness to any child anywhere. But surely John had some normal acquaintances. What had the police discovered? Gillies told me that according to the cleaners who looked after his house John Tunnock was 'a nice wee man who wouldnae hurt a fly or say boo to a goose'. His social life seemed confined to Tennants, a large pub on the corner of Highburgh Road and Byres Road where the regular clients were university students, people working nearby in medicine, law and teaching, retired academics, several long-term unemployed and owners of small businesses who avoided declaring their earnings to the Inland Revenue. Here John was recognized and respected, though his quiet ways drew too little attention to make him popular. His main acquaintance, Francis Lambert, was a retired university lecturer and more robust figure who in the 1970s had achieved some fame on BBC television by nearly winning a UK-wide general-knowledge contest.* He and John Tunnock were known to discuss politics and crossword puzzles while John drank half-pints of lager very slowly. The bar staff had never seen him intoxicated.

I brooded on this information, then asked if Tennants was a very crowded pub. Did it show football matches on television? Had John worn noticeable colours there? Mr Gillies understood more by my question than I knew it contained. The police had investigated that (he said) and found John Tunnock never wore team colours, supported neither Rangers nor Celtic, was neither Orangeman nor Fenian, Mason or Knight of St Columba. When asked what football club he supported Tunnock always said Partick Thistle, which in Glasgow is a code name for agnostic. This might inspire contempt in Protestant or Catholic bigots but not murderous rage. He had not visited Tennants on the night of his death. Next morning the cleaners discovered him on the staircase landing. A forensic report indicated he had died suddenly of a fractured skull about ten hours earlier, the fracture caused by abrupt contact with a step. There was no alcohol in his blood, though the state of the living room upstairs, together with fingerprints on glasses and bottles, indicated some kind of party with several individuals, one a drug user known to the police. He (Mr Gillies) had been privately informed that the drug user had confessed to pushing John away during an amorous struggle on the staircase while she attempted to leave, a push that resulted in his fall. The Crown Office had decided not to make a respected citizen's sex life public by accusing the girl of culpable homicide, especially when a jury would almost certainly bring a verdict of not proven.†

'Well,' I said, slightly disgusted with my cousin, 'since you have the keys to his house please take me there.'

I do not mention the address of the house, for houses tainted by suspicion of murder are harder to sell, but I found the surrounding

---

*The competition was for the title 'Mastermind'.
†This verdict unique to Scottish law enables jurors to dismiss the accused without punishment and without deciding they are innocent. A cynic has suggested it means, 'Go away and don't do it again.' Madeleine Smith (1835–1928), charged in Edinburgh in 1857 with poisoning an inconvenient lover, is the most famous beneficiary of this verdict.

architecture, gardens and parks pleasanter than many pleasant parts of London, because less grandiose. This did not prepare me for the interior.

The only part of John Tunnock's diaries I have read mentions a robbery that deprived his home of expensive bric-a-brac. I doubt if I could have faced it before that robbery. The clutter of dark mahogany furniture with dark, slightly threadbare upholstery, dark oil paintings in thick gilt frames, heavily ticking pendulum clocks, glass-fronted bookcases full of bound sermons, all seemed to press crushingly on me. The day was overcast. We switched on electric lights with frosted-glass shades that had been converted from ancient gas fittings. Over tables in the main rooms were chandeliers that could be raised or lowered by adjusting a central brass, cone-shaped counterweight. The lavatory was the biggest surprise. I had expected Victorian plumbing to be primitive, but here it was palatial, complex and gloomy in a way recalling Edgar Allan Poe. The vast bath was housed in a panelled chest ending in something like a sentry box with its own little vaulted ceiling. It had a dozen big brass taps, each with a label giving temperature, angle and force of a different spray. Their position suggested a servant was needed to turn them, a detail that struck me as weirder than the death on the staircase outside. The water was heated by gas burners under a tank in a wardrobe-like cupboard lined with what must have been asbestos. A smaller wardrobe-like structure in the living room had no visible doors but something like a glass porthole at eye level. Mr Gillies said this was the house's most modern article, being a 1938 television set manufactured by John Logie Baird's company. Of course it did not work. There was no other television set, no telephone or record player. There *was* an upright piano with an unusually thick case: a pianola or (as they say in the States) a player piano operated by rolls of perforated card. A player could work it in person using pedals and stops, or switch on an electric motor to play it automatically. A stand like a huge wine rack held several hundred rolls of work by composers from Bach to Gershwin. Labelled discs at the ends of the rolls named opera overtures and ponderous symphonies. There was also a radio in a two foot square cubical wooden case.

Despite my dislike of the place I saw it was a better example of nineteenth-century interior decor than many in well-funded museums. I considered offering it to Glasgow District Council to be maintained as a small local-history museum, but Mr Gillies told me another such house, more representative since not as opulent, was on show in a tenement near Sauchiehall Street, so Glasgow's museum service would not want another. After careful consultation I decided to sell through Christie's the Burne-Jones window and two dull landscapes I was told belonged to the Barbizon School. Through Sotheby's I sold the most valuable furniture, including the Baird television set, the pianola with its rolls and even the Edgar Allan Poe shower-bath. Through a local firm, West End Auctions, I sold everything else. Mrs Manning, owner of the firm, tells me the portraits of clergy and volumes of sermons will decorate a public house in Saltcoats called The Auld Kirk, in a building that was once indeed a Church of Scotland. These transactions will finally raise more cash than the million I expect for the house.

John Tunnock's papers were all that now remained to embarrass me. After old letters, receipts and bills were removed I had a mass of typescript and a large desktop notebook two-thirds full of undated entries in tiny, clear, almost sinisterly childish calligraphy, with strange curlicue embellishments. It would have been heartless to discard all that as waste paper, but what else could I do? The typed pages were historical novels, which I detest. I also dislike reading diaries, even those written for publication, and a sample of John's miserable confessions made me think them unpublishable – I now know this idea is old-fashioned and out of date. On Mr Gillies's advice I put the lot in a suitcase and left it at the University of Glasgow's Scottish Literature office, with a letter offering a donation to the department of a few hundred pounds in return for an honest assessment of the contents. Did anything in these papers deserve publication? I asked. Would a publisher consider them a commercial proposition if I paid for the printing? Or would Glasgow University, which in 1962 had awarded John an honours degree in the Humanities, find room for these papers in its archives?

A fortnight later the Head of the Department, Alan Riach, sent a courteous and helpful reply. He thought the historical fictions well written and entertaining, but the one set in Classical Greece lacked chapters connecting the start and finish, the one set in Renaissance Italy had neither start nor finish being three loosely linked dialogues, and the fictional biography of the Victorian clergyman had already been novelized by Aubrey Menen in a 1972 Penguin paperback called *The Abode of Love*. No reputable firm would undertake to publish such work by an author who was unknown, Scottish and dead. For the same reason no public archive would want them. If university and national libraries became repositories of unpublished fiction by unknown authors they would soon have no room for anything else. The notebook diary was another matter. The entries ran from 2001 to an abrupt ending in 2006. Its social and personal notes by one who had died violently might interest a publishing house, especially if I paid part of the production costs and the book was introduced and edited by a known author. With my permission he would show the papers to Alasdair Gray, a writer who lived locally and, with some success, had edited and published the papers of a late-Victorian public-health officer.

It was thus that I met Mr Gray, whose response to *all* John's papers was enthusiastic. The diary and historic fictions should be published together, Gray said, thus casting light on what he saw as a major theme, men in love. Tunnock, like many of his generation, was an old-fashioned Socialist and had planned the novels as a trilogy with a name suggesting the Marxist theory of surplus value. *Men in Love* would be a more eye-catching and accurate title, for it would connect Tunnock's love life with those of his heroes, and in an odd way balance them. These patriarchs in Classical Greece, Renaissance Italy and Victorian England loved their ideas of truth, beauty or God more than their women, but the women in Tunnock's love life had certainly dominated *him*.

'If you can call it a love life!' I said grimly. 'I have known many men, but none like John Tunnock. If you insist on publishing his diary along with the rest I insist that you call the book *John Tunnock*.'

Mr Gray, not very graciously, seemed to accept this. He said that if I paid for the printing out of John's estate, the book, edited as he envisaged, would certainly be distributed by Bloomsbury Publishing of London and New York, a highly successful firm that had done well out of J. K. Rowling's Harry Potter books. Mr Gray (who clearly had a high opinion of his talents) said he would decorate the book with John Tunnock's linear embellishments, 'in colour, if the money stretches so far'. He indignantly refused my offer of payment for his editorial work because, 'It is a privilege to be midwife to so unique a volume.' *John Tunnock* would never be a popular success (he said) but he would 'claw back' something from Bloomsbury in royalties if I signed a paper granting him possession of copyright. This I was pleased to do.

He differed from Alan Riach, however, by insisting that I write the introduction, because his own reputation as an occasional writer of fiction often led critics to doubt the value of his serious academic work. But Lady Sim Jaegar (he gallantly declared) was both known in US business circles and remembered in Britain as the glamorous wife of a popular American ambassador. My introduction would therefore do the book more good than anything by *him*. I need only describe my part in its production, and say something about his editorial method. He would use diary entries to connect the fictions. This would annoy purists but make the book more readable. The entries, though undated, were in chronological order, the first mentioning an event placing it in the autumn of 2001, the last from a day or two before Tunnock's death in late 2006. The manuscript diary and typed narratives had therefore been written in the same five years. Gray would also provide footnotes explaining details that might puzzle foreigners.

Writing this introduction has so saturated me in what seems a bygone era (though actually modern Scotland) that it tempts me to say that I now lay down my pen, satisfied in having done all I can for my unfortunate cousin's memory. But I am dictating these words to a secretary who sits beside me with her wireless-enabled laptop on the sunny patio of my Los Angeles home. It only remains to add that the publishing director of Bloomsbury, or perhaps her marketing department, insists for commercial reasons that the book be called *Men in Love*. I will now do my best to forget John

Tunnock, while hoping that Mr Gray manages to 'claw back' more from the publishers than he has led me to believe possible.

Beverly Hills, California
28 July 2007

Chapter One: John Tunnock's Diary, Autumn 2001

The time is now three in the morning after the most bemusing hours of my life. They started yesterday when I arose and, as usual on days when cleaners come, had to start by tidying away signs of female presence scattered over my floors from living room to lavatory: discarded garments, cosmetic tools, photographic magazines about the sex lives of beautiful rich people. All the women I once knew kept tidy houses – why are the young things who sometimes stay here so different? I always begin by showing them cupboards, drawers and the newspaper rack but when I suggest they tidy things into them they snort and ignore me. They love their messes like cats that have never been housetrained so claim a new territory by pissing over it. When serving breakfast to Niki yesterday I told her so. Her reaction was violent and I came near to apologizing for my honesty. Our parting was acrimonious.

Worked all day at University Library on Athenian economics, left late, called in at Tennants. It was buzzing with the communal elation that usually follows Scottish football victories, though the TV kept showing what seemed a Hollywood disaster movie. I joined Mastermind, who told me suicidal terrorists had made two passenger planes crash into the World Trade Center, totally destroying it and killing hundreds. He thought the elation in Tennants resembled the delight of mobs in Berlin and London who in 1914 cheered the start of the first great modern war – they knew the world would now change unpredictably, which gave them a brief illusion of freedom. I disagreed. The Twin Towers have been the main financial house of an Empire State whose bankers and brokers, according to the New York writer Tom Wolfe, believe themselves 'masters of the universe'. The people he describes do nothing but enrich themselves by manipulating the international money market. They have no interest in what this does to the rest of the world, but know they control it. Capitalists like that *should* learn they are not perfectly safe. Mastermind said I was wrong if I thought the atrocity damaged global capitalism, which is fully insured against the most horrendous losses of life and property. The calamity was an act of guerrilla war by folk unable to fight the USA with a conventional army and air force – folk from several lands where the USA had propped up dictators so that North American businesses could buy natural products cheaply. This propping had mainly been done through secret CIA funding with secret British assistance, so most Americans and Britons knew nothing of it. If President Bush reacts by declaring war on other nations another Vietnam situation will arise, which the terrorists probably want. Bush's richest supporters will probably want that too, as an excuse for seizing dictatorial powers unthinkable in peace. 'Interesting times,' concluded Mastermind, having turned my temporary elation into sheer worry for the future.

I came home and was at first pleasantly surprised, thinking Niki had recovered from her huff and tidied the house more thoroughly than I had ever seen it before she came. Several minutes passed before I saw she had finally left me, helped by a systematic partner or partners who own or have hired a van. They have removed enough from this house to equip another, also many small, valuable ornaments. I wandered from room to room in a kind of daze, wondering what to tell the police. My fondness for young things could lead to difficulties if Niki is under the age of consent. What *is* the age of consent? (Memo: find out.) Such thoughts, troublesome at first, are now eased by blissful relief *not* caused by sipping this brandy the robbers failed to discover under the pianola lid.

Yes, my life suddenly feels wonderfully simplified by the disappearance of Niki and familiar objects I now realize I never liked. The silver-framed photographs were especially depressing. Inside them our family history flowed through three misleadingly respectable generations: the grandparents I never knew, then my mother and aunts in their younger days, finally me standing between Isa and Maisie clutching my PhD scroll, capped and gowned, plump and po-faced like an alarm clock between two candlesticks. My aunts said that was the proudest moment of their lives but I hate being reminded of my appearance. I hope Niki and partners get good money for those frames.

The rising crescendo of our quarrels over the last month has been exhausting. Yvonne, equally messy, heralded her departure in the same way. I keep forgetting how each unexpected disappearance restores me to the hopeful freedom I first enjoyed after Aunt Maisie's funeral. Once more I am a man again. In fact more than a man – a writer! Remember the words of Vasari that inspired that bashful university student, poor wee John Tunnock: 'Nature has created many men who are small and insignificant in appearance but who are endowed with spirits so full of greatness and hearts of such boundless courage that they have no peace until they undertake difficult and almost impossible tasks and bring them to completion, to the astonishment of those who witness them.'* The years of school teaching and running a home for elderly invalids only allowed time to collect raw materials for my book. Since Maisie died I have sketched out many adequate chapters but completed none. Niki, Yvonne etc. were wildly distracting but necessary, for without the sexual pleasure they gave I could not convincingly describe passionate people. True, I found passion late in life, but so did Fra Filippo Lippi, also orphaned at an early age. He too was in his forties when he helped a young thing escape from a nunnery and began his great paintings in Prato Cathedral.

But at last, thank God, I am exiled from fleshly distractions. Silence, exile and cunning will now let me reveal, here in Glasgow, the European *Erdgeist* to the world in a vision of three unique civilizations. It will be called *WHO PAID FOR ALL THIS?* and when that Great Book Booms, none other will be left upstanding. Tomorrow, Tunnock, to work!

*This sentence introduces Brunelleschi in Vasari's *Le Vite de' Più Eccellenti Architetti, Pittori, et Scultori Italiani*.

Moniza Alvi

The Crossing

God, or someone, had parted the sea, and who were we
to say we weren't going to walk through it?

The cliff-like corridor, its glassy walls. We didn't dare
speak in case the great lift doors of the earth would close

and drown us – feared to touch the translucent sides,
shells and seaweed fixed to a screen.

Fish stared, large as cabins, small as fingernails:
the knife-like, the black funereal, the bridal-tailed.

We moved as one, as surely as if we'd sponsored
each other. And those of us at war with ourselves,

our different parts were fused together.
We were twinned with our own undulating faces.

Who could know how our dire and honourable world
would re-establish itself?

The sky was below us and the sand above us.
Bitter as chocolate, the east wind blew all night.

John Siddique

Inside # 1

'It is no use shouting'

There are poems to write which I am told should
not be written, almost as if to think
about a thing condones it. We are supposed
to say this is bad, this is good, this is evil.

I am part of it. We have the minds that could
make these things, but what interests me is the way
you hold your hand to your face at that moment, the
film of sweat above your lip. There is
an answer there.

Rahat Kurd

A Memoir of Modest Appearances

I bought a long black coat the summer I was twenty-four. It was August, and I was feeling unseasonably morose. Standing in front of a mirror in a shop called Tristan et Iseut, I could see the coat was too big. Its softly draping folds were like a cave I could retreat into. I didn't want to take it off.

The salesgirl helped me fold back the sleeves, to make cuffs. 'I've seen you go by here a few times,' she said. 'I like how you always wear a scarf. It makes you look so mysterious. Here, the fitted sleeves work better, don't you think?'

I was thrilled. This unusually poised young woman in a crisp white shirt, easily more sophisticated than all the bare-shouldered girls trawling glumly through the mall, said that I looked *mysterious*. The word lit up something in me, as if I'd been waiting to hear it. In seven years of covering my hair in public, I'd never had such a compliment.

Why was it so much more gratifying than the uninvited effusions of Muslim men, strangers who often stopped to tell me how happy they were to see me, how wonderful that I was setting such a good example for all womanhood? Scarf-wearing Muslim women who do not know each other almost never stop to smile or call out salaams or congratulations for adhering to the dress code. If anything, they avoid each other's glances. I used to be baffled by this when I first moved to Ottawa, but I caught on very quickly, becoming cold and withdrawn like the rest of them. *Yeah, I cover. Get on with your shopping.*

At the time I could not explain how this mutual wariness arose. But after being too often and heartily claimed by the overfamiliar presumptions of Muslim men, looking away from each other is probably the only way Muslim women can maintain some shred of individuality on the city street. The salesgirl's glance, on the other hand, was a respectful appraisal not only of my style, but also of my independence. She didn't know what it meant – that was the point. In her eyes, my scarf belonged to me alone.

My encounter with the salesgirl also reminded me that aesthetic details of the scarf I put on – colour, fabric and style – were just as enjoyable as the buying of new clothes. And like shopping for clothes, putting on a scarf was especially enjoyable in the company of women. Standing in communal bathrooms with my Muslim friends, in front of a mirrored row of sinks, we happily confided in each other as we rolled up our sleeves for ablutions before prayers. We put our scarves back on after drying our hands; watching each other pin and fold fabric in ways we wanted to try ourselves: pulled over the forehead, pinned above the ear, a long scarf loosely flung over a shoulder. We covered ourselves among friends the way other women fluff their hair and spray perfume across their wrists. We admired each other's unique styles; our gestures were no less absorbing, and gave us no less pleasure, than other forms of feminine self-adornment.

I was far more fluent in defending my dress code with the strident language of feminist politics than with the breathless enthusiasm of fashion. But it is fashion that seeks to make a person's appearance into something exciting and important. A scarf perfectly fulfils this goal. Whatever the religion or politics of it, there is no denying that the visual impact of a headscarf in a diverse secular city is more arresting than almost anything you can name. When I walked into politics class at the start of the semester or down the aisle towards my seat on a train, I felt it: in that moment, I had everyone's attention. What Hermès handbag or Prada shoe could ever achieve that?

I will never be as interesting to look at as I was when I covered my hair. I slowly realized this after my first few months of walking around the city bareheaded. Nobody looked at me strangely on the bus; no one looked surprised that I spoke with the same Canadian accent as everyone else. Strangers no longer wanted to stop me on the street, to jeer at my submissive delusions, or to roll down a car window and call out with fatherly warmth and a thumbs-up sign, 'Good for you for wearing the hijab!'

No one called me to ask for a radio, TV or newspaper interview. Journalists were no longer rapt as I expounded wittily on my feminist views. I used to take these interviews very seriously, because I had thought about these things in great depth. But most of the reporters I talked to didn't know what to do with the complexity of the ideas and feelings I was trying to express. The resulting article would invariably focus on the link between a perceived increase in Islamic fundamentalism or extremism in North America and the scarves my friends and I wore; a few snappy quotes proving my feminist credentials (and momentarily upsetting the stereotype of suffering victim) made my family and friends laugh with pleasure and pride. By the time I was twenty-five, getting media attention for this superficial flimsy thing was itself – painful to admit – unsatisfyingly superficial. Nothing I might do, say, think or wear in future would ever draw the kind of attention – the sustained critical interest, the open scorn, the warm approval, the love, the wrath – my favourite scarves attracted, with as little effort on my part. I had no doubt left that it was not me who was fascinating.

Ask any English-speaking public-affairs expert what that thing is that devout Muslim women wear on their heads. 'It's the hijab,' secular journalists and politicians in Toronto and London will promptly tell you. 'Hijab' is no longer even italicized in English. It is, however, often preceded by a definite article, 'the hijab', thereby assuming the sort of weight and gravity we most often ascribe to singular, universally known entities: 'the Bible', for instance, or 'the Parthenon'.

The hijab has no history, no origin, no connection to any geography or climate or season. Whether worn by someone in Islamabad or Indianapolis, the meaning of the hijab (Arabic for 'curtain') goes unquestioned; it is everywhere recognized as a fixed symbol of obedience to a religious dress code that is fourteen centuries old.

If someone says, 'She always covers her hair in public,' our impression is of an individual with a specific story we can ask questions about and perhaps understand. 'She wears the hijab,' in contrast, invokes the authority of a religious practice that, in its apparent lack of an English translation, is permanently foreign; it cannot be integrated and so must be either accepted or rejected whole. The woman who appears only as a correct, stern symbol of an abstract idea is remote and untouchable. The hijab is almost impossible to talk about in intimate terms arising from ordinary human motives.

When a Muslim girl in a North American or western European city feels like wearing a scarf to class, she becomes the immediate target of questions about international politics. Is it fair or reasonable to expect a gum-chewing American sixteen-year-old who wears a favourite blue scarf while rollerblading home from school to explain her choice of clothing in terms of post-Soviet tribal warfare in Afghanistan? If the girl were to talk about her cool aunt who studied engineering, who helps her with her maths homework, and taught her how to stare rude people down in the subway, and how covering her hair makes her feel brave like her aunt, what would happen?

Perhaps it's right that the news-makers can't answer this question. Perhaps it's time to turn away from deliberate fact-based portrayals of 'Muslims', and look to literature instead.

I bought the novel *Possession* by A. S. Byatt late in 1991, in paperback. I was twenty-one, a dropout from school, which felt like being in exile from the only country in the world where I knew how to speak the language. I had picked it up and looked at the many praises of the critics on the opening pages, during my increasingly frequent bookstore-skulking sessions. The story begins in a library, where a struggling scholar named Roland Michell comes across half-finished letters to an unknown woman written by the late-Victorian poet whose work he is studying. It was the intrigue of this opening scene that decided my purchase. *Possession* was the first Booker Prize-winning novel I had ever read. I made myself read slowly, putting off the last page for an entire day. I bought copies for friends, recommended it to several others and reread it several times. Even looking at the cover was a pleasure – I loved the way the word 'Possession' was printed on the front, in a scrolling slant that suggested ink from a Victorian fountain pen.

I was fascinated by the huge scope of the story, its several intricate layers, its genteel academic milieu, its descriptions – at least four different bathrooms are rendered in minute detail. At the heart of *Possession* is a nineteenth-century romance between two poets whose letters are discovered by two late-twentieth-century English scholars. The past is richly constructed, while contemporary scenes have a gratifying immediacy, such as when Roland comes home to a sulking girlfriend frying onions in a dingy London flat. The novel is completely empty of explicit reference to Islam or Muslims, except for a British Museum poster of an illuminated page from the Koran on the wall in Roland and Val's living room, a detail I found delightful. (Islam's holy book is unlikely ever again to appear in English literature as mere decoration.)

In 1994 two new collections of Byatt's short stories were published. I bought them in Hamilton while visiting my father. I still remember sitting on the train back to Ottawa and settling happily back in my seat with 'The Djinn in the Nightingale's Eye'. Of course I was curious about what kinds of references to Islam or Muslims the story might contain. It begins with an English woman named Gillian Perholt, who is on board a flight to Ankara during the time of the first Gulf War; she is met at the airport by her Turkish friend Orhan; both are presenting at a conference on the theme 'Stories of Women's Lives'; both are narratologists, scholars of storytelling.

'Most of the Turkish students were like students everywhere, in jeans and tee-shirts, but conspicuous in the front row were three young women with their heads wrapped in grey scarves, and dotted amongst the young men in jeans were soldiers – young officers – in uniform. In the secular Turkish republic the scarves were a sign of religious defiance, an act of independence with which liberal-minded Turkish professors felt they should feel sympathy, though in a Muslim state much of what they themselves taught and cared about would be as objectionable, as forbidden, as the covered heads were here. The young soldiers, Gillian Perholt observed, listened intently and took assiduous notes. The three scarved women, on the other hand, stared proudly ahead, never meeting the speakers' eyes, as though completely preoccupied with their own conspicuous self-assertion. They came to hear all the speakers. Orhan had asked one of them, he told Gillian, why she dressed as she did. "My father and my fiancé say it is right," she had said. "And I agree."' ('The Djinn in the Nightingale's Eye', pp. 107–8).

The Muslim women are mentioned briefly twice more in the story: 'and the grey-scarved women stared fixedly ahead' (p. 111) and 'the scarved women stared ahead motionlessly, holding their heads high and proud' (p. 135). 'Stared proudly ahead'; 'stared fixedly ahead'; 'stared ahead motionlessly'. Byatt makes it clear that the women are not listening, not interested in reading, in storytelling, or in finding out the meaning of stories about women's lives, whether in Chaucer or *The Thousand and One Nights*; and the motive for their 'conspicuous self-assertion' turns out to be unthinking submission to male authority.

As it happened, I was reading this story on a train journey, alone, with my own head wrapped in a scarf. I was amused that my hobby of pop-culture Muslim-sighting had found an object in a story by Byatt. But I couldn't suppress a feeling of disappointment, even hurt, as if the author were making explicit her disapproval of all scarf-wearing Muslims, including me; as if I'd somehow believed the author should have known or sensed that a Muslim scarf-wearer could be among her eager readers.

It didn't mean that 'The Djinn in the Nightingale's Eye' wasn't a good story – it was a very enjoyable, strange and dreamlike fable about the universal necessity of telling and listening to stories; about how old stories, retold to new listeners in new places, can echo in unexpected ways, resonate with subtle new meanings, so that both the story and the listener can never be the same again. But it set up a clear divide between the worlds of its characters, implying that what motivates the religious can never motivate the secular.

And suddenly, with a shock, I remembered the green silk scarf. Maud Bailey, the main female character in *Possession*, is wearing it when Roland first meets her. And I further recalled that throughout the book Maud, a feminist literary scholar, almost always covers her hair, that this habit actually becomes an important key to her emotional history, her personality:

'She was dressed with unusual coherence for an academic,' Roland thought, rejecting several other ways of describing her green and white length, a long pine-green tunic over a pine-green skirt, a white silk shirt inside the tunic and long softly white stockings inside long shining green shoes. He could not see her hair, which was wound tightly into a turban of peacock-feathered painted silk, low on her brow . . . She did not smile.' (*Possession*, pp. 38–9).

I had not, in my numerous readings of this novel, connected Maud's eccentric practice of hiding her hair with my own. I would most likely never have done so, if it had not been for the dismissive treatment of the very minor Muslim characters in the 'Djinn' story. I went through *Possession* again carefully, noting descriptions of Maud's scarves:

'Maud had driven out early and had arrived, keen and tense, before breakfast was over, well-wrapped in tweed jacket and Aran wool sweater, with the bright hair, visible last night at dinner in the Baileys' chilly hall, again wholly swallowed by a green silk knotted scarf.' (p. 128).

'"Tell me – why do you always cover your hair?" He thought for a moment he might have offended her, but she only looked down, and then answered with a kind of academic accuracy. "It's the wrong colour, you see, no one believes it's natural. I once got hissed at a conference, for dyeing it to please men."

"You shouldn't. You should let it out."

"Why do you say that?"

"Because if anyone can't see it they think and think about it, they wonder what it's like, so you attract attention to it. Also because, because . . ."

"I see."

He waited. Maud untied the head-square.' (pp. 271–2).

Possession is a multi-layered novel interweaving passion with serious erudition. Maud's eccentric dress habit as an act of self-possession, a serious desire to have her work taken seriously, is just one of its minor threads. Maud fears her standing as an academic may be undermined by her appearance, by her long blonde hair in particular, which is indeed, the author makes repeatedly clear, beautiful, and so has been a spur to feminist resentment:

'The doll-mask she saw had nothing to do with her, nothing. The feminists had divined that, who once, when she rose to speak at a meeting, had hissed and cat-called, assuming her crowning glory to be the seductive and marketable product of an inhumanely tested bottle.' (p. 57).

Yet it is an important thread within the larger story that contrasts the lives of women in nineteenth-century England with the contemporary lives of English and American feminist scholars. Two of the nineteenth-century female characters are portrayed attempting to build a life around the work they wish to do, despite the very real, very difficult obstacles and prejudices they face in rejecting conventional marriage and motherhood; a third woman, near the end of her life, counts the cost of decades of silent deceptions that sustained the respectable appearance of the life she made with her husband. By the late twentieth century, Maud Bailey is a full professor while Roland, a PhD, makes a part-time pittance and is largely dependent on his girlfriend's income.

Physical appearance is an ongoing preoccupation with Byatt's highly believable female characters. Gillian Perholt wishes for a more youthful body from the Djinn she releases from the ancient bottle; he grants her wish, and the professor is happy when she looks in the mirror. 'That was an intelligent wish,' she tells herself; no feminist guilt taints her pleasure.

In *Possession* we find literary scholars who are not above insecurity and professional jealousy; even feminist scholars do not always live up to the shining ideals of the sisterhood.

The incident of Maud's being derided for her attractive appearance by other feminists is recounted twice in the novel, once early on, by the omniscient narrator (as Maud brushes her hair before going to sleep) and much later, by Maud, in a conversation of growing trust and sympathy with Roland Michell. It is told in both accounts with suppressed feeling, as of something that gave pain and puzzlement that has still not been forgotten. (And pain and puzzlement, indeed, are the best words to describe what any woman feels when her actions in good faith are misread, taken as a contrived bid for male approval.) The other significant factor in Maud's decision to cover her hair is also revealed in both these instances: the end of an unhappy affair, a year before the story begins, during which her lover had dared her to grow the blonde hair she had, in deference to feminist conventions, kept short.

I know this is strange. I'm using minor details from an English novel published in 1990 that has nothing to do with Muslims to try to make a point about what it means when a Muslim girl in a western city covers her head. But it's a point that demonstrates exactly why great literature is so essential. It enlarges the world for its readers, beyond even what the author might have intended, because it gives us the freedom to imagine that fictional world and move around in it, draw our own meaning from it. Think about it: where would you rather find validation of your own ideas, feelings and experiences – in an enjoyable novel, bought and read at leisure, about a person with whom, despite differences of race, class and religion, you feel a strong connection? Or in some painfully earnest documentary about the plight of poor, endlessly traumatized women living under (name your tyrannical regime here) that you feel obliged, because of shared religious heritage, to sit through?

Maud's motives for her mysterious practice are revealed slowly, with sensitivity and nuance. Her green silk scarf turns out to be a sign neither of feminist rigidity nor of religious dogma. Near the end of the novel, encouraged by Roland, whom she has come to trust, she feels she can 'untie the head-square'. She is in no way influenced by Muslim practice – indeed, though I first read *Possession* as an enthusiastic and devout head-covering young woman, I did not think of this character as doing something 'Islamic'.

It is, however, the most sympathetic and believable portrayal in popular English fiction of the complex reasons for which a young woman in secular modernity might want, for a while, to cover her hair. Maud does not want to be defined by her physical beauty: she strongly rejects the simplistic notion that her appearance, her body, is the same thing as her *self*.

And because she uses a headscarf to make this distinction, Maud's character excites sympathy in the reader who has also covered her hair as a bid for a morally serious life. Certainly it is Maud's fiercely guarded independence, 'her autonomy', which inspires her to cover her hair in the first place. If wearing a head cover can be nothing more or less than one choice on the path towards the attainment of that confident adult self, that idea has seldom stood on its own in English-language treatments, whether in fiction or non-fiction, by Muslims or non-Muslims, of 'the hijab'. Muslim women are not yet allowed to be complicated human beings in cultural representations. Instead they must be anonymous bodies who exist only to provide a form on which the scarf or coat or chador can be wrapped: they must be stiff-necked with absolute scarf-consciousness.

And that image is at least partly true. We've all known people like this, full of their own 'conspicuous self-assertion', who don a sloganed T-shirt or carry a placard on the street, with the desire to be identified, if only for the hour the demonstration lasts, as the sign itself; in other words, people using their whole physical selves in public space to communicate a demand or a belief.

But who can hold such a pose all the time? No one. Not even the grey-scarved Turkish stiff-necks: eventually their shoulders will slump; they'll start worrying again about their mother's medical expenses; they'll yearn for a nice hot dinner. A Muslim woman wearing a scarf in public is always demonstrating, until she gets comfortable and, because her real life has become too difficult, funny, or absorbing for her to keep her attention focused exclusively on her appearance, forgets about it altogether.

Kate Rhodes

Four Things You Never Got to See

My new attitude –
chin up, nothing dents me.
Oh yes, I'm doing fine, thank you,
in my jacket of impervious leather.
That table, please, the one by the window.

The town I've borrowed
shot through with privilege and dirt.
Tourists like ice cream wrappers
littering themselves across the common,
as far as the eye can see.

The haircut that cost a fortune,
blonde, high maintenance.
It makes a Jean Harlow of me,
sends me on errands for sequins,
buttons and dancing shoes.

The underwear I bought
just before you left,
held together by willpower.
Red silk daisies, faces to the sun,
blooming in a field of lace.

Sharmistha Mohanty

The Sari

(novel extract)

The sari, as one knows it now, was not worn in this ancient land. Then it was a piece of cloth tied around the waist and reaching the knees, as in the frescoes of Ajanta or the sculptures of old temples. Women wore nothing over their breasts. Slowly, the sari began to drape its way up. The breasts were covered, by a piece of small cloth. With the coming of the Mughals women began to wear a longer garment below the waist, it reached till the ankles. Above, the piece of cloth over the breasts grew into a full bodice, with arms and shoulders covered. A cloth, the dupatta, fell softly now, over the head. It did not take much time for the bodice to close the gap between it and the skirt, for the dupatta to grow longer till one side was tucked into the skirt, the other end coming over the head, covering the bodice and reaching the waist. The lengthening of the dupatta was infinite. The sari finally emerged from a long dupatta, tucked into the skirt underneath at one end, going once around the body and then pulled all the way over the head at the other. Everything was covered now, the skirt, the bodice, the head. No skin showed anywhere. There was so much covering cloth that with the leftovers women created pleats in front. The pleats flew a little as they walked, on a summer evening full of released breeze.

Rob A. Mackenzie

Lighter

She never smoked but carried matches –
to meet interesting people, she said,
by which she meant
interesting men.

'Got a light, darling?'
She always had a light
for anyone.

I married her in a bright January.
She grew bold, approached
strangers in the street, non-smokers.
They understood the itch and scratch,
the flame glistening in her cheeks.

March, I took up the habit,
coughed my way through
a packet of twenty. She gifted me
a lighter.

April, she moved out.

What does a man do when love
isn't enough, when little by little
it burns to a butt-end
and drops to a car wheel?

I bought a pipe, packed it
with the finest tobacco,
spent years of evenings waiting
at the corner of our street.

Charles Lambert

Entertaining Friends

I'm not surprised when Sophie phones to say she's coming. I knew she'd invite herself the minute I decided to stay in Rome for the summer. Sophie still loves me, although she knows it's hopeless. After years of the direct approach, unexpected open-mouthed kisses, tears, pleading, bursts of fisticuffs, she's started to work on the 'us-problem' more obliquely, as though we were friends, as though friendship were also a sort of purge. She's swivelled things round until neither of us quite knows who or where we are. Together, we reel from bar to bar, giddy with emotion at first, eventually staggering with inexpressible rage. Her sexual love for me has been transformed into a passionate, possessive interest in something she calls my 'happiness'. 'All I care about is your happiness,' she says, as though happiness were a child I'd adopted and needed to be reminded of constantly, to stop it wasting away with neglect. As I watch her come round the corner from Customs with her overloaded trolley – how long does she plan to stay? – I'm already defensive. Sophie has made me feel there's something fraudulent about my happiness. It's all right as it goes, but it doesn't go far enough. In her eyes, adopted children are consolation prizes, which makes our love for them more complex.

By the time we're on the airport bus she's busily describing a man she met in London two weeks earlier. He comes from Rome, his name is Claudio, he's dying to meet me. I'm unconvinced. She seems surprised we don't already know each other. After all, we both live in the same city.

Friends from England are strange. They think the world outside is woven into a kind of basket for their annual holidays, each thread a known and loving face. Abroad, for them, is intimate and simplified, smaller than the trivial, mean-spirited island their own lives focus on. It's a trick of perspective, I suppose, like one of those maps where every country is represented according to its gross domestic product. I tell her that Romans always leave the city in August, and hope she lets the matter drop. I point out fragments of the ancient city as the bus speeds past. But Sophie's adamant he's waiting for her to call. As soon as we're inside the flat she drops her cases and races for the phone. I hear her shriek with laughter as I carry her luggage into the spare bedroom. The next thing I know we're meeting on Tuesday evening at the Circus Maximus.

Tuesday night is Kubrick night. The massive screen dividing the circus in two is showing *Barry Lyndon*. I sit between some soldiers and a group of German tourists and watch the film, struck, as the highwaymen rob him, by the bulge in Ryan O'Neal's knickerbockers, what Barthes might have called the *punctum*. Sophie goes off to find her friend, irritated that I don't go with her. When she comes back with him she seems disappointed, oddly I think, until I look at Claudio and understand. Claudio's shorter than Sophie and wearing tight white shorts and a singlet. His hair has been gelled into a feeble crest. He might be thirty, thirty-five, it's hard to tell. He takes his eyes off Sophie and stares with unwavering hostility into mine. She introduces me to him as 'the friend I told you about, you *know*'. His chief concern seems to be his fluent, but imprecise English, which he uses to little effect on Sophie, who squirms and pulls a face at me. 'I'm sorry?' she keeps saying. She tries to draw me into conversation, talking across his back towards me. His singlet cuts into the sweat-greased flesh of his neck and shoulders. When he rests a hand on the chair beside me, barricading Sophie, a tangle of moist black hair emerges from his armpit. I turn to watch the film.

Rome in August is usually an exhausted place, but this year there's a bubble-like delicacy to everything, a sheen. I can't get to sleep before dawn; I'm scared of missing something. As people begin to drift off after the film I give my spare keys to Sophie, who takes them with a wince, and wander to Monte Caprino, a tangle of winding paths, dead ends, mysterious descents, behind the Capitol. Steep flights of steps lead up to terraces surrounded by bushes I can't identify by name, but only by the pungency of their leaves, a scent I associate with sex.

The first man I speak to is someone whose friend had a brief affair with my flatmate, Gordon. The affair led us both into a circle of gay men in the 'art business', most of them escort-cum-lackeys for big-time art smugglers who know Valentino and like to be surrounded by the willing style-obsessed young. Roberto used to wear sharply creased trousers and a tie. Now he's bearded for the summer, with a baseball cap and dungarees. He's looking for contacts in Germany, he says.

It's past three o'clock in the morning, but the air is still warm, with a light breeze. Throughout the conversation our eyes are never still. We look at everyone who passes with flushes of interest, and anyone who doesn't know us might even think that nothing important is being said, that we aren't friends at all, that we value our friendship less than casual sex. Yet every word we say stays with me, even now, years later, as I write this, and know that some of those men I looked at and desired are dead. Everything in my life is being made here, in this now that is nothing, of nothing, of air and the scent of these dark, pungent bushes. In the shaft-like depth of the moment.

After about twenty minutes we split up, Roberto trailing a German accent to his left. I walk up a flight of steps that leads to the rock from which traitors were thrown. There is a cage down below where the city used to keep a lion. Or was it a she-wolf? Whatever it was, it's dead.

The bushes are denser here. They grow in a spiral like hair on some men's crowns. My eyes adjust to the dark and I see a man in the heart of the spiral. He must be seventy. He has taken off all his clothes and hung them on a branch. His shoes, with their socks rolled into balls inside, are side by side beneath a bush. He's arched back precariously, taut as a bow, wanking. His eyes and mouth are closed. There is an absolute stillness, apart from his hand, moving faster and faster until he comes with a splutter of watery sperm. He staggers forward as though the string that was holding him has been cut, and I realize that I've been holding my breath and gasp for air. Other men have been watching him as well, from the dark of other bushes. The old man opens his eyes, like someone waking up, and gets dressed, almost falling over as he slides his thin white legs into trousers. Without looking round, he walks out of the clearing and down the path. The members of his audience glance at one another, suddenly embarrassed, then melt away.

A few minutes later, as I walk back down the path, I notice a man in his early twenties, with cropped blond hair and sharp, fox-like features. He's wearing a grubby T-shirt and a pair of army shorts, with the kind of navy-blue plimsolls we used to wear at school. His legs are muscular, not tanned, covered with fine, almost white hair. I move towards him, but he turns his head slightly away and I know I'm not wanted.

Two hours later I see him again as he walks out from behind a bush, buttoning up his shorts. This time he stares at me and smiles. He looks younger when he smiles, and more attractive. I don't notice who else is in the bush.

'*Ciao,*' I say.

He nods and smiles again, then asks, '*Est-ce que tu parles français?*'

I thank God for Labelle.

'*Veux-tu coucher avec moi?*' I say, continuing, with more confidence, '*Ce soir?*'

He smiles again. I lead him down the path.

When we get back to the flat Sophie is splayed across the sofa, talking to Gordon. There is no sign of Claudio. An almost empty bottle of duty-free vodka stands between them on the table, beside the ashtray, a half-eaten peach and some water melon rind. Seeds lie scattered across the table. Sophie is talking with drunken animation to Gordon, whose eyes are heavy. As we walk into the room she stares up, startled, and pauses. It's clear that she has been talking about me, about us, from the embarrassed, almost pleading glance she throws at Gordon. It's equally clear that the vivid drive of her narrative has wiped my existence from her mind.

Then she sees that I'm not alone, and is suddenly at her ease.

'Eric,' I say, standing to one side, pronouncing it 'Orric', rolling my r's as best I can. 'He's French.' I looked at his passport in the lift after pretending I didn't understand his surname. I wanted to see how old he is. He is twenty-two.

He blinks. His eyelashes are coarse, long, blond. He seems to be surprised to find people still awake, while the sky outside fills up with milky light. Sophie shouts questions at him in English. He shakes his head, bemused, glancing to me for help. Gordon wakes up and begins to speak in laboured but comprehensible French. Eric seems relieved, sitting down on the sofa. He tells Gordon that he's a fireman, and I see him in uniform, a rubbery hybrid of boots and belt. Sophie has suddenly gone to sleep and is snoring lightly, her mouth falling open. As the sun rises outside and Gordon begins to concentrate on his tenses I pull Eric to his feet and into my bedroom.

He looks round and seems impressed. I glance at the rented furniture, which has nothing to do with me, and wonder what kind of person he is. We both have so little to go on. He pulls off his T-shirt and I reach out to touch him, his skin, the points of his nipples, but he is bending over to take off his plimsolls and I let my hand rest lightly on his back as though that's what I want to do. Then he straightens up and gestures toward the bathroom with his head. I nod.

I watch him shower. He turns the taps until the water is as hot as he can stand. His milky skin grows pink. He holds his head back and the water beats his face. I can see that he has completely forgotten me. He has no idea where he is, no idea that he is being watched. I stand by the door of my bathroom as steam lifts off him, knowing that I will never see any body more beautiful. I might as well not be here. I could be watching him through a window. He reaches to turn off the taps and I dart away, almost ashamed.

When we are lying on the bed he coughs nervously. I am hesitant, waiting for him to make a move. He asks me if I understand the words '*passif*' and '*actif*'. Reluctantly, I say I do.

'*Je suis passif*,' he says.

'*Moi aussi*,' I say, though that isn't always true. I think I just want to be possessed by him.

We lie together for some minutes and then he asks me if I have ever loved a woman. I understand the question after he has repeated it twice. I gesture towards the sitting room and say, or think I say, that I have slept with one. '*La femme ici*,' I say. He is startled, and I wonder what I have said. He closes his eyes and turns slightly on to one side, away from me. I wait until I think he's asleep and then begin to stroke his leg. I reach for his penis, feeling it swell in my hand. But he moves away with a sigh and I understand that he is still awake.

Next morning he tells me he is going back to Paris because he has run out of money. There is a brief silence while I think about this, and then I offer to take him to the station on my moped. He holds me tight throughout the journey with what feels like affection, resting his cheek on my neck. I feel his stubble scratch me as the moped jolts over the cobbles and I'm glad I didn't offer him my razor. At the station, to my surprise, he gives me his number and address in Paris. His writing is big, clumsily formed, the numbers like those made by a child. He asks me to get in touch. As he moves away he looks like a teenage boy in his grubby T-shirt and shorts, baggy round the arse. He should have a catapult sitting out of the pocket. I think of the body I have seen, and briefly touched, as it walks back into the world away from me. I feel where his stubble scratched my neck.

Sophie and I eat not far from the Colosseum. By the time we are drunk I mention that, talking to Eric, I had called her my *'femme'*.

'What does *"femme"* mean?' she says, staring up from her plate. She looks defensive.

'I think it might mean wife,' I giggle.

'You have no idea how much you hurt me, do you?' she says after a pause, her tone conversational. She's right, of course. It's natural for me to hurt her without noticing. It seems to me sometimes that hurt is what gives our relationship depth.

'Was he any good?' she says when she sees that I'm not going to answer.

'He was *passif*,' I say wryly.

'Does that mean you picked him up?'

'It means that too,' I say.

Later, when we are drinking grappa, she says, 'Can't we just be friends?'

'That's all I've ever wanted,' I say earnestly.

Then, after a third grappa, she begins to cry. 'All I want is your child,' she says.

'Please, Sophie.' I stroke her arm.

'Oh, fuck off.' Then, 'But you promised. Don't you remember? You promised.'

I take her home on the moped. As soon as she has let herself into the flat I go to Monte Caprino. The first person I see is Roberto. He's excited about the German man he tracked down last night. He'll be visiting him in Frankfurt in the autumn. Not to be out-done, I say that I'll soon have a chance to improve what Gordon has referred to as my 'schoolgirl French', and tell him about Eric. Roberto listens with interest, then surprise. As I describe Eric his surprise turns into poorly concealed amusement.

'What does he do?' he asks me. I tell him, with civic pride, that Eric is a fireman. Roberto pats my arm, clearly relieved.

'I didn't want to have to tell you,' he says, 'but it sounded as though your Eric was down there on the terrace.'

'What do you mean?' I say. '"It sounded"?'

'Don't worry,' says Roberto. 'The Parisian Eric down there sells life insurance. Anyway, he's nothing like as good-looking as the one you fucked.'

I go to the top of the steps and look at the terrace below. Eric is leaning against the parapet talking to someone. He is wearing the same grubby clothes he wore last night.

A month later I'm in Paris with Gordon. We're staying with Brigitte, a French woman we met on holiday at the beginning of the summer. Brigitte's flat overlooks the park of Buttes-Chaumont. We go for a walk there after lunch on the second day of our visit, by which time our conversation has become almost cloyingly inti-mate. Newlyweds are gathering on the grass to pose for their photograph albums. Watching a bride arrange her voluminous skirt around her, we continue to talk about fidelity. Brigitte says she would never trust a lover the way she would trust a friend. I instantly tell her about Eric while Gordon stares at the couples and thinks of his new lover in Rome. When I tease him, he snaps at me, pretending that he wants to know if I called Sophie back. Since her return to London Sophie has been using the office phone to plague the flat. Each time I refuse to answer the message becomes more spiteful. During the last tearful monologue she told Gordon I was less than 'well endowed'. Gordon dutifully reported back. I feel that Sophie is both far away in the past and waiting for me, a dark and brooding cloud, as I blithely, ignorantly, drift in her direction.

Later that day, after aperitifs, I search my wallet for the scrap of paper I haven't been able to throw away and we drive out to Eric's address. It's on the other side of Paris, a shabby late-nineteenth-century building with art-nouveau balconies that's been turned into a hotel. As soon as we park I know I'm too shy to go in. Brigitte, with an air of adventurous complicity I find faintly irritating, helps me write a message, which she delivers. The message is brief: her number and the times I can be found, either this evening or tomorrow morning. I put the word 'Rome' in brackets after my name, then watch her walk out of the hotel and run towards the car. Gordon hums critically in the back of the car.

'He really is a fireman,' she says, squeezing my arm, excited by this further proof of Eric's integrity. 'I asked the receptionist.'

I spend the evening waiting for a phone call. Some of Brigitte's friends come round for dinner. We speak about food and language, exchanging addresses for other summers, while Brigitte entertains in a high-spirited, unexpectedly professional fashion. Every now and again Gordon catches my eye and glances towards the phone. By the time we are drinking cognac I know that Eric will never call and feel relieved. I see his failure as another kind of faithfulness, to the moment.

So when the telephone rings at half past six the next morning I wait for Brigitte to answer. I hear her speak; with a shock I hear her say my name. She carries the phone into the room where Gordon and I are sleeping, then squats on the floor beside the bed, to listen. I shouldn't mind her being there. It's only fair that Eric should be common property, cement in the larger intimacy of entertaining friends.

'*Allo!*' I say.

Eric begins to talk. I recognize his voice by its tone, but the words mean nothing. He sounds as though he's got a cold. I begin to catch scraps of meaning. Finally I realize that he wants us to meet.

'*Je dois partir,*' I say, glancing at Brigitte to check my French.

She nods, but looks confused, disappointed. He asks me if we can meet for lunch.

'*Je dois partir*,' I say again. At this point Gordon wakes up. I cover the mouthpiece with my hand and say, 'It's Eric!' and for some reason we both begin to giggle. Brigitte goes into the kitchen to make coffee. By the time she comes back with a tray of cups and croissants I have lied to Eric for the third and final time.

Catherine Smith

The White Sheets

How wicked this feels, to sneak back
to our room mid-morning, windows open,
curtains drawn against the sun,
sheets smoothed, pillows plumped.
The bathroom's chrome shines like a gun,
the towels lined up like surplices.
We undress each other silently,
skin still warm from the street
where minutes ago we breathed in
slow-cooking lamb. Your mouth
tastes of melon, chorizo,
salami, dolcelatte, espresso –
and as you slide a pillow
under my buttocks, the white sheets
cool against my shoulders, I open
like the petals of a lotus.
I don't cry out, half expecting the manager,
neat and severe in her navy suit,
to rap on the door, point out
we're contravening some regulation
in the small print. We shouldn't
be inside, we should be exploring
the hushed cool of a back-street chapel,
breathing in incense, the Mother of God
regarding us mournfully as we light candles
for our dead. Instead we fuck
with the urgency of new lovers
in a dingy King's Cross hotel
on a wet Wednesday in September,
our wedding rings on bedside tables,
aware afterwards of the dull throb of traffic,
the scratches on each other's backs.

Robin Robertson

Territorial

She doesn't know I'm watching her,
that what I'm watching is a cat
opening up new territories to hunt and play.
She is grooming herself into life: deciphering
each stray scent, finding her fluency. Its code
already broken, she is starting to read the world.

When she sees me, she changes,
switches to a slow walk, her poise slipped
to a feigned interest. Why should I be surprised
she curls past, refusing to catch my eye?
Only back to get warm,
she has been learning how to kill boys.

Doris Lessing

In the National Gallery

My intention was simple. I had a free hour. Instead of spending it going from picture to picture until the time ran out, I would find one large enough to be seen well from the middle of the room, and I would sit quietly and look at it. Just one picture, by itself. It should be already known to me. And there it was, the Stubbs chestnut horse, that magnificent beast, all power and potency, and from the central benches I could see it well. There were not many people that afternoon, fewer than with the Impressionists next door. I might almost have been alone with the horse, but then a man sat down, on the other side of the bench's arm and he leaned forward, elbows on knees, and looked hard at the horse. He was about sixty years old, well dressed, a well-presented man absorbed in his contemplation. A second man sat down next to the first, who raised his hand, imposing silence. Then he murmured, 'There he is, a beauty, isn't he?' This second one was younger by a good bit. A son? A younger brother? Certainly a pupil for now the first began talking, telling him about Stubbs the painter, and about the horses he painted. He was talking in a low voice, not wanting to be taken as an official guide, but the people just behind on the bench were turning to listen, and I tried to hear too. How much I would have liked to know as much as he did, and to share this passion for Stubbs and the horse, but only phrases reached me.

The second man listened and looked and, as people passed between us and the horse, frowned at the interruption of his view. But he seemed restless, and soon was looking at his watch. The first man smiled at this and said, 'Come on, you can spare a few minutes.' The second man did sit on, for a little, then jumped up, smiling, apologetic, a bit rueful, like a pupil chidden by a teacher. The first man then flung out his hand, in a gesture of humorous resignation, and the young man snapped, 'You can't make a silk purse out of me, I keep telling you.' In the space of a moment the scene had turned ugly. The handsome young rough, revealed by what he had said and how he had said it, now seemed on the point of apologizing, retrieving the situation, but the first man had turned his shoulder on him. The younger one went fast to the exit, which led to the French eighteenth century, though it was unlikely he had meant to find himself there. He turned and sketched a little frivolous wave, as if saying, 'Oh, let's kiss and make up,' but his mentor was still not looking at him but past me to the end of this gallery.

The room was suddenly noisy and animated. Its tranquillity had been banished by the advent of some schoolgirls, identified by smart little scarves, worn just so, expressing individuality, with a uniform of black jeans and black jackets. They were French, ten or so, a group conscious of being one, and they stood together just inside the big doors near Constable's picture of Salisbury Cathedral. They were not looking at it, or at any of the pictures, but talked loudly and laughed, expecting attention, which they were getting. The man next to me was actually leaning forward, in his pose of elbows on knees, staring at them. He had not so much as glanced at the exit where his friend had vanished. What an attractive little lot they were these girls, glittery and shiny, as if from a fever, excited perhaps from the trip, but more from their being here together, with each other, on show. Any older female watching would look and remember the driving competitiveness in a girls' group; we would know that this flock of pretty, well-dressed girls was full of rivalries, best friendships, betrayals, a seethe of emotion. One girl stood out. She was 'so French' in her way of presenting herself, a package to be admired, in the French way with their girls, with a pert little face which must have smiled a hundred times to be told that it was like Audrey Hepburn's. Well, it was, quite a bit. She was the boss girl in this group, even if not officially a head girl or monitor. She was an original, the 'card', the wit, perhaps even the buffoon.

The man next to me now did glance to see if his delinquent friend was in sight, but did not seem much put out, for he was absorbed by the girls. Everyone was looking at them. How could we not? They were so vivacious, so lively, such a little bonfire of bright sparks. Now they were playing up to us, making of some private disagreement a real drama, a joke perhaps, but voices were rising and the chief girl stood in their midst, ready to arbitrate, or adjudicate. The man next to me was staring hard at her. Yes, she really was something, this little bit of a miss from France with her chic, her dark locks of hair, cut to be crooked, dark eyes, slightly angular eyebrows. She was altogether sharp and challenging, like a spiky female kitten before it becomes a serious cat, with measure and propriety. She stood there while disagreement swirled around her. She yawned. The man stared and seemed to hold his breath. And then, without looking at them, without saying anything to them, she broke away, came towards us, or rather, towards the man, and sat down near him, on the other side of me. She had not looked at him. He did not move. She slid forward on the slippery seat, pulled herself up, and then, as it were, dived, hands between her feet, and clasped her pretty ankles. She sat herself up again, and yawned and looked at the great horse looming there. Her mouth fell open, from astonishment probably, but that turned into another yawn and she fell asleep. Just like that. She slept.

The girls had scarcely noticed her departure. They were continuing their disagreement. The man near me was very still. A quick glance showed how he cautiously turned his head to look at the sleeping beauty, so near to him. His face might seem like that if it had been slapped. She was asleep. It was the delightful effrontery of it, as if she were really alone. But she was not, and had been pulled away from that group of schoolgirls because of how he had stared, focused on her, by the sheer force of his attention. And she had not once looked at him.

'Good God,' he remarked aloud, not meaning to, but then gave me a glance, and laughed. That laugh could have been put into words, thus: 'Yes, I, too, had that irresistible impossible vitality . . . where has it all gone . . . we don't think when we are that age . . . time does its work without any reference to us . . . yes, time . . .' And so on. And I would bet words something like these were running through the minds of many people in that gallery just then.

The girl slumbered.

He remarked, to me or perhaps to himself, 'She's like a girl I was in love with once. But I was just a boy.'

'And she?' I dared.

'She was sixteen, like this one here.'

'And you?'

'I was twelve.'

'Ah, then she would be in love with a young man of twenty and to her you would be just a little kid.'

Now he looked properly at me, took me in, decided I was worthy to continue.

'Exactly right,' he said, admitting to much more than the discrepancy. 'But has it occurred to you how often our grand passions turn out to be bounded by some silly cliché?'

'Well, yes.'

'Yes. Of course she didn't reciprocate. But I was useful, you see. I was quite a likely lad, well grown, as they say, and good enough to make use of.'

Now we stared, both of us, at the girl, who had not moved, not a muscle, while we talked about her.

'I took her to *The Third Man* all that summer . . . yes, exactly so, I didn't get it either. It took me years, when much later I saw the film again and it was all clear. With her, I don't think I saw much more than her little profile.' And he indicated, smiling, that delightful face. 'I thought she had a crush on Orson Welles. I certainly had, but do you remember how that girl at the end walked down that long avenue towards her admirer, one step after another, and he waited for her, and then she walked past him, nose in the air? Well, she was rehearsing, do you see? She wanted to treat her chap like that. His name was Eric, I seem to remember. Yes, she would walk right past him, just like the girl in the film and he would be torn up with jealous rage.'

'And did that happen?'

'Who knows? That summer went past, the way summers did in those days, slowly, and later she married someone or other. And I did too.' And he laughed again. It was an unscrupulous, relishing laugh and he looked at me to share it with him.

'But if the snows of yesteryear are your thing – here they are.'

'No, I don't think they are. I don't go in for nostalgia.'

'But?' I said.

'But she's just walked in – walked in from the past. And I feel –

well, let me choose my words, I don't want to exaggerate – yes, I would say there is a knife in my heart. You are laughing?'

'Not really, no.'

'No, you shouldn't. The passions of little kids are just as strong as the grown-ups.'

'But we don't like to admit that?'

'Exactly. I remember every detail of that summer.' He was thinking of that summer and not at all of her, who was breathing away there, at his elbow.

And I was thinking that he had not suggested that his heart might have been even a little discommoded by that nasty little scene earlier.

And then she was awake. Her eyes focused, on the great brilliant horse, so close, towering there on the golden canvas, on his hind legs. Her face did not reveal what she was thinking.

What could she be making of that so dramatic horse, with his discontented eye? Was she thinking, Is this a circus horse? Horses don't usually stand on their back legs. And what was he thinking – the horse? Surely, 'What a silly business. I am a serious horse, and why should he paint me standing here with my forelegs in the air?' One thing we could be sure of was that this horse did not know he was the colour of polished copper, and so very beautiful.

The girl waved at her group, and they ran up and were scolding her for going off to sleep there. There was something theatrical about these reproaches, loud and meant to be heard. Now she must reaffirm her rights over them. She stood up and went to stand in front of the horse, and flung out her arm. 'Look,' she cried, 'A red horse!' '*Voilà! Un cheval rouge!*'

They all looked at the horse. Something had to be done, and in the spirit of their exuberance, their abundant animation, she began to laugh theatrically. Girls have to laugh, they have to, for elation rises in them like bubbles in liquid and has to find expression. They stood laughing at the horse, led by the girl, and the man, the expert on Stubbs, got up and stood in front of the horse, as if defending it. But the girls did not really care about the horse and wandered off, towards the French eighteenth century. The man merely stood there, staring after them. And then she wandered back, not to him, or that didn't seem to be the case; she stood beside him and stared at the horse, which she must have felt she had affronted by her laughter. At any rate, she and the girls hadn't really behaved very nicely. Well-behaved girls should not mock and giggle in a public gallery.

He stood staring, yes, he stared, and that wasn't very nice either. He went off towards the exit, back to the Impressionists. Her group came back to her and again they stood together, disagreeing. Now I could hear what it was all about. They were tired. They wanted to find a café and sit down and have some coffee. But then, they wouldn't see the rest of the pictures in this world-famous gallery, and they had been allotted just so long to see the great masterpieces which perhaps they might never see again.

It could have gone one way or the other. Then the girl, *his* girl, decided for them. 'Come. We must have coffee. At once. Or I'll simply die.'

The man was standing at the entrance, or exit, looking at her.

The girls were going towards him, but as they reached him on the way to departing altogether, she swerved to the left and stood gazing at Salisbury Cathedral. I would swear that this was the first picture, apart from the Stubbs, that any of them had glanced at that afternoon.

Some of her group had gone through to the Impressionists. She stood staring at the Constable, a few paces from him. One girl came back and took her by the arm and turned her around so now she was face to face with the man who for the third time had drawn her – or his memories had – towards him. She stood just in front of him. And still she did not look at him. Young things do not see the elderly or middle-aged. She might be staring straight at him, but she didn't see him.

Her friend pulled her through the big doors. There she stood and looked back. Her face said that she was wondering if she had mislaid something . . . forgotten something . . . missed something?

Then she disappeared with her group.

Slowly, he followed. Oh no, I was thinking, he simply must not try and talk to her, attract her attention, impose himself. If he did, it was easy to imagine raised voices, ugly laughter, even an 'incident' that could reach the newspapers. There was a wildness in the air, unexpressed, and raw, and dangerous.

Moniza Alvi

Interior, Degas

We must save this room from itself,
from its wallpaper cage

streaked grey-green,
from the din of its silence,

from the door that takes his weight
as he blocks the keyhole,

from the floor that takes hers,
her half-bare back to him.

This room, closed as a body,
with no visible window.

The rug knows more about it all
than we do.

The oval picture saw part of it
with its dead eye.

The clothes, limp across the bedstead,
carry it like smoke.

The mirror can't save the room,
can't draw it in completely:

the woman who couldn't hold herself up
if she wanted to,

the hard-eyed man across the floorboards,
miles from her, in his trousers.

Jean Sprackland

The Stopped Train

She stands and knows herself for the first time.
This recognition comes to each of us

sooner or later. When a baby meets a mirror
it enters this same state of rapture.
That's how the train is: stunned
and passionate. She looks, and sees

energy, will, destiny. Sees that she
touches the rails, but is not the rails,
brushes the overhead lines and drinks in power,
is headstrong and pioneering.

Inside, passengers cram the corridors,
sucking ice-cubes, taking turns at the windows.
A woman shouts: Why must you all be so *British*?
The carriage is brash with daylight

like a terrible living-room
filling up with unsaid things:
no one can get a signal here
in this nondescript England of

sly ditches and flat fields, where some
experiment must be taking place and
the only thing moving between the trees is
shadow. This is the Interior,

and if they were to smash the glass with a shoe,
jump down on to the track, set off in a somewhere
      direction,
they would be struck down
like stranded motorists in Death Valley.

The train has forgotten them. She stands and ticks,
letting the heat leak and equalize.
She is accounting for herself:

steel, glass, plastic, nylon,
an audit of chips and circuits –
a tin can in the dust, rescinding.

Gerard Woodward

Seagulls

I'd moved back to the city after ten years in the south, and I was trying to set myself up as a puppeteer, but I wasn't having much luck. I'd lost touch with all my old contacts in the puppetry society, which seemed no longer to exist. I felt as though I was having to start again from scratch.

The city was an industrial one. I found it noisy after the quietness of the south. People's voices were much louder than I was used to because they worked in noisy factories. They thought nothing of blasting music at deafening levels through thin walls, and seemed genuinely surprised if you complained. Sometimes, in the street, you could follow several conversations at once if you listened to the shouting coming from different houses. They owned bow-legged, thick-jawed dogs that shat with arrogant indifference all over the children's playgrounds and barked as repetitively as engines for no reason. The women wore their hair pulled back in ponytails so tightly their eyebrows were lifted, giving them a permanent look of surprise. People were either shockingly thin or shockingly fat. The thin ones were on drugs, I was told, and the fat ones weren't.

They were capable of quieter moments of tenderness and contemplation, however. On Sundays they flew brightly coloured kites in the playing fields. The men went fishing on the canals, often with no more equipment than a single rod and line. Most of the families seemed to own small green songbirds with bright red beaks, which they kept in cages in their front windows, and which came, I later found out, from a pet shop owned by a very old man.

My first attempts at re-establishing myself as a puppeteer involved contacting local schools. They all replied that they already had regular visits from a puppet troupe called Small World. This outfit sounded impressive. They conducted puppet-making workshops and playwriting workshops. In the afternoon they would put on an hour-long performance of a play the children had written, using puppets the children had made. Small World, it seemed, had the puppetry scene in the city sewn up.

I managed to scrape by as a children's entertainer for a while, doing birthday parties and special occasions. Bookings were scarce, and it was heartbreaking work. The children were usually out of control by the time I arrived and would tear down the theatres before I'd even finished setting up. They would demand magic tricks, but I wasn't a magician. In the end the parents would suggest I put on a video. So I was paid a hundred and fifty pounds to push one of their own cassettes into their own VHS player. And the children did calm down, and seemed to value and relish the video all the more simply because I had put it on.

My applications to the local office of the regional arts board were fruitless. Every grant, award, prize or theatre residency had already gone to Small World. These people had a complete monopoly, a stranglehold, on puppeteering in the city. I suggested to the arts board that this was unfair. Their reply was to the effect that there was really only room for one puppet troupe in a city of this size. If I wanted a future as a puppeteer I should consider working with them. Joining them.

I found out that Small World gave weekly public performances in one of the city's central squares, behind an old Georgian church blackened with soot.

I had to admit it was an impressive show. Small World, as its name suggested, fused eastern European wooden and rod dolls with Javanese shadow theatre. They even had a Scaramouche, whose head was nested in its body. The finale of the show was a skeleton called Georgina, who did a spectacular dance of death during which her skeleton dismantled itself bone by bone, even down to individual vertebrae, until the stage was a crowd of bobbing, dancing bones that would, bone by bone, reassemble into a skeleton once more. The audience of tubby toddlers and orange-haired tots loved this, and screamed with delight at the rollicking skeleton. I was all the more amazed to find, at the end, that the whole show was performed by just two puppeteers, a husband-and-wife operation.

For some reason, I have to say, my nerve failed me on that occasion and I didn't introduce myself to the puppeteers of Small World. Instead I observed them silently from a corner of the graveyard as they packed away their stage. Mrs Small World was a fortyish woman with girlishly long hair. She was wearing a diaphanous tie-dye blouse over sky-blue cords. Mr Small World was quite different. A much older man, in his late sixties, I thought, a pallid, cadaverous, lumpy sort of creature with porridgy hair and biscuity skin, a lipless visage and sad, melting eyes. He wore nothing but grey, a damp, mushroomy grey, right down to his socks. I wondered for a while if they were father and daughter, but it soon became clear they were not. Once they'd lugged all their cases and boxes to their Dormobile, the cadaverous one drove off while the girlish one remained in the city, and they gave each other a parting, lingering lip-kiss before separating.

It was shortly after this that the scandal of the songbirds broke. The old man in the pet shop was discovered to have been painting ordinary sparrows with green and red enamel paint, the sort kids use on model aeroplanes. No one knew how he'd managed to trap these sparrows, but it raised a debate in the pages of the local paper about the continued decline of the species. The sparrow population had fallen by seventy-five per cent in some parts of the city. Surely one man couldn't be responsible, they said, while others pointed out that the sparrows' decline was part of a national trend.

I wondered what the bird owners did with their songbirds now that they'd discovered they were fakes. Did they remove the paint and continue the birds' domestic entrapment, but as ordinary sparrows? Some people said it was impossible to remove the paint without harming the birds. Most people, it was believed, kept them as they were, green and red, and were told that the paint would eventually flake away. Others said the birds would die a natural death long before the paint flaked off. Some suggested they should be released back into the wild to rebuild the sparrow population. This sparked further debate as to whether painted sparrows would be able to find mates, except with each other, and then would they recognize their young?

I had not got used to the way people looked at you in this city. They would stare at you, but with faces of dreamy indifference, as though their thoughts were elsewhere, or as if they didn't have any thoughts at all. Their faces always bore the look of blissful unawareness that you see on people who are sleeping.

I remember, the night after my first encounter with Small World, someone turned over all the brave, packed wheelie bins in the alley beside my house, spilling their rancid loads. They looked like the fallen, disembowelled dead of some medieval battlefield.

The next time I saw Mr and Mrs Small World at the graveyard, I realized I knew the man. He had joined the old puppetry society of which I had been a member, just before I left the city. I think his first meeting had been my last. He had been distraught, as I recall, because his father had just died.

I hadn't had the opportunity to speak to him on that occasion, but I had noticed his sickly pallor even then. I also remembered the general twitchiness, the continual but short-lived looks of shock and pain, as though an invisible assailant was repeatedly sticking pins in him. I remembered overhearing him telling other members of the society, 'My father died last week. I'm having trouble talking . . .' He wouldn't elaborate further, thinking his own manner sufficient testament to the grief he was experiencing.

I remember thinking it odd: your father dies, a cause of great sorrow, and the next thing you do is join a society of puppeteers. Did he hope to derive some comfort, perhaps, from manipulating the strings of a father-homunculus?

This time I spoke to them. Mr Small World, whose name was Seamus, claimed he didn't remember me. I couldn't say this was surprising as we'd never really met. Yet inwardly I felt annoyed that he should have made a much greater impression on me than I on him.

I tried fishing into their lives, trying to get a bite of something that I could use to draw myself closer to them, but Seamus remained very distant, secretive even. He said almost nothing about himself, while his wife said nothing about anything, busying herself with packing away the puppets and their theatre.

We did find common ground when we talked about the society of puppeteers to which the three of us had belonged. Many of the familiar old names had left puppeteering altogether, and most of the people who were involved with Small World now were new names to me. (Small World, it seemed, acted almost like an agency, contracting out to individuals or teams puppetry work that couldn't be done by Seamus and his wife.) But the odd name from the past did crop up in conversation.

And then I mentioned Henrietta.

'We haven't seen her for a long time,' said Seamus, 'though I think she's still around. She's changed her name, though.'

'What to?'

Seamus thought hard.

'It was a city, I think. She called herself after a city.'

'Chicago,' came his wife's voice from the back of the van.

'That's it – Chicago.'

'Henrietta Chicago? It's a bit of a mouthful.'

'No, just Chicago. She had it done officially via deed poll. She won't answer to anything else.'

Try as I might, I could not think of Henrietta, that small, sad vampire of mine, as Chicago. Absurdly, even though we hadn't spoken for more than ten years, I felt a little bit hurt, as if she'd been my daughter and I had chosen the name Henrietta for her. It must, after all, hurt a parent to have their child reject their own name, the name they'd spent nine months or more deliberating over, that they'd argued about in Mothercare, or over ice creams on a final walk of freedom on the playing fields. Name-changing, I supposed, was a type of linguistic cosmetic surgery – removing or altering something one is born with, replacing it with something of one's own choosing. A nose – a name.

Henrietta and I had had a very brief affair when I'd lived in the city before. It couldn't have lasted more than a month, though I seemed to remember it had a long, moth-eaten tail – no sudden cutting-off, just a series of ever briefer, ever rarer meetings and phone calls, until it faded away altogether. When I left the city we wrote to each other a few times, but her letters were always politely formal and full of irrelevant news – her brother passing his exams, her sister passing her driving test. What really annoyed me about them was the way they always ended, 'Sorry, must dash now.' Henrietta, that little gothic finger-puppeteer, never dashed anywhere.

I remember the turning point of our relationship distinctly. It was during a weekend we spent together at a B&B near Hadrian's Wall. Somehow it all went wrong over breakfast. I ate all mine – a generous dish of the traditional fried meat and eggs – while she only nibbled at hers. Somehow during the eating of that breakfast she'd fallen out of love with me. I wondered – though never said, it would have sounded too silly – if my carnivorousness had somehow repelled her. She wasn't a vegetarian, as far as I could tell, yet our romance had come unstuck over a full English breakfast. She must have looked at me tearing into those rashers and sausages and thought, My God, he's just an animal . . .

I found her way of eating rather cute. It can't be true, but it seemed to me that she made a shape with her mouth exactly matching the shape of whatever was on her fork, then simply slotted it in, like one of those children's puzzles. Decorous, that was Henrietta's eating.

Eventually Seamus remembered who I was and we spent quite a while sharing reminiscences of people who came to the puppetry society meetings. 'They used to talk about you a lot,' he said, 'once you'd moved down south. You were much missed. People round here even began to feel a little bit betrayed. They spoke as if you'd sold your soul to the devil, attracted by the bright lights of the capital. How did things work out for you down there?'

Not too good, was how I replied. But Seamus didn't share these small-minded thoughts, and almost straight away he started giving me work. I helped with public shows and school workshops. I met some old acquaintances, some of whom looked openly displeased to see me back. 'He thinks he can swan off down south and then come back when things don't work out, and expect us to greet him with open arms and balloons. Who does he think he is?' At least, that's what I imagined they might be thinking. The puppetry society had disbanded shortly after I left, and some people blamed me for that. Seamus had formed Small World from the rump of that society, hence his subsequent dominance of local puppetry.

I began to think I might meet Henrietta again, that she might turn up for one of the shows, or that we might have to team up for a school workshop. But her severance from the old life in puppetry circles seemed complete. Chicago, as I was never able to call her, had put her ten fingers to more productive uses. I just wondered what they were.

I did glimpse her once, from the top deck of a bus. She was leaning against an advert at a bus stop, looking worried. At least, I think it was her. I couldn't be sure.

Things were going too well. I was getting regular work through Small World. Then I was invited to dinner at the couple's house to hear some bad news.

I knew it was going to be bad news because so little preparation had been put into the dinner. They'd expended the least possible amount of effort, to the extent that when I arrived I sensed they'd forgotten about the invitation. Mrs Small World answered the door and took a second to comprehend my presence. I met Seamus walking down the hall with two milk bottles full to the neck with water.

'Our plants get very thirsty,' he said, pouring the water into the pots of various succulents. Feed the plants first, I thought. Get your priorities right.

All evening Mrs Small World would suddenly look at her fingers in alarm, as though something had just bitten her. Then she would put her hand to her mouth, flat with nails inward, and nibble. The dinner was cold, intentionally. Quiche and couscous with a helping of salad. I was very surprised to see one of the painted sparrows in a cage by the window. I didn't know if they knew that they were painted. Even from a distance I could see the colour on its beak was beginning to flake, the green of its feathers beginning to fade back to its natural brown.

'The thing is,' said Seamus, chewing insufficiently, so that his every word revealed a different arrangement of the food in his mouth, 'we're not sure we can use you in Small World any more.'

'Why not?' I said, shocked by his bluntness.

'There's a question of fairness,' said his wife, drawing herself away from careful contemplation of her fingers. 'There are people in this city who would give their right arm to be in your position.'

'Good puppeteers,' Seamus added, 'good men and women who've been loyal to us and to the city. I'm afraid your position with us has upset a great many of our loyal friends. Much more than I had expected . . .'

'We are both great admirers of your work but, like I said, it comes back to a question of fairness . . .'

Just then their daughter appeared. She was nine years old and had been playing computer games in her bedroom. On her arrival everything in the room changed. Her parents stiffened noticeably and looked concerned. Even inanimate objects – books, cups, pictures – seemed to react to her presence.

The daughter was cross, red-faced. She stamped around the room, telling her parents they were stupid. Something had gone wrong with the computer. It had run out of memory. Seamus, it transpired, had been promising to buy new memory for it for months.

'I'm sorry, I keep forgetting, darling . . .'

'You're so pathetic, Daddy!' She stamped.

'And memory is very expensive,' said her mother.

The little girl shivered with rage, clenched her whole body and shrieked at the ceiling, 'Why can't you be richer?'

And then she stamped out of the room.

I felt as though I'd reluctantly been let in on a secret, the secret being their daughter's hideous temper and her parents' helplessness before it. No comment was passed on the incident, even though the stamping and slamming could be heard somewhere high up in the house for several minutes.

I finished my cold couscous and made to leave. I didn't think it was right that this couple should hold the careers of the city's puppeteers in the balance, but all I could find to say was, 'Your bird isn't real. Didn't you know? It's just a sparrow that's been dyed and painted.'

I left them in their dining room and let myself out. I can still picture them as they sat at the table, shock on their faces as they absorbed my news, looking first at each other, then at their fake songbird, then at each other again. I could see it had all suddenly made sense for them – the fading plumage, the rasping tunelessness.

I carried on living in the city but I gave up puppeteering. I got a job as a postman and this gave me afternoons off, which I spent wandering aimlessly across the playing fields and along the canals. I never saw Chicago again, but I saw lots of seagulls, even though we're fifty miles from the nearest coast. They come all this way inland and congregate on the playing fields. Sometimes they rise up and circle about in a great rotating wheel, hundreds of feet across. This can carry on for hours, so high up that no one takes any notice. But sometimes I'll spend a whole afternoon watching the birds. They carry on in this wheeling motion, but they drift off slightly, so that eventually they are circling several streets away from where they started. Then an amazing thing happens. A few seagulls peel themselves away from the main circle and fly in a straight line back to where their circling started. In time the rest of the gulls follow, unspooling from the main loop to return to the original circling. So for a while there are two circles connected by a straight line, just like a vast tape recorder made of birds, until they have all returned to the original location. Then the whole process starts again. I see it nearly every day.

Tod Hartman

Dear Dear Leader

CYCLE
Camden Young Communists' League

15 April 2004

16 Ross Street
Camden
London
N21 3RD

To: Commander Kim Jong-Il
        People's Palace
        Pyongyang
        North Korea
        Post Code: 1

Dear Dear Leader Kim Jong-Il,

Let me take this opportunity to congratulate you on the occasion of the biennial celebrations for the commemoration of the Juche Idea, in Pyongyang, this year. You don't know me, but I hope that we will become firm international friends over the course of a long and meaningful correspondence. I realise that someone in your position must receive a huge amount of post, so if you have taken the time to personally read my letter, please allow me to express my deepest gratitude at this point.

I write to you as the official representative of the Romsey branch of (acting secretary) the Young British Communist League. Here in London, we have held study groups on several of your works, including *On the Emergence of Modern Revisionism* and *On the Decisive Role of Ideology*, the latter of which particularly impressed us with its trenchant attack on those who would disengage with the anti-imperialist struggle and yield to the Americans' policy of nuclear blackmail. Your words have inspired some of our own publications and manifestos. Hooray for the Revolution!

I would like to request, if possible, some small token of your person and the North Korean revolution – perhaps a signed photograph, that we could display in our party headquarters in Camden. If you would be amenable to this, you can reach me at the address above.

Once again, allow me to offer my deepest congratulations on this most momentous of occasions, and reiterate our undying admiration for the struggle of the true, Democratic Korea under your great leadership.

Yours sincerely,

Paul Cook, CYCLE (Acting Secretary)

9 May 2004

16 Ross Street
Camden
London
N21 3RD

Dear Dear Leader,

I wrote to you on 15 April of this year on the occasion of the biennial celebrations for the commemoration of the Juche idea in Pyongyang last month. I have yet to receive a reply.

You must allow me to make a small confession at this point. CYCLE is not an officially accredited institution, at least not in a narrow, capitalist sense. The members (or rather, the Member, Me) view it more as a personal project, a vision, to present and debate the concepts of the Juche idea and to paint a true, objective, portrait of North Korea and its government to people in the West.

Specifically, I seek to engage with and challenge those negative biases towards your person that are so prevalent in the British media, biases which have come directly from the poison pens of the American Imperialist agents in Seoul!

But if the reason you haven't been writing back to me is that you have discovered that there is no party branch in Camden, please Please PLEASE rest assured that I am no spy for Anglo-American colonialists seeking to gain information to destabilise your regime. I am, instead, you might say, your biggest fan!

I am pleased that we've now got that sorted out between us. Looking forward to receiving your next letter!

Best wishes,

Paul Cook

15 May 2004

Bloomsbury
London

Dear Dear Leader,

I fear the reason you have not been replying to my letters is that you suspect me of harbouring a bourgeois background. You are quite right to be cautious. As Mao Zedong said, 'it is right to rebel against the reactionaries'.

Let me put your mind at rest. I should explain first of all that I come from a humble background, just like you. My great-grand-father was the leader of the Ledsborough miners' strike of 1913, so revolutionary spirit is in my blood. My childhood was not easy. My parents were both hard-working people – my father sadly died when I was quite young in an industrial accident.

Because of my class background, I was forced to spend my childhood in a variety of institutions, subject to the biopolitical controls of the capitalist state, medicated to the point of unconsciousness in an effort to quell my revolutionary spirit. However, upon reaching the age of majority, I devoted myself to the study of

Marx and Lenin, Gramsci, Althusser, and of course your own seminal works, and have spurned the *soma* and the panoptical surveillance imposed on me by the medical profession and the American capitalist pharmaceutical industry. I have won a scholarship to read for a degree in Politics and History at University College, London as a mature student, and am well on the way to building a high-powered career in academic and media circles. I am studying primarily under the tutelage of Dr. Roderick Stuffer, a distinguished cultural historian and sociologist. My main project consists of a comprehensive theoretical study entitled *On the Bourgeois Treachery of Opera*.

Dr. Stuffer may come from a middle-class background but he is the epitome of kindness, as well as being a critically engaged intellectual fighting for the rights of the proletariat! He has even co-authored a volume entitled *Indigenous Rights: Property or Paradox?* based on his own fieldwork amongst the Yuhup tribes/peoples of Brazil!!

Perhaps we could exchange our work sometime, Dear Leader? Are you working on anything at the moment?

Yours,

Paul Cook

1 June 2004

Bloomsbury
London

Dear Dear Leader,

I am writing to tell you about a crime against the Working People, the Juche Idea and the spirit of the revolution and my reaction to it. You would be proud of me. At the first seminar on 'post' socialist studies here at University College, London, in which I intend to be a steadfast, if critical, participant, the committee had the unfortunate bad judgement to invite a practitioner of reactionary ideas!

Some ridiculous bourgeois 'intellectual' of the arrogant neo-liberal bent had the cheek to present a paper on the 'tragic irony' of the revolutionary project!! Here are my notes from the session (I was a little bit late as I was detained in the college bar for the obligatory pre-seminar drinks and meet-and-greet).

'. . . We have seen,' continues Dr. Hammond-Smith (PhD Vocational Community College of Hull part-time, *in absentia,* forthcoming), removing and then replacing her little pretentious black-rimmed horizontal spectacles (how *that* trend ever came to symbolise the feminist intellectual we shall *never* know, I personally think the French have a lot to answer for), 'that the communist system which seemed to be a dream for the workers in 1952 had turned to a nightmare by the end of 1962. The harsh realities of collectivisation had taken their toll, and from that point on there could be no return to Petre's Futuristic vision. The aesthetics of power had now replaced the idealism of . . .'

The bitch! What could she know about the hardships of the Prahovan worker? Doubtless the regime had been sabotaged – as everywhere – by capitalist bourgeois traitors seeking to line their own pockets on the back of the party. I have half a mind to stand up during question time and ask her if *her* great-grandfather was the leader of the 1913 Ledsborough miners' strike and if not what business the middle-class reactionary *provocateur* from Islington has speaking for the proletariat. But I restrain myself. After all, it would not do to make a bad impression on Dr. Stuffer, who is to be my academic supervisor and sponsor and letter-writer and key to a brilliant future in academic and media circles – and my instinct tells me that denouncing the speaker during Question Time might just do that.

Yet Question Time arrives and I can't help myself. Something strains, splits, separates inside me. Without raising my hand (Dear Leader, as you well know, the spirit of critical interrogation is within every anti-capitalist!) the words escape me, falling out of my mouth involuntarily. *Bastard! Traitor to the People! Pretender!*

A large, long silence extends through the room. Aware that my emotions have carried me away and I have perhaps gone too far, I smile a grimacey sort of smile at the group, as if I have just had to unavoidably expel a rather large amount of phlegm. Dr. Stuffer clears his throat loudly, and raises his hand to ask a question – gallantly identifying some point of interest in this academic nobody's work, effectively covering for my (warranted but unexpectedly sudden) outburst.

I know he protects me, as I would protect him in a similar situation. I know from our secret smiles and hidden coded conversation that we are complicit together, partners in the project of dismantling the capitalist hegemony!!!

I am sending you a photograph of Dr. Stuffer in this letter. You can see that there is snow in the background. In fact, this is a picture of Dr. Stuffer on a skiing holiday in Switzerland!!

Yours,

Paul Cook

12 August 2004

Hackney

Dear Dear Leader,

Hello. This is the last letter you will receive from me because tonight I have decided to end my own life. I have nothing left to hold on to in life of value (besides you Dear Leader and Dr. Stuffer of course) and my life has been nothing more than a tragic itinerary of unfortunate events. I have put my affairs in order and lined up the requisite quantities of sleeping pills and am getting ready for my final overdose.

I wish you well in all your current and future projects.

It would have been nice to receive a letter from you. But obviously it's too late now. Adieu then.

Yours,

Paul Cook

15 September 2004

Hackney

Dear Dear Leader,

Much has happened since that last time I wrote to you. The big news is that I have decided to give up my place at university and focus entirely on my political activities, writing and other projects. I have rather jarringly discovered that the path to building a high-powered career in academic and media circles lies not in burrowing oneself away in some reactionary and criminal institution such as the University of London. That's right, criminal! Not only is UCL complicit in crimes against the World's Poor, but they are intellectual plagiarists as well!!!!

As you know, I am halfway through writing *On the Bourgeois Treachery of Opera*, the book that will solidify my reputation as a high-flyer in academic and media circles. Obviously this work takes up a large part of my time and attention. This morning I was in the photocopying room in the Department of Political Sciences at the university copying both volumes of Marx's *Capital* (admittedly quite a large number of pages) when Dr. Stuffer suddenly burst in, staring at me as if I had been making lewd photocopies of some private part of my body! 'What are you doing?' he asked, 'I'm afraid the photocopier is for staff use only.' 'Why, highly topical and important work!!' I replied, somewhat indignantly. Is not the function of the mentor to encourage the student's creativity and initiative rather than stifling him with petty bureaucratic regulations??????? Apparently this is not the case in the University of London system. I was summoned later on that afternoon, as if to some fascist interrogation to confirm my imminent deportation to a death-camp, to Dr. Stuffer's office, to 'explain myself'. Explain myself for what? I asked. Is it true, replies this Hitlerian official, this disgusting collaborationist leech who I had previously thought of as my advocate in academic and media circles, it is true that you have not attended a course lecture or seminar in the past two months? This may well be the case I replied, but I am engaged in other, more pressing work! And at that moment, I happened to glance down at the miscreant's desk and see MY text of *On the Bourgeois Treachery of Opera*, mistakenly left in the photocopying room. The bastard was obviously copying it and would attempt to pass it off as his own work!!

There is a level of subjugation that one individual can stand, and at that moment I passed that level and went absolutely mad. Thief! I cried, Plagiarist! Please, please, articulated Dr. Stuffer, standing up and putting his hands out in front of him in that disgusting compromising way, that awful *just listen to reason* of the bourgeois liberal intellectual traitor. Please don't become agitated, he said. Agitated??? You have stolen the work of another! I yelled. And I must confess my teeth sank into the bone structure of his hairy fat real-ale-drinking reclining-bicycle-building organic-vegetable-eating shoulder and drew blood.

This is perhaps the principal reason I am now not allowed to set foot on University of London property (they call it an 'ASBO' here!). But let me tell you if this hadn't happened I would have withdrawn my presence out of choice!

I am now thinking of becoming a visiting fellow at Kim Il Sung University. Could you please send the relevant information or a prospectus? I would be willing to attend an intensive Korean language course provided I was given a stipend to finish *OBTO*.

Yours,

Paul Cook

1 October 2004

Hackney Central Library

Dear Dear Leader,

How are you? Things are fine here. We've had quite a cold spell here in London. Apart from that, I don't have much to report. Hope you are well. Oh, I may not be able to write for a few days as I need to go on a short trip to Paris as I am co-authoring an article with Jacques Derrida.

Â bientôt!

Paul Cook

8 October 2004

Café Les Deux Magots
Paris, France

Dear Dear Leader,

Hello from Paris. My visit has been an emotional roller-coaster, let me tell you.

As you know, I went to Paris with a copy of my article – or rather *our* article – awaiting JD's contribution – a sublime, powerful little piece entitled 'The Crisis of Modernity', which I had helpfully translated into French as '*L'impossibilité des choses*'. I had written to Derrida the week before and more or less expected his part of the writing to be done by the time of my arrival in Paris and our *rendez-vous*, which I fixed for 3 today. I am perfectly willing to collaborate with Derrida on this, providing he shows *some* enthusiasm. As you know, JD is battling with terminal cancer, and – let's be realistic, not morbid – it will benefit both of us to get this article finished quickly.

Would you believe this – when I buzzed Derrida's bell some arrogant assistant had the gall to have cancelled my *entretien* with Jacques, and claimed that there was no such meeting scheduled!! Doubtless frightened of a competitor for Derrida's attention (Me!). I had to insist that I did indeed have a meeting of top-level importance and that this secretary would undoubtedly face JD's wrath should I not be invited in immediately and offered a complimentary drink.

This individual I suspected was in fact JD's daughter, some poor dim-witted creature whose long-standing Ophelia Complex has left her devoid of any social skills. *Vous êtes mariée?* I asked, trying to make conversation. *Il n'est peut-être pas trop tard pour avoir des enfants*, I assured her encouragingly, trying to win her trust. *Comment connaissez-vous Jacques?* she asked. *Oui, nous nous sommes rencontrés dans le contexte d'un rencontre-débat et puis nous avons construit un partenariat intellectuel ensemble*, I replied, fibbing ever so slightly. Time seemed to stretch out uncomfortably as I finished a bottle of red she had produced at my request and then several supplementary glasses and she stared at me quizzically – as if drinking wine was some sort of unheard of custom – in France!!

At long last, there was the sound of footsteps on the stair and, after a rustling of papers and the sound of keys being deposited in some receptacle, Derrida himself appeared. I arose, my hand outstretched, determined to be polite and friendly despite the fact that he was now arriving *two hours* late for our meeting. *Enfin! Il est de retour* ... I exclaimed jovially, rising to greet him and was about to shake the withered, ill hand that presented itself when my foot caught in the corner of an Oriental carpet and I plummeted into JD, knocking him to the ground, taking several glass knick-knacks, a pile of *Pléiades* and a heavy brass lamp with me, before collapsing onto his supine, motionless body, as in some particularly vicious tackle from an American football game.

The full dreadfulness of the situation didn't become immediately apparent until I saw the daughter staring in horror as I rolled off JD and struggled to rise again while JD himself remained motionless on the ground, giving off faint, hoarse rasping sounds. *Qu'est-ce que vous avez fait? Qu'est-ce que vous avez fait?* the woman was yelling at me.

I admit I may have had one glass of wine too many, and perhaps my coordination was not what it should have been by the time of JD's belated arrival. But, Dear Leader, let us remember at this point that if Derrida hadn't been so thoughtless as to arrive late for our meeting, and I hadn't been forced to spend hours in the uncomfortable presence of this strange, dour woman, I wouldn't have had to console myself by drinking and then – through no fault of my own – having a small accident! (I once read somewhere that accidents that occur in the home are more common than any other kind of physical injury!)

At this point there seemed to be only one option: a quick exit, especially now the woman was screaming *A l'aide! A l'aide! Je ne me sens pas bien*, I muttered apologetically, as if I was a guest at her dinner party suddenly overtaken by diarrhoea and had to excuse myself discreetly from table, as if the corpse of the host was not lying supine on the drawing room carpet. *Merci*, I said, apologetically, as the woman was frantically making for the telephone. *À bientôt*, I added, jauntily – after all, why make a situation worse than it already is? What else was to be done? It seemed that Derrida would not be writing any more articles, either with me or with anyone else.

I'm off for *steak-frites* and a *chocolat fondant avec crème anglaise*. Wish you were here!

Yours,

Paul Cook

P.S. I hope you like the postcard. The picture is of the Quai de Montebello, some artists selling paintings outside, *Notre-Dame* cathedral in the background and just next to it the *Monument de la déportation*.

10 October 2004

London!

Dear Dear Leader,

How are you? I am back in London, thank heavens. I changed my ticket to come back earlier because the Louvre is shut on Tuesdays, I had a slight touch of diarrhoea and also I still felt slightly guilty about accidentally killing Jacques Derrida. (It's official by the way, JD slipped away on the day of our *rendez-vous*, although there was no mention of the exact circumstances of death in the papers. PLEASE don't tell anyone about that by the way – it is our secret. I am trying my best to put the entire incident out of my mind.)

I am going off the Haloperidol and other drugs by which the

panoptical gaze of the bourgeois state and its biopolitical controls seeks to tranquilise me into submission. I will write again in a few days.

Yours,

Paul Cook

26 December 2004

Bloomsbury

Dear Dear Leader,

How are you? I am fine. I tried to ring up last night but all I got was a kind of beeping sound, some clicks, and then just static. You had better check that you haven't left the phone off the hook! But, anyway, the reason I was calling (apart from just to have a chat), was to tell you my exciting news . . . . I am coming to visit! That's right! I am coming to Pyongyang in 2 weeks' time so we can finally meet!!

I will be waiting in Kim Jong-Il Square (your square!) on 15 January, wearing a green jumper and having a coffee, just like in the photo I am sending with this letter.

I realise you must receive a huge quantity of international mail. And service from London to Pyongyang undoubtedly takes a bit longer to arrive that if one sent it, say, to Guernsey. But honestly! It's been eight months since I started writing to you and I haven't received a response, not even a photograph with a mimeographed 'best wishes from Commander Kim Jong-Il' on it!

Anyway, if you ARE reading this now, it is probably down to the colourful pictures of farm animals I have sellotaped to the exterior of the envelope to get your attention. If this is the first letter you have read from me then please Please PLEASE stop now and find my first letter (postmarked 15 April), wherein I introduce myself, etc. etc. At this point I will assume that you HAVE read my earlier letters. Anyway, Christmas was unbearable. If you look at the date of this letter, you will see that it is December 26, Boxing

Day, one day after Christmas – which obviously means little to you, coming from a Godless society, but I can imagine that you have some idea of its significance in the capitalist West. Christmas was in some sense a double blow because I had to put up with my mother and her latest paramour Larry, *and* the public library was shut with the result that I have lost two ENTIRE days of work on *On the Bourgeois Treachery of Opera*. As a result, I am now back on the Haloperidol and can barely move from this room.

Dr. Stuffer has extended the olive branch, so to speak, and invited me to his house for some tragic vegetarian holiday tofu meal with a group of sad international students. But it'll take more than a tin of coconut milk and some Sainsbury's curry powder to get *me* over to his bachelor pad!! The old pervert probably just wants to pull my trousers down and . . . but I shall spare you the details, Dear Leader.

I must sleep now.

Yours,

Paul Cook

20 January 2005

Hackney Central Library

Dear Dear Leader,

I guess you will be wondering why I didn't turn up at our meeting – and the simple fact is that I hate Australians. I walked into the student travel agency and there they all were with their idiotic shell necklaces and their stupid backpacks and horrid little flags stitched on, and their annoying moral superiority. Australia, I need hardly remind you, is an imperialist pig that has oppressed its aboriginal peoples to the point of extinction. When the revolution comes to your region as a whole, Dear Leader, they will be the first to go. And anyway how are these people permitted to enter the country and chop away at the foundations of the British travel industry, selling cut-rate tickets for Thailand to German sex tourists??? I asked for a student flight to Pyongyang and you would have thought I had asked for a return journey to Mercury! Why, the individual with whom I dealt didn't even know where Pyongyang was and tried to sell me a backpacking tour through Laos, Thailand, Cambodia and Vietnam on 'The Big Red Bus' – obviously some sort of awful phallic metaphor for the penis of the Western imperialist penetrating the vagina of the subordinated indigenous female. I threw the 'travel' brochure on to the ground and stormed out of the office. I shall write a letter of complaint – NOT THAT IT WILL DO ANY GOOD.

I have had a pharmaceutical-free weekend but now the horror and the spectacle of these Australians has forced me back onto the medication and I am in a contemplative state.

Yours,

(in international correspondence solidarity – looking forward to your next letter!)

Paul Cook

3 March 2005

Glasgow, Scotland

Dear Dear Leader Kim Jong-Il,

Greetings from Scotland. Allow me to introduce myself. I am an experienced, independent international traveller with an interest in exploring the regions and states of the world that have been misrepresented by the Western media and travel guidebook industry. I am especially interested in visiting your country of North Korea in order to write a non-biased, balanced account of what life is like under true, democratic leadership.

In planning my trip, I have encountered a minor problem. I wish to travel from Kaesong to Kanggye, stopping for a brief visit to Hamhung on the Southern coast. Service from Pyongyang to Kaesong, as you are no doubt aware, is excellent and direct. However, in order to get to the Eastern Coast and to Hamhung I will need to switch lines, and there does not appear to be a connection between the two major lines, both of which cross the border into South Korea in parallel. (NOT a desired stop on my itinerary!) I assume there is some sort of complimentary shuttle service, but I'd like to be sure before setting off on my journey. Heading North, I notice that I will have a 15-hour wait in Wonsan before the Kimchaek-bound train from Pyongyang arrives from the West to take me to Hamhung, from which I will then go South again on my way to Kanggye. Can you recommend any interesting sights in Wonsan, or a good restaurant? Or, failing that, is there a bus service from Wonsan up the coast to Hamhung? I would like to avoid having to transit Pyongyang again on my Hamhung–Kanggye leg of the journey, but it is unclear if it will be possible to change trains at the junction of the Kyonggi line and the Kyongwon line and switch direction on the Manpo-bound line north towards Kanggye before they descend together into the capital.

Unfortunately, my region does not boast a North Korean tourist information office, and I was wondering if you could have this information sent to me?

As I will be temporarily in London as a distinguished visiting lecturer in Post-colonialism and Post-imperialist studies at the School of Oriental and Asian Studies (SOAS), could you please send the information to this address:

Mailboxes Etc.
8-17 Tottenham Court Rd,
London, W1T 1AZ
United Kingdom.

Thank you for any information you might be able to provide.

Yours in international friendship,

Hamish McFeely.

15 March 2005

Hackney Central Library

Dear Dear Leader,

Don't worry this is the last letter I shall send you. I am just writing to say thank you. Thank you. Specifically, thank you so bloody much for:

a)Not responding to any of my letters

b)Probably not reading any of my letters

c)Causing me to waste valuable time when I could have been building a high-powered career in academic and media circles

d)Causing me to lose faith entirely in the Juche idea and the worldwide Socialist project

I have seen your photograph, but up until this point I have continued to address you with respect despite the fact that you are a pathetic midget and I am nearly twice your height. In Japan, a person of your size would be immediately knitted into a soft toy and stapled onto some raver girl's Issey Miyake combat jacket as a fashion accessory!

Yours,

Paul Cook

15 March 2005

Hackney

Dear Dear Leader,

I am writing to apologise for the inexcusable things I have written in my latest letter to you. I am in an emotionally painful state at the moment as I am attempting to abandon the tranquilising prescriptions of the bourgeois capitalist state. I cannot be responsible for my actions for the next or previous 24 hours. Could you please destroy my last letter.

Please rest assured that I regard you with the utmost respect and admiration.

Yours,

Paul Cook

16 March 2005

Hackney

Dear Dear Leader,

There is a serial killer on the loose.

If you haven't already guessed, the assassin is me! That's right, using Lacanian psychoanalysis I am going to single-handedly deconstruct the edifice of Western capitalist media hegemony! Power to the intellectual and the pen and the word!!

I will just send you a few snippets from the notes I have made tonight and you can give me comments in your next letter!!

Let's get out our analytical toolkit!!!

If we examine the latest James Bond film, for example, entitled 'Die Another Day', (I don't think you would like this one, Dear Leader!) we see the narrative structure of what is nothing less than a modernist *palindrome*. Even the most shallow analysis reveals that textually – *and* ontologically – the beginning and the end of the film are the *same thing* in the sense that the onerous spectacle of 'terrorism' has not been averted but rather perpetuated in the course of the action. At the start of the film, where we see the invocation of the innocent, vaguely international sphere of decent 'citizens' that must be protected and opposed to the nameless *other* that is the foreigner, the sexually ambiguous (and therefore inherently evil) villain, the . . . . . .

. . . . . . but things get much more tricky towards the beginning of the third part of the film when we learn that what we have assumed thus far to be the protagonist's own perspective is in fact being narrated by his *suitcase* . . . . . .

. . . . . . At this point we hear the opening lines of Meatloaf's 'I Would do Anything for Love', with its 'dramatic' 'piano' beginning and racialised 'gothic/gospel' 'chorus' and I am moved to tears by the spectacle of it all, by the depressing yet strangely elevating 1980s/90s kitsch aesthetic, by the ultimate tragic paradox of the 'American Dream' and by my own insightful analysis of it and now must stop writing to have a drink and post this to you tomorrow.

Please translate this all into Korean and add it to the socialist library for the culturally-curious masses of your great state!! I will send you the full text in several days!!

Yours,

Paul Cook

17 March 2005

Hackney Central Library

Dear Dear Leader,

I have taken the decision of my life, and have used my remaining resources to book a flight to Beijing. From there, I will travel to meet you in Pyongyang. I can't write any more now as there are many preparations and much packing to be done. I'll contact you as soon as I arrive in Beijing.

Yours,

Paul Cook

21 March 2005

Novotel Xinqiao Hotel
Beijing, People's Republic of China

Dear Dear Leader,

My plan is to cross into North Korea from China in two days time, at the border near Sinŭiju. I have destroyed my passport. I shall expect a delegation from your government to meet me and assure safe passage to Pyongyang and our too-long delayed meeting. I look forward to the open arms of North Korea and your own warm embrace.

See you soon,

Paul Cook

Karen McCarthy

If I was a Buddhist I'd Chant for Your Happiness

One hare's head with antlers three inches long:
this will be my fork. I will dig down and bury
a Dogge Fish and find him a bone;
I will unearth a Grampus and weed out a Squeede.
For my fence I shall plant a row of unicorn horns
that spike the soil crust like silver asparagus spears.
This will demarcate the line.

I will propagate Sea Wolfes and watch them shoot
into my own army of glittering green gargoyles.
I will take a circumcision knife of stone and carve
out a herb-bed: alongside marjoram and thyme
I will also grow rue. I will wear two feathers
of the Phoenix tail upright in my hair as I dance
round my bonfire, scattering handfuls of myrrh.

I will shower the treetops with owls that swoop
at my command. I will water this Eden
with Blood That Rained in the Isle of Wight
(as attested by Sir Joe Oglander) and even mutter
in Latin if I must. I will transform to a four-footed
    beast.
Then I will abracadabra you invisible, compost
your white plastic table and obliterate that colony
of pots. I will do all of this, Neighbour, I will.

Kate Rhodes

The Conversation

They make it clear from the start
they're reasonable people.
All I have to do is listen,
be honest, give straight replies.

Soon the conversation will end
but there's no need to be afraid.
They leave me paper,
one silver pen for company.

Just one hour to record
every detail I can think of –
numbers, safe houses,
the codes I memorized.

Keys rattle questions in the lock.
Unlikely as a zeppelin
the pen is distended,
almost certain to implode.

Robin Yassin-Kassab

Marwan al-Haj

(novel extract)

Marwan al-Haj left his country for ever in June 1982. This was four years after the cultural blacklist, two years after the outbreak of war and three months after his release from prison. Looking back, leaving home was for him a release from the absurdities and irrelevance of his early life.

He had spent sixteen months in prison. Not a long sentence according to the standards of his homeland, but still long enough to repent being an Iraqi, or an Arab. And long enough also for his slight, well-proportioned body to stop being a source of pleasure and pride and become instead his enemy. Through his body they had broken him. With his testicles and penis and anus (he thought of these areas in such impersonal, faintly medical terms) they had humiliated him. By splitting his lips and ears, smashing his nose, crushing his spine and tugging out handfuls of his full hair, from scalp and pubis, they had taught him at once how physical he in fact was, despite his earlier disbelief, and also, or therefore, how expendable.

Part of the lesson was cleanliness. Being next to godliness, this was a supreme virtue, essential for his development. They washed away all the illusions concerning an expansive soul that had hitherto rolled about within him like lemonade in the belly of an overstuffed spoilt child. Which made things simpler. They washed, too, the uneven concrete floor of both his cell and the pain room with his blood and urine, bucketloads, really sluiced the place shiny so that he thought of himself in the end as a large blood blister, a viscous membrane containing too much red, sweet, sickening liquid. A surface. Something savagely, uselessly, physical, better burnt and buried and unseen.

They used his body as a door to his soul. They climbed in through it, keeping their boots on, found the soul and kicked it down to size. In quieter moments they reasoned with it gently, convincing it that if it did exist, it certainly had no right to. Then they hoovered it up, all except a grain, a peppercorn of hope. I will live, it said. I will see Mouna. She will make me better. We will start again.

When they beat him he would gasp or belch God's name. It meant nothing to him. It didn't help him. He had been too long out of the habit of seeking help in religious quarters. He didn't even intend to say it, but heard the sound on his animal breath: '*Ullahullahullahullahu*.' '*Maa ku Allah*,' the beaters said. 'There is no God.' They wrote it on the wall with his blood, using the wall as a blackboard and the blood as chalk.

After the first timeless beatings time settled into order. They beat him one day a week, except for the week before they let him out. Sixty-eight Tuesdays (he thought they were Tuesdays). He had no secrets to spill. They never even asked him questions, except rhetorical ones. There was no point to it beyond his metaphysical education, to satisfy the demands of routine, and his beaters' zeal.

This zeal he had to admire. They set about their work with unflagging dedication. Sometimes he detected exhaustion in their eyes, but they kept on at it. They did it as effectively as possible, so he supposed, although he was no expert. And a lot of thought had gone into his torture. The chair in which his back was shortened, for instance, was a quite ingenious device. Made in Iraq by Iraqis too, not imported technology.

Now he thought about it he realized how many people his being here depended on, what careful planning the whole complex system required. A network of informers, party men, officials, wardens, revolutionary guardsmen, police and soldiers. Taxi drivers were famous for listening, and the shopkeepers who opened early and closed late, and watchful tenants in every building. How many people? He estimated, from the number of suspects in his own neighbourhood and the population of the country, hundreds of thousands. All of them with families. All of them with some poetry in the soul. But he'd learnt about the soul now. He knew what human beings really were.

Out of prison, he found the city stunned by heat and war. He, at least, was stunned. He returned to his flat and sat on the sofa in a layer of dust, wondering vaguely what would happen next. Mouna and the children were not there. He waited for them, looking out of the window. The sky and the street were bleached by the sun. He heard amplified counting songs and patriotic anthems from the primary school at the corner. He heard the chattering of women in the stairwell and children's laughter among cars. He heard policemen's whistles and the crowing of cocks. He heard the prayer called five times a day.

Old men from the nearby flats came one by one to greet him. The young men were away at war. The fathers and grandfathers spoke softly, closed the door behind them before they embraced him. He held them without warmth and thanked them for their presents of food and tobacco. Many of the neighbours didn't come at all. He would have come, in their position, in his stupid days. But he wasn't stupid any more, and so he understood. He had some bites of the food, rice and beans prepared in pity, and smoked the cigarettes, for something to do.

On the third day his brother-in-law Nidal knocked on the door. Seeing him through the spyhole, his hollow cheeks and sharp jaw, Marwan's hope exploded in him. 'God is great!' he cried, tugging him into the flat. Resurrected thoughts ran about inside him. Mouna would come back with the children. He'd keep himself out of trouble. Life would start again. He wept with huge movements of his chest, like an old, rusty engine heaving into motion, the tears dragged from him in bursts and blusters.

Nidal stood back and watched with a helpless expression. He shook his head slowly from side to side. He raised and lowered his hands, and finally clasped them across his waist.

'She is dead,' he said. 'God have mercy on her. They beat her on the night of your arrest. We took her to the hospital but it was no use. They beat her on the head and she bled inside. God have mercy on her. There is no might and no strength save in God.'

Marwan stopped crying. It was hope not sorrow that made him weep. He blew his nose and washed his face while Nidal made tea. They drank the tea, and Nidal continued talking.

'Muntaha and Ammar are with us. They're fine. Of course they're upset, but they're fine. Muntaha's still going to school. Ammar has become a bit nervous. He cries a lot. That's understood. He doesn't really know what has happened. He'll be all right. Both of them will. You all will. We'll bring them to you whenever you're ready. Or they can stay with us. It's up to you.'

At the beginning of June a *mukhabarat* man rapped at the door. Marwan looked through the spyhole and the *mukhabarat* man looked back defiantly. Looking was his profession. His shoes shone in the absence of light. His trousers were so black they shone too. His polished leather jacket reflected the yellow ooze from the landing bulb. Marwan opened the door and stood with head bowed.

'You are Marwan al-Haj.'

'Yes.'

'Do you want to leave Iraq?'

'No.'

The *mukhabarat* man cleared his throat. He tried again.

'Do you want to go away?'

Marwan, unsure, whispered, 'No.'

'Nevertheless, it would be better if you went away.'

'Perhaps.'

'Certainly it would. Here is your exit visa.'

He removed an envelope from a shimmering inner pocket and thrust it towards Marwan.

'This is valid for one month only. Do not make trouble where you go. Wherever you go, we are there too. Go with peace.'

He spun with a squeak of the shoes and strutted to the stairs. Unheard, Marwan thanked the retreating back, and slid the door closed again, frowning, pensive. The future had been decided. He had no feelings about it either way.

The next day, returning on foot from the Jordanian Embassy, Marwan saw one of his former torturers at an intersection sandwich stand: a large man crammed into a small plastic chair on the pavement, legs in a diamond shape bowed outwards at the knees and converging at boyishly side-rolled feet, chest and shoulders bulging over a white plastic table, a water-coloured face, unlined and uncomplicated, sunk into the shoulders. He was looking into the traffic blankly, perhaps sadly. An ordinary man. Marwan stepped behind a tree and watched until a boy brought the torturer's order. A tightly wrapped sandwich and a tall glass of red juice. Fruit cocktail. The customer acknowledged service with a weak smile and a slightly timid nod, but the boy was already at another table. Marwan, out of sight, watched the torturer eating – he ate slowly, with both hands – and asked himself what kind of revenge he'd like, if it was possible. His response was, none at all. He wasn't even angry. He said a silent goodbye across the exhaust fumes and moving crowds, and went home.

He sold the flat to Nidal for as much as could be mustered in a week. He took Muntaha and Ammar and two suitcases packed with their clothes and toys. Also some photographs, for the children's sake, not his, and the album of their drawings Mouna had collected. He didn't take his books.

The children eyed him cautiously, circled him whispering incantations against doppelgängers and possessing *jinn*. Muntaha was excessively correct with him, behaving with a politeness he hadn't seen from her before, although at times she would forget and leap into his surprised, unready arms to nuzzle her face in his beard, or sidle up to him and slip her brittle hand in his. Ammar, much smaller, was governed by his sister. When she came close so did he, and then Marwan nodded to himself, ah yes, the children loved him. He felt the warmth of the memory of paternal love. He remembered how it had once brought tears to his gazing eyes, given him a sense of meaningless things like meaning and achievement. But he couldn't feel these things again. Sometimes, when his children touched him, he flinched. That enveloped him in nebulous guilt, but he fought it off, knowing it to be illogical. Greater than love or other abstractions, he had duty, and because of duty – to his children, his dead wife, to himself – he would do his best.

On the day of departure, Nidal made himself busy with the suitcases, and keys and addresses on scraps of paper. A hot wind blew up the stairwell against them as they descended. Dust was yellowish and thick on the roofs of their mouths. In the tiled entranceway Nidal turned around, panting.

'You should be happier than this,' he said. 'Good things will happen now. You'll see. And think of us.' A portrait of the president was pasted to the wall behind his head. 'We're staying here with this bastard.'

Nidal shut them into the taxi and leaned in through the

window, dispensing sweets, blowing kisses, fixing his brother-in-law with a significant stare.

'Go with peace, Marwan. It will be a new start. God be with you.'

'I've already made a new start,' said Marwan, his eyes on the windscreen.

The car pulled out into the noise of the street – children wailing, mothers screaming at children, a cart man crying his wares, television sets, pop music on tinny radios, patriotic songs, the *clank-clank* of the gas-bottle man. Tattered flags flapped in the breeze. An old man stood in the road rubbing his back and groaning. A harsh, indifferent sun glared, fixing details in memory, embellishing them with meanings to be retrieved later, meanings which they perhaps did not deserve.

The Immigrant

And the absurdity and irrelevance of his early life? Marwan had been a minor poet. Very minor. And very poet – in attitude, lifestyle and aspiration. There were lots of poets in those days, lots of young people, lots of words.

Plenty of cash. Iraq was the only Arab country with both oil wealth and a large urban population, the only Arab country where something constructive could be done with the wealth. Money flowed into the sandbanks of the two rivers and the future sprouted. You could see through the crumbling shrines and markets and under the surface of recent slums to a coming metropolis as greenly luxuriant as Haroon al-Rasheed's. The hospitals and universities were already as good as those in Europe, and cleaner, newer, more gleaming. Public housing proliferated, and art galleries (socialist realism blending with surrealism), and ideas. There was an infestation of intellectuals barking names – Fanon and Neruda, Mahfouz and Nasser, Marx and Mao – from their restaurant-kennels and as background noise at their constant parties. Parties characterized the city as mosques had done in the past. A cigarette-smoke and perfume miasma spawned vegetal words, verdant ropes and webs of words, of ... renaissance, progress, unity. Everything seemed to matter, every word.

Verses were currency as much as commodity. A well-aimed panegyric would buy you a job, a villa, a car. Verses came easily to Marwan, but he was an ethical investor who avoided direct toadying. He was able in good conscience to praise more generally, and the bulk of his poetry consisted of such innocuous fare: short laudatory hymns to the city, the nation, to brotherhood and other abstractions. He lovingly ornamented the present and future, and also conjured the dusty town he'd grown out of, representative of the primitive past.

He sat on the editorial committee of *Revolution in Words*, a state-sponsored literary review for a coterie readership. The editors played their roles as seriously as method actors through flashing afternoons of theory and whisky which ended in table-thumping to punctuate socio-poetic points, and then laughter. They belonged to a class which had liberated itself from rural inhibitions. They were open about their girlfriends and boyfriends, their atheism, their experiments with hashish and opium. Wild love and intoxication, they said, defined Baghdad in its Golden Age, and would again in this age of black gold.

Mouna was one of this group, Marwan's girlfriend before she became his wife, his wild lover, his accomplice in experiment. The object of erotic verses.

Marwan, secular and romantic, believed he was a model citizen of the new Iraq. He made no mistakes in his writing or living, not that he was aware of, not until he made the mistake he must have made in order to be arrested. He thought on this when he had time between Tuesdays in prison, and afterwards, and decided his blunder had most probably been to copy and circulate the wrong poetry. Of course nothing directly political, nothing he expected would cause offence, but he'd copied poems by disappeared communists, translated Iranians, sectarians. He'd used the *Revolution in Words* photocopier and distributed the poems to friends and visitors, who accepted them out of politeness and in most cases never read them; Marwan standing up when they were sitting, waving his hands the while, becoming overexcited, babbling too loudly about modernism and radical diction and liberating the unconscious and God knows what else. Frothing a little at the mouth, dribbling and loonish. For such noble activity he'd murdered his wife and lost his country. If he could feel anything he'd feel shame. For his absurdity. But then the copied poems may not have been the mistake. Someone may have made a false report about him and, in that case, his arrest had been a mistake. And he asked himself, could Mouna's death have been caused by a mistake? Could the death of his own soul and the orphaning of his children and the end of consequence and depth in the world which left only silhouettes where there had been well-dimensioned people and houses, could all this be mistaken, or was there a reason for it he could not perceive? A logic which determined events? A set of rules?

In Amman, from a rented house on a rocky hill, Marwan wrote to Jim Clark for help. As poet and editor he'd had such international acquaintances. Jim Clark: former cultural attaché at the British Embassy in Baghdad, Arabist and Arabophile, who'd arranged bilingual poetry evenings in the British Council garden and translated Marwan's poems for London magazines. Marwan posted the letter and waited for a reply.

He sat on a mattress in his bare accommodation. Without the furniture of books and words his life was as empty as the house. *Better like that*, he thought. *Free of illusions. Simpler. Uncluttered.* On Friday he walked to the nearest mosque and half-listened to the sermon like the other men, cross-legged and nodding on the tired carpet. He prayed the congregational prayer for the first time in twenty years. Stood and bowed and knelt and prostrated in conformity with the crowd. He bought fruit in the street outside and carried it back. During the week he stayed in the house. He didn't read. He didn't pray.

The following Friday, and the next, he returned to the same mosque. He took pleasure in the uniform movement of the praying men, and hurried away from their extended hands and questioning glances as the mass splintered afterwards. He didn't wish to know them as individuals. As individuals they would be sharp as shrapnel.

In three weeks Jim Clark arrived. He had come promptly, as soon as he received the letter, loyal to poetry, loyal to loyalty (he held this to be an Arab value), sweeping sweat out of grizzled eyebrows with the back of a heavy hand. He attended to Marwan's every gesture with the grim sympathy he judged due. Marwan –

exile, torture victim, persecuted artist – was unable to play his roles properly, or to reciprocate Jim's friendship. But he did what needed to be done; was taken to doctors who noted and recorded his limp, his twisted spine, his sudden bald patches, and to British officials who regarded him with the same focused attention as Jim, dispensing with paperwork, patting him cautiously on the shoulder, afraid he would break.

Jim, tree-tall next to Marwan's withered shrub, explained that political asylum had already been applied for. A formality. In the meantime, here were three visas, and plane tickets. Marwan could pay him back later. It was the least he could do.

'Call yourself lucky,' said Jim, flinching from the inappropriate adjective. 'I expect half the country would like to get out.'

'They would,' said Marwan, 'and they wouldn't.'

'Yes, I know, I know.' Jim puzzled over it. 'It's our fault, of course. It usually is. Us and our American friends. He's our man, you see. Keeping the communists down yesterday, knocking the Iranians about today. He can do no wrong. It's a sorry state of affairs.'

Ammar wheeled around the adults on the mattress with a peal of high laughter. A screech of brightness. Muntaha followed with a water pistol. Jim was talking about the poetry Marwan would write in London. Marwan gazed at Jim, and at the abstractions like steam clouding his face. At the dead layers of his grey skin. *Overcooked adults*, he thought. *Hope and soul burnt away. Some absurdity remaining in those who haven't suffered.* And he thought, *If I'd died at thirty I might have died happy. My eyes might have entered paradise open, still searching for something. I might have had the smell of paradise in my nostrils as I died.*

The next day they arrived in London.

It astounded Marwan. Stately-solid, autonomous, indifferent, history bowed before it. He tried to compare. More prosperous than Baghdad but harsher, tidier but more desolate, it revealed Baghdad as a ramshackle shapeshifter, built in haste for a shuddering moment, all its wiring and dirt showing. London, in contrast, was sculpted and seamed like a fortress, for permanence, with its rolling acres of pavement and wall and its tunnels underground channelling sewage, rats and trains, everything functional enclosed coffin-tight and buried again in stone. With its big stone houses, its blocks and rows and crescents, its entire streets carved from the same rock, its red zones and its white zones, its brick-work, the tremendous trunks of its trees, the city could withstand anything. Even its dwarfed and cowed inhabitants, who seemed to be there by accident. Was that it? Baghdad was an accident that happened to its people, but the people here were an accident happening to London. Crawling over its face like unwelcome insects. Getting in the way. Including him now, Marwan and his children accidents too.

Could people be merely accidents? Was it humility or arrogance to think so?

Everything was tied down in its proper place. The streets had names. No discrepancy between the written and spoken names. Even the dogs, labelled around the neck, had names and addresses. Squirrels, less timid in their residence than Iraqi human beings, lived unharassed in the trees which burst from the pavement at regular intervals.

He didn't sneer, not even at the combed and collared dogs. There was nothing wrong with order. Order meant safety. Order kept people within limits.

And there were people, he gradually understood, who belonged in the city more than accidentally but as part of its fabric, people made of stone flesh and cold stone blood. Of every colour and class, arriving from everywhere, for every reason and none, and staying when they came in the shadows until they moved invisibly into death, and even the shadows were fixed, and the air hanging between the buildings, the exhalation of lungs and engines, the cloud and the metal sky in permanent residence, fixed in situ for ever and ever and ever.

Unrelenting, eternal London. A piece of the earth's crust reared up and separated from the rest of the planet. A stone mountain.

Wonder soon hardened into resentment. He cast bitter glances at the imperial centre, at Buckingham Palace and Whitehall, the great museums and opera houses, at banks, theatres, department stores. *Why don't we live like this?* he asked the emptiness. *Do we not qualify? Are we a different species? Are we not human beings? Or are we human beings and these the gods?*

But he was giving up metaphysics. Rarely did he consider the city a mountain or the people gods. He developed a sense of perspective. Weaned himself away from symbols and observed the world by its letter and surface. He attended to his hours as assistant librarian in the Arabic department of the School of Oriental and African Studies (Jim had guided him into the job). He paid the rent for the small house Jim had found in west London. He attended the local mosque. He bowed like the others – the Turks, Indians, Nigerians – prayed as he'd been taught as a boy, before abstraction set in. His prayer was not meditation but a habit establishing itself, a practice and a rhythm, the string attaching him to his place in the city.

There were other sides to London he discovered only as time passed. After a leaden winter he found less reason to be jealous of it. He noticed shabbiness, hollowness, randomness. How the lives hurtled into collision, unplanned, each scouring the other's surface. A sandpaper world. People tied individually to the city but not to each other. He wasn't the only one to avoid meeting eyes in the street; the natives too were foreign to each other. He read in the free newspaper stuffed through his door how an old man had sat dead and rotting for three months in his flat, in the armchair in front of a loud TV, before a neighbour realized. The weather had to warm up before the smell made the neighbour call the police. The neighbour didn't know the old man's name. More chance of knowing a dog's name.

Marwan watched the aggressive youths, beer cans in knuckly hands, navels exposed, sometimes pierced, and remembered with shame his own extended youth in Iraq. And for that association among others he didn't miss it. Any happiness there had been illusory. A mistake. Mistaking hell for heaven. *The world is made of the same material, London or Baghdad, it makes no difference. Once you disregard the whispering of the deceiver. All hell.*

One humid evening walking from the tube station Marwan passed a blood-sticky body hugging the kerb. Matted filthy beard and tangled long hair. Passed it and half-turned his head, his peeled eyes. Nobody else was stopping. So with the now characteristic hard-set turned-down expression about his mouth he went back and crouched, holding his breath to keep his lungs unsoiled, and slowly rolled the corpse face up. And the corpse came to life, spitting froth from its lips. Marwan sprang back upright. 'Fuck you,' groaned the corpse. Marwan walked on quickly.

He stayed inside when he could. But inside was no relief. The little rooms were dark and damp. Varieties of mould tattooed the walls. He had that mushroomy sour smell always in his nostrils. The windows didn't open unless you unscrewed anti-burglar locks, and the air outside was anyway gusty and cold, and tasted of beer and traffic. Gusts like the squalling tears of a derelict. When the wind rushed along the street the windows rattled. In the winter, ice formed on the inside of the panes.

Marwan's room, downstairs, guarding the entrance hall, also served as dining room and living room. In the daytime his bed became a couch. No pictures or books. He had the TV, which revealed further little rooms and compartmentalized English people gossiping and whingeing within them. Through the window he heard the immanence and distance of the world outside.

The children were upstairs out of harm's way. A room for the girl and a room for the boy. They cut pictures from magazines and stuck them to the walls to reflect what they imagined inside themselves. They were allowed to jump around and make noise. Marwan was not an unkind father. He questioned them about their schoolwork and the friends he never saw. He worried about them and warned them away from danger, but never beat them or raised his voice. He did his best. He played his part.

He would pray at home and at work as well as in the mosque, measuring out the day by the allotted times. He performed fifty press-ups and fifty sit-ups in the gloom of each morning. He memorized sections of the Qur'an as an exercise to maintain his mental health. With a sort of quiet pleasure he felt age descending upon him.

Once on the tube he intervened in an argument between a man and a woman. They cursed in one of the stranger accents. Irish? Scottish? Subdued swearing burst into shouts, and then shoving and flailing hands. As slaps became punches Marwan found himself standing, stretching an arm between them. 'Madam, how may I help you?' He heard his croaky foreign voice and his diction suited to the British Council garden or to Shakespeare seminars thirty stale years old. Bleating ridiculously, 'Madam, Madam . . .' until the couple interrupted themselves and looked at him with shocked disgust. 'Piss off, you old Paki fucker,' the woman said, and pushed against his face with a wet hand, a fingernail scratching blood from the corner of his eye. Marwan leaked tears back to the house, locked the door and shielded himself from Muntaha's concern.

Thereafter, in the English phrase, *he kept himself to himself*. He hid away in the dry, bare room inside himself, inside the damp, bare room in the house. Took refuge in silence. Didn't presume to interfere in anything beyond himself. Not in the city's life, not in the children's lives, not after he'd dutifully warned them. More useful English phrases: *that's your business. That isn't your business. Keep your nose out of what doesn't concern you. No point fretting over what can't be changed*. It was easy to separate what concerned him, which wasn't much, from what didn't.

He began reading again, but not poetry. He read the pamphlets he picked up at the mosque or in Islamic bookshops concerning the laws of God established and fixed by the Righteous Predecessors. The laws by which God made Himself known in the lives of His servants. These were straightforward, plain texts. Facts you could be sure of. No mistakes or accidents. Nothing elitist or vague.

The pamphlets provided another reason not to miss Iraq, which they said was the realm of unbelief as much as London. No country could call itself Muslim if it refused to submit to God's laws. And no individual. Marwan remembered his soul-bloated former self mocking the laws, how in his foolishness and arrogance he'd assumed men to be angels. Worse, he'd attributed to men qualities owned only by God, such as interpretive control over life, such as absolute independence. 'I seek forgiveness from God,' he repeated. 'Forgive me my faults. Forgive me my faults.'

It was clear to him that the laws offered a solution to the agonies of the grimy city and its brawling populace. That the laws could tie the people together with the twine of common humanity and shared purpose, could tame them with humility and restrain them within proper limits. Strict punishments and the prohibition of drugs and alcohol could establish peace and safety. Modesty and honour in sexual matters could allow men to regard their fellows as brothers rather than competitors. Then the city could be clean. Not sandpaper, but harmony and balance. Five times a day it would pause its commerce and bow as one body to its Creator.

But that wasn't his business. He ordered his own life and left the people to their fate. If it was God's will to guide them, they would be guided. But he still felt a kind of pity as he walked at a distance behind them, striving for invisibility. He raised his eyes under lowered lids as the Londoners flitted or staggered from pub to betting shop, those most commonly in the poor areas, or wandered blank-faced and numb in shopping centres, or stood nervous at cashpoints, guarded, locked into themselves. Marwan followed them breathing quick and shallow, worrying his prayer beads, either seeking forgiveness on their behalf or protecting himself from repeating their sin. '*Istughfurullah*,' he muttered. '*Istughfurullah*. I seek forgiveness from God, I seek forgiveness.'

Computerization and cutbacks, meanwhile, made Marwan redundant. He wasn't sorry to lose his job, for two reasons. First, he found himself incompatible with the bookish, youthful environment of the university. The undergraduates – noisy, brash children – he could bear. But the ever-drawn-out youth of the graduate students and unkempt professors he could not. Their academic froth of visions and revisions, their satisfaction with unreality, they mirrored too much his younger self. Not a mirror he wished to look into any longer. And secondly, this: in his former academic life, back there, he'd been a student and, more or less, a teacher. Student and teacher of nothing much, but at least those, an agent with knowledge as his supposed object. He'd been made a fool of only by himself and God. Until his imprisonment. Whereas here, he himself was an object of study. In this respect undergraduates were worse. They peered thoughtfully over the tops of books into the middle distance, not into space but at him, the Arab. Sometimes they would ask for his point of view on a particular issue, not because they respected his opinion but from a desire to hear an Arab voice, any Arab voice. It spiced up their day. Saved them a trip to Edgware Road. Just standing nearby could authenticate things for them. Breathing the air he'd breathed was like treading the Mesopotamian soil, like waking in a goat-hair tent. An undergraduate once asked him, with admirable honesty, 'Mr al-Haj, what's it like, being an Arab?' He didn't say, 'It's not like anything. I have no perspective. I know nothing.' He was never more than formal with them, although they were often too friendly with him, these sons and daughters of a cold, uncourteous people, introducing their sexual partners as if he was interested, or badgering him into group photographs with their large arms around his shoulder. In some way he couldn't define and therefore couldn't repulse, they recorded him, fixed him, pinned him down. He expected at any moment to be dissected.

So it was a relief to be freed from this. His health was degenerating too. As loyal as a sheepdog – a dog to the English is a fine and trusty animal – Jim Clark arrived to organize another transition. Shaggy, stumble-footed, he led Marwan between hospitals and government offices to confirm again the official existence of his bad back and persistent limp, plus now the laboured beating of his heart. Jim did the talking, ponderously, with significant nods and movements of the eyes.

Marwan qualified for Housing Benefit, Supplementary Benefit and a disability allowance. It was good of the state, he said to Jim's not-at-alls, good of Jim, good of the English to help him. It was more than he had the right to expect. Jim asked why Marwan hadn't been to visit him in the country. Marwan said thank you, thank you, and shrugged. They talked awkwardly about outward, impersonal things, the weather, the traffic, the state of public transport. Once or twice Jim summoned a Baghdad memory and Marwan summoned a stiff smile in response. He knew how Jim felt – that his protégé had failed to fulfil his potential. Jim as embarrassed as if he'd found Marwan incontinent. Weakness was apparent in his grey English face for the first time, his expression of fortitude wavering, his body stooping as if it found itself suddenly too tall for his soul. The man was grievously disappointed. *But what could you do?*

Marwan's retirement present was a cup overflowing with empty time. What would he do with the yards and folds of it, the time to be disciplined and made to pass? He interested himself in the children's homework and exam revision. He expanded his daily routines, walking to the mosque for every prayer and spending twenty minutes after each glorifying of God on his prayer beads. He did press-ups in the afternoons as well as the mornings. He reread his collection of pamphlets, finding comfort in the repetition. He memorized more of the Qur'an. Still there was time.

He explored further afield, on wide-ranging circuits of Arab London. To the Syrian grocer's on the Uxbridge Road, where he bought olives and salted balls of cheese. To Moroccan stalls on Golborne Road, where he drank steaming bowls of *harira* against the weather and listened to the gruff, almost incomprehensible Franco-Arabic of the market men. To cafés on the Edgware Road or upstairs rooms in Kilburn, where he smoked a *narghile* – his one occasional vice – between voluble Egyptians and Lebanese. He stepped around plotters, journalists and other exiles, and closed his eyes to the vulgar young Gulf tourists.

He walked alone, troglodytic, uncherished, but the city softened to him by degrees. He expanded his acquaintance. Before long he had hand-shaking knowledge of more than two dozen men. Shopkeepers, security guards, eternal students and tourists who'd lost their way home, a poet, businessmen, embassy staff, waiters and managers of restaurants. He knew their names and origins, the storied versions at least. He presented himself as a mild critic of his country's regime, but a patriot, who'd settled in London for the sake of a good job (perhaps he exaggerated its importance) and was now waiting for his children to finish their education before returning home. Most of them talked of going home, even the Palestinians from disappeared villages.

They bought each other lunches or glasses of tea or pipes to smoke through bawdy or fantastical narrations of Haifa or Beirut, Cairo or Riyadh, or of London itself, what scandals they had heard or seen or imagined. They talked a lot of politics, but seldom involved themselves in the opinions they gave, cloaking every thought in so many layers of irony or parody that even the speaker of a statement rarely felt sure of its intention. They preserved the survivalist suspicion they had brought with them. There was a lot of laughter in these meetings, and the steam of vain words again, but Marwan allowed himself the indulgence. He wasn't engaged to words this time. That was the difference. He didn't have faith in them any more.

On warmer days he would walk on to Hyde Park or Regent's Park or Queen's Park, worrying his beads to excuse himself from the café's frivolity or from the corruption of the streets. On these days women were more than usually naked and lovers more than ever intent on flaunting the drunkenness of the body. He would choose an unoccupied bench and flick non-committally, inviolate, through a pan-Arab newspaper until he fell into a doze punctuated by cloud-interrupted sun. Then he would awake from kinder parallel worlds into a brief bitterness, sour and cramped, before he remembered himself, stood up and limped towards the nearest mosque.

It was in the Regent's Park mosque, after Friday prayers, that marriage was proposed to him. He was kneeling far beneath the dome, as the congregation picked its way past those still stationary in prayer or meditation, when the face of Abu Hassan, a huge and craggy Baghdadi, loomed close. Eyes burned from deep sockets in Abu Hassan's bone-white cheeks. Tufts of brownish hair sprouted from his ears and nostrils. He wore a grey suit and an open-collar pinstriped shirt for the mosque, but Marwan saw him always as he usually encountered him, with a triple-extra-large Union Jack T-shirt pulled shiny tight across his barrel chest. Such was the uniform Abu Hassan had selected for the staff of his Queensway shop, which sold royal regalia, novelties and tourist goods. In among the plastic patriotism that made his living, the policeman's hats and postcards of Mohicanned punks, Princess Di dolls and rubber caricatures of the prime minister, he looked like a toy himself, with his simple movements and uneven proportions, like a bear-sized, vastly overgrown child. Like many people that big he was an unexpectedly gentle man, happiest at home with his little wife and his shipwrecked sister Hasna. It was for Hasna that he clutched Marwan's arm in the mosque and announced, 'My brother, marriage is half of religion.'

Hasna's first husband had been an officer and Ba'ath Party member who at the close of an illustrious career of casual barbarity had committed the folly of idealism. He had intervened to avert an entirely irrelevant act of murder or torture. As a result, he was exiled from home, property and reputation. In sullen recognition of her duty Hasna had obliged herself to go with him, to London because her brother was there, leaving her adult children behind. It was hard for her to forgive her husband, so she didn't. She put her energy into building a shrine to Iraq in the tiny flat they bought, representing her sacrifice in an iconography of lost bliss, in photographs of family and in traditional craftwork items she'd never been interested in before. She bemoaned her reduced circumstances and ignored her husband until, with admirable promptness, he was thrown down dead on the linoleum kitchen floor by a tremendous shaking of the heart. Then she kept the shrine for religious purposes only, and moved into her brother's house.

Marwan seemed to her a steady, uncontroversial man who would spring on her no surprises, and she was largely right. He made few claims on her. She found him regular in his habits and respectful, if also uncommunicative and on occasion suddenly harsh. The children were polite, although secretive and wayward, and at least half English, particularly the snake-eyed boy, who refused to speak his own language. She moved Ammar into the living room and took for her and her husband, purged of its supernatural posters, the bedroom he'd occupied. She did her best with the dank little house, which was not much more than stairs, corridors and cupboards. She double-glazed the rattling windows. She painted the living walls, but the paint never really dried. She overstocked the kitchen with food, and invited guests at least once a week.

Marwan remembered to thank God for his blessings. Hasna was a handsome woman, large and white, round-eyed, round-faced, round-bellied. Her breasts were rich and heavy circles. She contained as much femininity as he could bear. He felt properly human when he was imam for the prayer at home, with his wife praying behind him, as if his body carried weight and consequence.

Sometimes at night or in the deserted hours of the morning when the children were at school and habit made him think himself alone, she found him weeping without noise or reason. It was only because she saw him that he realized he did it. In such ways she made him more lucid. He was thankful for the light, this shrivelled man who did his duty and tried to do his best.

Wayne Burrows

Under Surveillance

Landscapes Glimpsed From A Midday Train, Nottingham to
Birmingham, August 2005

(i)
Cut hay dries out in even rows,
each field a barcode
scanned by the sun.

Woodland strobes the eye
with light, reads the iris
as the lens adjusts.

Pupils dilate, like ponds of dark
in fields of green,
reflecting cloud.

(ii)
In the gap between hawthorn,
scrub-grass and pine,
constellations of flowers on elder twigs.

Nightshade and early blackberries merge
with shadows cast
on breeze-block walls.

Among these flints and cinders
on the railway line,
lush dock leaves, nettles,

bindweeds spread –
blend poisons, cross-pollinate
as winds blow cold.

(iii)
Pallets of sacks – potassium
and chicken feed – are piled like sandbags
round warehouse doors:

closed shutters painted
in high-gloss black
mirror the darkness of a storm to come.

As the onboard air conditioners hum,
numbers – *12, 9, 16, 1* –
fly by like random, encrypted mail.

(iv)
The landscape falls through container parks
where steel bridges span gorse
and poppy slopes –

curve downward into half-built estates.
Saplings strain to put down roots
through sheets of mesh.

Pantiled homes with conservatories
stand like Lego, abandoned
on a lawn in drought.

(v)
Lavender and rhododendrons bloom
where neglected sidings
sprout CCTV –

a woman in an oversized Disney shirt
huddles with luggage
on a bright green bench.

When pigeons explode from a disused shed
cameras follow them
to the platform's edge.

(vi)
A fountain watering
a field of beet
spurts arcs of water, an arterial pulse.

The grasses' plumage of ochre seed
breeds ostrich feathers
in nettle beds.

A pond loops footage
of ducks and swans
adrift in the blue between cumulus clouds.

(vii)
Cooling towers, like machines
for making clouds,
stir air and water to slow-moving white.

The line ends here.
A tannoy crackles. Thunder breaks.
The evening sun is a sinking lid.

Karen McCarthy

War's Imperial Museum

Auschwitz is shrunk to an icy cake,
pristine and architectural.
I have seen this blueprint before:
the who, how, what, where of
stuffing everybody in.
This is what scares me.
Not the emaciated corpses tipped
into mass graves like landfill.
Nor the reality of shoes.
Or the fact that Roman Halter,
who buried hope with his father,
still goes to synagogue but cannot pray.

Mercy is a muzzled dog as I meander
from Genocide – 1st Floor to Genocide –
Lower Ground, before arriving at
Crimes Against Humanity: Level 4.
Pol Pot, Kurdistan, Rwanda: touch-screen
technology enables the death counts
to scroll like football scores.
Now it is the 21st century, I wonder
if soon we will be required to dismiss
that which has happened the century before.
Who remembers Armenia now?

The name has changed but
inside the old asylum it is still Bedlam.
Departure is harder than I think,
it takes time to exit this predatory basement.
Out past jaunty fighter planes that dangle

in the atrium. Out past the thrusting
guns, two of them, long as a street.
Out into the air, grateful for frost
and buses, which glow like lamps,
luminous in the dark afternoon.

John Siddique

Inside # 2

'There is no more time'

9.47, the peak of the morning rush is
beginning to subside, though the tube is
closed so he's taking the bus to work.
A woman at the front of the bus is
on her way to her course. There is
a girl on her way to the dentist, and
a cleaner on her way home. A bus full
of people like this and more.

Then there is no more time, just a flash.
No time for fear. Here then gone, or
unconscious, or at the edge, or screaming.
All fixed in their own heads a moment ago,
busy being late for things, tired, looking forward
to a cup of tea, or just getting there
to get out of this traffic.

9.47 lasts for ever and ticks on for the rest of us.
Before and after the application of words. Divide
the hour, divide the minute, subdivide the second,
keep on dividing and time ceases to exist.

Fiona Sampson

As If to Move the Air Is to Disturb It

(After the Wellcome Archive of Refugee Clinicians' Testimony,
Oxford Brookes University)

The *ticker-ticker* of a tape.

Nasal cavities fill
                    something soughs round corners.
Bruised knees of childhood
                    aaah –
houses rebuild themselves –

And could you tell us something about your parents,
                                        please?
Where they were from? What were their occupations?

the street beginning to form – he steps into it
shopfronts composing themselves
Zalewski outfitter's
Goldstein maker of walking sticks
cigars in the corner window, mucus-yellow with age;
lucent glaze of gobstoppers.

Where were you born?

All of it:
        bright cold mornings
stab and jar of feet racing
and Latin, golonka, ploughlines of wet comb,
a boy who loved history.

                    *

Some words:
                    Porky, dirty Judas
outside the pink-and-white torte of the church
head to stone on the Lenten cobbles.
As if listening:
                    ticker-ticker.

My father was in carpets. Import-export.
Even in the Depression, every Thursday at four,
pani Pawelska, little heels clicking, came with cash in
                                        a briefcase
by the end it was a suitcase
Mamushka immediately turning it into
soap starch apples chicken. Hard currency.

Life is inequitable
and stars tip
                    over a Polish city

                    *

then my friends said *come and study with us*
it'll be marvellous
                        a marvellous life
so I went, my parents paid,
I went to Lvov

                    you can't imagine
the marvellous life we had there as medical students
                                    before the war

ticker-ticker

the summer-holiday tick
of crickets in cloudless
nineteen-thirty-nine

when, on the third of September,
without saying goodbye

(my brother gone already, his bed tidied)
we step out the stunned house at three,
Willi and Nix and I
with our bicycles like coffee-grinders

into the long landscape.

                         *

Tracks
          birch-groves.

Tiredness is a point
that pinions the nape

                         a bullet-point
between branching tendons –

when the roar from a fattening sky
is a fighter
coming for *us*.

Shock of your
              first time

and shaky fingers touch steel touch the handlebar again;
your skin leaks sweat.

Train tracks line the road
and when a crowded carriage
slows

we slip breathless into night,
                              moon licking the treetops;
by the third day
              eyes ears throat buzzing
                                    sleepless
seeing death in trees haypoles the movement of water.

                         *

At the Front we volunteered for a Field Hospital.
Wards full of the torn white strips of beds.

Eight days later the Russians arrived,
moustaches, boots, clamour of requisition
and our officers
                              not exactly hostages
their white dressings white feathers
we traded for civvies

letting the kitchen door swing unattended, nights,

steel jumping in all the drawers
the night Nix and I and Willi
took our bicycles out into the darkness

                              *

to squeeze between lock and key
                                             breathing
neither Russian nor German.

                              *

Lvov again. Turning its silver back.

Without money you make yourself indispensable.
Days of queues rumour barter
of hands cutting air
                              bread
potato

but even New Year with pani Hubicka all milk and
                                                                butter
little Rosa
                  her salt-meat tongue
our parents' lives were
in the German shroud.

                              *

February.
Our bicycles lean together to graze.

Beyond yellowish grass
we see
      the other Poland.

At dusk we move quietly,
willing the body to a quality of dark.

In the fourth field a voice thrown up close by is a
                startled bird

Stop!

we stop

      Stop!

        the shot sounding round us
we raise our hands
        cautiously
as if to move the air is to disturb it
as if the dark is mined.

        *

Night burns on.

At last they line us up
empty our pockets
        bootlace pebble penknife
           harmonica
Give us a tune!
      the little harmonica Katya gave me
the enamelled rose
      at my mouth
like a cold lip.
      I played a Russian song
and immediately the mood in the hall

silence

      burning crackle

the tape's tail racing through all eyes

                            ticker-ticker

entering the library where a bored *ticker-*
the old man's sitting-room
(tea tray forgotten on footstool)
ticker- a requisitioned hall surprisingly bright
where the laughing commander says
In Russia, we pay your medical studies!

           *

Silent pig sheds.
A pile of pallets, straw,
a propped spade.
The stranger watching from the corridor says *These*
    are the boys
who helped me get out the Field Hospital

showing a brown jacket

Remember this?
             No.
                But he gets us across
Willi and I
        wade
           the shocking current
our bodies are sticks.
               Except Nix can't swim
Boys, I –

Where did he go?
          Afraid
              back to the empty farm
                   alone

and then?
East to Lvov east to
                    in the middle of war
                                        Russia?
I imagine him sometimes –
                    an old man
                                with his tea tray
somewhere in Russia.

                    *

When I came up our street and knocked the door
my mother screamed
she thought
we were both dead.
Strange. I had a brother.

Nix.

They were very much reduced had no money
but Willi's father
was not a Jew, you see.

They were taking the young men rounding them up
so Willi's father
because I was also blond I had *good looks* I could
                                        pass
and we would take rolls of film
and false papers.

                    Why us?
                                I don't know:

history's like that, it takes away with one hand gives
                                with the other

            *

but he knows
            under lizard skin

under old tendons strung like knitting wool
bones' long shadows:
                              Willi's father.

                    *

Night-trains bump between sidings.

Across Pannonia wild flowers rush the line.
At Novi Sad a peasant eating bread and cheese
cuts us crusts.
                    We take the first boat

                    *

coming in before dawn,
                              the death hour.
Italy was hard walking,
                              fascisti everywhere.
In villages, faces pointed at us like suspicions.
We kept to the hills.
Stone everywhere. A pebble could slip
the sheer flank of a hill
and peasants far below look up
one of them with a rifle
raising rabbit-scuts of dust.
Behind a stone cistern.
Waiting in the shadow of trees
till we became like trees.

One time taking a ham from an outhouse –
its lover's weight under my arm.

Finally, in France,
the speeding, requisitioned train
station masters at blurred attention;
in Paris – pale shocked streets –
                              the General
giving us to understand
                    how *very* –

What did I feel? I *felt:* yes.

*

A Polish vessel slipping unlit
out of Vichy Marseille
                               into dawn.

*

No, I don't tell.

*

Oh, after that I began to live
like an ordinary man
                               like –
                                         gesture –

*

That's dignity, that's privacy
(though I have to be
                               toileted like a child)

*

you see?
            Fog in the channel
of the throat.

When I was a boy, I was in love with history.
Membranes gleam.
As a doctor, so many slip through your hands.

Willi
went in '44
on Fire Watch: the warehouse toppling
stones on his grave
                               who wasn't Jewish.
Willi

whose parents survived the war.
                                    I wrote to them
enclosing his watch
condolences and respects of the whole crew
a brave and very dearest friend.
                                    Willi
who might have stayed in Poland and lived

with his binoculars thermos lucky photo of Claudette
                                              Col –
the warehouse roof
folding him with girders
paper-bags and other waste.

We hadn't drifted apart it was hard we kept in touch.

Who saved my life; whom I persuaded to volunteer.

Anthony Joseph

The Bamboo Saxophone

The Barrel

My brother and I, we in jungle now. We roam wide country look-ing for sacred bamboo. Thick, tapered, brown and wet, the bell end was full up with buds of fungus; remind me of ringworm that ate my dog's ear. The other end, to blow, was a soft seam of black crapaud truffle. I used a stick and said 'back off this!', and lumps of old tar balm and gutty oil, bits of wood liver, a little blood, came out when I poke it under. All this kept the sound hid, sealed and holy. The wind gauge made true scale, but I preferred a reed, a fipple reed, so we kept on.

Soot

At some dusk burning bush
   In the back ground
      Yard fowl rake in in in
The dust, dirt and soot
Limetree root
   – bare naked fruit
      of cocoa and zaboca
the sikyé fig and the green plantain
the old man in his Wellington boots
     with his cutlass stab in in
the soft dirt beside the dasheen stream
its blade glint   ** sparks **
colonial iron
colonial black
rubber heel
    ./mud

the leaping tongues of flame
conversing, pleading with the darkness
to wait.
      night is a secret

a promise to keep
the black pepper soot
of burning
leaf and feather
fan in   in the flame
then standing back to gaze
on the fire crackle in
and upwards
to the moon.

Nii Ayikwei Parkes

Afterbirth

(novel extract)

'On this dunghill we will search among the rubble for our talisman of hope'

This Earth, My Brother, Kofi Awoonor

kwasida – nkyi kwasi

The birds have never stopped singing. If you look you will see that whatever happens the birds will sing their song. Things are not the same. In my grandfather's time the forest was thick thick and higher; we didn't have to go far to kill a hog. Ah, their spoor began at the edge of the village, I remember well. The taste of boar meat was like water to us, we ate so much. Now they have gone deep deep, the boar. But all things are in Onyame's wide hands. Only Onyame, the shining one, knows why a goat's shit is so beautiful. We are not complaining. When I go to forest I can see that the world is wonderful. The birds are all colours colours. Red, sea blue, yellow, some like leaves, some white like fresh calico. What creatures can't you find there? The smallest catch I have ever brought home is adanko. (Ndanko are not hard to catch. Even when they hide their ears stick up so you can see them. If I created them I would have put their eyes on their pointed ears to keep them safe, but then I wouldn't be able to catch them. Maybe hunger would consume me. Ah, Ndanko. They are fast, but traps catch them all the time. I have many traps. That is a hunter's life.) So we are not complaining. The village is good. We are close to the chief's village and we can take any matters to him. But we have just twelve families so we have no trouble. Apart from Kofi Atta. He is my cousin, but before I learned how to wear cloth my mother told me that he would bring heavy matters to us. I remem-

144

ber; my father had brought otwe – *antelope* – the night before and she was cooking abenkwan.

Yaw Poku, she said, when you are playing with your cousin look well, ooh.

Yoo.

Yaw Poku! (My mother said things to me twice.) I said look well when you play with Kofi Atta. You hear?

Yoo.

She took my hand and put hot soup in it for me to taste. Then she said, you don't know that the woman who helped his mother lost his umbilical cord? She shook her head. It is not buried. The boy will bring trouble someday.

So maybe I shouldn't be surprised, but I forgot. We don't think of these things. They are like light. In the day there is always light and we don't think about it, but I, Yaw Poku, am a hunter so light surprises me. I am used to the dimness of forest, the way the light falls on me like incisions from a knife when I move. When I go to forest sound is brighter than light, so light surprises me. The same way I was surprised even though my mother warned me to look well – *be careful*.

We were at our somewhere when they came. First it was the young woman whose eyes could not rest. Hmm, since you are here let me tell you. The ancestors say that the truth is short but, sɛbi, when the tale is bad, then even the truth stretches like a toad run over by a car on those new roads they are building. I, the one who crouches, the one who watches, I, Yaw Poku, who has roamed the forests from Atewa to Kade, seen every duiker, hog, cobra and leopard that turns this our earth, I was surprised. But let me tell you the tale before it goes cold. It was my grandfather, Opoku, the one whose hands were never empty, who told me that the tale the Englishman calls *history* is mostly lies written in fine dye. This is no such tale and, as the wise weaver of webs did not sell speech, I shall tell it.

It was kwasida, nkyi kwasi – just *one week* before kuru-kwasi, when it would be a taboo, sɛbi, to speak of death and funerals. Nawotwe before we were to pour libation for the ones on the other side. I am sure of the day but if you think I'm lying you can check with the Bono, who have kept the days for the Asantehene for centuries.

We were at our somewhere when she came. The one whose eyes would not lie still. I myself was coming from the palm wine tapper's hut. (The woman who sells palm wine doesn't open on kwasida. She went to live in the big city, Accra, for six years and when she came back she refused to work on *Sundays*. Before she went to the city she used to sell tomatoes at the roadside, but that is another story.) The palm wine tapper gave me a large calabash of his *special* and I was going back to my hut when I heard the woman scream like a grasscutter in a trap. I don't play with my palm wine, no, no, so I went to put it in the corner of my hut, then I came to the tweneboa tree in the village centre.

She was wearing these short short skirts some. Showing her thighs, sɛbi, but her legs were like a baby otwe's front two legs – thiiiin. (It was later that I found out she was some *Minister's* girl-friend. Hmm. This world is full of wonders.) Her *driver* was wearing *khaki* up-and-down like a colo man and he wanted to hold her but the woman was shaking her head and screaming. And there she strengthened herself and ran towards a pale car at the roadside. The *driver* followed her rear like dust.

When I asked the children, Oforiwaa, Kusi and the twins – Panyin and Kakra – who were playing in the village centre, what happened, they said the *cream Benz* parked and the woman was following a blue-headed bird (it is true that our village has many beautiful things) when she held her nose. She called her *driver* and they sniffed the air like dogs until they got to Kofi Atta's hut. They said 'Agoo,' but nobody answered. Then the *driver* raised the kɛtɛ and held it up and the woman went inside. That's when she screamed. It was still morning and the sound made the forest go quiet. But it's what happened after they left that's wondrous. It is true. Even the eagle has not seen everything.

The sun was at its highest, sitting hard in the middle of the sky. I was resting on the felled palm by the tweneboa tree, listening to my *radio* (these days I catch this new *Sunrise FM* from Koforidua), drinking some of my palm wine and watching the children play when they came. The first car came towards the tree at top speed and screeched to a stop, raising sand like rice husks. There were two aburuburu in the trees. I'm telling you, they flew off, making that sound like pouring water in their throats and flapping wildly as the other cars stopped near the first. It was five cars in all. *Police* cars. The first car wasn't even like the *police* cars you sometimes see. It was a *Pinzgauer* with a long *aerial* on top; that's how I knew it was a big matter. *Pinzgauers* are what the army use when they go into jungle for training; I have seen them while hunting.

The big man in *mufti* got down from the *Pinzgauer*. He was wearing a big black abomu over his *jeans* and he was eating groundnuts.

Who is in charge here?

The children pointed towards the giant kapok tree beyond Asare's farm. *The chief lives in that village there.*

The other *policemen* had come down from their cars, all in black-black. *Policemen* one, one–nine, in our village on this young day. The one in *mufti* looked left and right, then I saw him looking behind the tree at my mother's blue sanyaa basin that I put on top of my hut after she died. I remember she carried water with it until it was full of holes, then she took it to her farm to harvest vegetables until there was just a big hole at the bottom. I put it on top of the grass on my roof so I can see my house from far when I am coming back from forest. When the *policeman* looked, I looked too. And there he looked at me and pointed.

You, do you speak English?

Ah. I thought this man either doesn't respect or because, sɛbi, I have shaved my hair he can't see my seventy-four years. (Chewing groundnuts while speaking to me!) I didn't say anything. I raised my calabash and drank some of Kwaku Wusu's palm wine. (It was good. Kwaku Wusu is the best tapper in the sixteen villages under our chief and the twelve villages under Nana Afari.)

You. The *policeman* walked towards me, while the children jumped around him. Oforiwaa started singing a 'Papa *Police*' song (that girl is always singing) and clapping. Kusi was standing by the eight *policemen* in uniform, touching their guns while they tried to push him away. (These *policemen* carry guns all the time, everywhere. Even I, a hunter, I put my long gun down on kwasida.)

His name is Opanyin Poku, said the twins.

Ah, said the *policeman, senior man*. He showed his mother's training and swallowed his groundnuts and put his hands behind him. Opanyin Poku, please, do you speak English?

I smiled and finished my palm wine. Small, small. I go for Nkrumah adult education. OK, listen. I no get plenty time. I dey house for Accra wey I get call say some woman find something for here wey e dey smell. You know something for the matter?

Ei, the elders say that news is as restless as a bird but as for this! The woman had come in the morning and it was still morning, afternoon had not yet come, but these *policemen* were here all the way from Accra, as if there were no *policemen* in Tafo. I shook my head.

You see the woman?

Oh yes *police*, I see am. Thiiin woman like so.

The *policeman* smiled. But you no dey smell anything?

No, I no dey smell anything.

Ah, ah. He turned to look at the other *policemen. Do you people smell anything?*

Yes, Sergeant, it stinks like rotten meat.

Thank you. He turned to me again. And you no dey smell anything.

No, Sargie.

He shook his head. So where the woman go?

Accra.

No. Which side she go for here? He raised his arm towards the tweneboa tree.

I pointed at Kofi Atta's hut.

He brought his hand down to hold the black stick in his abomu. *Let's go.*

The other *policemen* followed him. After a little distance he stopped and turned to me. Opanyin Poku, I beg, make you come some.

I called Kusi to come and get my calabash and radio, put them at the door of my house and tell Mama Aku that I'll be back later. Then I stood up and walked to join the *policemen*.

The Sargie was trying to send the other children back but they were still singing and refused to leave. He looked at me.

Children, I said. Stop your silliness and go home.

They stopped following the *policemen* and turned to leave. Suddenly the Sargie clapped. *Children, do you smell anything? No Sir, Sergeant.* They laughed and ran off.

The Sargie frowned and looked at me. Opanyin Poku, why say we all dey smell something wey you people for here no dey smell anything?

I laughed. Sargie, make I talk something for Twi inside?

Oh, Opanyin, no problem.

Then listen, Sargie. Sɛbi, our village is like a vagina. Those on the inside have no problems with it; those on the outside think it stinks.

The front of Kofi Atta's hut was untidy. There was a heap of bidie near his fireplace and a broken water pot by the door. The obsidian from the water pot was lying under the kɛtɛ like the lost eye of a giant bat. The Sargie and the other *policemen* held their noses and looked at each other. I could see they were scared. Sargie pointed at the kɛtɛ and the tall red *policeman* raised it. I went inside and all the *policemen* one, one–nine came inside. None of them thought of holding the kɛtɛ so the sun could come in. As for me I didn't care. It was dark but I could see. There was a little space in the grass in Kofi Atta's roof so some flimsy sun was able to squeeze through like the deep deep forest. I could smell old palm wine. (Kofi Atta liked to store his palm wine until it became bitter and strong.) There was something on Kofi Atta's kɛtɛ, about the size of a newborn otwe.

Kai, Sargie shouted. *It stinks in here.* He took a *torchlight* out of his abomu and switched it on.

And there, all the *policemen* started shouting, Oh Awurade, Ei Yesu, asɛm bɛn ni, which would have made me laugh because they were all speaking English before that, but it's true that what we saw . . . it's not something you see every day. Even I, Yaw Poku.

The thing lying on Kofi Atta's kɛtɛ was quivering. It was black and shiny, but when the tall red *policeman* stepped closer it was wansima, about apem apem, *thousands*. They took off and the hut was filled with their buzzing. I ran towards the wall, but they surrounded the *policemen*, who stamped around trying to brush them off. I turned and removed the cloth from Kofi Atta's window hole and all the wansima left, except for one or two that kept hovering around. The sun entered the room and we all saw what was on the kɛtɛ. It looked like, sɛbi, a skinned adanko, but it had no bones and it was very red, like a woman's monthly troubles.

It's a dead baby, said the tall red policeman.

Sargie shook his head.

Another policeman, dark, but not dark dark, with a gap between his teeth, said, *This is not natural.*

Sargie stepped back and put his hands in the back pockets of his jeans. *All right, officers, let us not forget our duties.* Mensah?

The tall red one turned to him. *Sir.*

Cordon off this abode. He turned to me. 'Opanyin Poku, weytin you know about this thing?'

Nothing, Sargie, I told him. (Because truly I was shocked. I was not meant to see what I saw, sɛbi. No one without the right powers was supposed to see it. I knew I had to pour libation as soon as possible. All this because of some woman in a short short skirt with thiiin legs. Ah, the elders did not lie when they said one palm nut spoils the enjoyment of the palm wine.) I walked out of Kofi Atta's hut and stood outside holding my head.

Sargie came outside with all the *policemen*, leaving the tall red one inside. He took a *radio* from his abomu and pushed something, then he spoke:

Inspector Donkor, Sergeant reporting.
We suspect human remains, sir.
We are not sure.
With respect, we can't be sure, sir. We are not qualified.
Sorry, sir. Yes, sir, we will try harder.
Of course, sir. We can get a pathologist. We'll try Koforidua.
Sir, we will begin interrogation shortly.
Yes, sir. Yes, sir. I'll update you, sir.

We were at our somewhere when they came; first the woman and her *driver*, then one, one–nine *policemen*, then a drunk *patho-*

logis. And now they had left us with one tall red *policeman*, a Ga man, I think, and a *police* car that the children climbed in the evening. And they said the next day a *graduate* was coming. (I had to tell the chief in the morning.) We waited to see. Man has his plans and the ancestors also have their plans, and sometimes they are not the same. The needs of the earth are greater than the needs of us. We are not complaining. My father and his father before him were hunters; that is what was chosen. My own two sons have not followed me; they have gone to their mother's family in the south. So I am the last hunter in this village. I have seen all the wonders of the forests and rivers and I have told many of the young men, but they all want to go to the cities and make money. Even the story of how I followed the Densu river; rode it in a dug-out canoe learning the birds' songs as the current carried me down, watched the many-patterned butterflies flutter on the river banks, ran my hand in the water like a fish swimming all the way down to the mangroves of the south, where I saw my wife bathing naked in the waters; her buttocks wide and dark, her legs strong and bowed, her beauty greater than a royal python's. Even that story does not entice them. They say there are beautiful women everywhere now. And I tell them that it is not just about beauty because beauty doesn't pay debts; but do they listen?

The medicine man, Oduro, can't find an assistant, and the young ones don't trust him any more; they want *tablets* and he gives them leaves.

Things are not the same. But night had fallen just the same. I had been out too long and it was time to go to my wife. That red *policeman* was smoking something. I could smell it. (If he wanted to stay awake he should have chewed cola; smoke does not keep the eyes open. Oh, Kofi Atta! Because of you all these people have come to do what they like in our village.) My eyes had seen what the mouth must not speak, but one must not let the sight of death, sɛbi, stop one from sleeping, and so I went home. Those who have lived know that darkness is only temporary; morning brings its own light.

abomu – belt
aburuburu – wild doves
adanko (*pl.* Ndanko) – rabbit
bidie – charcoal
kɛtɛ – a woven mat with many uses
nawotwe – an Akan week
sanyaa – enamel
sɛbi – an expression used when one speaks of things they usually
wouldn't speak of

Sharmistha Mohanty

Tornado

(novel extract)

On the day the tornado came, my grandfather saw a buffalo fly through the air. Not gently, its large body resting on the flow of the breeze, but sudden and swift, like an afternoon sleep's oversized dream. It was so close when it went by that he could have reached out and touched its frightened face.

My grandfather, in a long white shirt and dhoti, was on his way back from a walk. As the breeze intensified, his dhoti swirled around his legs. The black umbrella he always used as a cane was sucked away from his hand. There were red and yellow flowers, broken from their stalks and flying over the fields. The flower filled wind threw my grandfather against a banyan tree. On all fours, little by little, he made his way home. On the way he saw a cow on a peepul tree and small silver fish on bushes. He passed the neighbourhood pond from which this wind had drained all the water and loosened it on the land. The pond was empty now, a large bowl of weeds and silt.

All night, the wind. All night the sound of falling trees, breaking branches, dancing twigs, flowers hurled against one another. In the lantern light, full of shadows, my grandfather sat silently. No other sound, no other action, except the wind's had any meaning. So he made only the most necessary of movements – stretching a leg, waving away a fly, leaning his head against a wall. His mind hovered in a region beyond fear, beyond wonder. The wind had entered in him through nose, mouth and ears, and had begun to move him inside, gently but powerfully, a slow, rocking wave forming from the sea of his blood.

A window flew open towards midnight, and my grandfather, looking out, saw a large crystal chandelier floating through the dark, all its swaying pieces tinkling loudly against each other. The zamindar, my great-grandfather, was slowly losing his riches to the wind. The chandelier was like a star flung down from the sky, stark against the tornado night blackness. The world had changed, thought my grandfather. In the passionate wind, things had been cut loose from their moorings. The chandelier was simply a low hanging star, the buffalo a bird, the pond a crater, the land a lake.

The wind transformed things, gave them new names. And not only new names. It gave them new possibilities. The chandelier knew how it felt to be a star, and the silver fish what it was to be a bird on a green smelling bush. My grandfather opened his eyes in the tornado to a new vision of the world. He saw that only things loosened from their moorings became truly real, like a ship throwing off anchor to set sail.

When my grandfather came to the city, he carried the wind with him. In the big city house, he was the one who breathed most easily, sitting on the bed with his back straight, his hands on his knees, silent. There were large balconies in the house but still too many walls, and the wind entered here only in small wisps, like a child's excited breath. Once, only once, it had knocked over a glass.

Henry Shukman

The Call

All these years and I still don't understand
how it works, how the signal gets through
the bones of my hand, the bricks of this house,
the bank building opposite, and across miles

of suburb and field, pylons and roads,
hills and four rivers to precisely you,
in another city, another house, another room,
hunched by the bath with your phone in your hand,

sobbing. You can't bear to feel so split,
you gasp. Downstairs you hear
a chair scrape, a man's voice.
He laughs, in dialogue with another ghost.

But I understand how light works.
Earlier your back gleamed like a guitar.
The last leaves on the sycamore
flickered like a school of mackerel.

Later I will go out in a leopard-coat of light
without you: just me and the trees baring themselves
for winter, and the marbled paving stones,
and my empty hand shining.

Upside Down

On the school field
We tipped our heads back
to see the bell tower hanging
into the sky. Trees floated,
green clouds in the blue air.

We were pinned like beetles to a board.
Who divided the day into hours?
The birds don't know it's Monday.
Why four walls, not eight, or three?

It was spring, all the leaves new,
the ground beneath us firm and dry.
The grass smelt of mowing,
sweet like French beans.

Who cut the world into countries?
I could have yellow shoes.
Or big white boots. We repeated
our names until they meant nothing.

Feeling light as seedballs
with our half-hairy heads
we moved in our two-beat way
towards the trees, who knew all along

what we saw now. We touched
their rough dark skin and agreed
to trust only them and the sky,
none of the things men did in between.

The school bell pricked the dream,
calling, Hour, class, book,
and again we left the world,
passed under the lintel of brick.

Adam Marek

Batman vs the Bull

Casey ran through the leaves and light, skipping over tree roots and ducking under branches. He could win this game. He'd covered more ground than anyone else, venturing deeper into the forest than anyone else dared. His bag of rubbish was already bulging. His friends were all far behind.

The sunlight flickered in the forest, and a cloud snuffed out the sun, revealing a man standing a few steps away, playing with the loose skin around his flabby throat. His leather shoes were broad and firmly rooted in the soft earth.

'What's the outfit for?' the stranger said.

Casey stared at the man for a long while before replying, 'Batman.'

The stranger raised his eyebrows and his head at the same time, like they were being pulled from behind. 'What you got in the bag?'

Casey looked in the bag, even though he already knew that it was full of torn-up envelopes. Casey didn't reply, but looked sideways, hoping to see someone familiar nearby, but the woods were empty.

'Is it sweets?' the stranger said.

Casey looked at the leaves around his feet and shook his head. He felt compelled to linger in this man's shadow, as if to walk away would invite him to become angry. Casey opened the bag so that the stranger could see inside. He didn't know why he did this. The man was a big man. His dipped a hairy hand into the bag to open it wider, then knelt down in front of Casey and looked inside.

The light that had slipped between the trees earlier was gone, and Casey felt cold in his stomach. How long had he been? The party was far away and happening on fast forward. Games were being played in the space between handclaps, and his friends were locusts at the buffet table, cleaning plates between blinks.

'What's that for?' he asked. 'A game?'

Casey nodded. 'I'd better get back,' he said. 'I'm late.'

'You collecting rubbish or something?' the stranger said.

How could he have known this? Had he been at the party? Casey scanned through his memories of the last few hours, trying to remember if this man had been one of the adults there. But Casey only remembered two adults: his mum dropping him off, and Kelly's mum handing out the plastic bags.

'I'll help you,' the stranger said. 'I'll help you win the prize. There is a prize, isn't there?'

Casey nodded. 'A *Finding Nemo* DVD,' he said.

'Wow,' the stranger smiled. 'You could win that. How much rubbish do you have to collect?'

Casey shrugged his shoulders.

'Listen, there's a massive pile of old papers over there. I'll show you where they are. Come on. Follow me.'

The stranger walked on a few steps, then turned and seemed confused when Casey didn't follow. 'Come on,' he said. 'I'll help you win that DVD. The rubbish is just over here. You'll have more than all the other kids.'

Casey took a few steps towards the stranger. His feet took three paces, but his body moved ten, as if on a conveyor belt beneath the early-autumn rot. The space between him and the edge of the wood, which butted up against Kelly's garden fence, swelled, filling up with frosty air, becoming thick and slowing down movement. This dense air pushed against Casey's back, nudging him towards the stranger, and the steep bank of earth towards which the stranger was gesturing. Casey's cheeks prickled and he felt a little sick. He didn't want to upset the strange man, who was now walking towards him with his hand outstretched, reaching to take his own hand, to lead him towards the bank. To help him gain his prize.

The stranger's hand moved around Casey's small fingers. The light in the woods inhaled, swallowing all the shadows, blurring the trees at the edges.

The man's hands were clay, the palms hot and slippery. He pulled Casey towards the bank. Casey felt the tug at his elbow and shoulder. The stranger wasn't looking at him, but at the brow of the mound.

The bank was steep, and Casey tripped. His hand flew out to break his fall, slapping his bag of rubbish against his cape, but the stranger lifted him up by his arm before his bag even hit the ground. His feet levitated, and when they came down again, the stranger didn't give him time to find his balance.

From the top of the bank, Casey saw a steep drop, and a hollow, like the imprint of an enormous fist.

'I can't see any papers,' Casey said.

The man's fingers tangled as they sought to renew their grip on Casey's hand. Casey snatched his hand back, dropped the bag and fled, a flash of pain shooting up his arm as a fingernail raked the top of his thumb.

Casey ran, his mouth open with a soundless sob and his cheeks rippling with the stampede of fear around his body. His legs felt weak stumbling down the bank, and they had to fight to move through the dense air that had filled the forest. He'd moved so far away from the house. His body was too light. The gentlest breeze was blowing against it, but he was tissue paper and it lifted him back through the air where the stranger was waiting to catch him. His breath burned in his chest and throat.

He flashed a glance behind, long enough to see the man, red in the face, charging through the forest, steam pouring from his nostrils. His face was bloated and red, the eyes invisible because the brows had sank so low over them. The ground shook as his feet pounded. He was so fast and strong, ripping through the air without effort. His arms were long enough to reach forward and almost touch the back of Casey's neck. He was burning up the forest with the heat of his rage, dead leaves flying up at his feet.

And then Kelly's gate was before him.

But as he thundered towards it, pistons exploding, the edges of the gate began to melt into the surrounding fence. The handle shrank into the wood, as if retreating from a cold touch. With a terrible sucking sound, the gate became fence.

Casey bounced off it, bashing his elbows and pushing the Batman helmet over one of his eyes. The ground shook below him as he fell. He scrambled up and smacked the fence where the gate had been with his palms and then his fists. His face grew sore with screaming for Kelly's mum to let him in.

Gravity changed. The earth was pulling him to the ground, and he knew that the stranger was behind him. The man was engorged, muscles ripping his clothes and meat spewing out of the torn seams. Two great horns curled out of his forehead, and his eyes filled with black ink. His shoes disintegrated as the cloven feet within split the leather.

The bull stomped the ground and knocked Casey down. It was right over him, its enormous balls swinging between its legs. Its whole body went rigid and its bones cracked as they set into new positions. It roared again, hot air and spit firing from its mouth.

Casey scrambled in the leaves to stand up, but the bull cuffed him with the bottom of its fist. It was a light strike, but it sent Casey sprawling. He closed his eyes against the pain, and put his arms over his head, expecting another blow. A weight pushed into the centre of his back, like a car had rolled on to him. It pinned him to the ground. He tore a fingernail off scratching at the dirt to escape. He couldn't twist to his side. His feet kicked at the ground but were useless. The bull's breath was hot on the back of his head.

And then he remembered his utility belt. He flicked open one of the small yellow pouches and pulled out a penknife keyring. He drew the knife out of the handle with his teeth, then slashed it about at his side, hoping to get lucky.

The bull pushed so hard against his back that he thought his spine would snap. The blade caught something and the bull yelped. Casey aimed for this spot again and again and the knife sank into its ankle. The bull stepped back to avoid another stab, and Casey rolled over and backed up against the fence, panting to get some breath.

The bull thrashed its arms around, back arched, head tilted back, firing noise from deep in its throat up into the trees. Casey went into his utility belt again. Of course, the samurai sword.

The forest was ash grey, spots of rain dripping down through the branches and turning to steam on the bull's back. Tiny lights from fireflies made grottoes of the dying bracken. Casey gripped the samurai sword with both hands and held it before him. A security light in the garden behind him flicked on, and the light bounced off the blade, stunning the bull for a second.

Casey ran between the bull's legs and slashed the blade along the inside of its red thigh. He didn't stop to see the damage, but continued round to the bull's back and swept the blade diagonally across its calf muscle. It unravelled like fistfuls of string, spraying dark blood over the ground.

The bull swung round and its howl knocked Batman off his feet. It lunged forward, pulling its head to the side, like it was going to drive a horn into Batman. But the gouges in the bull's legs slowed it down, and Casey leapt to the side. The bull's horn thumped into the ground where Casey had been, and while the bull struggled to pull it out, Casey swung the samurai sword down on its neck.

Casey felt the blade cutting through the air, could see the exposed neck, could feel victory thumping in his arms, but the sword hit the bull's shoulder and glanced off, slicing a neat but ineffective cutlet of flesh. The cut was enough to show the bull how close it had come to defeat, and it went crazy, bucking its back up and down, screaming and spitting and whirling its fists, stamping the ground and charging at Casey. Casey ducked to the left and the tree he had stood in front of snapped into splinters beneath the bull's shoulder. Casey leapt backwards and the hoof that was aimed for his head sank deep into a rotted tree trunk.

Fear filled the bull's face for the first time as it struggled to pull its hoof from the trunk. Casey saw his opportunity. He ran to the side and drew the blade back behind him, winding himself up. He leapt into the air and uncoiled, the blade spinning around, street-light glinting from its bloodied surface. He slashed the blade through the bull's penis and blood erupted everywhere. The bull's scream was so loud and high that Casey only heard it for a fraction of a second before he went deaf beneath the sound.

The bull writhed on the ground, snake-like and spasmodic, a red fountain spewing from between its legs.

Casey ran along the fence, occasionally glancing back to make sure the bull wasn't following. The trees came to a stop at a path that was lined with amber lights. A car moved past, leaving an orange vapour trail on the inside of Casey's eyelids. Casey wiped his sword on the tufty grass growing at the base of a concrete bollard, then slipped it back into his utility belt. He wiped the bull's dark blood from his face with his cape.

Stumbling along the street, Casey soon came to a junction that led to Kelly's road. He could see lights through the front window of Kelly's house, and two balloons dangling from the front door. The sound of laughter spilled out of the letter box.

Casey turned away, skipping homewards, keeping to the shadows. Fireworks exploded overhead, muffling the sound of his footsteps.

Jason Kennedy

The Sandwich Factory

In keeping with my station in society, and having been rejected by the bowling alley, I took a low-paid job at a sandwich factory. I worked at a sandwich factory where a mad kid worked. He would leer through a hatch and wave a knife at me. One day he ran after my car waving a knife. I figured he wanted to scare me. Or scare and then kill me. I would sit at home in the morning, listening to Joy Division, compensating for the lack of meaning in the coming shift, and wondering if I was going to be killed. And then I would have to have a thought equivalent to, 'Don't forget your hairnet.' Because you had to wear a hairnet, a disobedient blue mesh that embodied your sacrifice to the needs of the company. The hairnets were supposed to be issued at work, but the hairnet box was often empty. And the penalty for not wearing one was so harsh that everyone took hairnets home with them. A fistful of hairnets. And because of this, one manager was constantly saying, 'Where have all these hairnets gone?' as he looked into an empty hairnet box, projecting agitation and concealing confusion. I pictured him at his management training. 'Remember, never look confused. A confused manager is a vulnerable manager. And a vulnerable manager is an inefficient manager. And an inefficient manager is an unemployed manager.' Allowing this to sink in. 'So, a sandwich can come down the line with no filling, but don't you ever let a confused look pass across your face. Instead, use anger, use the face that says, "Someone is going to get fired soon."' And then pointed to a slide projected on the wall. It was a man with three arms. Everyone looked confused. 'By the end of this seminar, you'll be able to look at a picture of a three-armed man without betraying the slightest trace of confusion.'

Packing away, the trainer marks each employee, considering the placement of each checkbox, drinking coffee. Someone always has

163

to be rated excellent; he always chooses whoever had the best legs. Today it was all men. He marks them all as 'poor'.

There was a woman there named Dot. I am never sure why somebody wants to render a child insignificant by naming them Dot. How about Speck? Smidgen? Nano? Or Dash. The Dots and Dashes could form themselves into an unconscious SOS in the staff canteen. Dot wore her paper suit with a tear and had mastered leaning forward to spill her breasts, transferring them into the nearby male minds. I would think, 'Don't transfer your breasts into my mind. Each breast is fifty years old, that's a century of breast tissue . . .' These pre-decimal breasts made me think of everyone riding around on bicycles, of cobblestones and the first sub-four-minute mile, and the Mods and Rockers fighting on Brighton seafront. Dot was a female lech, who had presumably had one of the top teeth at the side removed, so that when she laughed at something about sex, you would see an awful black space where a tooth should be. It was a terrible shame that it was 1994 and Dot lived in the Midlands, as she would've been an excellent pirate, giving blow jobs on the high seas and making all the pirates sandwiches. But the high seas were a long way away and so Dot gave blow jobs in and around The Embassy, a seedy nightclub she went to each week. I would think all this and then look around, panicked, for the madman at the hatch. Was he there? Waving his knife . . . And then a quick feel around my side and back, checking there was no knife stuck in me. Or stab wounds. There was a guy opposite with terrible skin who always appeared deeply surprised if I spoke to him. Turning three-sixty degrees, saying, 'Hey, is there a knife sticking out of my back?' He had a scared look. I carried on working.

The work was carried out beside a conveyor belt. Sandwiches came along the conveyor belt. Dot was 'on bread', splitting loaves and setting the pace for the other workers. Each of us would be there with an ingredient. If you were lucky it would be lettuce or ham or egg, but if you were unlucky or new, it would be tomatoes. It was after a few days of this job that the tomato dreams began, formally pure, endless tomatoes passing silently, a note of agony sounding through them. The tomatoes were chilled in enormous boxes, pre-sliced. There was undoubtedly another factory somewhere, the tomato-slicing factory, where similarly bored and unhappy workers attended daily to make sure that enough tomatoes were sliced to satisfy demand. The acid in the tomatoes would bite into the fingers after a while, making them sting, stinging the soul. All kinds of bitter thoughts filled me then. With bread flying past and the constant grasping of cold slices of tomato, the hectoring from any passing manager, and the burning fingers, all the ingredients of a Greek punishment were in place. A whole factory full of workers who would bite your arm off to push a rock up a hill for eternity (so long as you gave us £4.50 an hour and the weekends off). I entertained a vision of one day being rich and hiring a bunch of faded paunchy managers to recreate the myth of Sisyphus in my back garden, as I sat in a director's chair, watching them push boulders up a home-made hill. There'd be conveyor belts, too, arranged confusingly in the manner of an M. C. Escher engraving, so you had no idea which direction the bread and ham and tomatoes and slices of lettuce were coming from. I'd yell into a megaphone, 'Boulders down! I want sixty thousand egg salad and I want them now! So move it!'

Locked doors were a feature of the sandwich factory. The managers would lock everyone in if we were behind schedule or there was a larger order than usual. Someone would come back to the conveyor belt and whisper, 'They've locked us in. Locked us in until British Rail have another six thousand ham and egg.' And the word would go round. All the previously very unhappy workers now had the extra knowledge that they were locked in. There were three ways to respond to being locked in. Firstly, no response, keep working at the same rate. Or start working faster, so the work would finish sooner and the doors would reopen. Or finally, accept that you were here till the end, and slow down, collecting more pay. Although overall productivity was largely unaffected by what choices the workers made, the fact we were diverging in our approach now made all sorts of problems appear. And these problems manifested as poorly made sandwiches. Sandwiches with no lid, sandwiches without tomato. Ham and tomato sandwiches with no lid, no ham, and no tomato (in extreme cases).

The locked doors thrilled the madman at the hatch. His red face and ginger hair appeared. And then the knife. He drove a forklift, too. Men who drive forklifts are revered as demi-gods in these factories. You will hear people say, 'A forklift driver gets X' and X is two and a half times what the other workers are receiving. There is a 'forklift swagger' to these men (and occasionally a woman). There is a 'forklift face' as they lift a pallet. And there is a 'forklift arm', a particularly fast and dispassionate way of spinning the tiny steering wheel, like the wheel on a speedboat. I had no thoughts of attending forklift truck drivers school, but other workers were saving up for it. They would sit in the canteen with a little leaflet, dreaming of when they had money enough to take the test. The leaflet was pure seduction: the cover featured a tanned, smiling man in the prime of life, removing a heavy pallet from the top of a stack while a manager with a clipboard admired the process. If there had been bikini women on the pallet, oiling themselves and pulling horny faces, this little group of forklift dreamers would've gone straight to heaven.

Dot wanted someone to have sex with me, when I hadn't left after a week. Most people left before they made it through a week. Dot was concerned that I did not say much, that I didn't try to 'get into the girls knickers' and she searched for a girl who would sleep with me. I had zero confidence with women anyway, but it's even harder to engage in courtship wearing a paper suit and a blue hairnet. One lunchtime, Dot's designated girl came over and tried talking to me, smiling and saying hello. But it was no use, she was behind some mysterious pane of glass. I was on my side, with my Joy Division records, my Camus novels, halfway through *Confessions of a Mask*. And she was there in a paper suit and a little cap, smiling. And that's all there was. Then I heard the words, 'I love your car' and I tuned in. 'What was that?' 'I love your car. Can you give me a ride home?' And that's what happened, in the dreamlike way it will, where you are always alone and then suddenly you are waiting for someone to change out of their work clothes and come with you. And as we drove away, the madman with the knife ran towards the car. And I pulled away hard as he slashed at the air. The girl looked back, astonished. 'Does he always do that?'

I brushed it off, careful not to sound unconcerned about violence full stop. I had a reputation for being weird already (simply for being quiet and not looking down girls tops), without making it sound like I gloried in casual violence. We drove to the girl's house. It was a predictable location she had given, one of the one-word names that designated an 80s housing development, a knife's edge away from council housing. Foxglove, Harebell, Angelica, Sorrel, these bastions of fear and loathing had all been named after plants. And yet there were no plants and no grass spread through the twists of tarmac and concrete, the overflowing wheelie bins and the gutted cars. The houses abused accepted design, standing strange as Easter Island statues, with the front door opposite a concrete shelter for trash and no downstairs windows. Built of unfaced blocks, in a charcoal shade designed to reveal any predisposition to mental illness, they had always scared me. The white Mini Cooper stopped and I had no idea what to say. She knew I lived nowhere nearby, so any offer of a ride to work tomorrow would mean a lot more than it might. 'I'll see you at work.' She touched my hand and climbed out.

Later that week I fainted, hypnotized by the conveyor belt. I sat recuperating, the one female manager having been assigned 'tea and sympathy' duty. I could imagine a manager saying, 'Make sure he doesn't stagger into a machine and kill himself. We don't need a lawsuit. When the doors are locked, you don't want them to start escaping chopped up in the sandwiches. They'll all be at it.' And the managers laughing at this.

When I had recovered, I drove home and I never went back.

Zoë Strachan

The Secret Life of Dads

Shift patterns make avoidance easy. That's my excuse. For all of my life, and most of his, my dad has worked in factories. It seems shameful to admit that, aged thirty, I had little idea what he actually did. He didn't speak about it, I didn't ask.

When I was a child he was employed by the Glenfield and Kennedy metalworks in Kilmarnock, making water control valves. For the past twenty-one years he has been a process operator in a chemical plant in south Ayrshire, making vitamins. Half of his life has been a secret, measured in twelve-hour shifts.

Once an interior just like that of the Glenfield appeared on the six o'clock news, a vast warehouse dotted with hulking pieces of machinery. It was illustrating a story about the accidental deaths of workers in initiation rituals. I asked my dad if such things really happened, and he said yes, but he had never taken any part in them. That was when it struck me that at work he might not be the dad I knew from home but someone else, someone who had to find ways of staying true to himself in circumstances alien to me.

Recently the chemical plant was sold, and the new owners have started implementing a 'socially responsible' redundancy policy. A third of the workforce must go. As my dad is fifty-eight years old, I realized it might be my last chance to take a peek into his secret life. To see behind the logo on the effervescent vitamin C tablets I used to crave, to meet his colleagues, to discover what fills those twelve-hour shifts.

So I rang him, ventured my curiosity. He agreed to speak to his line manager. His line manager spoke to the MD's PA. I spoke to the MD's PA. Finally the MD's PA spoke to the MD. It was decided. I could shadow my dad for a day at work.

'I was going to say we'll spot it a mile off,' I told the minicab driver who'd brought me down from Glasgow, leaning forward to squint through the heavy early-morning mist. A sudden slow convoy of orange and cream buses crawled past in soft focus, as if they'd driven straight off a poster in a transport museum, then houses rose beside us and we entered the village of Dalry.

'Oh well,' he said, 'we'll stop the first sensible-looking person and ask.'

We spotted a youngish boy, still up from the night before (and I mean up), and I wound down my window and called out, ''Scuse me!' He stared at me with flying-saucer eyes, then hared off down a side street.

An elderly man with a lugubrious golden retriever proved a better bet. I enquired after the factory, using the old name rather than the unfamiliar, post-takeover one, mispronouncing the continental vowels for clarity. We couldn't miss it, the man assured us, offering precise instructions and distances, brimming with an obvious sense of pride and utter acceptance that we'd be seeking this important place at five-thirty in the morning.

Steam from the cooling towers penetrated the thick morning haze and huge twisted metal shapes loomed ahead. There was nothing else it could be but a chemical factory. Cold morning air percolated in my lungs as I scurried towards the gatehouse. As I signed in I commented to the guards how massive the plant looked.

'Yes, but how long will it be here for?'

The Health and Safety officer, who had the same name as my dad, collected me and took me to a meeting room to do an induction, along with a new contractor. Contractors were conspicuous for their red boilersuits, I noticed, and were not allowed in certain areas. 'NO CONTRACTORS' said a sign on one bathroom door, printed large and laminated. Previously all work had been done in-house.

We watched a video, ticking boxes on a multiple-choice questionnaire to prove our grasp of emergency procedure and good working practice.

'It's like being back at school,' I said.

'Worse.'

Question followed question: about entry permits and hot work permits and confined spaces permits. The latter reminded me of *Star Trek*, my dad and I watching as Chekhov crawled along some narrow, claustrophobic tube in a brave effort to remobilize the ship, Cap'n. I don't know how many permits they use in China, where production will be transferred to if this factory closes.

The new contractor was absorbed into some other part of the plant, while I was kitted out with a labcoat and a gigantic parka emblazoned with 'VISITOR' (in case anyone was wondering) and escorted over to Building 69. Everywhere appeared deserted, yet 550 people worked there (excluding contractors), manufacturing ascorbic acid, panthenol and other vitamin mixes for use in pharmaceuticals, animal feeds, cosmetics. Those on day shift like my dad were all around us, concealed behind 'NO ENTRY' signs and windowless walls.

'You can go for twelve hours and not see five people,' my guide commented as we walked along roads named after famous chemists through a futuristic city, a mini-Metropolis sophisticated enough to have its own railway, but with bicycles leaning casually against each building, for raising the alarm between sections in an emergency. I wondered how delivery men managed when the night shift phoned for a takeaway. Perhaps someone drew the short straw and bundled on their parka to make the lonely walk up to the gatehouse.

Building 69 was a bare rectangle, grey in the gloom. Four tall levels with fire escapes at each corner, linked by external walkways. The passenger lift was broken, and we weren't supposed to use the goods lift, so we climbed the stairs to level four. My dad never brought his work home with him, though I remember my friend Audrey being round one evening, greeting him as he came through the door with a bright and bubbly, 'And how was your day?' and him replying, 'Fucking awful, thanks.' This before the days when it became acceptable to swear in front of your children, and pleasingly illicit, but within minutes the stress was gone, or hidden away somewhere we couldn't see. I didn't know what to expect as I put on my helmet and safety glasses, and swung through the double doors on to the factory floor.

Immediately ahead was a metal shower. No cubicle or curtain, only the industrial-looking shower unit. Below that what I took for a drinking fountain until I saw the notice 'EYE BATH'. Did anyone ever strip off and leap under that shower? Or, panicking, douse their eyes with cold water? I had seen my dad brought home after inhaling chlorine gas. Answered the phone to hear he'd been taken to hospital to be checked over. To the right was a mass of machinery and noise, outsize and scary, which I scarcely registered as we walked past it and into the glass-walled control room, because there finally was my dad.

He jumped up to kiss me hello, our helmets and goggles colliding. It had been a while since we'd seen each other, and his dark-blue boilersuit disguised the muscles I knew he'd developed from golf and hill-walking, making him look different, more slender.

The process my dad oversees makes nature-identical sodium ascorbate, or vitamin C. As we explored together he talked, keen to make sense of the tangled network of pipes; the huge, mystifying vats; the quivering, clanging equipment. Light poured through the high windows, but any view was obscured by the machinery and dust on the glass. Dad used another vocabulary at work, peppered with jargon: the mother liquor, the tank farm, the silent hours. I imagined glances over shoulders, hurried sign-language confabs between identically dressed workers.

Water containing sugary crystal, the mother liquor, is prepared elsewhere on site and piped in to Building 69, where it is heated in a huge crystallizer. The resulting lumps fall into a Pannevis filter and are mixed with ethanol to make a slurry. This is filtered and fed into a fluid bed dryer. Dad wiped clean small portholes so that I could peer in at the brittle snowfall of powder moving slowly along a conveyer belt, cracking as it dried.

The dry substance is shaken in an immense mechanical sieve ('EAR PROTECTORS MUST BE WORN') to achieve an especially fine grade of powder, which is acknowledged as superior within the industry. Samples are taken to the lab for quality-control testing at regular intervals. I followed my dad along the corridor as he went to collect the results, into a quieter place where a radio played gently and people wore white labcoats like mine rather than blue boilersuits, and the windows were low enough to look outside. He searched out a burst package of powder. Rabbis even visit to certify the process as kosher, he explained, as I ran soft handfuls of the finished sodium ascorbate through my fingers.

Building 69 is considered quite a cushy number, for its relative lack of physical labour. Controlling all the gurgling and shaking and sieving is a computer which would run or halt the process even if nobody was there, a variation of the HGV's dead man's handle. Most of my dad's twelve hours are spent in the control room, monitoring screens which show the entire system. These are much bigger than normal computer displays, and encased in resilient boxes which tremble if the machines become particularly energetic. A colourful 3-D-effect diagram – kind of future retro, as if Fred Tomaselli had designed an album sleeve for the Beastie Boys – shows each stage of the process. Dad worked through it, isolating each part of the system, checking the levels in the vats and the speed of production. After allowing one container to refill, he let me press F1 to Resume Normal Running. Machines roared into life and the walls started shuddering.

There was nothing personal in the control room. Company notices were pinned on the board, but no postcards or kids' drawings or funny stories clipped from the newspaper. Radios, personal stereos and mobile phones are forbidden in case the tiniest of sparks flies into the most flammable of flammables. The silent hours must be as eerie as the name suggests, save for the constant shake of the machines. Four shifts use the room, round the clock, four days on, four days off, every day of the year.

The only time I was left alone was when my dad went to the toilet. John, another member of B shift, asked me if I thought I'd like to work there. I said that I found the machines and the noise a bit scary.

'I did too, at first,' he confessed. 'Have you been to a chemical plant before?'

I told him I hadn't, apart from the open day here, years ago.

'Och, they're all same. My wife doesn't even know what I do and it's hard to explain – I open a valve, click a button.'

I asked John how long he had been there.

'Twenty years to the day,' he replied, looking slightly stunned. 'But will there be another twenty?'

Being in the same job for forty years was the ideal, something to be aspired to. After all, you left it behind you when you walked out the gates. With allowances for overtime and unsocial hours, process operators in this factory earn between £28,000 and

£30,000. Their time and energy are traded for family, a house, a nice car. Children at university. Gambling too sometimes, dope, ridiculously expensive wallpaper even. My dad has started travelling, to Iran and Ethiopia, Thailand and Nepal. There isn't an expectation of enjoyment from the work itself, except maybe a satisfaction at being able to do it effectively and diligently. There's no pretence either.

'Everyone gets trapped somehow,' Dad said.

I told him about it being an anniversary for John and later, as his colleague left the control room, Dad said to him, 'Twenty years to the day, eh, John?'

'Aye.'

We fell into a routine, patterned by trips to the mess room for tea, and lunch, and tea again. 'One man in the canteen at all times,' I heard someone quip, but there wasn't any opportunity for skiving. You could always be located if necessary in that bleak home from home, with its stainless-steel work surfaces and plastic chairs. Posters warned of the dangers of excessive drinking the night before operating heavy machinery and I noticed scribbled nicknames on some of the lockers, a few old Panini football stickers here and there. In a side room someone had written high up on the wall in marker pen: 'Cunty McFuck'.

When my dad was the age I am now, he was working constant night shifts. I was two years old. Later, when he switched to continental shifts, the rota was pinned up in our kitchen, highlighter pens colour-coding early, night, back. Seven days on, two off. Tea happened at four, six or ten p.m. No noise before three thirty on nights, or after ten p.m. on earlies. Forgetting your house key and ringing the bell at two a.m. on an early-shift night was a bad thing, though my dad laughed after the event. Occasionally I got up with the alarm at four fifteen and dressed for school, sleepily meeting my dad as he made his cup of tea and realizing my mistake. And like other night-shift children, I'd sleep in the bed with my mum sometimes, then get up before six and creep back to my own cold sheets.

It was, Dad said, much better when he started working four days on, four off. Now a return to the continental pattern is being proposed, with extra hours spent on call. The money will be reasonable, but Dad is unsure how it will work for some of the men with young children. He is concerned that they'll turn round one day and wonder where the years went.

After lunch we walked around the plant. It was still quiet, no people in sight, but the mist had burned away so that the tall white buildings were glowing, reflecting the sunshine of a gorgeous stuck-in-time late summer's day. We agreed that it would be a great place to film *Doctor Who*. Especially as there was an edge to the atmosphere, a knowledge that it was a place which might not always be there. The doomed planet, the spacecraft heading for the sun. If the plant does close, it is uncertain where people would find alternative work. Oil rigs. Saudi. Iraq. There isn't anywhere else nearby.

'Remember the salt mountain?' Dad asked as we passed a huge wooden shed. I had seen inside years before, on the open-day tour for families of employees. I used to picture my dad in one of the little diggers, scooping up salt and driving along the roads between buildings at night, but he hasn't done that for years. He told me about a family of rabbits who burrowed into the salt. Naturally mummy rabbit got squished by the digger. The night shift scooped the babies into a cardboard box and dropped them off at a local animal sanctuary the next morning. The rabbits survived, and as a thank you someone organized a fundraiser for the sanctuary. A burst of quirky humanity amid the anonymous, precisely timed process.

We kept walking, past monumental corrugated sheds and shiny white vats full of hydrochloric acid, across narrow metal grates over channels full of glistening pipes ('You wouldn't walk across these when you were wee'), past the building which contained the cyanide process, a large orange windsock on its roof. With cyanide, it's good to know where it will drift if it leaks.

Production started at the factory in 1983. It was inaugurated by the Queen, and although she didn't come along to the open day everyone dressed as if they were going to a garden party. My mum wore a pink two-piece she'd made herself, and smelled of Arpège. The mood was jubilant. The iron and steel works which had supported the area for 150 years had closed, collapsing the local economy. Many people believed they would never work again. But then, incredibly, what looked to be jobs for life. The government incentives required to lure a European company into the area made them the most expensive jobs which had ever been created in Britain. If new employees went to borrow money from their bank, the manager would just ask them to name their sum.

'It was like finding the Holy Grail,' Dad told me, 'getting work here.'

He had lost his job the year before. The personnel manager of the Glenfield, who had interviewed every man there, and known many of them since they were boys, was asked to use his knowledge of the workforce to identify 100 candidates for redundancy. He agonized over this, but finally did it. When he presented the list to his new bosses they told him to add his own name to the bottom.

It was hot in Building 69 when we returned, illicitly using the goods lift, which had 'WELCOME TO HELL' scrawled across the inside of its immense doors. I've seen this on other lifts, but this one was by far the biggest, darkest and creakiest. The kind of lift that might have conveyed miners deep underground, not far from here, men like my papa, Dad's dad, who had to leave school at fifteen without taking exams. I am very glad that he moved from the village he grew up in, so that my dad never had to work in a mine. Papa hid the medals he'd won during the war away in an old shoebox because he didn't want to be reminded of what he had to do to get them, or so I was told. One afternoon when I was seven we sat at a small Formica-topped table in his kitchen, and he taught me how to play chess and that I liked pickled beetroot. He later worked in the Glenfield, like my dad, and everyone else's dad who wasn't at Glacier Metal. I've stood on manhole covers with the Glenfield stamp on them in far-flung countries, wondering if someone in my family helped make them.

At two o'clock an alarm sounded in the control room. Any after-lunch sleepiness disappeared in an instant. The mechanical shaker which sieved the sodium ascorbate powder was clogged, and had to be shut down, taken apart and cleaned. My dad and John rushed over and began releasing the metal belts which held the layers of the shaker in place. There was no heel-dragging, no talk of doing it later. The system could not be stalled for long.

Each section was chained to gurneys running along girders in the ceiling, safe to 500 kilos, and swung out the way so that the thin layers of mesh could be removed, then washed and dried with a high-pressure hose. The shrill of the hose didn't drown out the impatient rumbles and clanks and *wheeshts* from the rest of the process. Reassembling the shaker needed another man, so Dad collected someone from the canteen. It took all three of them to propel each gigantic piece of metal back into position. Their blue boilersuits against the silver equipment were like an image from a 1930s propaganda poster. 'Productivity!' the slogan would say. As his two colleagues steadied the chains, Dad stretched right under the dangling machinery and replaced dozens of small plastic circles like cookie cutters, which dislodge clumps of powder in the mesh.

Once the shaker was operational again, he and John fetched mops and buckers and meticulously cleaned up the powder which had been spilled all over the floor. Afterwards they had to go out on to the fire escape to cool off. You would want your dinner on the table when you got home, I realized, and then to collapse in front of the television afterwards.

After an hour or so more gazing at the screen and a wander around the floor to listen for any untoward creaks or rattles from the machines, we took a final break. When I went to the toilet I knew my way about well enough to say that I'd join Dad back in the control room. On my way up the stairs I met one of his workmates, who said, 'He's waiting for you.'

When I reached level four Dad was sitting on a table in the hallway. He praised me for being good at remembering my goggles and hat. I still couldn't figure out the tone of his colleague's voice; didn't know if he had children too.

As the end of the day got nearer, activity heightened. Production figures and measurements were logged. A chemist bustled in to advise of handover issues which had to be written up for the night shift. No bells rang to signify the shift change, no whistles sounded, but when everything was in order my dad and I went to our respective locker rooms and showered. Most shifts make their own arrangements, swapping over at prearranged times within a set half-hour period.

Outside there was no surge of bodies rushing homewards, only a few handfuls of men ambling towards the car park. The fading sun was still belting between the buildings, and it seemed absurd that I had needed the big down-lined visitor's parka twelve hours before, in the early morning. We met the man who would take over from my dad walking towards Building 69, lacklustre about the long night ahead, to be spent staring at the screens, clicking on F1. I wondered if people talked on night shift, had those 4 a.m. conversations which are outwith the normal sphere, not to be quoted. What they told each other and what they kept secret.

Trees and bushes line the perimeter of the site. Dad explained that they were there to help monitor any chemical emissions. As always he spoke with respect for the ingenuity of the company that employs him. At first I'd thought the trees were an ineffectual way of screening a potential eyesore from the village, but I'd come to understand a different way of looking at things. In the evening light, the plant seemed beautiful.

I could hear the day falling from my dad's voice as we approached the gates.

'I like to throw a flaky every now and again, so they know I'm not an automaton,' he said. 'But when it comes down to it, it's just a job.'

Lucy Eyre

Brand Ethiopia

In the mid-1800s in Texas, every cattle owner would brand their herd with an individual symbol to distinguish their cows from those of other ranchers. Samuel Maverick made a decision not to brand his cows. It would be simple to identify his herd: any cattle found without a brand must belong to Samuel Maverick. Once this scheme was known, all other ranchers had to make certain that their cows were safely branded to prevent them becoming 'Maverick' cows.

These days a brand has a different meaning. It does not mean 'these cows are mine'; it means 'these customers are mine'. A successful brand creates an allergy to buying an alternative product. The standard economic argument for the existence, indeed necessity, of brands is that they ensure that the market functions; in the parlance, they 'make trade happen'. It strikes me that the country where I live, Ethiopia, is not particularly brand-conscious. National music and 'cultural' food are a much stronger presence than imported music or food. Even when pasta is eaten, Ethiopians might use injera – a patriotic spongy pancake which serves as a plate, cutlery and starch for all Ethiopian meals – to scoop up the spaghetti. Non-Ethiopian music is rarely heard, unless in a restaurant or hotel aimed at foreigners. Many people wear the national dress and can be seen swathed in white cotton shawls. In so far as there is any cinema, much of it is home-grown and in the official Ethiopian language, Amharic. The majority of the billboards advertise local shops and products. There is certainly a strong national identity at work, but, of course, poverty is effective at restraining global brands. With fifty per cent of Ethiopians living below the poverty line and a very localized economy of small traders, paying extra for branded goods is inconceivable.

An interesting consideration is whether the lack of Western brands supports the distinctive national identity; which, if Ethiopia develops as it hopes, might turn out to be fragile after all. Evidence that poverty is behind the lack of brands, rather than a strong national identity, is provided by the litany of fake brands. You might choose to stay at the Mariot in Addis Ababa, feeling that an international chain cannot allow standards to fall – even in the Ethiopian capital – in case you subsequently refuse to visit its Paris branch, unless you realize that one less 'R' and a missing 'T' can make all the difference between quality assurance and free-riding. There is Abibas merchandise, Crust toothpaste and even a T-shirt promoting the Boing 737.

Rich Ethiopians are no more immune to the lure of brand identity and the easy route to whatever image it provides than anyone else in the world, including the first world. There is no McDonald's (although there is a McDils burger drive-in, and a Burger Queen with a similar logo to the more common masculine version). There is no Starbucks, but there is Kaldi's café. Yes, its logo is a motif in a green and white circle; though it contains an Ethiopian-style coffee cup and some beans, rather than Starbucks' more familiar mermaid. Ethiopia's traditional coffee ceremony (which is not exactly a ceremony, but it does take a long time) is more common, yet Kaldi's is full of smart young Addis Ababans consuming cakes, lattes, frozen caramel moccachinos and the like. To be more accurate, it is not always full because rich Ethiopians prefer to be served and drink their coffee sitting outside the café in their cars.

Coke and Pepsi are here, of course. Arguably the most affordable consumer good (far cheaper than sports shoes, iPods or cars), cola is perhaps the first to arrive in any developing country. People in Ethiopia have become brand-conscious about cola in an interesting way. Pepsi production in Ethiopia is owned by a half-Saudi, half-Ethiopian businessman who owns many other factories, including garment makers, and the Sheraton (it's the real thing). He is perceived as being close to the government, though I would like to know which beyond-wealthy businessman can afford not to be close to the government in a country where he owns half the manufacturing capacity. Ethiopia's government is unpopular after recent elections and subsequent troubles; hence so are its allies and so, therefore, is Pepsi. Apparently people have been switching away in such numbers that Coke is considering building another factory. This is the only way in which political messages impinge on brands – by buying less. This switch suggests that, although people are aware of what they drink, they are not brand-loyal. You order a *leslassa* – the name for all soft drinks – and see if you like what comes: be it Coke, Pepsi, generic orange or lime.

The strongest Western brand in Ethiopia, by a long way, is the English Football Premiership. It is very common to see a ten-year-old boy herding goats with a ragged – or even pristine – Manchester United shirt; a twelve-year-old 'Thierry Henry' pushing a wheelbarrow of rubble up a hill; or taxi with 'I love Chelsea. Jose Mourinho' painted by hand on the back windscreen. In the middle of nowhere, a small boy will materialize wearing a (last season only) Wayne Rooney shirt. Local blue and white minibuses might label themselves 'O$_2$' in honour of Arsenal's sponsor; impressive brand awareness, although useless in a country where the government owns and controls all telecommunications.

The obsession stretches slightly wider than the Premiership: the occasional Barcelona FC shirt, for example. David Beckham is everywhere: a large batch of red T-shirts printed with his fuzzy face has somehow found its way to Ethiopia because I have spotted them in several towns hundreds of miles apart. Is David Beckham perhaps the most famous man in the world? It makes one think that footballers' stratospheric salaries are almost justified if their names and faces can reach this far. I flew to Jinka in the south of Ethiopia, where the plane was required to land on the local grazing area (the livestock were temporarily cleared). Even here, we counted ten Chelsea, twelve Arsenal and sixteen Manchester United shirts before we gave up. I tried to arrange a meeting but no one was available that afternoon because they planned to watch 'Bolton vis-à-vis Arsenal' in the local bar. Later that evening several people filled us in on the score. In an even more remote area of Ethiopia, several hours' drive from Jinka, I met a young man, Baila, from the Banna tribe. He walks two hours to market each week to sell cows and butter. He was wearing a traditional, (very) short wraparound skirt, beaded earrings and headgear decorated with feathers. He also wore a Juventus shirt. This is serious brand penetration, I thought, but when I said 'Juventus' his face was blank. This time, it was all about image in its purest form: he simply loved the white and black striped design.

What about Ethiopia itself? These days every country has a brand, though some (Rwanda perhaps?) might prefer not to. How does the word 'Ethiopia' sound to you? Perhaps like a door opening – and, no doubt, quickly shutting – on a bare room. The place in your mind which refers to this country is unfurnished. Or, more likely, there is something in that room: a starving child with a distended belly, wide-eyed and desperate, too weak to brush the flies off her face.

In some ways Ethiopia is a maverick country: unbranded. Or, fairer to say, mis-branded. Your most powerful impression of Ethiopia is almost certainly the famous famine in the mid-1980s. Over twenty years on, people sometimes discreetly enquire when booking with Ethiopian Airlines whether there will be food available on the flight. Ethiopia has been 'branded' with the famine, in accordance with the *OED*'s second definition of that word: 'stigmatize'. Its association with the famine makes Ethiopia the poster child for poor, starving Africa. Many people eat well in Ethiopia, and famines occur elsewhere too, but brands are about the media and one of the most powerful global media events of the past few decades, certainly the most high-profile event by far to mention Ethiopia, is Live Aid. Brands are about reinforcing quick, simple associations: Ethiopia = Famine.

It would be easy for the lazy, uninformed mind for whom that equation is obvious thus to see Ethiopia as an epitome of all that Africa represents to the Western mind. Ethiopians would not see it that way, of course; and not just because there is so much more to their country than famine, nor even because they are too proud to acknowledge dependence on external aid. No, the problem is the troubling association with Africa. Ethiopians speak of it as Britons do about Europe: as a friendly place to visit but not a category to which they belong. 'When did you get back from Europe?' a man in London might say to a friend. Ethiopians tend to view Africa as a continent of black, pagan, colonized slaves. Not the only people to have thought this way, perhaps, but surprising from the country which petitioned for, and won, the privilege to host the headquarters of the African Union. I heard a story of a delegate to the African Union who offered money to a beggar in Addis Ababa. The diplomat, a dark-skinned man from West Africa, spoke a little Amharic and so understood the beggar's response: 'Why would I accept money from a slave?'

Kwame Dawes

The Magic of Monarchy

for Julian May

Come next year, the rains
cover the palace with silence.
it is as if the Emperor has travelled,
but worse. Now cows graze
on the palace lawns, the fanfare
is silent; all ceremony is reduced
to the ritual of an Emperor
picking his painful way through
the echoing walkways, before
they gather him and place him
in the villa surrounded by
soldiers. There in the chapel
a servant reads the psalms of David,
the prophets, the patriarchs,
all fallen men lamenting the jackals
slinking through the broken walls
of the ruined palace. He prays
with slow lips while silence
hangs over the world. It is
the season of new things,
the courtiers are dead,
the nobles slaughtered,
the ministers, the sweet, sweet
children all gone, while soldiers
wait for the magic of majesty
to make them die.
The world will not understand
the quiet of an empty court,

the Emperor's thinning beard
and the blank of his eyes
like Jesus who knows that silence
turns the ordinary to monarchy;
eyes that see the cross ahead.
Jesus, though, timed it well,
or at least the crowd was hot.
Here, the palace is dead,
the people have returned
to the routine of starvation,
the city has lost its way.

Pam Zinnemann-Hope

On Cigarette Papers

Extract from Poem Sequence

Foreword

In 1935 my parents, represented here as Kurt and Lottie, eloped from Hitler's Germany to Kharkov, Ukraine, in the USSR. Kurt was Jewish. In 1937 they were imprisoned during the Stalin Purges. They were released in 1938 and came to England via Krakow in Poland, where Kurt had an uncle.

Headingley, Leeds 1990

The Attic

In the attic
I find my mother has left
her two black fabric travelling bags,
with the exact space between them

for her –
slightly bending her knees
as she lets go the handles.

*

I find
fifty pencilled recipes,
on cigarette papers, in Russian.

And I wonder, did my mother
collect one from each woman
in her prison?

What were their names,
what dish did each dream?
Kiev, nineteen thirty-seven.

                      Kiev Prison 1937 and London 1990
On Cigarette Papers

'*Russische Kochrezepte, nicht wegwerfen,*'
Russian recipes, don't throw away;
I tip them out of their small envelope,

wonder who saved the papers,
where she found the pencil
since writing was forbidden;

the flimsy pile sits soft
in my palm, till I hand them over.
Each edge is foxed.

        *

The translator is trying to decipher
the Russian through a reading glass;
she might smudge the rhythms

of my mother's hand as she shuffles
the fifty slips, turns some over to scan
the writing on the reverse . . .

She tells me, 'Here's *kvass*,
a national drink, illegible
at the end; lemon jam, unfinished;

twice *kulebyaka*, both incomplete;
varyeniki, lazybones curd parcels,
with half the method, served with butter, sprinkled
    with sugar . . .'

        *

In the cramped space
on the stone floor
my mother and her

cell-mates live on
black bread and cabbage;
they call up

the normal kitchen chat,
the swapping of recipes
out of their cavernous hunger,

making feasts.
In her neat Cyrillic
my mother is noting

a dish from each woman,
practising the language
to hold her mind.

*

'Your mother's notes are misspelt,
her verbs – infinitives,
hurried, furtive . . .'
I think my mother hopes
she might get out, be in
a kitchen, gather ingredients:

here's food from Latvia,
Georgia, Greece, Ukraine, Russia,
Jewish herring, fish in aspic . . .

her lists on cigarette papers;
my only map
of who is with her.

My Mother Recites a Litany

My birthday.
The Jewish New Year
(though all religious festivals are forbidden),
Yom Kippur – The Day of Atonement –
Sukkot.

His birthday.
Hanukkah,
Christmas,
New Year.
Purim,
Pesach – Passover –
Easter.

Kiev Prison 1938 and Headingley 1965

My Mother Dreams

I can almost remember
the feel of my green linen tablecloth;
flowers,
a little honeysuckle perhaps,
a *Rose à Parfum de Bulgarie*;
make it a bouquet
and a little cut glass vase to put it in
and place it in the centre of the table with the green
   linen tablecloth.
Let my cloth have embroidery.
Give me the smell of frying onions, please,
and the sight of the steam rising
– like wraiths from the broth.
Let the broth be thick,
let it come out of a tureen
so full that whatever I eat it can't be emptied
and let the rolls be white and light and covered with

poppy seed and served with butter.
And let the next course come.
let it be *schnitzel* in pastry,
Crimean aubergines, potato pie.
And for dessert I'll pipe white heaps on to rice paper,
bake them at a hundred and thirty;
I'll serve meringues on a plate of blue sky.

                    en route, May 1938 and Headingley 1965
Release

                        1
My Mother Tells about Leaving Russia

The wheels clank their slow way;
the couplings are whistling
the same two flat notes.

My underwear, my fur coat,
my hat and my rings –
is all they gave me.

Your father
with his shaven head
sits upright beside me

starved
and deprived of sleep
for two weeks.

'*I confessed to nothing
because,*' he says,
'*your life depended on me.*'

The couplings still whistle
the same two flat notes.
The train pushes us over

the Polish border –
like one flesh – we get up
and step off.

I, swollen
from malnutrition,
in my furs,

your father, thin,
thin, in a suit.
An elegant couple!

ll

My Father Tells about the Polish Border

We are given tickets to Berlin
– compliments of the Führer –
and money for one day's food.

A ride to Berlin
is a ticket to death,
for a Jew that's married a German.

Nazis (or not)
the Red Cross trade money
for your mother's gold rings.

[Note: Many German scientists and engineers went to work in the Soviet Union. The majority were imprisoned in the Stalin Purges. Hitler signed a non-aggression pact with Stalin in which he demanded their return.]

lll

My Father Tells about Warsaw

Another train. A change of gauge.
A different destination.

I take a chance,
ask the German Consul,

'Please can you lend me forty dollars?
My father in Frankfurt will repay it.'

This man, knowing, shakes my hand
– the hand of a Jew –

gives me the money,

'Ich wünsche Ihnen Glück,'
I wish you luck.

Robin Robertson

About Time

In the time it took to hold my breath
and slip under the bathwater,
to hear the blood-thud in the veins,
for me to rise to the surface,
my parents had died,
the house had been sold and now
was being demolished around me,
wall by wall, by a ball and chain.

I swim one length underwater,
pulling myself up on the other side, gasping,
to find my marriage over,
my daughters grown and settled down,
the skin loosening
from my legs and arms
and this heart going
like there's no tomorrow.

Robert Ewing

Rapture of the Deep

Here is the Human Zoo, in this old theatre-turned-dance venue. It's a big space, with adjoining bars, plenty of room to groove and breathe in. The DJ's John Kelly, over from the UK. You see him up on stage behind the decks. He's playing a totally wild-school mix. It's def. It's rad. It's nearly too much to bear. There are stacked speakers either side of him, and lasers illuminating the crowd, scanning upwards out of sight.

Everyone – in front of you, beside you, dancing in the auditorium behind you – is going crazy. And you're in the steamy centre of it all. What a guy! You turn to see these people rising behind, and you think: this is the Human Zoo. This is where all the mad animals come to rattle at their bars and foul up their cages and bite at the hands that feed them. Here are the strutting peacocks and the vainglorious stallions and the preening meerkats and the baboons with their mad arses and hallucinogenic faces; here, all of the skins of the world, black and white and yellow and reds and in-betweens, all with the same wide smiles. Look at the movement, look at the colour, the outrageous clothes, luminous bikinis and silver romper suits and Superfly wigs and naked torsos and tattoos and T-shirts with logos on them like 'Orgasm Donor' and 'Fucker' and 'Betty Ford Clinic'.

Your name's Marcus. You were born here in Sydney and grew up under its oceanside spell, and you have the sun-kissed skin and easygoing charm to prove it. You're a very beautiful young thing. You make top dollar working as an IT consultant for a PR company on the sixteenth floor of a very shiny office block in the heart of the CBD. You like Aussie rules and vodka Red Bull and sushi and casual sex and going to the movies stoned. You smoke hydroponically grown Sydney skunk, and you blast coke Fridays and Saturdays, with diazos for the heavy comedowns. And you surf: at

Maroubra beach weekday evenings, maybe the southern beaches on the weekends when the swell's on, provided you're not languishing at a recovery party somewhere.

You have a luxurious condominium in Double Bay. In your garage there you have a quiver of ten boards to choose from, including, in pride of place, a nine-foot-two-inch, custom-shaped, hand-painted Bob McTavish, worth a cool twenty-five hundred bucks. You also own a BMW Z3 roadster, a Toyota Prado and an immaculate 1964 Ford Futura, which does for cruising out of town.

Tonight your clothing is the hetero side of camp. Sleeveless white Lycra top, cargo pants, denim jacket, moosehide moccasins. Hugo Boss underwear.

Most important though, there's a Chupa Chup lolly in your mouth. They're *de rigueur* in the clubs at the moment. Your one is strawberry-flavoured. You suck hard at this lolly; waves of kickass saccharine pinch your cheek. Sucking stops chewing, which stops teeth grinding. Your teeth are *soooo* beautiful. You have to protect them. Chupa Chups are free at the bar. Most folk have them twisting around in their mouths.

How dangerous could it be to suck on a lolly?

There's a change in tempo: Kelly mixes in a particularly slamming track, and you and the rest of the crowd respond with frenetic dancing. The club goes off its rocker – for a while there you were flagging, but now you're resurgent. All around you, facelift, wind-tunnel smiles. You're whooping and thinking, *Where does the warmth come from? Why's it not always here? Where do I end? Where do I begin? Why do we go back to the same old scene on Mondays, exchanging polite convo, always keeping the respectful distance? We need to change ourselves; it could and should start HERE.*

This and much more of the same. The music washes near and far. You get all removed. Your head becomes a new planet with its own red spot and ring system and coterie of moons. The faces of the people around you register pain, confusion, but you're way in control. A warmth, a sensuality rising into your neck, then you're gone, thoughts tunnelling ahead, mind gone, ego dissolved, eyes upward, following the tracers, people in strobing standstills, the music distant and happening somewhere, not here.

The sexiness is so great that when you reach around yourself to check you're still there, you fall in love with your own caresses. You forget everything outside of your own singular heaven, and perhaps that's what heaven's about: a vaunted detachment, nothing to reach you, nothing to annoy or frustrate you, inhabiting a vast, empty space, a space of time and light which belongs only to you, never sleeping, a chemical pharaoh, like Anubis watching from twenty miles up the unimportant people of the world turning circles swerving colliding like bumper cars on Arctic ice floes –

Huh? Hold up.

Hang a U-ey. Bumper cars on Arctic ice floes?

You try to remember how you got to this thought – but the way of your thoughts, the path, the process, is gone. You think, *Whoa. What a trippy pill.*

Then you're back. Kelly mixes in a new uptempo song. You and all the others detonate into life. It's too awesome. What a world!

A wild guy, tattooed neck, shaved head, blue shades, dances like a feral rabbit with myxomatosis behind you. He rocks around so hard in fact that he misjudges, and his elbow strikes hard the centre of your back.

The Chupa Chup lolly that you were sucking on falls into your mouth, and is pulled with a gasp of inspiration into your throat.

The lolly lodges a good way inside, stopping just over your vocal cords, preventing completely the flow of air into and out of your lungs.

You try to cough, bent over, hands at your neck, face red, the veins on your forehead standing out. You're shocked into reality. You pull vainly for breath. The Chupa Chup will not shift. Unhappily for you, the lolly stick has lodged into one of your throat muscles. The stick is, if you could see it, acting as a wedge against expulsion.

Your hands tremble at your neck. You keep trying to cough, but the lolly doesn't shift. Your panic becomes extreme. You push around the dancers, reaching for their help, pulling them by the arms, grabbing at their funky clothes, but they're gone – blind, lost inside their own raptures. You gesture to your throat, but no one will see. Some spangled guy even tries to dance with you, giving you a damp hug, shouting, 'Yeah, man!' and copying your agonal movements by dancing with his own hands agitating at his neck.

You recoil, try to scream, but of course you're unable to do so.

You have a pressure in your head: the burn of a forced breath hold. Your stomach muscles convulse, moving in concert with your diaphragm. You stagger away from the crowds, the dance floor, and you try to reach the door, get to a quiet area where people will *notice*, but your legs are way too weak. Your eyes brim with tears. Sounds swim as if in the distance, or underwater. You look down on a floor covered in plastic cups and lolly sticks and cigarette ends and this seems odd, an abstract, meaningless mess.

You stumble, fall to the floor.

There you lie with your chest heaving.

Vital seconds go.

Someone's face swells into view. Shouting into your ear, repeating, asking rather hopefully, 'You all right, mate? Mate, you all right?'

Yeah, of course I'm all right. No worries! I'm just a little tired, you fuckin' drongo.

The voice startles you. It's loud, internal, yet removed. Is it yours? God's? The devil's? Then you understand: yeah. It's yours. Or rather, it's the voice of your superego and your id combined. The same scathing accent heard every morning at the mirror; the same gloating voice beside you as you thrust over your conquests.

A scrum of faces above you. One person runs for assistance, while another helpfully slaps you in the face. The penny begins to drop that you're not all right: in fact, you're definitely not very well at all.

You're dragged from the dance floor, legs sliding inelegantly behind you, to the light and lesser noise of a corridor. There are individual voices: shouts, someone calling for help, urgent interrogations.

'What's he taken! Has he taken anything?'

'Is he breathing?'

'What the fucking hell's going on?'

Now you can hear your friends, their voices small, panicky: answering questions, admitting to your ingestion of ecstasy and coke and even, from the sublime to the ridiculous, a wee bit of dope. You picture their faces, their self-reflected concern, hands at their cheeks, wondering if it's bad form to slink away.

Party's over, dudes! Enjoy the show. Hur-hur-hur.

You curse the voice and wish for more time, wish times ten that you had more time. You promise to be a better citizen, a More Giving Person, selfless to a fault.

'Is he hot? Does he feel hot?'

'He's not breathing! He's not breathing! How much water has he had to drink? Didn't you hear me, he's not bloody breathing!'

'What else did he have?'

'Could the coke stop his heart?'

'OOHH! I had the same coke! Will my heart stop too?'

'I heard that ecstasy can cause your lungs to fill up with fluid and you die. Your eyeballs explode and your heart splits in two.'

'There was this article in *GQ* about this coke fiend whose legs and arms went black and he had to have them amputated . . .'

'Oh my word! What about me? I dropped at the same time as him!'

This is great. Having a debate about the potentially life-threatening side-effects of recreational drugs, while I lie here dying. And no one has even considered the lethality of choking on a Chupa Chup.

'Does he have a pulse? Oh Marcus!'

A voice, butting in: 'Is that a dead guy? Seeek, mate!'

'Get lost, asshole!'

Another voice: 'It could be a case of hypertrophic obstructive cardiomyopathy, you know.'

'Who are you – bloody Doctor Kildare?'

The voice admits, 'I'm a medical student.'

'Then do something!'

Silence. Then, 'I don't know CPR.'

'You're fucking joking! Does anyone know CPR?'

The shout's taken up. It appears someone does. An irritating alpha-male voice replies, 'I know CPR!' You feel fingers at the hollow of your neck.

'He's got a pulse.'

No shit, Sherlock. I coulda told ya that.

'Is he breathing?' A hand on your forehead, another firmly gripping your jaw, tilting your head back. 'No breathing.'

Pursed lips, rough stubble, sour breath, the alpha male blowing into your mouth.

This is a bit better. Now let's see how long it takes him to work out I've got a Chupa Chup stuck here bang in my windpipe.

Alpha male tries another couple of breaths. No chest expansion. Then are another two breaths, then a flummoxed silence. Alpha male thinks aloud through his ABCs.

'Did you call an ambulance?'

'An ambulance? Anybody? Hey you fuckin lame-os, an ambulance?!!'

'It's on its way, chill out.'

'Erm . . . danger . . . responsiveness . . .'

As you lie flaccid and awaiting resuscitation, the numbskulls in your head play a naughty, cruel trick: they put on the jukebox in your mind.

'My Girl Lollipop', by Bad Manners, comes on.

Ha, ha, very bloody funny. What an idiot I am.

It has been three minutes since your last breath. You are reminded now of the worst surf hold-down you ever had: pearling on the lip of a massive set wave, in four-times-overhead conditions on a howling day at the Fairy Bower, Manly.

The ocean boiling. Paddling hard. A dark impossible shape beyond the wave you just crested. You pull for it, pull into it, strain as it lifts you, then gasp to see the guts of the Bower opening up way below. You take a short drop, then nothing: then the violence begins, down and up, over the falls, over again and down, down, *down*. Held there in the darkness, pulled along underneath, almost surfacing, but then hit by the next wave as you claw through the foam. Pulled along by this wave underwater way past the point, forgetting to relax and desperately trying to climb up your leash to the surface.

Being held down beyond the point was very heavy indeed.

But nothing like this.

The alpha male recovers himself. He gives more breaths. Then he wonders aloud, 'Is there something stuck in his throat?'

Bingo! Check out the big brain on Brad!

You feel your mouth being opened and a finger pushed inside, poked around.

'Come on, there must be something . . .'

The alpha male sits astride your hips. He puts his hands together in the middle of your abdomen, asks everyone to stand back. Performing abdominal thrusts!

Come back to daddy, come back, my boy . . .

Now your body tightens around you. You begin to shake, the onset of a fit. It's been four minutes since your last breath, and soon you'll begin to die. You've entered a bloodless limbo, where you flex between disconnected serenity and moments of consciousness and panic. Thoughts form in your mind, but you can't register them, and will not later remember them.

Please, oh please, not me, not here, not now, please . . .

You don't experience the stock-in-trade near-death phenomena: floating above and looking down on your recumbent body, or ascending through a black tunnel to a blinding white light. Nor do you relive your life in moments, in a flickering series of snapshots, back and back to wind-whipped sunshine days of ice cream and *slip slop slap*.

Instead: you're underwater. Warm salt water. The sea. Opening your eyes, you see a tropical realm of immense undersea boulders. You drift over these monolithic stones which form hillside slopes and crannies and grottoes and pinnacles for countless types of fish. The stones are dotted with corals: soft corals, gorgonian fans, sea pens and whips, all caressed by the currents. The fish sashay around you. You swim on your back, looking up on the shifting mosaic of light formed by the water's surface, and you turn again, look down to a sandy sea floor with coral bommies dotted around.

The water's so clear that you can see a hundred metres in every direction; the deep blue eliding with depth and distance to black.

You hear the steady crackling of a million, million coral mouths. This sound will be the last impression within your dying nerve cells, and it's really not a bad way to go.

One, two, three –

Explosions.

The alpha male is delivering sets of five liver-splitting thrusts to your upper abdomen. He pushes up and into your chest. Fireworks go off underwater.

Dynamite shattering the coral.

A high-pitched whine in your ears, then:

The Chupa Chup is dislodged. It appears with a froth of vomit at your blue lips. Alpha male falls backwards, amazed, triumphant. He holds up the lolly.

You take a harsh breath. You cough, breathe again. Your breathing falters, then returns to regularity. There are calls for oxygen, and applause.

A rude consciousness slips around you, the strangest wakening of your life, lying in a star on the floor of a corridor with a huddle of strained faces over you. Pain in your head, nausea. You try to speak but cannot. You wonder where you are, what this is.

Things happening. People looking at you. Someone saying, just like in the movies, 'You're gonna be all right, mate.' Then being lifted by some other people, moved down a stairway on some kind of stretcher. Pretty blue lights. A fast drive across town.

You'll be admitted to hospital for investigations. Your voice will return in a few hours, a whisper at first, then a croak. Visitors will come and cry to you.

The sun will shine on and on in your window. Flowers in vases will flourish on your windowsill. Nurses will soothe your early nightmares with sleeping pills.

You'll be discharged from hospital after three days. Then you'll stay at home for two weeks, anxious, haunted by what has happened. When you first return to work, on commute you'll panic at the sight of Chupa Chups on display in the newsagent's. But this will get better.

And you'll be driven by an odd desire: to throw it all in, quit your highly paid job, quit the cars and the boards and the condo and take up scuba-diving instead.

Jean Sprackland

Birthday Poem

A roll of blue silk
left on the edge of the counter.

Above, in the fluorescent light,
a soft equation shimmered. Then

the silk moved, or the spool relinquished it –

unsleeved
slowly at first, then
gathering confidence
spent itself faster and faster, a torrent
flashing over and pooling beneath

and dragged the spool thumping to the floor.
The assistant turned, too late.

Halfway through my life I think of it.
That roll of shining stuff.
Its choice to spill.
Acceleration. Rapture.

Bracken

Lives by its own rules, obeys
a single imperative: *Swarm*

Can smell the space a mile away
where trees have been cleared

Claims squatters' rights
from Norway to Tasmania

and has been seen through telescopes
on the surface of Venus

Closes over the heads of children
where they lie waiting to be found

Spins long curled arguments
tentative as fists

that drink in confidence
thicken into dogma

grow brown and esoteric
waiting for the moment

to pounce on the accident
of the discarded match

Sudeep Sen

Mediterranean

1

A bright red boat
Yellow capsicums

Blue fishing nets
Ochre fort walls

2

Sahar's silk blouse
gold and sheer

Her dark black
kohl-lined lashes

3

A street child's
brown fists

holding the rainbow
in his small grasp

4

My lost memory
white and frozen

now melts colour
ready to refract

Sue Rullière

The Sound of Flies

Adèle squirms at the table, fighting the grip of the chair. It won't let her go. Her eyes flit from the clock to the doorway, to her mother's face and back to the doorway. The strips of coloured plastic hang there stiffly: there's no wind today, no air.

'*Mange donc*,' says Francine, pushing food towards the child. Adèle glares at her mother, grabs a handful of lettuce and stuffs it in her mouth. Keeps stuffing until her mouth is full of lettuce and her chin shines with oil. Francine has words on her face but doesn't say them. The room stays as silent as before, with just the sound of the clock and the flies.

Adèle flicks her eyes back to the doorway. With her gaze fixed on the curtain, she wipes her chin with the back of her hand and smears grease across the table. The oilcloth is worn in the places where they sit, with tiny nicks in its surface where knives have pierced and plates have rubbed and torn. Adèle picks at a crack and makes it bigger. She worries at a hunk of stale bread, digging grooves in the crust with her nails and making crumbs. Her legs swing and kick. Glancing at her mother, she tells her legs just to do it, but they don't, they won't.

And then it happens: she breaks free, slaps her feet down on the floor and runs across to the doorway. Clutching the strips of plastic in a sticky hand, she leans out into the stabbing heat. Behind her in the darkness her mother's words cut through the silence but Adèle doesn't hear.

Francine watches as a fly picks its way across the table. On the edge of her vision a wedge of sunlight breaks in through the gap Adèle has made in the curtain. When Francine closes her eyes, the light's still there inside her head. The child is pulling too hard, her hand is squeaking on the plastic. One of these days she'll drag the whole lot down and there'll be more flies in the room, more heat.

Francine unsticks her forearms from the oilcloth and peels the backs of her thighs off the chair. She stacks up the plates and wipes crumbs off the table. There's no point in trying to brush away the flies.

A mirror on the wall catches her as she passes. Her face is tired and drawn, and her hair, cut short, dyed blonde, looks strangely disconnected from the cracked brown skin beneath it. Francine thinks of Adèle, whose skin is soft and smooth. The child who churns up the air like wind from a storm and has claws that scratch at her heart.

They'd sat together at the table. Adèle smelt of talc and freshly sunned skin. Balls of coloured glass rolled off her fingers as she sifted through beads in a tin, picking out the crimsons and pinks. Crimson to match her tasselled shorts, pink her skimpy top. Bare shoulders, bare midriff – the child's too young for that, but it's all she'll wear. And Adèle's hand was shaking as she cut through string with scissors and threaded on the beads, one by one. Francine watched. Longed to help. Was glad she'd kept the beads all this time.

Adèle sits on the track by the house and draws shapes in the dust. She doesn't see what she draws: all she sees is the cottage at the end of the track. The *gîte* that looks asleep with its shutters closed against the sun. She wants to pick it up and shake it, make its secrets tumble out, let her mother see them scattered on the track.

There's no shade. Adèle's skin prickles in the heat and the beads feel sticky on her neck. Around her the air quivers with the rattle of cicadas and somewhere a dog is barking. The one she always hears but never sees.

A cat skulks on the track, its eyes narrow and its head too big for its body. Adèle throws gravel and like a shot the cat is gone. She wishes it had stayed. She throws more gravel, watching it jump and fling up dust. Brightness screams inside her head. The things the black girl has told her scream there too. Crawling closer to the wall of the house, she puts out a hand and feels the sunshine trapped in the stone. And when she touches her head, she feels the heat that's soaked in there as well and she wonders what will happen if her brain gets too hot: will it melt or catch fire?

A lizard darts across the wall and is swallowed by a crack in the stone. At the far end of the track, the *gîte* still sleeps. Adèle smacks the wall to scare the lizard and swipes at a fly that keeps landing on her leg.

'It's time for your *sieste*,' says her mother from the doorway, barely parting the curtain. Adèle doesn't move. She doesn't want to sleep. She needs to stay there on the track, just in case.

The man is wet with sweat, his shoulders twitch and his hands hang large and dirty by his side. A strange, dark creature that walks in and changes the feel of the room, saying nothing. Adèle can taste him in the air.

In the screened-off corner where they wash, his stream of urine hits the water noisily before he flushes it away. Then he fills the basin, with the cold tap flowing thicker than the hot. In one movement he peels off his shirt and lets his shorts fall to the floor. His buttocks are tight as he soaps himself, his breathing heavy. When he's done he rinses round the basin with a cloth, wipes the floor and dries himself roughly with a towel that smells of sweat.

Adèle pulls her eye away from the screen, away from the chink between the fabric and the wood. She slinks on bare feet to the cupboard, stands on a chair and reaches up. Her fingers feel their way along the shelf, nudging jars and grains of rice. She's searching for a crinkle of foil, a flat slab scored with lines that she can feel through the foil where it's smooth.

The piece she breaks off doesn't follow the lines, it's not a proper square, it's got bits jutting out. Perhaps it's bigger than a square – she hopes it is. She throws herself down in the armchair, her legs higher than her head. The chocolate starts to melt in her hand and saliva floods her mouth. She puts a finger to her lips. The sweetness mixes with her spit and seeps down through her body. She licks each finger slowly with her long, moist tongue and then, with lips curving, sinks her teeth into the chocolate.

The man steps out from behind the screen in fresh cotton. As he comes towards the child, she turns her head away and pulls her knees in to her chest. Her eyes are tightly closed as his hand strokes the side of her face.

The table's clear. The dishes have been dried and put away. Dishcloths hug the backs of the chairs and there's the sound of flies, the ticking of the clock and distant barking. Francine is slumped in the armchair, listening for gaps between the sounds. Moments when everything goes quiet. Silences where nothing happens.

Outside there's scuffling. The strips of plastic clatter and a mess of white fur crashes in, paws clacking, tongue panting. Francine feels a shifting of the air and rough fur against her leg. She hears voices on the track and grips the arms of the chair. The black girl slides into the room, tall and sleek and breathless, with a sheen on her clothes and her skin. Next comes Adèle, bringing dust in on her feet. She's screaming and tugging, needing to touch the black girl's skin and feel her clothes. And then the boys are there too, spitting insults, lashing out, jumping up to touch the black girl's breasts – just hints of breasts beneath the silky fabric. '*Racistes!*' screams the girl. '*Racistes! Racistes!*' And the boys keep trying to touch while the girl spins and twirls, pushing them away towards the flat-chested child. Adèle squeals and runs to her mother, pulls her forwards and hides behind her in the chair, grasping on with sharp fingers, nails digging in.

The dog skids on the tiles and scampers out, and soon the boys are gone too. The girl wants to follow but Adèle rushes over and holds her back, clinging to her silky clothes. She drags her up the slatted steps to the space she calls her room, and soon music shudders loudly and the ceiling jumps and thuds. Downstairs the air still swirls, like dust shaken from a cushion into sunlight.

Francine sits in the armchair. Waits for the dust to settle.

When bubbles break the surface of the water, Francine wraps a dishcloth round the handle of the pan. The water spits and hisses as she pours. She dunks a teabag in the bowl and stirs it with a spoon to spread the dye. The bag was used the day before, once or maybe twice, she doesn't quite remember. It has little colour left.

The music has gone quiet. There are giggles and muffled whispers from above. When Adèle and the black girl tiptoe down, their lips are smeared with lipstick. There's colour on their nails and sparkle round their eyes. They dance around the plastic curtain, weaving in and out, holding hands, until the girl breaks away and leaves the child in the doorway, feet still dancing, as she runs off down the track.

Francine holds her bowl in both hands and blows to cool the tea. The man is sitting opposite. She knows she must tell him. It's been ten days now, she can't be wrong. But there have been enough storm winds already for one day. It can wait. She can tell him tomorrow.

He leaves empty bottles on the table and a smell of cigarillo in the air. Francine doesn't ask where he's going. She takes the crumpled notes he's given her and hides them in a jar in the cupboard. Then she sits with the tea that's still too hot to drink and lays a hand, warm and heavy, on her belly.

The sun has moved across the sky and the track, in shade, is less hot now. Francine comes with a jug and pours water on the bonsais in their pots. Adèle watches as water trickles out across the dust. She fiddles with the beads around her neck that taste of lipstick and salt. Her mother snips at the stunted little trees, shaping them with scissors that used to cut her daughter's hair.

Adèle won't let her do it any more. She wants her hair thick and long like the black girl's. Dark and frizzy like the black girl's. She looks down the track to the *gîte* where the girl is staying, and he's there at the door, coming out. As he strolls back up the track, the shutters of an upstairs window open and the girl appears, just like she did the day before and the day before that. She stands there, peering out, running her fingers through her long black hair. Adèle's eyes go misty. She blinks and rubs them, and when she looks again the man's still walking but the girl has gone.

Francine has her back to the child. She's put the scissors down and is picking wilted leaves off the bonsais. Without turning round she tells Adèle to wipe the colour off her face. Adèle doesn't move. She sees the man coming closer, hands in pockets, kicking dust. Francine speaks to her again, saying the colour doesn't suit her.

'*Putain!*' screams Adèle. 'Go fuck yourself!' And when she feels the hand strike her face, feels the pain her mother's given her, she grabs the scissors and stabs her mother's arm, puncturing the skin. The blood's the same colour as her own and she wishes that it wasn't. The plastic curtain flaps as Francine rushes back inside the house.

Adèle sits with head bowed, her tears falling into the dust. She hears the man's shoes scuffing on the track and sees his shadow slide along the edge of the shade.

In the morning, Francine carries her daughter down from the space beneath the roof where they sleep, and where the man sleeps too sometimes. The space was too hot though for sleep that night, filled with dead air left behind by the day. Its window doesn't open wide enough: it's just a crack through which Francine and Adèle can see the stars when they lie there on their backs, looking up, trying to dream.

Sleeping now, Adèle is heavy. Francine sits down at the table with the child flopping against her, pressing on the wound on her arm, and she strokes her daughter's hair and gently kisses her head, smelling the night on her skin, breathing her in. 'The man may not come today,' she whispers. 'He may not come.'

The sun is slicing through the strips of coloured plastic in the doorway. The flies are starting to annoy. The child stirs in her mother's arms.

Lisa Fugard

Shangri-La

In the moments when neither of us speaks, the sound of Mommie's breathing grows raspier and I imagine I've crept up to a large sleeping animal. I think of Piet when he's hunting, how quietly he raises his gun to take aim. A Winchester Magnum is heavy, but in his hands it looks light as a feather as though he's not even lifting it, as though it's floating up on water or some invisible force. Then I hear the springs of her sofa groaning and I remember it's Mommie at the other end of the phone. She's sitting in her house in Bloemfontein, the green and black and yellow blanket that I crocheted for home-economics class draped over the back of the sofa, just so.

'How hot is it there?' she asks.

Three, four, sometimes five times a week she telephones me and we talk about the weather.

'You watch TV,' I say. 'You read the weather map.'

'They lie.'

Through the window opposite me I can see the ragged banana leaves shaking in the breeze. I've tried Fahrenheit, the way they taught when Mommie was in school, and I've tried Celsius. Numbers mean nothing to her.

'Is it hot by you?' I ask.

She laughs. But it sounds more like a cough or a bark.

I know it's hot in Bloemfontein because I saw the weather map on TV last night, and I know she's laughing at me, thinking I made a mistake marrying Piet and moving to a hunting lodge in the northern Transvaal, thinking that soon I will be asking her if I can come home.

It's nine in the morning and the curtains in her lounge must be open. She's probably staring at the blue gnome who fishes in the sea of gravel among the thorny plants that never need water.

Everything in the garden is coated with dust and surrounded by a concrete wall topped with fins of amber glass from the bottles of Castle Lager that husband number two used to drink.

She hated the way I never called them by their names, but I didn't ask for all those stepfathers. This rotten one who worked on the railways, that drunk one who was fired from his job as a foreman. How can you be fired as a foreman when all you have to do is say, 'Dig here, dig there'? I used to see number two on the road near my high school, drinking his Castles in front of the municipal bakkie while all around him the Africans were dripping with sweat. As for number three? I don't even think she married him.

I can hear a humming over the phone. She's moved to the air conditioner Piet gave her when we got married three years ago. 'The air conditioner still works well?' I ask.

She doesn't answer.

Outside my window an empty Simba chips packet blows across the lawn with one of our maids, fat Queenie, huffing after it. The wind gusts again and the banana leaves show their dull green undersides and suddenly I'm filled with a feeling. Sadness, but not quite, more like a knowing of sadness to come. The humming fades and I hear Mommie breathing again. She's straining as if moving across the room is an effort.

'It's a funny day here,' I tell her. 'We've got a hot little breeze blowing.'

She grunts.

'Like the devil is farting on us.'

'*Bokkie,* that is now too hot!' She laughs again and tells me to keep wet hankies in the fridge.

Mommie doesn't know the heat never bothers me. When I see the mercury rising as if some thirsty beast is sucking it right out of the thermometer, I say, hooray! I dare it to keep rising.

I hang up the phone and for a second the lodge feels too quiet – I'm standing in the same kind of stillness that Mommie's sitting in seven hundred miles away in Bloemfontein. I walk barefoot down the hall to the bar, where I get a ginger ale. Queenie keeps the bar spotless and we don't have guests every night, but the bar still has that smell about it, as if every hunter has left behind a gust of his brandy breath.

'Open sesame!' I whisper and I push open the wooden door that leads to the garden. It's carved with every animal a hunter can shoot in South Africa – elephant, rhino, kudu, lion, even the little ones like duiker and klipspringer. Everything except a kaffir, Piet's older brother Kobus likes to joke.

Outside, the pool is gurgling and Joseph the garden boy is watering the cannas. The lawn is mowed so short it's like walking across a soldier's head. It's paradise, which is why Kobus named the lodge Shangri-La. There are no thorns here, not one duiveltjie in Shangri-La, just birds and flowers and the huge mountain tortoise that Piet found in the Karoo and brought home in the boot of the car.

'The water's disgusting,' my sister-in-law, Charmaine, says from the shallow end of the pool, Cosmo balanced on the edge. 'Like babies' wee.'

'And you're sitting in it, Charmaine.'

She mumbles something and I couldn't care less. I walk into the sun where a lion with hairdryer breath grabs me between its paws and breathes into my brain. Today will be a scorcher, and like a boxer getting ready for a fight I find that special place inside of me and firm it up. I grit my heart.

Piet and Kobus have driven into Jo'burg for the day and it's just us girls at the lodge. And the father and son from Germany in bungalow number six. They flew in a week ago for a safari and Piet and Kobus took them into Zim because there's too much trouble here on the game farms with terrorists laying mines along the border. They came back yesterday afternoon, dirty and smelling of blood, and, like I did when we first got married, I sat on the edge of the bath and shampooed Piet's hair. I tried to bring him back to me. I watched his freckles slowly appear from beneath the grime on his shoulders, but it was too late. Already he was thinking about the animals, the two buffalo and the kudu, their skins salted and rolled up, waiting for him in his taxidermy shop.

Across the lawn Queenie is singing while she wanders through the garden looking for glasses and bottles from last night's party. Princess, our new maid, walks behind her, carrying a cardboard box.

'Is that the bottle song?' I ask Queenie. The Africans have songs for everything.

Queenie says something in Sotho to old Joseph, who laughs so hard he drops the hose and water sprays into the pool.

'Shut up!' Charmaine yells and everyone goes back to work.

I check the thermometer nailed to the fig tree; it's in the shade but still it reads thirty-four degrees. That's ninety-three for the American guests. Take the Celsius, divide by five, multiply by nine and add thirty-two. I don't need to do that all the time. I know the big numbers by heart.

There's a beer bottle jammed between the branches above the thermometer. One of the local farmers probably stuck it there, they were so *vrot* last night. Not the Germans, though: they drank just as much as everyone else, maybe even more, but they didn't get stupid. Hunting does that to men for a few hours, makes them all quick as hawks.

'Princess! Come here,' I call.

She hurries over. This is her first week, make-or-break time when it comes to learning good habits. If you work hard, we'll treat you right – that's the motto at Shangri-La and Queenie is our shining example. She's a hard worker and, present grumpy company in the swimming pool excluded, we all like her voice. Whenever a hunter is here on his birthday, Queenie sings 'Happy Birthday' in Zulu and presents him with a ball of elephant dung covered with icing.

Princess holds the cardboard box filled with glasses and bottles close to her chest. Her face is heart-shaped. Both Piet and Kobus think she's part bushman. Charmaine thinks she's stupid. I'm not sure if she can even speak.

'Princess, we have wild parties! You must look everywhere for bottles.' I mime for her to look under the bushes and in the trees, then I point to the beer bottle in the fig tree as if I've just seen it. Princess doesn't reach for it.

'Do you understand? *Verstaan jy?*'

She nods rapidly and the bottles in the box rattle.

'So take the bloody bottle!' I grab it and clunk it on top of the others.

Just then the door to number six opens and the Germans appear. They arrived white as fish fillets, now even their scalps are sunburnt. All their swagger and steel from the night before have vanished; they're hung-over.

'*Guten morgen*,' I sing out. '*Slapen zi wel?*'

One of them squints helplessly in my direction.

'Breakfast is that way!' I point to the dining room, where ceiling fans and ostrich-egg omelettes are waiting for them.

Charmaine sloshes out of the pool and doesn't bother to reach for a towel.

'Anneline will be coming round that corner in two secs,' I say and, sure enough, there she is in a tight white dress with blue straps and a big blue anchor over her right boob. She's talking to Queenie and waving at us, pretending that she's just driven over from Messina, that she hasn't spent the night with a German.

'I bet she slept with the father,' I whisper and Charmaine glares at me. She thinks Anneline is the closest thing we've got to a war hero, her husband having been killed in Angola, and on a secret mission no less. Closest thing to a stray cat as far as I'm concerned, showing up in our garden every few days to check out the new hunters.

Charmaine picks up her glass of Coke, takes a big sip and spits it out.

'Maybe she slept with the son as well.' I watch Joseph water the cannas, knowing my sister-in-law is double disgusted. Warm Coke and crude jokes.

Anneline curls into a chair beside one of the patio tables. She unclips her blonde hair so it falls behind the chair, and closes her eyes.

'Hot ride from Messina?' I ask.

Charmaine is about to explode

'Did you see the cheetah? The boy who delivered the milk told me someone hit a cheetah on the Messina road.'

'Blood and spots,' Anneline murmurs. 'You must put that Queenie on a diet. She doesn't come fast enough with the tea.' She wearily stands up and wanders across the lawn, moving from the shade of one tree to the shade of the next.

I step into the sun. '*Ja*, it's getting hotter.'

'Why do you do that?' Charmaine demands.

'Do what?'

'Tease Anneline. She lost a husband, you know.'

'I'm interested in lies. I like to see her make things up.'

'Well, Cookie,' Charmaine says, 'that's not a good thing to be interested in.'

Good or bad, there's plenty of lying going on around here. Piet putting a baboon's tooth in the mouth of that impala he was working on, Queenie taking those three Cokes from the bar, and Kobus, Charmaine's husband, sneaking out of Princess's room last week.

Eleven o'clock and it's ninety-seven degrees. The maids are still inside serving breakfast, and Charmaine is dozing, her mouth open for flies. I walk to the far end of the garden, where the bananas and the pawpaws grow – camouflage so guests won't see the servants' quarters – and I push my way through the rubbery leaves until I reach the wall. The veld on the other side is brown from the drought and dust blows around the tin-roofed maids' rooms. Everything is restless, not calm and still like it was five days ago when I spied Kobus.

It was the middle of the afternoon and I was hunting through the bushes for the tortoise because I wanted the Germans to see it on the lawn when we had sundowners. I glanced over the wall and there was Kobus leaving the last room, the one where Miriam with the baby that died used to live, the room we'd given to Princess. He looked around, spat and then strolled towards the lodge whistling. I ducked down before he could see me. No, I thought, it's not what you think, she's a thief and he came to search her room. I crawled towards a banana tree and stood up, hidden by the leaves. I wondered if I would also see Princess leaving the room, then, suddenly frightened that I would, I bolted out of the bushes.

I had tea with Charmaine and the Germans, who had been oiling their guns, and I barely drank a cup before I had to excuse myself because my stomach was doing cartwheels and I wanted to see Piet. His taxidermy shop is a quarter-mile away from the lodge, behind the small general store where Kobus and Piet sell groceries and curios, and I set off down the road. That's when I saw Princess leaning against a tree near the shop and holding something white in her hand. She *is* stealing. Flowers! And then my heart thumped hard because I had an even stranger thought. *Kobus gave her an arum lily?* She bent down as if to smell the lily, then she saw me and moved fast as a ghost into the veld. I hurried through the yard behind the shop and into Piet's workroom and found him sitting at his table scratching through the tooth tin for a spare.

'Are you all right?' he asked.

'*Ja*, I'm just hot.'

'Hot? Cookie? Is that you talking?' He was making a sexy joke, but in that nervous way of his, hoping that I wouldn't pick it up.

'That's not what I meant,' I said.

'I'm done,' he said and he quickly covered the impala head on the table with an old dish towel. He knows I don't like his work.

The first time I saw my husband do it, slip his hands into an animal to remove the skin, I felt sick. It was the expression on his face, so soft, even his eyes were fluttering. He didn't know I was watching. 'Piet!' I whispered, and he pulled his hands out as fast as if they'd been inside another woman.

Later that night in the bar I watched Kobus, all showered and shaved and smelling as though he'd poured three bottles of cologne over himself. He got the Germans nicely tanked and then he led them to the door and asked them to guess which South African game animal was missing. 'The safari's free if you get the answer.'

Mountain gorilla, said the son, which was no surprise. Give a foreigner enough drinks and Africa becomes one big blur, all the animals and countries muddled up. Even Charmaine chuckled. 'Sita . . . sita . . .' said the father, trying to spit out 'sitatunga'. Piet caught my eye for a second and smiled and frowned and then stared at his flip-flops. He knows what I think of his big brother's jokes. Another look to see if I was really mad and then he hurried to Kobus's side. Which is worse, I thought, being married to a weak man, or one who's too strong? I left the bar and searched the garden for arum lilies. There were none. Thank God I woke up the next day to find everyone gone on safari and Charmaine in bed with female complaints.

Mud and rotten flower juice squeeze between my toes as I lean against the wall and watch a little piccaniny who's peeping at me from behind the corner of one of the maids' rooms. Kobus and Piet don't like this. They say we're not running a hotel for the blacks and their children must go stay with families in the townships or wherever the hell they live. But I won't tell. Just then I hear Charmaine calling my name and I duck down. My blood is thick and heavy in my ears, and I feel as though all the insects in the garden are making a racket in my head. Safe! I think. But then I ask myself, why the hell am I hiding when I've done nothing wrong?

When I see Charmaine head for the lodge I make my way back to the pool. I rinse my feet and check the thermometer. We're up three degrees. The heat is like a slow-motion slap, a golden hand forcing me down. 'Not today,' I whisper, and slide back into the shade.

The screen door to the dining room slams shut and Charmaine scuttles across the lawn with two slices of milk tart. 'The German's are coming!' she hisses and she plonks the plates on the table next to Anneline. She flops down on a lounge chair and closes her eyes, pretending to be asleep.

A minute later the Germans pass by, fat with impala sausages. They wave and I know that in a few minutes we'll have company.

'What do you think the professors will talk about this morning?' I ask and Anneline looks at me as if I'm speaking Swahili.

It's predictable, though. First night back from a safari everyone flirts with us, forgetting they've been tramping around in the bush with our husbands, one lucky hunter getting stray cat Anneline. The next morning, to make up for the night before, we get lectured on either politics or animal behaviour.

'If it's another wounded-buffalo story, I'll scream,' Charmaine says, eyes still closed tight.

The Germans reappear with smiles and armfuls of newspapers and magazines. After the usual 'Do you mind?' 'No, we don't,' they pull up two chairs, making sure they're well out of the sun. There's no flicker of anything between Anneline and either the father or the son. This, Charmaine will tell you – and she thinks she's got a degree in affairs of the heart after reading so many Barbara Cartlands – is proof that there is nothing romantic going on in our bungalows. Who says it's about romance? is what I say.

'We have reading materials,' the German father announces. 'Would you like them, to catch up? You are so far away here in South Africa.' He spreads them across the tables and Charmaine, still stretched out on the chair, cranes her neck and eyes them warily.

'You are in the headlines nearly every day,' says the son.

'Really?' Charmaine sits up, making sure to suck in her stomach.

Just then Princess trots over with fresh tea for Anneline, the teapot rattling away as she sets the tray down.

'Thank you, Princess,' I say.

'Princess,' says the father, who has more hair than his son. 'That is a pretty name, but what is your tribal name?'

'She doesn't understand English,' I say. Before I can translate it into Afrikaans for her, she says something with about ten high-pitched clicks and hurries away.

'Sounds like a bloody dolphin,' says Charmaine.

'This is so interesting,' says the son and he rubs his chin as if he's thinking. 'Did we not have Queenie serving us breakfast?'

I'm surprised. Usually it's the Americans who have to ask the name of every African who serves them.

'That's right,' says Charmaine. 'All we need is the Duke of Wellington with a broom and we'll have the royal bloody family working for us.'

There's a glance between father and son that tells me we're not in for a buffalo story.

'I think in South Africa it is you and Cookie who are living like the royal family.' The son clears his throat. 'You have a lovely world here, but I'm not sure how long it will last with boycotts and sanctions.'

'Sanctions?' says Charmaine.

'*Ja*, other countries participating in the economic boycott of South Africa will eventually . . .'

'Well, it's not working, *meneer*,' Charmaine snarls, 'because let me tell you just last month Cookie and I went to Jo'burg and we came back with shopping bags full of perfume and make-up. Picasso, Clinique, Borghese.' She snaps her fingers. 'What else, Cookie?'

'Giorgio,' I remind her.

'That's right. Of Beverly Hills. In America. Sanctions, *se gat*,' says Charmaine. She settles back in her chair. 'And in case you're feeling smug let me tell you that the glass eyes Piet's putting in your buffalo head and your kudu come from Germany! So much for sanctions. Unless you brought a suitcase full of eyes with you.'

The father snickers and says something in German.

'What? What's that you're saying? Just like the kaffirs, always talking in another language,' huffs Charmaine.

'I'm telling my son it is time for our siesta,' says the father. 'The ladies have worn us out.' With a nod, he and his son head back to their bungalow.

'Sanctions!' says Charmaine, her eyes glittering, her mouth fierce. 'I showed them.' She reaches for a copy of *Der Spiegel* and flips through it. 'Thinking that they're doing us a favour, giving us magazines like we're poor. Look at this, they spend so much time looking at this –' she slides the magazine across the table, open at a photo of a woman sunbathing topless on a yacht – 'that they don't know their elbows from their arseholes!' She shakes her head. 'Excuse me, Anneline,' she says and she stomps off to the pool.

I know what comes next. A quick toe dip and, '*Sies!* Queenie, it's too bloody warm!'

Minutes later Queenie and Princess are standing at the edge of the pool with buckets of ice. They tip them into the water around Charmaine, who oohs and aahs and calls for more. Back into the lodge they race to fill the buckets and when they return Queenie has dark patches of sweat under her arms and on her back.

'Shame!' Charmaine cries, suddenly taking pity. 'You take some.'

Poor Queenie. She kneels down and scoops up handfuls of ice and presses them to her face. Princess giggles and puts several cubes into her mouth, water dripping down her chin as she crunches them. Her smile falls away. She stops chewing and I follow her gaze and see Charmaine staring at her.

'Spit it out,' Charmaine says.

Princess lowers her eyes.

'*Spit it out.*'

Queenie rattles off something at Princess and the girl cups her hands and spits the ice into them. Charmaine glides over, easy as a crocodile, until she's in the shallow end, staring at Princess, who is staring at the paving stones.

'Cheeky,' Charmaine says in a squeaky voice and she slaps the water with her hand.

Queenie jumps back, but several drops rain down on Princess, darkening her pink uniform.

'Cheeky!' Charmaine shouts, punching the water hard so that Princess is splashed. Now Charmaine's slapping and hitting the water, trying to grab armfuls of it to throw at Princess. The girl is drenched. Her outfit dark pink, her shoes soaked.

Whoosh! Charmaine plunges underwater. Queenie screams at Princess and waddles towards her, her arm raised as if she's going to hit Princess, and then, as Charmaine surfaces at the deep end, Princess runs into the lodge. A wildlife photographer could not have snapped more exciting pics if he'd witnessed a kill at a water-hole.

The tortoise plods across the lawn, and old Joseph pretends he hasn't heard a thing. Anneline raises her sunglasses. 'Who's coming in next?' she asks.

'No one for a few days, then on the weekend two Americans. Kevin and Tammi. They want a pair of cheetahs.'

One o'clock and it's 104°. Princess has not returned – perhaps she's hitching a ride back to South-West Africa, perhaps she's roasting in her little room – so it is Queenie who trudges across the lawn with glasses of Rose's Lime Cordial and thin slices of Marmite toast for Anneline. The air conditioner in front of bungalow number six starts up and Charmaine complains loudly. 'As if it's not hot enough, now we have their air conditioner pumping hot air.'

'A leopard for tea,' I say, peering into the shade where she sits, brooding like a bullfrog. 'What do you think?'

Her laugh is nasty. 'Cookie, that's a great idea.'

'We've got the bait right here.' I nod towards Anneline, who briefly stops her search for split ends and asks me, if I see Queenie, to tell her that she'd like a soft-boiled egg.

Inside the lodge I find Queenie standing by the ice machine as it rumbles and clanks and coughs up cubes.

'We don't like the Germans,' I say.

'Bad men,' she replies.

'You mean the Germans?'

She puts her hands on her hips, faces me head-on and chatters away in Sotho for at least two minutes. The wrinkles on her face are squiggling in every direction and she speaks so fast it sounds like she's hammering something with her tongue. I catch all our names – Baas Kobus, Baas Piet, Madam Charmaine, Missus Cookie.

'I'm sorry,' I say at the end of it. She doesn't answer and I want to apologize again but that won't do any good.

'So, Queenie, we're playing the leopard game. Warn the others.'

Queenie nods her head vigorously.

We've only done this twice before and Piet and Kobus would probably divorce us if they ever found out. There's an old leopard in the back of the taxidermy shop – one of Piet's first – '*suur lemoen* leopard' I call it because he made such a mess of the mouth – and we hoist it into one of the trees in the garden and have Anneline sit underneath. It's always interesting to see how men react when they don't have their guns.

I unlock the iron door in the wall that surrounds the lodge and the gardens and step outside. The road is the colour of ash and I set off slow and steady. I wish I had a portable thermometer because it must be at least five degrees hotter out here. If Mommie were to visit I'd make her walk this one with me. This is how hot it gets, I'd tell her, this is the truth.

But she won't visit; she barely leaves the house these days. After number three left she got so fat. Week by week there was more flesh between her and the world. As much as I hated one, two and three I felt scared. 'You'll never get a good one this way, Mommie,' I said to her while she changed moods – angry, sad, angry, sad – fast as a traffic light. She kept eating, frozen dinners and cakes and take-out chicken with the crispy skin. We weren't going to have a maid cooking us dinner any more.

'Did you smell it?' she'd asked when she barged into my room while I was doing my homework.

'Smell what, Mommie?' I'd lied.

I knew exactly what she was talking about. The Doreen smell on number three. I had smelled it earlier. I was on the phone taking a message for Mommie, when I heard the kitchen door open and seconds later I smelled that mix of Sunlight soap, sweat, paraffin and a sprinkle of talcum powder. As I finished scribbling the message I said, 'What's for dinner, Doreen?' She didn't answer. 'Doreen?' I turned around and saw it wasn't Doreen opening the fridge, but number three getting ice for his Southern Comfort.

The next night at the dinner table Mommie sat there, sniffing. It was just us, number three and our chicken à la king, and yet it smelled like Doreen was having dinner with us. I kept my eyes glued to my plate of white chicken in its white sauce on the white rice. Only once I glanced up and Mommie was staring at me. I'm sure it was written on my face, the way it was, big as headlines, on hers: 'NUMBER THREE IS BOFFING DOREEN'. I didn't do any homework that night, I went straight to bed. Still she came in, just to sit in a corner and breathe. 'It's the only room in the house that doesn't smell,' she said. A week later number three was gone. And so was Doreen, her back room empty; even the bricks that she used to raise her bed so the tokoloshe wouldn't get her were gone.

I've almost reached the shop when I see Princess sitting on an overturned petrol drum in the shade of the side wall. Her pink uniform is dry and she's holding another white lily. Then I see that, no, it's an ice-cream bar. And that is even stranger, because I've never seen an African eat an ice cream. She's hungry, taking long licks, until she sees me and her hand jerks almost as if she's going to throw the ice cream away.

'No, no,' I mumble, 'it's good. *Dis lekker.*'

But now she won't eat it and we're standing there like idiots, both of us watching the ice cream melt into her hand.

'Stupid! I'm telling you to eat it!'

She starts to cry. Because I'm on the verge of giving her a good *klap* I ignore her tears and head for the shop.

Moses must have just closed it for the afternoon, but I have the key and I unlock the front door. Seeing the bags of chips and neatly stacked bars of chocolate and cool drinks all quiet like that makes me feel like a thief. From the rear of the building I hear African music and I open the door behind the counter and walk down the passage to Piet's workroom. Moses is dabbing black paint on the pink epoxy inside of a baboon's mouth to make it look natural.

'I've come for the leopard,' I say.

Moses laughs. 'You want to make trouble, Miss Cookie!'

He's a good African and Piet lets him work with the animals. His favourite soccer team is Morocco Swallows but he didn't know Morocco was a country in Africa until I showed him on a map. Still, he's smart, he's always reading. Once I caught him with *Cosmo*. 'That's not for you, Moses, that's for women only,' I said and I took it away. Charmaine was furious. What did he think he was doing, reading about orgasms and dating? She wanted to report him to the police so I lied and told her I gave it to him.

The *suur lemoen* leopard is light because of the fibreglass forms that Piet uses, and I carry it through the shop and Moses hurries in front and opens the door. He shrieks. Gliding through the bougainvillea that reaches above the entrance to the shop is a green boomslang. I scream and the leopard falls to the floor. If the snake could scream it would have. It spills out of the bougainvillea, then loops back in. Moses grabs one of the carved knobkieries that we keep stacked next to the door and tries to knock the snake out of the tree. Now it's sliding down the stick but Moses gives it another good shake and the snake lands on the hood of Kobus's old diesel Mercedes that's parked in the shade in front of the shop. He's about to bring the knobkierie down on the snake when I yell, 'Moses! The Mercedes!' Both of us are panting, I'm clutching his arm and the snake is whipping and sizzling. Right in front of our eyes the reflected heat on the bonnet of the car starts to cook it.

Next thing I know I'm leaning against the ice-cream freezer, my head floating in a strange prickly blackness. I can't see Moses. He's like a magician. I just hear his deep voice. 'Drink, madam.' A neon-orange Fanta appears in front of me.

The phone rings and rings.

'The phone,' I mumble.

I hear him answer it. 'Oasis general store,' he says in a formal voice. I hear a tiny shriek. 'It's missus, Charmaine,' says Moses' voice and I feel the phone nudging into my hand.

Charmaine is hysterical. 'I heard screaming! Are you all right?'

'*Ja.*' I can feel myself wanting to cry and I gulp the Fanta. 'Just a snake. I'm OK, but it's too hot to walk back. I'm going to stay in the shop for a while.'

Now I can see Moses. He's squatting right next to me. He takes the phone out of my hand, places it back on the cradle and stares at me.

'Go back to work!' I yell at him.

The faint feeling leaves me and I crawl behind the counter, where I cry and cry. Next thing I know I've got the phone in my hand and I'm dialling Bloemfontein.

'Hello, Mommie,' I say when she answers the phone. I can't go any further. I can't talk about Princess stealing flowers and eating ice cream, and Kobus coming out of her room and Piet, who will do whatever his big brother does. 'Mommie,' I finally say, 'it's so hot here a snake fell out of a tree just now – this snake, Mommie, it landed on a car and began to cook.

'A snake,' she says. 'Are you all right?'

'*Ja.*'

'Sounds like hell,' says Mommie. And then, after a long silence, 'You want to come home?'

It's what I was going to ask, but hearing her say it startles me. Scares me. She must be big as an elephant by now, and moving so slow, using up all the time in the world.

'No big catastrophe,' I say, 'nothing a wet hanky can't help.'

We sit for a few moments like that, me saying no inside and her just breathing. I can still hear her when I move the phone away from my ear, when I hold the receiver above the cradle. Then click. So still. As though the wind that's been blowing all day suddenly stops.

Catherine Smith

Prayers

Because you promised
to process his application for
the caretaker's position
as quickly as possible,
he's including you,
nightly, in his prayers.

He rings next morning,
to check; you assure him
the paperwork's in order.
He tells you he'll include
your parents and brothers
in his prayers.

That night you imagine him
kneeling on the floor
in a bed-sit in Hounslow,
the sour orange glow
from a streetlight
seeking out his tight hands.

When he rings you
two days later, he sounds tired.
His prayers, he tells you,
take him a long time.

There's his own family
to consider – his wife,
who longs to join him,
his brother, whose feet
still suppurate from
after the arrest,
the beatings. His country,
he tells you, is a place
where bad men come
in the night. And

the nightmares, still.
From now on, he'll be including
your aunts, cousins,
surviving grandfather,
friends, in his prayers.

Next morning you wake
in a room flooded with sunlight,
drink hot tea and hope
his lips aren't cracked –

and when he rings
he apologizes for bothering you,
but tells you again
how much this job
would mean.

This job. You are
a kind English lady,
and tonight in his prayers
he'll include, lady,
your future husband,
and your future babies,
if you are so blessed.

Kerri Sakamoto

The Mongolian Spot

(novel extract)

Chapter One: The Priest Who Lost His Followers

They gathered before the priest on the dock at Yokohama, his gaggle of followers. They were cowed among the throngs waiting to board the ship but conspicuously motley. He was sad to be leaving them, and afraid for them being without him. Whereas his wife, Momoye, was happy. She was irked whenever he brought them home. Each had something wrong with them in some way or other according to the families that hid them out of shame or abandoned them to save one mouth to feed. The something wrong wasn't always obvious. But sooner or later it showed itself and they would be cast out or shut in.

There was the handsome man who, no matter how often he bathed, gave off a sulphurous smell that burned the nostrils; another who flapped his arms and cawed every few minutes; the bitter soldier who'd returned from the Manchurian front with no forearms; and the old man with a peach-sized growth protruding from his forehead. There was the stuttering man, the boy silent with sadness and the young woman withered from fear. More recently, a lonely spinster had joined the congregation and so, too, had a family of untouchables banished from their nearby village after the father died of leprosy.

Then there was the girl with the crooked spine who lurched and swayed when she walked, threatening to topple or snap. She'd appeared at the priest's doorstep one morning, waiting for him as if they'd had an appointment for which he was late.

At the priest's request, Momoye altered a dress to prevent it from slipping off the sinking shoulder of the girl's bent body. The dress would pool around a stunted leg, tripping her at every step. At thirteen, the girl was growing tall on one side while disappearing into a bottomless marsh on the other. Momoye was tempted to yank her upright just as she would a hen with a lopsided gait.

Likewise, she wanted to pluck the bulbous growth from the forehead of the old man and cure him once and for all. Her eyes were drawn to it constantly; her fingers twitched. When the poor man tried to shrink himself from her sight, the thing loomed larger, eclipsing his head. On the street, he wore a misshapen hat that Momoye had sewn for him, also at her husband's request.

Momoye contented herself with plucking the coarse hairs from the spinster's chin and powdering the woman's sallow cheeks. She arranged her sparse hair using ornaments to cover patches of her scalp. Momoye often smacked down the flapping arms of the cawing man, and tugged upward at the downturned corners of the sad boy's mouth. She had no patience for these misfits and their ailments, and even less for her husband's prayers to heal them. To her mind, they indulged their own weaknesses, and their families were right to turn them out or shut them in.

They longed to be healed. They'd all heard of the miracle the priest had once performed. It was said he'd brought a woman back to life for her grieving fiancé. But that was long ago, when the priest was a young man, barely more than a youth. Now it seemed to him all a dream, or an accident, and he bore the burden of his followers' yearning hope. He had yet to give them any faith or relief truly; he'd merely given them one another. They might realize that once he was gone. Maybe when he came back, they wouldn't need or want him at all; they might not even like him. They'd grown a touch rebellious lately, ever since he'd told them he was leaving.

One night, when too many people passed before the temple without dropping a single coin into their palms, they became defiant. It began with the old soldier, who poked the stumps of his arms out of his sleeves to scare one passer-by. The others then brazenly displayed their something wrong on the street like wares for sale. The old man cast off his hat and thrust the peach on his forehead into the face of a woman, who screeched in fright. The spinster grinned and tugged at a hair on her chin that Momoye had missed. The sad youth lifted his head from his leaden melancholy with a fleeting smirk.

Once the priest had promised to take them on the pilgrimage to Shikoku. They'd heard the miracle stories of limbs and hair sprouting anew (in the right places); of moles and tumours shrivelling, fading like stones worn smooth by the tide; of general and sundry healthful regenerations. There'd been talk of women's refurbished passageways and men's members buffed and sprung to new life. The priest warned his followers against vain wishes; he implored them to pray to Buddha to show them the Path to Enlightenment.

Time passed and still he hadn't taken them. Why, he didn't know, except that he was awaiting a moment of readiness that hadn't arrived. The followers' interest dwindled along with, if not their inconstant faith, then their will to believe. One by one, the idea dropped from their hearts and minds, just as the last strands of hair fell from the spinster's head. Now the pilgrimage was rarely mentioned, recalled only as a thing to not be mentioned. Now the priest was leaving and who knew when he'd be back, if at all? In the crevices of his heart, the priest despaired of fulfilling the task set by Momoye's mother of finding her capricious son. Nobuo was adrift somewhere in what seemed the limitless horizon of a New World they were poised to sail into, perhaps to become lost themselves. Nobuo had left only the faintest trace: a postcard sent two years ago from Hawaii, the place for which the *Empress of Japan*, this very ship he and his wife were about to board, was bound.

He would miss the girl. She followed at his heels, prayed and recited whatever the priest bid with wide, unbelieving eyes. While the others swayed and swooned, letting themselves be taken in the moment, she stood untaken, she who swayed most easily out of lameness. Her eyes made him wonder if he himself believed, even as he chanted and prayed for his followers until he was emptied, poured into the bottomless, faithless pit of her eyes. She never begged for alms. She hung back behind the others, later accepting with neither a solicitous nor a thankful word what they gave over. The spinster was sure to give her something; she, who was stingy with everyone else, mistook the girl's passivity for timidity, and was touched by her own charity.

The girl made people reach beyond themselves to something greater – or lesser. For immediately the priest would sense his own foolishness, his grasping nature. She humbled him. He wanted to keep her close as a talisman that would make him a good priest, bring miracles to him, keeping his straining vanity in check. But in that very desire, he betrayed himself.

He wanted to bring the girl with them. When he dared broach the idea with his wife, the muscular black wing of her eyebrow began to rustle and swoop. This, he'd learned on their wedding night, was a sign of something raw and vulnerable sniffed out; he glimpsed his tender desires splayed as carnage below him.

Later, onboard the ship, the priest stared out to where the water flatly met the sky and envisioned the girl perched there, her left side sinking into the sea. She was his anchor to home. He would, he must, return to Japan after their task was done.

The voyage went back and forth from darkness to light but without correlation to night or day. Once Momoye awoke to the sun exploded across the sky and thought they'd gone too far, to the end of the world. She slept to wake in pitch starless black; slept still more. She woke and stood amid a maddening sameness of blue sea and sky with frothing waves and clouds, no up or down. She grew dizzy and sick, and the priest lay her down. The clouds and waves rose as smoke, as her own breath out from inside her, forming a shape like one of the priest's mysteries in which she refused to believe. The smoke became him in his dark robe, faced out to sea on the ship's deck. He was unnatural: a blot on the horizon. Hands from out of that robe at night, spidering up her thighs, dry and parched. How could he ever enliven deadened limbs and spirits?

The marriage was a punishment meted out by Momoye's mother. From birth, she had disapproved of Momoye. To not glimpse her own austere beauty in the child and, worse, to see her estranged plump husband in miniature. Momoye grew in spite of the meagre meals she was fed, savouring every crumb. Her mother pinched the girl's meaty calves, buttocks and burgeoning breasts to nip them in the bud. She bound her in sashes so tight the girl feared her tender breasts might grow inward. But she could not stymie her daughter's bursting flesh. She detested and envied the fullness of the girl, her appetite and avidness. That was why she married her off to the priest.

The priest was dry and Momoye was wet. She gushed like a fountain but had no desire for him. She was grateful to not yet be pregnant. She was a flood and knew she might one day drown him.

But before she did, Momoye's mother wanted her son restored to her. He was her prince, who, unlike Momoye, was moulded in her image: the diminutive stature (which he despised, more so when he was found to be an inch short of the five-foot requirement for soldiers in the Emperor's army), the fine, brittle bones. Mother and son's fair, pellucid skin revealed the pulsing beneath it, to be read like a map. In the son, you could chart the design of his emotions, anticipating caprices even before he could. In the mother elaborate machinations swirled; her veins coursed with the thickest, purest samurai blood.

Yet she sat utterly still always: still as the Buddha at Kamakura that was hollow at its core. This unnerved the priest. Only once he saw the stillness shaken and it was the day she asked him to marry her daughter and, pleading for a miracle, to find her son. He had no family and was penniless; he was not worthy of her daughter but she threw herself at his feet, weeping so violently he feared the delicate bones of her face and dainty clenched fists might shatter. It was Nobu she wanted, and Momoye was the offering.

'Take her, take her,' she wept, 'and find my Nobu.'

For she had heard of the priest's miracle, his one and only miracle, the one that had restored his faltering faith and burdened or blessed him with followers. He dared not enunciate it for fear of diminishing it.

'I saw you,' the mother said accusingly. 'I saw.' She set him the task of a second miracle, of finding her beloved son, who'd not been heard from in the New World for nearly two years. He was now made complicit in the sadness of her life and responsible for alleviating that suffering.

The priest had never given a thought to marriage, having consigned himself to an ascetic existence. He had even contemplated the life of a monk in perpetual pilgrimage, but had not yet succeeded in shedding worldly concerns in meditation.

He could only consent therefore, and the woman instantly fell back into repose, restored to an exquisite whole. He, on the other hand, felt himself and his ambitions splinter apart, skyward and earthward. He glimpsed tiny ants scurry in dirt from the crush of his monstrous feet, and gazed on himself as one of those pitiful insects.

On the ship, the priest's unceasing chants of 'Namu amida butsu' resounded with the ship's engine in Momoye's heart. As they neared land, she became more certain that Nobu would not have remained in Hawaii, only to be taken back to the place he'd longed to escape. As a boy he'd disappear for hours with a friend; return giddy and famished for dinner, clothes twisted, lips swollen. Nobu's fingers played in the palm of the other boy, spelling out secrets. In time, that boy went to war, leaving Nobu behind. His moods brought downpours of rain and snow and endless clouds. But soon he found a new friend. When that boy went to war, Nobu sailed away. He must, by now, have found a New World friend.

He'd sent his sister only a picture, no letter. He wore a white cowboy hat on his head and spurs on his boots with mountains behind him. It was a painted mountain and borrowed hat and boots but she never showed their mother if only because of the smile on his face. He'd wanted to be new in this New World, and shameless, and she did too.

When they landed, Momoye gulped the air and tasted the sticky sugar and pungent blossoms. The heat let out its steamy breath all over her. She was drenched but sucked dry. She stepped into a field of tall swishing grasses, then a sudden clearing where women and men hacked at the stalks and slung them aside.

When night came she went to the bath with the women. In the steaming water she marvelled not so much at the darkened ends of all their bodies – their feet and hands, their necks and faces – but the whiteness of what was covered by day from the sun, as if this torso was the place left behind, pristine and unchanged in memory. As if this was Toyama or Yokohama or Yamanashi.

Immediately the priest began to gather misfits around him, no different from the ones he'd left behind. There were Picture Brides yearning for home brought here by the Lonely Old Men who'd deceived them with photographs of themselves as young men. Then there were the Ladies with Many Visitors who'd once been Picture Brides too. They all chanted fervently to the priest instead of to Buddha. They cried for their wretched lives stretching out into the vast sugar-cane fields with no end or sea in sight. Their desires, sticky and knotted and thwarted, plunged inward like a blunt fist that even the Ladies with Many Visitors could not unclench.

One afternoon the priest returned to their tiny hut – a place deserted by an ageing farmer who'd saved enough for his passage home after twenty years away. He had news of Nobu. The priest often walked through the fields of workers clutching a picture of Momoye's brother and this time met a young Filipino boy. Nobu had been here, the boy seemed to say, but months ago sailed north to a city named after the Queen of England, a place where precious flowers – marigolds, peonies and petunias – adorned the streets. The Queen herself was coming to open a grand hotel named after her – the Empress Hotel. Nobu went to catch a glimpse of this divine being: her crown and gown, the sceptre clasped in her royal hand.

Momoye and the priest packed their belongings. The dolls she'd brought from Japan had been eaten from within by moths so that their cheeks or noses were caving in like ruins; their silk robes eaten ragged or coated with a cloud of mould. One had always reminded her of her mother, its imperious beauty, but now its right eye had been eaten and the doll seemed to wink at Momoye in mischief and abjection.

Once again the priest waved to his new followers on the dock – the unmarried Brides, the Old Men, the Ladies – but this time knowing he wouldn't see them again. Yet he felt pleased with himself in a small way because the one Bride he'd helped get to Honolulu had met a young man there from her own hometown in Japan. She sent a photograph of the two of them before a painted tableau of mountains. 'I am finally a Bride,' she'd written on the back. A modest miracle, the priest told himself. Not as big as the first, but a miracle just the same. He prayed as the ship moved away from shore. Momoye waved limply to no one in particular. Anywhere that was not Japan could be home to her, she told herself.

Sarah Hymas

A Wise Man Builds His House on a Rock

Mt 7:29 Harold leads the Plymouth Brethren to Filey, 1919

Call me Canute for choosing this cliff
for our house, like the locals do. But Hannah,
I know it will weather the rain and salt wind
of the North Sea. Just as my brother,
a diviner, is drawn to where he bores his wells,
I can smell the grit and lime within the clay.
Our walls will still stand a hundred years from now.
No one understands frontiers like a man
who's seen the godless gold rush of the Yukon.

I was glad to return goldless. Hannah, this is the place
and the time. With our John back home, safe
from Dublin, with the glory of not killing a soul,
he can handle the firm. In this post-war stutter
of building, he knows haulage is the road forward.
Let him orchestrate our boilers to Bradford.
I will build here at weekends with bricks, twice as quick
as the union rate. The workman is worthy of his meat.
We shall feast on cockles to keep our eyes clear.

Here the Methodists are ready to listen,
Hannah. We will be welcomed. Your piano will inspirit.
The rows of seats, facing the preacher in worship,
can be turned inwards, in equality in meeting.
For who are we if unable to sit square
around our Bible, bread and wine, to let whoever
has the gift of speech, thought or prayer
stand and lead us to be wise as serpents,
harmless as doves? My fire is fuelled, Hannah.

And yes, you may look at me, with doubt
as you did when I told you of my father's suicide,
but did I follow in his weakness? I remind you
of his eight children and how, despite your desire,
I knew one would support and fulfil us,
as if he were eight. Your faith in me and God
was well placed. Have I not led us well, unflinching
in my service? Now I say, as a family, rising
from yard dust into this sea air, we shall be pioneers.

Andrew Crumey

Livacy

When my father was around twenty years old, doing compulsory national service with the British Army, he found himself posted to Christmas Island in the South Pacific. While his former school-mates back home were square-bashing in the rain, he was spearfishing in the Blue Lagoon or watching land-crabs scuttle across burning sands. He was an avid stargazer, and at night he trained his binoculars on treasures of the southern sky – the Magellanic Clouds, the Jewel Box – which he described to me years afterwards, instilling in me a fascination that was to form the basis of my adult career.

Along with his fellow conscripts, my father was one day ordered to stand on the beach, close his eyes as tightly as he could and hold his clenched fists over them. He knew what was about to happen. As a safety measure, the men had all been instructed to wear long trousers that morning, rather than shorts. It was a beautiful, calm day, my father told me. They all stood there, heard the countdown, and thirty miles behind them, a hydrogen bomb exploded.

My father said that even with his back turned to the fireball, and with his eyes closed, he could see the bones of his own hands. A few seconds later he turned and saw the rising mushroom cloud; a ball of incinerated air convected so swiftly into the upper atmosphere that sparks of lightning flashed around its rolling flanks.

Then the sound arrived: a shockwave that knocked the young soldiers to the ground. As the spectacle continued to unfold, the disrupted air above them curdled into black rain clouds, drenching them with viscous bullets of water. When it was all over, they showered and changed, got on with their daily duties and later enjoyed a laugh and a pint at the regimental club's tombola night.

As soon as my father was released from the army he married the girl in Glasgow he'd been writing to every week since he was called up. A year later they had a plump and healthy son, my brother Ken, who now works as a civil engineer. After another two years, I came into the world; but at first the midwife wouldn't hand me to my mother. Instead she called for a male doctor, who had a look at the little bundle he was presented with, took it away for closer inspection, then came back to report his findings to my anxious and exhausted mother.

'It's a little boy,' the doctor told her. 'Unfortunately he's blind.' My mother asked how he could possibly be so sure, and he told her that since I had no eyes there really couldn't be much doubt about it, could there?

That's how my life began: I told the new girl about it today. She's called Jagoda and says the hours and money are fine; she'll clean and iron, do a bit of cooking if need be, read the mail. She comes from what used to be the other side of the geopolitical divide, now vanished like a dream, that caused my father to be soaked in fallout. The bomb he witnessed was meant to damage people such as her, but instead made me.

'Do you regret what happened?' she asked in accented but perfect English, and I laughed, for how could I ever regret being born? I was a love-child, after all. Had my father not been so passionate about the stars, he would never have applied for a posting where clear nights and southern constellations attracted him more than puffer fish or gooney birds. Had a high-energy photon from the nuclear blast not severed a chemical bond inside his body, sending a free radical on its hungry, damaging course, then I might have been born sighted, and perhaps I would have been unmoved by the stories he told me about the mythical beasts and heroes which wheel above our heads each night and go unnoticed by people for whom the flicker of a television screen is more compelling than the glimmer of distant worlds. I might never have become a cosmologist – and Jagoda would have needed a different employer.

'Let me show you around,' I offered, then took her on a tour of the flat, which didn't take long. 'The only rule,' I said, 'is that you don't move things, otherwise I never know where to find them. So no tidying. Other than that, treat it like any other place.'

'What about the lights?' she asked. I didn't know what she

meant. 'They're switched on, though it's the middle of the day. Do you leave them on constantly?'

I realized there must be something wrong with the timer; the lights are meant to come on at night to reassure callers and deter burglars, but perhaps my young nephew had fiddled with the control at the weekend when my sister came to visit. I showed Jagoda how to make the necessary adjustment. 'You see how much trouble I have to go to for the benefit of the sighted?' I explained. 'It costs me money to keep you folk from being in the dark.'

'Perhaps we should try living in darkness like you,' she suggested.

'Oh no,' I said, taking her back to the living room so we could finish our tea. 'There's no darkness in my life.' She thought I was being metaphorical, but such things don't come naturally to a scientist like me; I was merely stating a fact. 'What's behind you right now?' I asked once we were seated.

I heard her turn to look. 'A door, some bookshelves.' Her voice echoed against the far wall.

'Now face me again. How does the bookcase look to you?'

'It doesn't look like anything – I can't see it.'

'Exactly, and that's how everything looks to me: neither dark nor light, but invisible. I'm sure you've never felt you were missing out by not having eyes in the back of your head; I feel that way about eyes in front. I've never needed them and I don't want them. I only wear these artificial things so that I won't frighten people.'

Throughout my childhood I had to go to hospital regularly to have new eyes fitted. They prevented my sockets from closing up, but couldn't keep pace with my growth; so on countless unpleasant occasions I sat stoically while gel was squirted into each empty orbit and left to set, providing a cast for my next set of custom-made eyes. In a medical school drawer somewhere, I expect my youth is still mapped out by a forgotten array of ancient discarded blobs staring blankly in every direction.

In the old days, I told Jagoda, the world's false eyes were crafted by German glass-blowers renowned for their unmatchable skill. The one-eyed Prince Christian of Schleswig-Holstein, maimed in a shooting accident, had a different eye made for every occasion: proud, lascivious, sleepy, hung-over. A man's soul, it is said, is written in his eyes, so I share with Prince Christian the opportunity for self-creation; but my eyes are not glass, because the Second World War cut the supply line, and when Spitfire pilots fell from burning, shattered cockpits into the safety of military hospitals, there was nothing to plug their ruined faces. It was the Perspex shards embedded in their flesh that saved them. Found to be biologically inert, the plastic proved a perfect substitute for glass, and henceforth the nation's artificial eyes were moulded in a workshop in Blackpool, which is where mine came from, made to simulate real eyes, with matching irises and pupils, so that I can look relatively 'normal'.

'They're very realistic,' Jagoda told me. 'When you came to the door to let me in, I thought at first that you were someone else, because you'd told me on the phone that you were blind. It took a few moments to see there was something different about your eyes.'

'They don't move or blink – you can only do so much with two lumps of plastic.'

'I think they make you look very distinguished,' she said tactfully. Perhaps mine came from the same design catalogue as Prince Christian's. Posing as a child for successive generations of these impostors meant sitting patiently in a leather chair, holding my mother's hand while the gel went firm in my sockets. When the casts were ready, the cheerful whiskery doctor would extract them delicately, but never without some of the gel adhering to my own tissue – like stripping an elastoplast from under the tongue. There were consolations of the usual hospital kind: a chair I could swing in as much as I liked; a stethoscope with which to probe my beating heart; inscrutable gadgets of cold, smooth steel, drawn randomly, it seemed, from the doctor's menagerie of disposable spares. None of these, however, could counterbalance the ominous sense of dread I felt whenever we walked down the echoing hospital corridor with its sickly smell of undefined despair; its heavy swing doors; its stock of conversational snippets, momentarily caught from passers-by as Mother and I marched to the eye clinic. Those fragments of unknown lives, falling into my ears like fluttering relics, seemed all the more poignant by virtue of their sheer triviality. This was a place where absolutely no one wanted to be –

even the doctors would doubtless rather have been in the pub. And this was the place where I had to come and have false eyes pushed into my head so that to sighted people I would not appear too monstrous. And like any child, I accepted it.

My escape, I told Jagoda, was to think. In the doctor's leather chair I would avoid the discomfort by fixing my mind on an idea, a memory, a hope. I would hold it with the same tenacious grip that kept my comforting mother close beside me.

'Did you ever wonder what it would be like to see?' Jagoda asked.

'Of course, just as I've wondered what it must be like to be a goldfish or Napoleon – or a woman, though I'd never undergo surgery to find out. I don't suppose you'd want to go round wearing Perspex testicles, would you?'

'What a horrible idea!'

'False eyes are about as much use to me, and real ones appeal even less. Certainly I'm curious about sight, but only if I could have the experience for a very short time, and be sure it was reversible. More tea?' She'd drained her cup with a slurp, and accepted a top-up.

What's it like to see? No poet has ever described it, though accounts abound of what things look like, for the benefit of those who know already. There was even a congenitally blind poet, Thomas Blacklock, who impressed eighteenth-century sighted contemporaries with striking visual evocations of a natural world he never saw. Aristotle offered something more useful in his theory of how the eye works. Rays fly out of it, he claimed, strike distant objects, and in this way give the sensation of vision, so that sight is really a form of touch: a beautiful confirmation of what any blind person suspects. Uncontaminated by the later knowledge that light is a wave flowing into people's eyes, Aristotle constructed a theory based only on what he genuinely felt.

'What else did you think about during those hospital visits?' Jagoda asked.

All sorts of things, I told her; but most of all I wondered why any of it was happening: the leather chair, the gel, my entire life occurring in just the way it was; and why the unfolding narrative, like one of the Braille story books I was then learning to read, should have reached the point it had, precisely then. Was all of time a moving finger, pointing at the tiny dots that make up our lives? Is the rest already written? This was a feeling for which our language has no word; the sensation of being alive, here and now, and of being surprised by it, as one often is in childhood, though the wonder fades with the habits and distractions of age. I made my own word for it, 'livacy', so that whenever the rush of fearful joy overcame me, a sense of death as well as life, I had a name I could hold on to, as reassuring as my mother's hand.

Perhaps Dad felt it when the bomb exploded behind his back, its invisible light strong enough to crowd straight through his head. He could see the bones of his own hands, he told me, even with his eyes shut; and as a child this didn't strike me as extraordinary because the bones of my own small hands made an equally clear impression when I held them to my face. But I noticed the strange pleasure he took in recounting the scene of beauty and destruction he attended. We know life only through its juxtaposition with death.

My life is without light yet knows no darkness. Jagoda found this strange; all sighted people do, which is why I enjoy explaining it to them as much as my father liked recounting the scorching flash; the momentary, all-embracing burst of creation; the rising pillar of involuting cloud that was a brain, a tree, or a thousand other resemblances to the awed onlookers watching from many miles away through smoked glass, being irradiated by human ingenuity.

I was in the back garden with my father one night, holding his star map for him while his binoculars licked the cold sky, when he explained to me how it all worked: the fusion of hydrogen atoms, releasing so much energy that for a brief moment the fireball was like a piece of the sun brought down to earth. He was an engineer by trade, and the universe he described to me was one of machine-like intricacy and perfection. A hoarder of spare parts encountered in his work, he had filled a cupboard in our house with knurled cogs, bits of clocks, greasy gears and tangled wires terminating in sandwiches of plastic and solder that smelled of unknown factories as romantic to my mind as Ursa Major or Canes Venatici hanging far above our heads. He was a hoarder of useless knowledge too, and the workings of bombs and stars lay heaped in the reckless jumble he shared so eagerly with me.

We are all made of atoms, he told me, whose centres are like little jack-in-the-boxes. The lids are held down by nuclear force; the electrical repulsion of protons inside the atoms pushes against this restraint like a pent-up spring. To close a jack-in-the-box, you need to push down hard on the spring until the box shuts with a click. Squeeze lots of hydrogen atoms together and the force makes a trillion clicks: fusion's thunderous roar.

It was enough to knock my father to the ground, this energy from mating particles carried through seared air into his youthful body. Yet only a single click – on a Geiger counter as he emerged from the shower afterwards – was enough to decide my future and his. For me, it was the blessing of being who I am. For him, it was the cancer that killed him three years ago.

I didn't tell any of this to Jagoda; she'd come to offer domestic help, not hear my life story. But she wanted to know what I do for a living, so I explained how one thing had followed another, like particles communicating their quantity of motion, or like the harmonious interlocking of a succession of toothed wheels. I was born from a hydrogen bomb and so is everyone, since the sun or any other star is a bottomless ocean of hydrogen whose atoms, compressed by their own sheer weight, fuse unavoidably, sending parcels of light burrowing haphazardly through the thick and perilous mantle, out into space, across distances of unimaginable emptiness, traversing the cosmos without incident until at last a few of them might fall, like unexpected snowflakes, upon the innocent lens a human aims towards the place were they were born.

Those nights in the garden when I stood with Dad and gave him the loyal audience he elsewhere lacked were the means by which that feeble starlight entered my life, keeping me company during visits to the hospital and prompting the first stirrings of livacy that stayed with me as native wonder turned to scientific curiosity. How fortunate I was, I realized, to be able to experience something no sighted person can truly imagine: a universe in which neither light nor dark exists, though this was how everything began, in a condition lacking even space and time which we only fully recover when we come to be deprived of every sense, like my father now.

If the stars hadn't taken him to Christmas Island he would probably still be alive, and I wouldn't have wasted an hour telling Jagoda his story. She starts next week; there'll be plenty for her to do, and before she left she asked me one more thing. Since you're a cosmologist, she said, can you explain to me what started it all in the first place? Why is there something rather than nothing? That's the oldest question of all, I replied. I wish I knew the answer.

M. R. Peacocke

Simile

Like waking on a clear day early, satisfied with sleep,
and stretching, when the stretch takes you and widens
     you further
than the narrow arches of the body knew they could
     go,
widens you and flings you softly to your furthest of
     touch –

this simile that I know and don't know, that won't
     attach,
that's like the moth I found on the floor, white,
     plumy, perfect
except that something had gone out of it; or else
     perhaps
a flawless immobility had crept in; and this moth

resembles the dream whose loss I wake to, that's
     telling me
the vital thing I need to know which waking
     displaces,
like the smell of a loved body that once seemed like
     the smell
of love itself and now you can't, can't recall. Can't
     recall.

Helen Dunmore

At the Institute with KM

I lie and bathe in the warmth of the cows. That's what I'm here for, or rather it's what the cows are here for. It's beneficial to inhale the mild steam of cows. Everything happens for a reason at the Institute. Even lying down has its purpose. I want to resist it, but I haven't the energy any more.

I lie on my couch in the hayloft. Down below, the cows shift and stir and tear the hay from the manger, and send up billows of breath. They shit as they eat, and the shit smells both sweet and acrid as it spatters down their legs and clots the hair of their tails.

The cows are beautiful. I could think about them all day long. Their movements, their long shuddery sighs, the noise of their teeth, the sensitivity of their lips, the long strings of slobber that drop from their jaws. They are benign. We lie in a row and think about the benignity of cows.

I wish I'd been chosen to learn to milk, but I wasn't. I used to work in the vegetable garden. Last summer we produced more than two thousand pounds of tomatoes. Sometimes I think of those tomatoes, too, as a change from thinking about the cows. They are not quite like the tomatoes on market stalls. They are thick-skinned and warm. As the vines shrivel, the pungency of tomatoes grows until you start to imagine that they are the fruit Adam ate in Eden.

But we don't eat tomatoes very often at the Institute. No doubt there's some reason against it.

I worked hard in that vegetable garden. Even when the sun was full in the sky I didn't rest. My hoe scritch-scratched up and down the rows of onions and I watered the tomatoes evenly so that their skin wouldn't split.

If my mother could have seen me, she would have rubbed her eyes.

I used to be a strong child, I know that. I wasn't always like this. I was a stout, four-square little boy in my white embroidered smock and loose trousers. Doesn't my mother remember that? It was only later on that this filthy disease took hold of me and made me what I am now.

I'm twenty-seven, that's all. I look at myself in the mirror and I know far too much about myself. The bony skull and the big teeth that make me look as if I'm heehawing like a donkey. Why didn't my skull have the grace to stay hidden? I'm still alive. I don't want to see it.

Some days there are as many as ten of us, lying in a row in the hayloft, absorbing the shit-sweet breath of the cows. I stare up at the pictures on the ceiling. Mr de Saltzmann painted them. They are beautiful and funny and they do exactly what they are meant to do: they divert us.

It wasn't my choice to come to the Institute. It wasn't my vision. Gurdjieff has been very patient about this. He could tell instantly that I wasn't a disciple. It was my mother who wanted me to come, and in the end it was too much trouble to resist her. I thought G might throw me out, and even after a few days I was afraid of being thrown out. But he didn't. He said I could work, and join in the fast.

Fasting is strange. If you've never done it, you've no idea how it will make you feel. Ever since I've been ill, people have been urging me to eat.

My mother most of all. She can't bear my thinness: literally can't bear it.

I don't blame her. It's disgusting to be so thin. I disgust myself. I took off all my clothes and stood in front of the mirror and there I was. Collar bones like coat-hangers. Rounded shoulders and sucked-in ribs. My feet were bony and enormous. My elbows – why should anybody have such elbows? And for God's sake, my knees. I looked at it all for a long time and then I covered it up again. These days I prefer to contemplate the cows in all their fullness.

My poor mother with her little pancakes filled with cream and chocolate sauce, her nourishing soups and her sudden frenzies for the blackest, most expensive caviar or for dried reindeer tongue which has to be bought in slivers which are more expensive than gold leaf.

'In Lapland, they just heal themselves, quite simply, with berries and moss and reindeer tongue.'

I'm sure they do, my dear mother. But what I couldn't bear was the frightened, pleading look on your face as you ordered yet another dish of sweetbreads or quails' eggs or whatever it was that offered a day's hope. I turned away. I always turned away. I literally could not swallow it.

'Please, my darling, just one spoonful for me.'

She has been frightened like that, and pleading, since I came back from the war. Pleading with me not to know the things I know. Frightened that they will burst out of me in a rage that nothing will be able to extinguish.

Maybe that's what everyone over the age of forty really feels. They want to silence us. To stop our mouths with food.

So I fasted. I can't tell you what a relief it was. Everything else dropped away. We began the season of fasting with enemas. It doesn't sound too pleasant, does it? But soon we were empty. Transparent. It didn't disgust me at all. Would you ever imagine that an enema could have the eloquence of a ritual?

We did eat during the fast. I can't remember the exact progression. One day there was vegetable juice, I know that. I was so purified, and I was strong. I could have walked out into the fields and worked.

You might ask, What on earth was going on? I did at first. It made me laugh to think of us fasting. There we were, already skeletons, gargoyles.

Why add to it? But after a while – a few days, maybe more – I began to see the point of it. I felt stronger. I was doing to myself what even my sickness could not do, and by my own choice. Not only was I still alive, I was more alive than I had been for months. Years.

G didn't say anything. Didn't even smile or look a little satisfied. In fact the next day someone said to me in passing, 'You're to come off the fast today.'

And I was sick with disappointment, if you can believe it. Because I'd been so close to where I wanted to be, so empty, so pure, having so little and needing so little. And it wouldn't have taken much longer for me to understand so many things. Maybe only another two days of fasting would have brought me to it.

I kept awake all night long during the fast. I didn't need sleep any more, you see. I'd realized how unnecessary they were, all these things of the body that we cling to and can't imagine living without. I listened to the cows pulling the hay from the manger and then tearing it, and chewing it slowly, for hour after hour, sometimes shifting from one foot to another. I could hear every hesitation in the rhythm of their feeding. I understood that the hesitations don't break the rhythm: no, it is the hesitations that make the rhythm.

I was so close then. If I'd reached out just a little further I would have touched what I wanted to touch.

The Englishwoman is asleep. She's not really an Englishwoman, in fact.

No, it turns out that she comes from the other side of the world. Her nose has the sharp, nipped-in look that means she's going to die soon. I understand that look very well. I'm not sure yet whether she knows its significance. But very likely she does.

She works hard. She likes to be outdoors. All the English here prefer to work outdoors. She speaks French, but we don't talk much, even when we're lying side by side. Sometimes I know that she's lying awake. You can always tell. But I don't say anything. I expect she prefers listening to the cows, as I do.

I've talked about fasting, but I haven't really explained about working.

Sometimes I shook and sweat sprang out all over my skin and I couldn't see anything but blackness. But that's not important. When I did my work I was strong.

'Be careful. Rest. Don't try to do too much.' Ever since I've had this filthy disease, that is what they've been telling me. Go south in the winter, go up into the mountains, take your temperature night and morning, swallow this medicine and that medicine, pay over fat coins to fat doctors (my mother paid so many coins, I can't begin to count what she paid), take a raw egg beaten up in milk night and morning, weigh yourself before eating or weigh yourself after eating.

Your life is so precious suddenly. Isn't it comical? After those years of trying to kill us, now they want us alive.

Avoid stimulation and over-excitement. An absolutely regular life, fresh air, plenty of sleep. And of course give up any thought, my dear boy, of ever marrying.

Here at the Institute, I do too much. I work until I drop. Sometimes I really have dropped, out there in the fields, in the hot August sun. And I can tell you that when you drop it isn't the end of everything. There you are, flat on your face among the stalks and roots. Slowly the blackness parts and the ringing in your head stops. You notice some little insects scrabbling at the base of the stalks. There's a noise of crickets. You've dropped, but everything's still going on and your body fits against the earth as if it's been made to lie there.

After a long time I got up and found my hoe where it had fallen. I picked it up, and drove it into the earth again. The sun was hot on my back.

I'd worked until I'd fallen, and then I'd got up and now I would work again. I imagined G watching me. Of course he knew nothing about it, but that was what I liked to imagine. That he was watching, and perhaps approving. That he might find something harmonious in my fall.

One of the cows isn't happy. Her udder is too full. If I knew how to milk, I'd clamber down the ladder from this hayloft, and sit on a stool at her side, and ease her pain. It looks so easy when you see somebody else milking a cow. You almost imagine that you know how to do it yourself.

The Englishwoman stirs, and turns towards me. Her face is still asleep.

I shouldn't call her the Englishwoman. I know her name perfectly well.

'You're jealous, that's what it is.'

How well I can hear my mother saying that. 'You're just jealous. Jealousy is an ugly emotion. It even makes you look ugly. Go on, go and look in the mirror and see if I'm right or not.'

It's true that I was a jealous child. Always wanting too much of something and spitting with rage when I didn't get it. I would lie on the ground and beat the floor with my strong boots, because my sister was praised more than I was.

I'm jealous because the Englishwoman is going to die before me. She's farther on the road, she has fasted more resolutely and worked herself into the ground more obediently. She's got rid of everything, you can tell that.

Even her husband. She has a husband, but she's rubbed him off like the husk on an ear of corn.

G likes her. She's one of his favourites, anyone can see it, even if she seems quite unimpressed by it.

She hasn't really noticed me. Why should she? We're just lying side by side, listening to the cows, and she's asleep. So worn out and so weary and so close to death that anyone but me would feel pity for her. I don't feel any pity. She is closer to it than I am, almost within touching distance.

She has stopped clinging to life, although perhaps she doesn't yet know it.

How I envy her, because in spite of everything I've said, I am still clinging like a sick monkey who doesn't know how to let go.

When my temperature goes up I can scarcely breathe for panic. I calm myself with the thought that it's natural to run a little fever after dark.

I keep imagining that I'm putting on weight. Sometimes I'm even weak enough to say to someone else, 'Don't you think these trousers are getting a little tight for me?' and then they have to hide their look of pity and astonishment as they murmur, 'No, no, the trousers are fine, they're a perfect fit.' The trousers are hanging off me, of course.

G told me once that it was purely a fault of the organism, that it couldn't recognize its own death. He looked at me, not with pity, but as if waiting for me to learn a difficult lesson that I kept failing over and over again.

Her lips are slightly open. She's been asleep for a long time now. The cow moans again. Soon someone will come in and milk her. I hope to God they will. I would rather shoot the cow than listen to her moaning all night long.

I had a haemorrhage two weeks ago. It wasn't very big. The thing is that you mustn't be frightened and start to think that you won't be able to breathe. You can breathe right through it. I stared at the patch of blood on my pillow for a long time, as if I was looking at a cow.

Please don't believe that I'm feeling sorry for myself. That's the last impression I would want to give. Very often I stop feeling jealous entirely. It empties out of me, quite late in the evening, when it's dark and a chill rises from the earth and I realize that the tomatoes have all been picked a long time ago and it's not summer any more, or even autumn. You know that feeling when you're playing a game of hide-and-seek out of doors, and it's growing dark, thick grainy dark gathering all around you, and one minute the yard is full of children and the next they've melted away. But you are still in hiding, waiting to be found. It sounds forlorn, but it's exciting too.

Only you, out of everybody that was playing, still out in the dark. The dark thickens, thickens. You don't know if you want to hear a voice raised up, calling your name, or if you want to stay out in the dark for ever.

The Englishwoman's eyes are open. She's breathing very gently, in through her mouth, out through her nose. The line of her nose is sharp. Yes, she has a line all around her now, defined and dazzling.

I want to say to her that it will soon be over. All the horror of it.

The rotting stink of your own breath. The labour of walking. Creeping from the chair to the door, resting, gathering strength to turn the door handle.

The ugliness of it all. Perhaps I don't need to tell her. Perhaps she knows. She looks quizzical, but she says nothing. Is the husband coming soon? He'd better. But however soon he comes he will never get this moment we've got. The cows below us, big and square and warm-breathing. The scent of the packed hay. If I were not myself, I would be jealous of myself. The thought is so ridiculous that I smile, and immediately the same smile lights her face, as if we're two children sharing a pillow.

'It's raining,' she says.

'I know.'

I've been hearing the rain for hours. Not listening to it exactly. The rain isn't music and it doesn't require any attention from me.

'It's pouring,' she says, as if the thought pleases her.

'Yes. Good for the soil.'

'Yes.'

If it were not for the rain, and the mud, and what it did to us, I would not have this disease. I am convinced of it. I was so glad to be alive, to have outwitted everything that tried to kill me. We drank, and drank, and drank. I can't tell you how we drank. Until we were barking at each other like dogs. The war was over, and we were not.

'*C'est foutue, la guerre!*'

'*Et moi, je m'en fous de la guerre!*'

Yes, the rain and the mud. You never forget the smell of it. Rank, raw, clayey, clinging. It sucks on your boots like a lover. Fall in it and you're finished. That's what I used to tell myself when I was slithering along the duckboards. Fall in it and you're finished.

But I've forgotten all that. I never think of it. It's not good to think of it, if you want to get the better of this filthy disease that seizes on every weak point. You know the way a butcher cleaves a rib of beef into chops? He finds the weak point first. A gentle chip of a cut, and then up with the chopper and whack!

So I never think of any of it. Only the noise of the rain reminds me sometimes.

'I wish I could feel it falling on me,' she says.

I don't say anything. A black bubble of bitterness has lodged in my throat.

I want to cry out. I want to say to her, 'You'll feel it soon enough, don't worry. You'll be out in the rain for ever.'

But I don't. I look sideways down the row of beds, all empty now but for hers and mine. They've left us here together, in the hayloft. No doubt there are exercises in progress in the room with the parquet floor. The Dervish Dance, the Big Prayer, the Enneagram. Everybody will be gathered. G will sit there with his expression of wise calm. I can picture it so clearly that my absence doesn't matter at all.

Yes, it's raining heavily. The shadows are big. We have only one small lantern to light us up here. You have to be very careful in a hayloft, in case of fire.

'I wish I could feel the rain,' she says again.

I can't think of any answer now. The black bubble shrinks, shrinks and finally dissolves. I can breathe a little more easily.

She's lying on her side. Her nose is sharper than ever in her sunken face. Her eyes are fixed on me. I can't even distinguish her pupils in the darkness, but I know that look.

I have become someone else. I've seen it happen many times when a man is dying, and now it's happening with this woman. I don't speak. I don't want to break the spell of being the person she thinks I am.

I reach out. Her hand is as cold as I thought it would be. But it's not time yet, not quite, not for either of us. In a minute her vision will clear and she'll see me for what I am. Someone she doesn't know, who has about as much meaning as a signpost in a language you can't read, on a journey that seems as if it will never come to an end. And your feet have got to labour on, until the mud reaches your lips.

Nothing can change what's got to happen. But all the same, I fold her hand in mine.

Fiona Ritchie Walker

Inviolata

Near the end
she said she could feel
her bones go,
pictured
iridescent shells
in pieces,
the fragmented skeleton
of a wren.

This, she said,
was necessary,
so the morning breeze
could carry her
through the open window,
over trees and traffic,
to where bodies don't matter
anymore.

Moses Isegawa

Major Azizima in Hot Soup

(novel extract)

Major Azizima and the boys arrived at the cabbage tree at around nine o'clock in the evening, but there was nobody waiting with instructions from Brigadier Balo, their boss. Sergeant Kabalega examined every inch of the trunk but, counter to expectation, found no message in its bark. This troubled Major Azizima deeply because, for the second time running, Brigadier Balo seemed to have disregarded an appointment. It alarmed him, for if his boss went down he would go down with him. And at this moment all he thought about was his promotion. Fear gripped him that maybe Brigadier Balo wanted to drop him.

He imagined Brigadier Balo standing in front of him, the pet python coiled around his neck. He addressed him. 'Have I displeased you in any way, sir? Have I unknowingly broken an important law? I followed all the instructions you gave me and always waited for your orders. Has somebody turned you against me, Brigadier? I am your most loyal servant. I am nothing without your love and protection.' Brigadier Balo kept quiet after listening to his words. In fact, it seemed as if he was offended, then he opened his arms and invited him for a fraternal embrace. He heard him explain that it was all one big misunderstanding. Major Azizima felt tears of joy flowing down his face.

'It is so much unlike the boss,' Lieutenant Wandera was saying. 'He has kept his word for the last seven years. How can he break it now?'

'Let us go and find a good place to spend the night. We will be back here at dawn,' Major Azizima said.

They travelled several kilometres in the direction of the

depopulated areas and spent the night in a large hole shielded by the roots of a massive tree.

Dawn found them back at the cabbage tree, but there was no sign of either Brigadier Balo's messengers or fresh codes on the trunk. Major Azizima ordered Lieutenant Wandera to call like a jackal in case the messengers were still on the way, but there was no response.

'They will be here soon,' he told his boys, sure that by letting out the words he was increasing the chance that they would become reality. 'It can't be any other way.'

They took no chances. They waited a distance away from the tree, now atop a tree, now in the high grass, to avoid giving anybody a sitting target. To dilute the tension which hung in the air like fog, they told each other stories.

Lieutenant Wandera told them about the immensity of the Second World War, the millions slaughtered, many of them children in combat, and the contribution East Africa and Uganda had made.

'Who told you all that?' Major Azizima asked.

'My grandfather fought in that war. It was the most important thing he ever did. He talked about it all the time. In fact, he talked about nothing else.'

'But why would white people want Ugandans to go and fight for them? Didn't they have the strongest army in the world?' Sergeant Kabalega asked.

'Look here,' Lieutenant Wandera said testily. 'It was called a world war because nobody could fight it alone. Understood? It was so big that the whole world was involved in it.'

'Did the Ugandans win?'

'What do you mean? It was not their war. How could they have won it?' Lieutenant Wandera asked irately.

Sergeant Kabalega, who came from a cattle-herding family, told them about cows, the best way to handle them, to milk them, to make them productive and to spot sick ones.

Major Azizima asked them to explain why one of the Holy Spirit Army rules said, 'Thou shalt have two testicles.'

'Maybe in some tribes every male has one testicle and the Holy Spirit Army found that distasteful and wanted to keep that particular group out of its ranks,' Lieutenant Wandera conjectured.

'Do you want to know the truth?' Major Azizima asked. 'Many Holy Spirit Army officials think that a man with one ball cannot procreate and is cursed. In order to avoid having such types in our army, they outlawed it.'

'Is it true that children can't live in a single ball? Why do men have two balls, anyway?' Sergeant Kabalega asked.

'I don't know,' Lieutenant Wandera replied. 'Why don't you cut off one of your balls and see what would happen?'

It went on like that all day, but Major Azizima's heart was not in those exchanges. He had weightier matters on his mind.

While the boys were thinking about other interesting things to say, Major Azizima worried that it was just a matter of time before the hippos, as government soldiers were called in the Holy Spirit Army, arrived and tried to punish them for killing two of their colleagues. Consequently he brought all laughter to an end and ordered Lieutenant Wandera to climb into an observation post and look carefully in all directions.

Major Azizima waited impatiently, stamping his feet, chewing on his lower lip, now and then looking up at the sky.

Lieutenant Wandera came back after a short while, only to report that apart from the trees and the birds he had seen nothing of interest.

Major Azizima followed the sun as it went down, the uncertainty in his chest pressing harder with each passing minute. They could not wait for messengers for another day. By and by, nocturnal creatures started asserting their authority. The noise became so overpowering that they seemed to be operating inside his skin.

'We've waited all day but nobody has shown up. We have one alternative now and that is to enter the base.'

'It is very dangerous at night,' Lieutenant Wandera said morosely. 'Why didn't we go earlier?'

'It is even more dangerous to stay here,' Major Azizima explained in an unsteady voice.

At night it was very hard to walk without making noise, and every twig they broke made them look over their shoulder, in case it was actually a gun being cocked. At every turn Major Azizima thought they were going to be shot by hippo snipers hiding in the trees. From the snipers his mind went to patiently laid ambushes, which he thought the hippos had spent the whole day perfecting. His mind kept telling him that the Regional Commander would not take the loss of his two soldiers lying down.

In the places where they expected their comrades to be on the lookout, they stopped and called like jackals. But nobody called back. Mystified that a base could be approached to within two kilometres without encountering guards, they trudged on.

For the first time in the past seven years, Major Azizima became afraid of the dark, no longer seeing it as an ally, or an integral part of him, but as a sanctuary for his enemies. His heart palpitated when he saw trees, which he believed to be people waiting to harm him.

When they came to within one kilometre of the base, they saw a big light flaming into the night. It looked as if somebody had made a fire and forgotten to put it out. Major Azizima shuddered to think what Brigadier Balo would do in the face of such a danger to their community. Fire was one of the holiest things at the base; it was handled with the utmost care.

They approached the fire very cautiously. It was obviously a trap, which they wanted to spring without being caught. 'Thou shalt not approach a fire in the night' was one of the rules a recruit got on the first day. If, for whatever reason, they broke it and were caught by Brigadier Balo, or any other officer for that matter, they would suffer dire consequences.

'I think I see girls with Uzi machine guns, Major,' Lieutenant Wandera said to his boss, who was behind him.

'Yes, you are right,' Major Azizima said with a sinking heart.

'The Eyes, Major,' Lieutenant Wandera said, a note of awe in his voice. 'It must be the Eyes of the Generalissimo. They are here already!'

'But why did they remove the guards? Why has the base been left so vulnerable?' Major Azizima wondered aloud.

'At this moment, nobody can tell,' Lieutenant Wandera replied, his heart racing. 'What options do we have, Major?'

'To declare ourselves. To retreat. Or to wait till morning comes.'

'I think we should declare ourselves before they find us. The hippos or those girls,' Sergeant Kabalega spoke for the first time.

'I would rather hand myself over to the girls than fall into the hands of the hippos,' Lieutenant Wandera said. 'We don't have anything to hide from our "Sudanese" colleagues.'

'Let us declare ourselves then,' Major Azizima said gravely, his heart heavy. 'Lieutenant, start crying like a jackal. If it is the Eyes, they will respond.'

Lieutenant Wandera started his jackal calls, which were answered by leopard calls. Lieutenant Wandera called back like a civet cat, the code-name of the group. The roar of a lioness that ended the exchange was an order to come out of the dark.

Major Azizima, hands in the air, led his group to the makeshift quarter guard.

The girls were smaller than he had thought. Could it be that the Sudanese government no longer gave food aid to the Generalissimo? Or had it become impossible to raid southern Sudanese villages and take food back to the Base of Bases? Major Azizima wondered as a tiny girl searched him. Finally it occurred to him that the smallness of the girls was due to the 1,000-kilometre journey they had made on foot to come here. He watched as the girl took away all his weapons, handling them with such supreme irreverence it made him want to scream.

'Strip,' the girl ordered in a shrill voice that made him think of a cicada.

A wave of incredible shyness attacked and immobilized his limbs; he had never stripped in front of a girl before, let alone a group of girls. Riding on top of the shyness was a feeling of great outrage. He felt like raising his hand and slapping this wisp of a girl so hard she would faint. Yet something in him warned him to stay his hand.

As he took off his clothes, he tried to tell the girls who he was and what he had done for the Holy Spirit Army. But they were not in the least interested. He found it hard to believe that they had never heard of the great Major Azizima.

He noticed that they were wearing new uniforms and new boots. His uniform, after many days and nights of service without a wash, looked terribly dirty. And to add insult to injury, he saw one of the girls hold her tiny button of a nose and spit at it.

'I don't know how these bushie fighters live!' he heard her exclaim and shake her head, as if she lived in a palace.

When it came to removing his underwear, Major Azizima hesitated, hoping to draw the line there. He looked down at the girl who had given the order, hoping to hear that it was no longer necessary. But she pointed and indicated rather impatiently that everything had to come off.

'I am a major in the Holy Spirit Army,' he said, using up much of the courage left in him. 'I deserve to be treated with proper respect.'

But before the words were out of his mouth, the girl who had spat at his clothes came up to him and slapped him hard across the face. The shock and the impact made his legs buckle. He could not believe that such a thin arm could generate such force, for it felt like being clobbered with a steel claw. Amid an ignominious disintegration of will, he knelt down, an explosion of colours dancing in front of his eyes. Steel Claw slapped him again, harder than before, and he made a valiant effort to absorb the pain without crying out.

In the end, he fell on his side and saw the fire and the girls spinning round and round. He heard himself calling his mother for help. But before any maternal help could come, Steel Claw started kicking him again and again. Humiliation burned in his bones, worse than the pain.

After approximately a dozen well-placed kicks that seemed to make a hole in his stomach, she stopped, took his hand gently and helped him up. Major Azizima, tears mixed with blood and snot flowing down his face, managed to get on his knees. He felt dizzy and his stomach seemed to be rushing to his throat with each breath. He shook his head several times, blinked repeatedly and took several breaths. Gradually his stomach calmed down. He steadied himself with one hand and stood up, his underwear still in the other.

Steel Claw, who had now taken over from the Cicada, ordered him to remove his rosary, something he believed would expose him to all kinds of malevolent forces. He was convinced that she was mad, in which case he needed Mother Mary's protection more than ever. In spite of the pain in his head and stomach, he tried to explain to her why he could not surrender the rosary.

Steel Claw slapped him again and he fell on the ground, one

hand clutching the rosary, one thrust between his legs. This time, though, she did not kick him. She ordered him to stand up, and he rose slowly, unsure what she was going to do next.

'When your superior gives you an order, you must obey without question,' she said in her disquietingly mature woman's voice. 'You are not in one of those disgusting militias where members smoke drugs, drink alcohol, rape women and shoot whenever their fingers feel itchy. This is the Holy Spirit Army led by Generalissimo L, God preserve him.'

'Yes, Colonel,' Major Azizima stammered, a violent spasm cutting through his body.

'I am not a colonel. I am a corporal. In our group there are no inflated titles like major or colonel. Our sergeant is better than your colonel.'

'Yes, Corporal,' Major Azizima heard himself say.

This kind of discrimination was new to him. Hitherto, he believed that all soldiers were equal before the Holy Spirit and the Generalissimo. It was the basis of his love for the army, knowing well that he was a brother to everybody in uniform, man or woman. Holding this great love above everyone's head was the Generalissimo, who cared about each and every one of his sons and daughters in the Holy Spirit. Without this great love permeating each and every division of the army, whether in Uganda or in Sudan, he felt there was little left other than the fight for power, for influence and for riches. Without it, he believed, the Holy Spirit Army would be just like the hippo army, a bunch of people without honour.

Steel Claw took his rosary, looked at it once and handed it back.

'You are lucky it is a rosary, not one of those stinking fetishes fools like you tend to wear. I would have made you eat it,' she said insouciantly.

He murmured words of thanks and put the rosary round his neck.

'Kneel down and tell us your story,' Steel Claw commanded, her voice inflected in such a way that he thought he heard his dead mother's voice in it.

'Yes, Corporal,' he agreed in a small voice, burdened with fear that his mother might have turned into this tiny girl to torment him for being a member of the group that killed her.

Major Azizima felt very intimidated by the prospect of talking about himself in front of this type of audience. In a bid to buy some time and steady his nerves, he carried out a cursory survey of his face. He felt his left cheek, which had ballooned, and his nose, which was broken. When he probed one of his teeth with his thumb, it fell out. He felt grateful that he had not bitten his tongue. He spat a mouthful of blood and bile in the grass and felt slightly better. When he wiped the snot running down his face with the back of his hand, the girls made sharp noises of disapproval.

'These bushies!' one hissed. 'It will take incredible effort to take the bush out of them.'

With each negative comment they made, Major Azizima's sense of belonging to the Holy Spirit family waned. There was only one unbreakable rock left on which all his faith rested: Brigadier Balo. He knew that as soon as the Brigadier appeared on the scene, golden python gleaming around his neck, everything would be all right, and one or two of these girls might get punished. He tried to imagine the kind of glee he would feel to see the worst of them brought low. He imagined the Brigadier ordering him to cane them himself. He could already feel the muscles in his arm dance with pleasure as they brought down the whip. With each lash he would say, 'We are not bushies, you fools. We are your equals, if not better. Take back your words. Now.'

It cost Major Azizima a number of attempts to get his voice in shape to tell his story. But, by and by, his voice held firm and he told them about recent attacks on civilians and the two soldiers they had killed a day ago in an attempt to extract information from them.

The girls made sneering voices, which he took to mean that they thought he was telling lies. This infuriated him greatly.

'Major,' he heard Steel Claw address him, unadulterated mockery in her voice. 'Your holiday in these bushes is over. You are going to join the Generalissimo's main force in Sudan. You are going to be retrained. And then you are going to do some real fighting. You are going to face the Sudan People's Liberation Army. And then you will see the true face of combat.'

Major Azizima shook his head a few times to make sure he was hearing right. It occurred to him that if he went to Sudan without

Brigadier Balo's support and protection, things would go badly. He would be just cannon fodder forced to rush headlong into battle against the SPLA. All of a sudden the face of the future looked grotesque, like the scars of a leper. He felt trapped. Behind him was the frothing wrath of the hippos, in front of him the unspeakable might of the Sudan People's Liberation Army.

'Tell us about Brigadier Balo,' Steel Claw demanded.

'He is the greatest commander and tactician I know. He has been my boss for the last seven years and whatever plan he makes works.'

'Stop boring us and I think you should know this. Your beloved greatest commander and tactician is dead. We killed him yesterday,' she said proudly, looking into Major Azizima's eyes, which had become large as saucers.

A huge spasm, like a powerful electric shock, went through Major Azizima's body. He felt faint, as if he was about to disintegrate into his composite parts. It occurred to him that at the time they were waiting for emissaries the Brigadier was already dead. Major Azizima's whole body sprouted with goose pimples as big as peas, and his teeth chattered so much that he had to hold his jaw to avoid biting his tongue. Many things made sense now: the messengers who never turned up; the codes on the tree trunk which were not there; and the lack of security at key approaches to the base.

'Don't you have anything to say about what you have heard?' Steel Claw asked.

'Nothing, Corporal,' he said.

'Good. We are going to investigate you. If you were part of the plot to steal the Generalissimo's gold, you will be hanged before the sun goes down.'

'I don't know anything, Corporal,' Major Azizima pleaded in a small voice. 'I was never part of that group. I was always in the field fighting and promoting the interests of the Holy Spirit Army.'

Steel Claw raised her index finger to indicate a need for silence and he kept quiet. She ordered the boys to take off their clothes. They obeyed without question and stood before her, their penises shrunken to little knots, their eyes downcast. She ordered them to kneel along the path leading to the base. They complied with utter docility and fell prey to the chill, the mosquitoes and other sting-ing insects of the night.

At dawn Major Azizima and the boys were ordered to put on their clothes and march to the base. They walked in single file, legs buckling, teeth chattering, heads heavy with unshed sleep. The journey, so familiar, so short, now seemed unbearably long. The dew falling down the leaves overhead made them shudder, as if touched by the tongue of a snake.

They were detained at the gate for a very long time, as if the person in charge had forgotten all about them. The gate was opened when the sun had already appeared and the play of light on the leaves and on the huge trunks of the trees provided a splen-did sight.

They were marched into the main square, in the middle of which stood a big cross supporting the body of Brigadier Balo, his innards hanging out, blue and green flies protesting loudly at the interruption to their meal.

Major Azizima's stomach turned so violently that his mouth filled with vomit. Afraid that he would be slapped if he spat near the dead, he swallowed, his eyes watering. He did not believe that his boss had tried to cheat the Generalissimo. Nobody dared. Not with so many spies everywhere. He believed that Brigadier Balo was killed in order to close the base with no resistance from any corner. And with the Brigadier dead, his men would be frightened and easy to lead on the 1,000-kilometre journey to Sudan.

Major Azizima and his boys were ordered to stand in front of the cross. Other soldiers joined them, till they were about fifty. They were commanded to chant, 'Holy Spirit, have mercy on us, even if we are only unworthy dogs. Forgive us, Generalissimo L, for we have badly abused your magnanimity.'

Major Azizima spent the next twenty hours in front of the cross. He kept calling Brigadier Balo's name over and over again, asking his forgiveness and asking him to stretch his protective hand over him. 'Let me avenge you if revenge is what you need to rest in peace in the next world,' he said again and again.

The worst moment was when birds came. They pecked out the eyes and, using razor-sharp bills, tore gouts of flesh from Brigadier Balo's body. Out of the corner of his eyes, he saw a number of birds tugging at strands of intestine. They twisted in the air, much to the chagrin of the dislocated flies, which roared like football fanatics. Major Azizima tried to look away, but his eye went back to his fallen hero. With each strike of the beak, his anger lit up; with each morsel of flesh that was taken, the hatred in him multiplied. 'I will avenge you, avenge you and avenge you,' he kept saying to the Brigadier, who could no longer give the illusion that he saw him because his eyes were gone; who could no longer give the impression that he could talk to him because the birds had pulled out his huge tongue and fought an epic battle over it; and who looked like a man whose work was done.

Saradha Soobrayen

I Will Unlove You

I will unlove you and become hollow,
undo every feeling from its hold.

I will restrict blood flow and circulate the cold,
deflate my heart and become shallow.

I will numb my tongue and choose not to swallow,
tie up my larynx, let love go untold.

I will scrub sensation from every fold
and squeeze the tenderness from my marrow.

But will I still be your *Saradha* tomorrow?
What becomes of us when love lets go?

Anita Desai

The Landing

The moving company's truck, emptied of its load, now turned around in the driveway, using the single immense hemlock tree as the pole on which to turn, and went lumbering down the dirt road on to the highway below, and slowly withdrew.

Then the silence began to ring in her ears. Louder and louder till it practically shrieked.

So she thought it best to turn too, and go into the house to see what distraction it could provide from that insistent ring.

It was, after all, very new to her even though it was very old: 1743 was the date carved into the beam over the entrance. But she had entered it newly and now had to learn every plank and brick and beam in it, one by one till all became familiar and she could move about without hesitation.

She paced the length of it and then the breadth, going from room to room. In one the floor sloped, in others the boards creaked, and the height of the ceiling changed from high to low. Some were well lit, others shadowy. They all belonged to her now, and she had to show them she was mistress. She said to herself, 'Hmm, I will put my desk here' and 'I will need some shelves there' but there was something hollow, not quite convinced about these intentions. That was because she was growing increasingly aware that there was an opposition to these intentions that was also growing, and that she was not in command of the house so much as it was of her. By entering it, she had subjected herself to it.

When she recognized that, she shook a little, a small shiver running down her neck and through her shoulders.

She had bought the house and established herself in it – but now it was projecting a powerful suggestion that it was not so amenable to her purchase as she had imagined. She had not asked for its consent, after all, and it struck her that the house was withholding it.

Of course this was absurd. How could the house, an inanimate object, possibly contain feelings or make them apparent?

Reason would not support such an intuition, however strong.

The house *was* inanimate, surely; a thing of stone, brick, board and beam. Mortar and lath. Sheetrock and slate.

But there was also the air entering it through the windows. She had gone around opening them while the men from the moving company unloaded their boxes and brought them in.

And it was these windows that let the air in – let it in, let it out, in, then out. It was not the house breathing, she told herself. That was an illusion, she said, and continued to prowl through the house she now owned.

Having learnt the dimensions of one floor, she grasped the banisters and went up the stairs. They were wide and hollowed out at the centre, as one might expect: through the years, many had climbed them and climbed down. Generations. The banisters provided safety and reassurance: these stairs could take more.

It was the landing that invited pause. It was somehow, inexplicably, more than simply a place to stop and catch one's breath before proceeding. Evidently bare and empty, yet strongly suggestive of more. She stopped to study the whitewashed walls and wondered if there weren't traces of openings that no longer existed and were covered over with plaster. Some heavy timber beams entered those walls, then vanished. They suggested that once they had led to, and supported, another space, perhaps a room that had once led off the landing.

If so, it no longer existed – all was bricked up, plastered over and painted.

What was it concealing?

She was certain that the landing, comfortably large as it was, was reduced from a formerly large space. She could not have said why but had the clear impression of another, yet undetected chamber that had for some reason been closed off. Why?

Baffled, she continued up the stairs to the upper floor. This too she carefully paced, measuring it with her stride. Here the ceiling was lower, the windows smaller, as were the rooms. All in all, they gave an impression of greater intimacy and friendliness than the rooms downstairs. What linked them to those places was of course the staircase – and the landing.

When she thought of how the landing separated and demarcated them, the image that came to her was of a landing stage on a river, or lake, where such a structure marked a point of transition between earth and water, one element and what was distinctly another.

Then there was the other landing, the long strip of tarmac trembling in an excess of light and heat, on which planes landed and from which they took off; she thought of such a strip in the middle of a forest, or plantation, or grassland – a kind of scar or scab marking the point of departure and arrival.

This had never before been suggested to her by a house.

Perplexed, she went back downstairs – and found all the windows shut. She had not heard them bang in the wind, and they were securely fastened.

Perhaps she had not opened them, after all, only thought she did. Surely that was the explanation. It was not a good idea, she knew, to start imagining ghosts in the house, or intruders.

Still, she went upstairs to check and found the windows that she was sure she had not touched, now all open. Breathing the air in, breathing it out. Perhaps they had been open all along.

It was both irritating and intimidating to find that her memory had begun to play tricks on her. Entering the old house – 1743, was it not carved in the beam over the door? – she herself had suddenly aged, with a failing memory, she told herself, and shook her head at the absurdity of it all.

But perhaps it was just being entirely alone, in that ringing silence, that made her imagine things. Hallucinate. She would have to take care.

As she might have foreseen, it was all even harder at night. Once darkness fell, she could not look around and reassure herself of what was there and what was not. She could have switched on lights and done so of course, for in place of the lanterns that must once have hung from the hooks in the ceiling there were now electric lights. But she never turned on more than one light at a time, and if she went from one room to the next, she turned off one light as soon as she turned on another. To have all the lights on at once and have every room blazing would have been a sign, a blatant show of panic. To light just one at a time was like taking a candle from room to room. As she might have, would have, done in 1743.

In that way she lit the way up the stairs to bed. On the landing she paused again, to see if the beams still gave that effect of going through the walls to another space, and if a bricked-up opening could still be deciphered under the pale layer of plaster and white-wash. But there was no light on the landing itself, only one at the bottom of the stairs and another at the top, and it was too dimly lit for her to see such traces. The walls and the stairs were mute, giving away nothing.

She had a bed upstairs – she had bought a few pieces of furniture along with the house: this four-poster bed and a chest of drawers upstairs, a kitchen table downstairs, all too large and heavy, obviously, for the previous owners to have removed and taken with them. Now she made up the bed for the night, and changed into a nightgown she had brought up in a valise. She put out the light and climbed into bed, actually glad for the darkness so that she could not make out any details – whether the closet doors were open or shut, the ceiling low or high – and perhaps they would no longer trouble her but allow the erasure of sleep.

She fell deeply into oblivion as if falling into a pit that had opened suddenly under her: she was tired. But soon, suddenly, awoke. In that pitch darkness she had a strong, throbbing sense – like a pulse beating in her temple – that someone was standing at the foot of her bed, watching her. She could distinctly hear it breathing, heavily and unevenly. It made no motion at all and she herself felt paralysed, incapable of any. It took a sudden lightning flash of will – Off! On! – to leap up and switch on a light.

The space revealed around her bed was empty of course. There was no one there. What she had taken for somebody was one post of the four-poster bed, at the foot. That was what had stood there, watching her. And it was her own breath, struggling to heave itself out of her sleep, that she had heard and taken for another's.

So she sat back on the edge of the bed, weak with foolishness. Then lay back and waited for day.

When it appeared, almost imperceptibly, as a silent dissolving of darkness, she went barefoot down the stairs to the landing. Here the presence – or intimation – of what had existed before and no longer did had become strongest. It no longer was but had left a grey and insubstantial after-image.

It could not be verified because there was no evidence of a door or window that might once have opened on to an additional space. Yet here, at what was arguably the heart, or centre, of the house, was the most powerful sense of what had once been the heart and centre and still marked a transition that had been made – from earth to water, land to space, night to day, life to death. That was what left behind an after-image, as a boat leaves a wake in water, a plane a trail of vapour in the sky.

She passed her hands over the surface of the walls to see if she could detect what her eyes could not: traces. Apart from her certainty that there was a chamber to which the presence that had watched her sleep had withdrawn, there was no other clue.

Perplexed and frustrated, she went back up the stairs with nothing but a sense of absence and bereavement.

When she went in to work, colleagues asked her, carelessly, as if not really interested in her replies, if she was 'settling in'. She kept her replies suitably brief and cryptic. Yes. She was. Settling in.

Once she went to the water cooler for a drink because she had had such an urge to shout, 'No! I'm not! Settling in!' and to ask some of them – some of the nicer ones in the department – to come and see for themselves. And an aged man who was something of a ghost of the department – he had been there for so long that he had almost been forgotten – came out of the hall to collect his hat and coat, looked at her briefly from under ashy eyebrows, and asked, 'Well, and how are you liking the house on the hill?' She wondered if he had ever lived there himself but she had never spoken to him before and could hardly start questioning him or inviting him to tea so that he could see for himself. That was what she might have done but he was already shuffling off down the hall, head sunk between his shoulders like an aged turtle. The house might have suited him, she thought as she collected her own coat from the stand; perhaps he would have been more attuned to its message and vibrations and been able to decipher them.

On returning to the house, she took a few moments to pace the grounds, looking at the walls, eaves and roof from outside, studying them to see if there were traces of an extension that might have existed. That could have provided an explanation of sorts of her suspicion that there had been one and that, like an amputated limb, it lived on, making itself apparent in her discomfort, her distress at its absence.

But all she saw was a tile coming loose, a ring of mossy green damp rising along the foundation and a spattering of bird droppings across a windowpane, but no clue that might give her direction for further search.

She turned to go in and suddenly a scattering of black rooks fell out of the hemlock tree with an astonishing volume of sound – flapping of wings, ruffling of feathers, indignant caws – and sat on the ground beneath the tree, trying to get back their balance, then stalked off across the drive into the shrubs, complaining of her intrusion.

She watched them till they were gone and only the rustling in the shrubs betrayed their passage. Gradually her own alarm subsided, and she went in and unpacked the groceries she had bought onto the kitchen table and made herself a meal, determined to keep herself occupied. It was the empty stretch of time and the empty space that night and darkness hollowed out of the visible world that let out the presence that came to watch her, audibly breathing, when she lay on the four-poster bed. She knew that, but it manifested what was otherwise invisible.

She was not afraid. Oh no. It was only that, while she had imagined the house she had bought and moved into to be vacant, it proved not to be so. There was this presence occupying it – and eluding her.

It became a nightly ritual to get up and pad on bare feet down the stairs to the landing, both to escape it and to confront it there. It was the landing, she knew, that the presence inhabited. Slipped through its walls as if they were porous, curtains rather than walls – in and out, in and out, like breath.

There was another chamber, she knew it, but when she touched the walls, they were just that – solid, not porous, cool and smooth to her touch like a blank face turning upon her, saying, 'Did you want something?'

Because she so much wanted that meeting, that confrontation, she began to try to entice it into the open – by setting a place for it at the table, by leaving a light on in a room she had left, or by placing a chair across from the one she occupied.

She did not talk to it, not yet. She held back that final communication. Not because it was too difficult, but because it would have been too easy. To talk to it would have been to acknowledge it out loud – and she would not do that; it would too closely resemble defeat.

But when the voices of the rooks startled her out of sleep at daybreak, she wondered if it was actually trying to talk to her in those harsh, jagged syllables. Perhaps it was making the attempt to break through that final barrier that she could not bring herself to make.

She started staying at work later and later, pretending she had paperwork to deal with after everyone else had gone. But the sense that it was waiting for her would grow steadily more powerful and more irresistible. Besides, she would be tired and want her tea and want to be home, by herself. Eventually she would give in, drive back and stride to the front door in a rush – to find it shut but unlocked, making her question herself: surely she had locked it on leaving? Or else find it double-locked when she was certain she had not done that – why should she? Always the door yielded reluctantly to her push as if the air, the emptiness behind it, were pushing back to keep her out.

This was too much – it was *her* house, after all. So she set down her bag and spoke to it, finally. 'I'm leaving.'

She did, at great expense and in great discomfort and, worst of all, a sense of acting foolishly. It made her angry to have bought and moved into that house and angry at now moving out. Her colleagues at work expressed surprise but also sympathy. The old man, who, she now felt, had something malevolent in his lidded eyes, twinkled darkly at her, 'Too lonely up there, eh?' and she very nearly snapped back, 'On the contrary, not lonely enough,' but caught herself in time.

The wretchedness of the transition was increased by the fact that the alternative accommodation she found was a set of small rooms above a row of shops in town. She chose it because there was simply no room here for any presence other than hers. She filled it completely with her furnishings and belongings. She could barely turn around among them. When the heat of summer drummed down on the low roof over her head and beat at the vinyl panel on the outside, it became suffocating.

Lying awake on the narrow couch – actually just a metal fold-up contraption – she thought of the big house on the hill, and the presence in it prowling from room to room, looking for her, waiting for her. If she returned, would it emerge from its secret chamber and ask her into it at last, in welcome?

She turned on to her side and closed her eyes, imagining that welcome. She felt neither triumphant nor relieved at having escaped its embrace; she only felt bereft at having abandoned all possibility of it.

Just under her window, on the street, a lamp glowed with ferocious zeal; some insects revolved around it in a rumbling drone while others hurled themselves at it with piercing detonations. If she drew her curtains to shut out the demon light, the room became so oppressive that she could not breathe.

She stood leaning out of the window, her palms pressed upon the sill, and waited for someone, some presence, to appear, even if only a cat prowling by night. But there was no one there at all. Till a car appeared, raucous with music and drunken voices. It slowed and someone flung a bottle that smashed against the wall just under her window. The shards burst outwards into the light, then showered down. There was laughter, a shouted expletive. That was the message, for her. It left her trembling.

Eventually she returned to the house, as she knew she would, her small car laboriously climbing the hill, seeming to remember the potholes and exposed rocks and roots, then arriving with a sudden, inexpert swerve. She tried hard to think of what she would say to the present owners if they saw her and came out to see what she wanted. Perhaps she could ask for some object she had left behind the house by the woodpile, or some garden tools propped up against the shed. Yes, she could do that.

What she had forgotten were the rooks, the way they yelled in alarm when she appeared under their hemlock tree, tumbled out of it as if they were going to launch themselves into the sky but fell to the ground instead and waddled away in their ungainly, lumbering way, darkly muttering.

Other than them there was no one around, although the new occupants' car was parked in the open garage.

She stood there uncertainly, letting her eyes rove, waiting to see if anyone would come out and talk to her. No one did. No one ever did. She had missed the meeting on the landing.

She returned to her car, turned it around the hemlock tree and slowly withdrew.

Henry Shukman

Backs of Houses

Behind Kingston Road ivy leaves shine with recent rain.
A concrete path between garden walls has mossed black.

Here in the peace no one owns the birds are at home
whistling their tunes, sprucing their wickerwork.

An unhinged gate leans its weight on weeds.
The windows of an empty house are solemn.

Untended place ripe with neglect, a stone's throw
from the grinding road, give us rest.

Jane McKie

Tin Quartet

Coffenoola

The open-work mine of an owl
is a Wesleyan killing – a shrew
shred to its backbone, an aerial view
of small black intestines laid out.
Owl-marks litter the land, claw-
grooves and mineral-rich pellets
displayed like an Old Testament
on the lectern of Penwith.

Crease an Pocket

That crease in the kerchief
folded in half; it is deep,
that pocket of land, it yields
bucket-loads of tin.

That crease in your pocket
folded in half; it is light,
that kerchief of cloth, mined
of its stitches, threadbare and thin.

Wheal Maria

Bless this bal-maiden's apron,
her white boat of a hat. She
tugs it low on her forehead
overwhelmed by heat and light.

She has worked with a miner's lust
powering her to uncover wonders.

Wheal and Howl

In the dark there are
candles, and a bird;
six wicks: each man
has his allowance.

A small sun, an 'o',
a howl. The bird chirps
into eternity. The sun
dwindles to a silent perch.

Henry Shukman

Four a.m. in Icy Mountains

This is the hour when the troubled man
hears the call of a train looping up a valley
and knows he must leave his home,
and also that he won't.

The desperate wife clutching
her robe at the neck
bathes herself in the light of a fridge,
having nowhere else to turn.

The poet looking out her window
at the dark world feels she must
resolve her loves once and for all,
but only writes another poem.

Ice-hard ruts whisper as you pass.
Dark bushes listen.
Already a big dog lifts its *woof* into the air.
Something smaller answers: *yap-yap*.

The stars will withdraw one by one,
and milk lighten the coffee.
Soon there won't be anything left
but ordinary day.

No one would guess not an hour ago
creation was laid bare
like the open back of a watch,
and an early waker walked right through it.

Boyd Tonkin

Shelf Doubt: The Intimate History of Bookshops

I'm browsing in a London bookshop on a bright afternoon in summer. This place feels like a refuge, but not a retreat. Scraps of chat drift in through the open doors. An elderly customer has a non-standard enquiry, and the young assistant has the time to give a non-routine answer. The store belongs in a small group – more a handful than a brand – known for arranging its stock, fiction and non-fiction alike, in distinct geographical regions. So the eye, and the mind, slides from France to India; from Latin America to Greece. Dante rubs spines with a guide to Tuscany. At the back, in the children's section, a woman reads to a gently rustling gaggle of under-fives. She tells them about Angry Arthur: a choleric kid, created by Hiawyn Oram and visualized by the Japanese illustrator Satoshi Kitamura, whose infant fury threatens his whole world. At this point Arthur is merely revving up his rage. 'Is he angry enough yet?' the reader asks. 'Naaa,' yells her audience, contentedly.

A satisfying bookshop, as always, can trigger a quiet riot of sensations. Adventure rubs covers with nostalgia; glimpses of a remembered past and an imagined future coalesce; security mixes with excitement, and self-discovery with self-forgetfulness. This could be somewhere to hide but, equally, somewhere to grow. The spun-out pleasures of drift and distraction may be consummated in a purchase; but maybe not. Just one impulse seems alien to this scene. In a city that grows more ill-tempered by the year, there's little here to anger Arthur.

But with that glow of quiet fulfilment comes, for me, another familar sense: of nagging unease, and even shame. After all, I'm shirking, not working. This spell of stationary globetrotting ranks as recreation, not research. If this is a guilty pleasure, it seems to be an inseparably complex one. The satisfaction and the shame arrive at once.

Few writers respect the intimate history of bookshops. Their presence, or absence; their plenitude, or poverty, feeds a stream of feeling that runs through the lives of people who read, and who write. They nourish and withold. They gratify and disappoint. They reward curiosity with serendipity. Responses to their opening and closures, their makeovers and takeovers, compile an index of emotions stretching from agony to zealotry.

Yet authors often feel compelled to foul the nests that nurture them. In novel after novel, from George Gissing to Vikram Seth, bookshops and their staff shrink into sketchy cartoon shapes. Alarmingly often, they feature as boringly unwholesome temples of dullness and delusion. Why should this be so?

Perhaps because, even after centuries of mass literacy, the constant reader – and the constant writer – stand accused of a vice. Any literature unredeemed by fame, utility and riches (in other words, almost all of it) will carry the taint of anti-social frivolity. Libraries redeem themselves with civic virtue and scholastic endeavour. Hushed like churches, they stand for something and they lead somewhere. But to the ever-busy Protestant spirit – or, for that matter, the ever-busy Confucian spirit – a bookshop can still look like a brazen monument to lost time and squandered cash.

One famous example of the writer ashamed of the place that gives his mind a home came out of this same parade of London shops. At the end of this road once stood a second-hand store called Booklover's Corner. There, over seventy years ago, a youngish George Orwell briefly worked. His 1936 essay 'Bookshop Memories' shows up its author as a bit of an Angry Arthur, sneering at the nuisances and nutcases who supposedly haunted the premises and asserting that the horde of 'not quite certifiable lunatics' who tramp the capital's streets 'tend to gravitate towards bookshops'.

Anyone who knows their Orwell can spot what's happening here. Already a veteran of the Burma police barracks and the Paris dosshouse, soon to leave for glory and danger in the Spanish Civil War, he finds in the shop a dusty epitome of the mad, stifling

England that he wanted both to conquer and to flee. To him the bookshop and its 'sweet smell of decaying paper' are redolent only of 'paranoiac customers and dead bluebottles'.

Orwell's biographer D. J. Taylor looked into the historical reality of Booklover's Corner. He found evidence of a lively location owned, staffed and used by progressive types. But the fretful author so keen to shake the dust of a dying country off his shoes can see only a toxic corner of the national asylum. To him, the British belfry feels full of old bats. You sense that 'the decayed person smelling of old breadcrusts' who plagued the ever-fastidious Orwell at his post must have been none other than Old Ma Britannia herself.

That corner site where Orwell served and seethed stands on a ragged square as grand Hampstead slides down into grittier Kentish Town. Later it became a café where ageing émigrés from the storms of mid-century Europe would gather for long and frequently silent games of chess. Now it has dwindled into a marginally upmarket burger bar. And just over the road, since the 1970s, has loomed the great white hulk of the Royal Free Hospital. Everyone grasps that hospitals operate as factories of feeling – humming production lines of dread and despair, of hope and renewal. Poems start here; novels finish here. Television soaps take up residence on wards and never leave. Pity and terror – and their humbler but sharper cousin, relief – flow day and night out of these power plants of catharsis. No writer would ever feel ashamed of a hospital scene, while even the most ambitious will find a way to make private trauma into public drama. Solzhenitsyn's *Cancer Ward* is Stalin's Russia in morbid microcosm.

So literature haunts hospital corridors like a chronic case. But it shuns or scorns the shops where it will thrive or perish. Ian McEwan's novel *Saturday*, with every detail of its neurosurgical operations so lovingly researched, is only one rich example of the tributes that writing often pays to healing. You have to read much wider and harder to discover the bookseller as hero. A recent French bestseller, *The Girl from the Chartreuse* by Pierre Péju, almost pulled off that feat. Étienne Vollard is a 'walking library', a hulk with a heart, who 'not only sells books but consumes them' in 'a never-tiring cycle of delight'. Yet the shambling giant from

Grenoble tempers his nobility with the standard flaws of introversion and eccentricity. His role in a terrible traffic accident leaves him commuting between bookshop and hospital ward, 'maintaining a strange liaison between two different universes'.

More typical are the rancid and rancorous bibliophiles who fill the pages of Iain Sinclair's fiction: noxious sociopaths driven doolally by the whiff of printer's ink. In London novels such as *Downriver* and *Radon Daughters*, Sinclair has built a baroque subgenre out of the book lover's disgust at the objects of his worship.

Now, writers spend a lot of time in bookshops, speaking, signing or (incognito) surreptitiously shifting their own titles from some high dark shelf down to the front table by the door. They always claim to love them, and make a dutiful noise of protest when pressure from dominant chain stores, supermarkets and the internet reduces the number and variety of outlets. But bookshops in books often sound like squalid, even shameful places, with Sinclair's fusty middens merely the extreme case: abodes of unhygienic pedantry at best, downright insanity at worst.

In Britain, at any rate, the palette that colours the imaginary bookshop seems to be mixed from many different shades of shame. And as a literary impetus, shame – with its outriders of desire and concealment – may have a lot to be said for it. In any utilitarian society, an aura of faint scandal will surround excessive private reading. Unless they're lucky enough to come from an artistic or academic family (sometimes even then), every brightly patterned adult 'book lover' will once have suffered as a grey-skinned adolescent 'bookworm'. In spite of the obligatory cult of Harry Potter, the level of reading for its own (rather than for school's) sake still tends to fall off a cliff at puberty – a more modest tumble for girls, but a sheer drop for many boys. Books are cool, purr the trend-seeking teachers, the visiting authors, the jolly retailers, the worthy agencies of state. They lie.

From the age of twelve or so, books are not cool. They mean games unplayed, gossip unshared, bands unheard, clothes unbought. Loving books counts among the most florid symptoms of the teenage 'social death' that Jonathan Frantzen recalls with a shudder in his Midwest memoir *The Discomfort Zone*. All the same, writers and readers, at a level below conscious conviction, can come to cherish the oddity that clings to them. And any kid whose passion for books persists through the hormonal blizzards of their teens will already know something about scorned and secret loves.

My formative bookshop memories mingle guilt with grace. In the beginning, as for most welfare-state children, there were no bookshops; there were only libraries. Plundered every week in the company of parents, to the limit of its rules for borrowing, this was the only true Eden of print. The highly waxed, chocolate-toned issues desk first stood above my head; then level; then below. Bathed in the scent of polish and approval, the library meant reading without sin. So to haunt a bookshop already felt like fall.

Even with a wholly encouraging home, I felt a twinge of trans-gression when I spent what little cash I had on grown-up books that played no part in formal education. And a deeply ordinary suburban stationer-cum-bookseller was still enough to launch the gravity-defying reader into orbit. From easily digested moderns like John Steinbeck and H. G. Wells I moved into more rarefied atmospheres: Kafka, Sartre, Camus, Huxley, Solzhenitsyn, Woolf – nothing uncommon for the time, but all fairly superfluous as far as exams and lessons went. Hardly surprising, perhaps, that I absorbed so much entry-level existentialism at that time: this undi-rected reading was the ultimate *acte gratuit*.

Soon the guilt, as guilt often does, gave way to tremendous excitement. These engineers of modern souls cabled the placid here-and-now to the front line of every twentieth-century battle over ideals and identities. They made a small world feel very big indeed. Fronted by some seductively strange painting by Dalí or Magritte or Die Chirico (chosen, I later learnt, by the great book designer Germano Facetti), the battleship grey of the Penguin Modern Classics' livery became the colour of desire itself.

Far more than libraries, bookshops can also allow the curious adolescent to find out at their leisure about literary sex. Now, lit-erary sex can sometimes have precious little to do with the kind encountered anywhere beyond the covers of books, especially for suburban adolescents. Here a different kind of shame kicked in: not of forbidden knowledge but of woeful under-achievement. It wasn't the knowing, or the finding out, that caused the injury. After all, my parents even owned a copy of the Penguin *Lady Chatterley* (given to all her friends, in a burst of post-trial euphoria, by an exuberant Australian divorcee). At school I had profited from the Platonic idea of an inspiring English teacher, who would chatter learnedly about every topic shunned by the Victorian hostess: sex, politics, science, religion and always back to sex again.

No: the bookshop shame came from a failure to measure up. Lawrence and Henry Miller, Anaïs Nin and William Burroughs: such paperbacked incendiaries showed the way into a world of erotic discourse that set mind-bogglingly high standards of exoticism and sophistication. Again it was the bookshop, by this time the cavernous and shambolic clutter of the unreformed Foyle's in Charing Cross Road, that promised a key into these dark corridors. Here was a Gothic castle, like some dust-caked wing of Mervyn Peake's *Gormenghast*, where desire and delirium could hide. Somewhere in this paper labyrinth lurked legendary bowers of bliss: *Tropic of Cancer*, perhaps, or even *Delta of Venus*. Its special brand of shame – for a late teenager in a liberal-minded epoch – came not from opening the creaking doors but from not yet being able to enter.

As a student, bookshops – or rather one in particular – delivered another hammer blow of humiliation. For a while, I literally lived above the shop. My hall of residence incorporated, at street level, a sleek academic superstore. After a while its post-Bauhaus glass-and-steel styling somehow fused with the technocratic rigour of the structuralist and deconstructionist schools of criticism then coming into vogue. Especially in the cool cubicles that housed literary theory, the staff terrified me more than any don. This was a shop that would sell out of studies of Saussure on the morning of publication. Every visit would prompt a small squall of panic. I hadn't read enough; I didn't know enough; the critical engines would go on grinding away to leave me helplessly stranded in their wake. With its synthetic carpets and fittings of tubular steel, this bookshop liked to punctuate the browser's time with tiny electric shocks – pinpricks to remind me of books still unread and ideas still unplumbed.

But, as with sex, so with scholarship. To feel left out, left

behind, found shamefully wanting, sharpened the pleasures of longing and hoping. Life is elsewhere, as the title of Kundera's
wonderful novel about the strandedness of youth affirms.
Bookshops at least showed you that 'elsewhere' meant somewhere,
rather than nowhere. They supplied the destination, but not the
itinerary. That you had to find all by yourself. So the shame of early
bookshop memories has another face. Not only has it to do with
sloth and sloppiness: with wasting time, and thought, and money.
It is the shame of the uncompleted consciousness, dreamily in
search of all the missing parts that may finish the jigsaw of the self.

So when writers mock the places where their own careers may
stand or fall, I can grasp their ambivalence. We live in a culture
that professes to admire good books, and their makers, but which
in reality deplores 'bookishness'. Save for the odd spontaneous
genius and the larger platoon of formula-driven hacks, one of literature's darker little secrets is that you don't, all that often, find
one without the other. 'People say life is the thing,' fluted the
Bloomsbury aesthete Logan Pearsall Smith, 'but I prefer reading.'
Not true, even in most writers' case; but the reading may help
shape the life with a force that upsets Romantic beliefs in the pri-
macy of 'real' experience.

Yet modern bookshops seem intent on liberating books from
the taint of bookishness. Especially since Tim Waterstone launched
his eponymous chain in Britain in 1982, this approach has made
them brighter and cheerier, saner and more welcoming. Surely,
only an oddball or outcast would object. In place of the sort of
mildewed oubliette that so disgusted Orwell, buyers and browsers
can enjoy the shadow-free serenity of a clean, well-lit place. Dark
wood (or at least a veneer to that effect) still lends grandeur and
gravitas to their shelves. They mimic, perhaps deliberately, the
stained-teak sobriety of the mid-century municipal library. Here, as
in so many other British institutions, the marketplace has con-
quered and stolen the virtues of the public sector. In fact, the
new-wave bookshop may almost function as a crèche. Strewn with
plastic trains and furry animals, children's corners emit a daylong
hubbub of chatter, giggles and screams.

Back amid the adult shelves, individual booksellers write hand-
written notes praising much-loved titles: little literary billets-doux

meant for everyone, but also just for you. The stacked tables of discounted paperbacks blaze with strident colours and famous names. Celebrity chefs, celebrity sportspeople, celebrity novelists and (these days) celebrity celebrities beam from the latest hardback covers, inviting buyers to share the splendours and miseries of their already illustrious lives. Many of them will have signed the books on display: small spoors of authentic contact that temper the mystique of 'personality'. Here Roth and Rooney can cohabit in the equal light of fame.

In the better-stocked branches, carefully crafted tables will lay out the mysteries of Surrealist fiction, or sociobiology, or Spanish history, in a multi-coloured patchwork. Horror and Erotica, like Computing and Cookery, may well enjoy their neatly labelled and well-ordered niches. Invisibly sustained by data systems that trace and ticket every book, this kind of store has wiped out all trace of bookish secrecy – and of bookish shame. Indeed, the cleanest, best-lit bookstore I know gives shape to a Utopian vision of enlightenment even in its architecture. The pioneering Finnish architect Alvar Aalto designed the Academic Bookshop in central Helsinki. Vast and airy, clinically stylish and formidably stocked, it feels like a well-scrubbed hospital where no one ever cries or dies. Here stands a Nordic democratic dream in strict subject order. And only an oddball or outcast could object . . .

I suspect that shame and secrecy still nurture many great readers – and, possibly, a few great writers too. No bookshop has ever picked an apter name than the much-loved London science-fiction specialist Forbidden Planet. Without the faint odour of forbidden fruit, bookshops can flourish as spotlit temples of education and recreation. But can they alchemize the furtive browser into the addicted reader and (perhaps) the committed writer? It could be that, from now on, the murky recesses and concealed shelves in the infinite warehouses of Amazon, Google and other sites will take on the bookshop's role. It could be that, apart from a handful of mavericks and throwbacks, those bookshops that survive will exhibit only the solid civic merits that public libraries once did. The figure of the mad bookseller will vanish from our cultural lexicon. Literary outcasts will now meet, and hunt, online. Even Forbidden Planet itself has morphed into a thriving, spotlit chain with a vast array of non-book merchandise: model superheroes, DVDs and toys from outer space.

That loss of a space for creative shame would be itself a shame. Browsers may skulk around bookshops, as I did, in search of absent or unformed parts of themselves. But an obsession shared can be an obsession, not cured, but socialized. Years ago, before its literary festival had established Hay-on-Wye in the Welsh borders as a Whitsun playground for the well-mannered reading classes, I once travelled more than 300 miles in a day to browse, quite uselessly, in the seething bookshops there. Before the photogenic chart-toppers and moralizing ex-presidents arrived, the town had a reputation only as the unholy shrine of demented bookishness. Here, in a string of raggedly converted cinemas, chapels and garages, the 'King of Hay', Richard Booth, had built his network of second-hand emporia.

So on that day I visited his kingdom with my girlfriend and our driver, her father, a teacher in a comprehensive school and lifelong communist, raised in the Jewish East End, who first taught me that book-devouring scholarship could happily live alongside both sociability and social conscience. We drove from Wembley to the Marches early one morning. We browsed and we bought: for me, a few tattered novels; nothing fancy, nothing valuable. We had a drink in a low dark farmer-filled bar still years away from the gastropub it would later become. And in the evening we returned from Hay's forbidden planet of books, secure in our pact of pedants against a disdainful world. It was a shamefully wasted day. It was a perfect day.

Listening to the kids learn about Angry Arthur, and about how anger can boomerang to knock out its generator, it is hard to imagine they will ever see bookshops as anything other than the homes of sweetness and light. If, that is, such stores survive in the age of high-definition, hand-held electronic readers. If not, then the search for a perfect work to download will transform the culture of browsing, just as much as the iPod has with recorded music. For now, the bookshop still feels like a semi-public place for unruly private impulses, and so the site of inextricably mixed feelings where thrills can fuse with guilt and serenity with shame.

A short walk away from this particular shop is a well-known pub where, half a century ago, there took place a much-mythologized crime of passion. Outside the Magdala, Ruth Ellis shot her abusive lover and so became the last woman ever to be hanged in Britain. True-crime bookworms may know that both her daughter and her sister have published their accounts of Ruth's life and death, but for many the case survives in the second of two movies made from it: *Dance with a Stranger*. Since the 'Forbidden Planet' franchise is taken, this would be my preferred name above the door if I ever ran a bookshop. In a good bookshop, you should always dance with a stranger. And that stranger is yourself.

Julian Barnes

The Case of Inspector Campbell's Red Hair

Novelists vary in how much, and how soon, they need to 'see' their characters. Some work 'outside in', unable to begin without a full physical presence; others (like me) tend to work 'inside out', starting from functional or moral significance. In the latter case, a character may be active in a novel without yet having a settled outline; then, at some point – even, with a minor figure, fairly late in the writing – the question of appearance needs attending to. Hair colour? Eyes? Stooping or erect of carriage? And so on.

How you make the reader see the character is a separate matter. A great portrait drawing – by Ingres, say, or Schiele – usually contains far fewer marks on the paper than we imagine possible. Our eye completes that cheek, neck, forearm, in ways the artist silently compels. And it's the same with fiction. It would be disastrous (not that this deters some writers) to list all the physical attributes of a character. You need to provide enough for readers to complete the imagining themselves. Flaubert evokes Emma Bovary mainly through her extremities – feet, hands, eyes, tongue, hair – and by a constant touching of them seems to whip her into existence and action like a top. Ask two different readers what she looks like, and you will get Emmas of their separate contriving.

Further, what a writer knows – and needs to know – to imagine the character is not the same as what the reader needs. In a famous letter of 1866 to Taine about the creative process, Flaubert says,'There are many details that I do not write down. For instance, Homais as I see him is slightly pitted by smallpox. In the passage I am writing just now, I see an entire set of furniture (including the stains on certain items); but not a word will be said about all this.' Ironically, in the ten years since completing

Madame Bovary, Flaubert had slightly forgotten his own book: he had in fact mentioned Homais's pockmarks. The principle, nevertheless, remains true.

When real people are introduced into fiction, these ways of working must inevitably be ditched, both by the 'outside in' and, even more, the 'inside out' novelist. Appearance (and to some extent character) have already been determined and are often, if not always, verifiable. So how much do you describe these people who really existed? Can you assume readers might know already what a few of them looked like? Should you describe them in exactly the same way as you would with invented characters, thus signalling their absorption into the world of fiction? Or go to the opposite extreme and include pictures of them, both as a short cut and to emphasize their factuality? How truthful must you be, and how malleable are their personalities? Do you, as a novelist, have the same or a greater responsibility to characters who really existed?

Of course, you don't pose such questions as directly as this; but they hover around, nudging you from time to time. My novel *Arthur & George,* set mainly in 1903–7 and based on a miscarriage of justice in Staffordshire, is filled with real people. At first, this had certain advantages. The 'Arthur' was Arthur Conan Doyle; everyone knows who he was, and many know what he looked like. There are images of him from cradle to grave. If he had been lightly pockmarked, there would have been no keeping it to myself. His appearance was non-negotiable; thus he always wore a moustache, which I was therefore forbidden to shave off – at least, not without making my novel deliberately unreliable or fantastical. There are also many photographs of those close to Doyle: parents, first wife, second wife, children, friends, associates. So there was no trouble working out what they looked like. Or was there? Take the second wife, Jean Leckie. She is never photographed smiling, even on her wedding day. I showed her photograph to friends, and asked what they thought she might have been like (the printed record tends to be thin and uxorious). 'I wouldn't mess with *her*,' said one (a woman, by the way). But was she stern, or humourless, or unhappy – or just shy and unrelaxed? I referred the matter to a Doyle biographer, who suggested that she was quite possibly self-conscious about the size of her teeth. Presumably she smiled in private, away from the intrusive camera – and the intrusive novelist.

There is a tyrannous assertiveness, and selectivity, about photography: as if there were no other life away from the one it records. After Conan Doyle's death, one of his sons boasted to the *Daily Herald* that 'there never had been greater lovers' than his parents. Even after twenty years, he filially blabbed, his mother, on hearing her husband return to the house, 'would jump up like a girl and pat her hair and run to meet him'. Such behaviour seems untypical – out of apparent character for the rather sombre, matronly figure who presented herself to the camera in later years. You find yourself trying to image-morph an uncooperative photograph. Is this how she would have smiled? How girlish did she become? And exactly how did she raise those stolid hands when patting her hair? This can feel harder than making it all up in the first place.

The photographic record on George's side of the story is much sketchier. There are perhaps half a dozen images of him, and none from his childhood. So George Edalji exists – that's to say, can be physically corroborated – from the age of about twenty to sixty. In other words, from the time he was – or was about to become – a young solicitor charged with a heinous crime, to when he was an old, white-haired, exonerated solicitor. A photographic record which would have been looked at by many with one question in mind: is, or was, this man innocent or guilty? And the awareness of such public judgement presumably affected how George sat for some of these pictures. Did he think about this? Did he try to look 'more' innocent? He too never smiles.

With George there was a further problem which pressed more directly on the novel. Several early readers asked me, 'Just out of interest, how dark-skinned was George?' It is a pertinent question, both for a reader trying to imagine a character and because the Edalji case turned on a largely unvoiced racial prejudice. The best answer I could give was a feeble 'I don't really know.' George's father was a Parsee (a light-skinned race), his mother Scottish. Old black-and-white photographs are unreliable indicators of skin colour. In some, George looks quite 'Hindoo', as local newspapers chose to describe him. But there is also an extraordinary photo – taken surreptitiously, and against court rules – of him in the dock at Stafford Assizes, leaning forward and listening intently to the evidence (or perhaps even the verdict). Behind him stands a uniformed policeman, also leaning forward attentively. The officer is a little older than George; both of them wear moustaches; and both of them – it may be a trick of the light, or of photographic processing, or it may be true – have the same skin tone. The more I looked at this image, the more I thought that if you reversed the two men, then George, in uniform, would have looked a plausible Staffordshire copper, while the officer could well have passed for the defendant. So the final answer to 'How dark-skinned was George?' was perhaps the one most useful to a novelist writing a story involving prejudice, misreading and ambiguity: that George was as light or dark as whoever was looking at him wanted him to be at that particular moment.

Below the level of the eponyms and their immediate circles, the question of authentic likeness arose less urgently, and less predictably. So, the first scene that I drafted was a violent exchange that occurs towards the end of the novel between Conan Doyle and the Chief Constable of Staffordshire, Captain Anson. I needed this in place early, to lay down the novel's key arguments and lines of battle. I wrote twenty pages or so with the carefree swiftness (no, that's putting it mildly – the deluded joy) that often comes with finally getting down to work. I finished, read it through and realized that I couldn't possibly proceed to a next draft until I knew what Anson looked like – and for that matter, Anson's house, where the encounter took place.

It wasn't just that the Chief Constable was an important character – I knew that already; it was more that I couldn't properly animate a scene in which I knew precisely what one participant looked like but had no idea about the other. (Why was this not so rebukingly clear when I began that first draft? Partly sheer zeal. Partly because novel-writing isn't architecture: you don't make a plan and then build to it; sometimes you just build, and then the plan begins to suggest itself.) A few weeks later the archivist of the Staffordshire Constabulary assisted me with my enquiries, and laid out in front of me various images of the former Chief Constable.

This ought to have been a more straightforward moment than it proved. Yes, I now had Anson's likeness; but at the same time, I was barely able to look at it objectively. I had already written part of him, and more or less decided his moral function (establishment villain and devil's advocate). So his image confirmed my preconception: 'Oh, he looks just like the sort of man who . . .' In this I was about as fair-minded as the jury member who admits, 'I could tell he was guilty just as soon as he stepped into the dock.' Unjust, of course; though in the context of what my novel was about, not unfitting.

The archivist also showed me a group photograph of the Stafford force at around the time of the Edalji case, with Captain Anson sitting in the middle of the front row. The detectives wore suits and bowler hats; the policemen had brass-buttoned uniforms, peaked caps pulled down low and enormous moustaches. They looked to my eye suspiciously as if they might – just possibly – be riddled with institutional racism. Because of the occasion – and photographic exposure times – they were rigidly posed, as if bodying forth an inflexibility of mind and method. This corporate stiffness was confirmed and mocked by the little dog at Anson's feet, whose head was a subversive blur of movement. A corpulent figure sitting next to the Chief Constable was identified to me as Superintendent Barrett. He had only a tiny part in the novel, as the officer who made police objection to bail at the magistrates' court. It didn't matter what he looked like, but even so I noted him, and, when his moment came, described him as accurately as a single photograph allows.

The most important character for whom I had no visual evidence – he wasn't in the Stafford line-up – was a certain Inspector Campbell. He was less important than Anson in the novel, though far more substantial than Barrett. He was also, in my book, the cleanest of the investigating officers (though not exactly impeccable). Obviously, he would need a physical description at some point. I suppose I could have gone looking for a real one, but I felt I had reached the level of personnel where appearance could be decided by either documentation or invention. Something about Campbell – or about the way I wrote him – made me think of him as red-haired, and his at times ponderous approach to matters suggested him as being 'camel-headed' and 'long-backed'. I didn't come to this physique easily – nor did I press it – but I wanted a description which would make him stand out in the reader's mind.

I mention the physical side of things at such length because it is an analogue for the mental and moral side. As with appearance, so with biography. At first it seems that the more you know, the easier it must be. If this person had this mind and this temperament, and this is how he/she behaved in a known situation, then this is how he/she would behave in a fictional situation. But such knowledge swiftly becomes a hindrance: established fact and character box you in as a novelist, give you less room for manoeuvre. My two main characters illustrated this perfectly. Doyle was world-famous, inspected, biographed, autobiographed. George Edalji left few traces except in local newspapers, in Doyle's brief character-sketch of him and in his own solitary publication, *Railway Law for the 'Man in the Train'* (1901). With Doyle I knew inhibitingly much; with Edalji hardly anything. I even found myself reading through *Railway Law* – a sprightlier book than it might sound – looking for clues to its author's temperament.

With Arthur, I was constantly discarding, cutting him and his life down, deciding if I needed this incident, that characteristic; with George, I was constantly building him up, awarding him a childhood, imagining his relationships with parents and siblings, inventing his emotional life, wondering about his sexual life. With Arthur, it was a moment of relief and breakthrough when I found a vital area – vital to him but, more importantly, vital to me – which had never been described in any detail or properly accounted for: his nine-year relationship, during his first wife's long illness, with the woman who was to become his second wife. The novelist in me was delighted to discover that all their love letters had been destroyed, and the secret relationship (before marriage and respectability struck) airbrushed from family history: at last, the imagination was free. As it was most of the time with George. Here I was constantly extrapolating, making key decisions on what a biographer would find flimsy evidence. Even in the broadest terms, his inner life and temperament were unclear. A local newspaper, for instance, referred to him as looking confident and at ease during his trial; whereas Doyle, in his autobiography, characterized him as 'very shy and nervous'. Was the journalist or the novelist correct? Or were they (as I had the freedom to decide) both correct? Why not? One explanation could be that Arthur only met George after the latter's release from prison, and George could have lost his self-confidence during incarceration. Possible, yet not persuasive, since George had throughout his ordeal displayed great tenacity in trying to re-establish his name and credentials. A more convincing explanation might be that George was at ease in a legal setting (even an extreme one called the dock), where he understood the rules, yet rightly shy and nervous when confronted in tête-à-tête by the large and vastly famous Sir Arthur.

Just as fictional dialogue is quite different from theatrical dialogue (as many play-writing novelists have painfully discovered), so fictional facts are quite different from biographical or historical facts. Fictional facts can't just – or rather, shouldn't just – be themselves, with their own truth and virtue enough to sustain them. They must do extra work, advance things, thicken character. For instance, it is a well-known biographical fact that Conan Doyle went to the South African War: he set off as a doctor and a patriot; he returned to be a historian and propagandist. Any biographer will have to cover this over several pages. But my novel had little to do with Doyle's political and imperial views. So I could choose to ignore the episode completely, pass it by in a parenthesis, or see if closer examination might yield something to my purpose.

My novel is much concerned with Doyle's view of death, and with his spiritualist belief in the life thereafter. In his own account of the South African War I discovered a resonant fact with definite potential. One day, riding across the veld, Doyle came across the body of an Australian soldier, which he helped transport for burial. This fly-attended corpse of a man sent thousands of miles to die young in the cause of Empire did not disgust or depress Arthur. On the contrary, death in a 'fair fight' for a 'great cause' under a wide sky struck him as the best possible exit for a man. That he remembered this Australian soldier twenty-five years later in his autobiography struck me as significant. For him it was a brave imperial death. But perhaps, given its continuance in his memory, I would be justified in making it something more: a touchstone, a running reference point when he thought about mortality.

This in itself was promising, but not enough. Was there perhaps a broader use for South Africa? It struck me, when reading about Doyle, that though he was unequivocally a 'man's man' – loving sports, mechanical inventions, science, clubland, authorial camaraderie (and opposing female suffrage) – I couldn't see who his close male friends were. Did he have any? Further, though his attitude to women – formal, chivalrous, unintimate – was old-fashioned even for the period, his closest relationships were with his domineering mother, his invalid first wife and his second wife-in-waiting. I imagined him feeling enclosed and smothered by this to him unfathomable world, and yearning for manly simplicities. And so I decided to let him go to South Africa, not for the official biographical reasons, but as a cleansing masculine pause – filled with cricket, joshing and war – before plunging back into his fraught life among women.

Writing fact-based fiction you ideally need just enough to get your imagination going, not so much that you are constantly being issued with correctives from the 'real' world (though your own has become the more real by now). George was perfect in this respect, while the red-haired and camel-headed Inspector Campbell was not far behind. Most of his official actions, and some of his words, in the Edalji case are recorded. But for a character in a novel, this left much to be filled in. What was he thinking and feeling through the case? How much did he suspect George on his own account, rather than on Anson's instructions? What family, if any, did he have? And might there be something in his life – that's to say, something I could invent – which might have had a particular impact on the case? I blocked out a back-story. Useful, I thought, to make him an outsider, so that he could discover and reflect upon rustic habits and backwardness, in parallel with the reader. I therefore had him start work in Birmingham, then move to Staffordshire on the plea of his wife, who wanted to return to where she had grown up. I also made him a modern, professional policeman, sceptical equally of Anson's upper-class autocracy and the low level of intellect and efficiency of the typical Staffordshire copper. Yes, that was the sort of Inspector Campbell I needed.

The main problem of incorporating a large number of characters with a greatly varying factual-fictional mix into the same novel is making sure they end up with the same plausible density and the proper specific gravity. There are also countless joins to cover up where fact meets fiction: you begin to imagine the reader as a Holmesian figure, knocking on the wainscot, hunting suspiciously for a panel with the wrong echo. Everything must have the same solidity. But from early on, and despite the fact that I had found the story elsewhere, it became jealously mine; the characters likewise. I did not want to go against known fact – except in minor instances – but my responsibility to these 100-year-old originals became a responsibility to what I was using them for. I was selfishly relieved that neither George nor his sister Maud had any direct descendants; also that the Doyles, though more procreative, had offspring who were much scattered (none of Arthur's five children produced any in their turn). It's sometimes helpful to anticipate comeback to what you are writing; though here, my portrayal of both Arthur and George seemed to me sympathetic and true. (Possible comeback from hardline Sherlockians was another matter: I imagined one or two of them finding lèse-majesté in a scene involving Arthur's under-linen.) I certainly don't recall specifically asking myself whether I had any responsibility to the descendants of the originals in my novel. If you had pressed me on that, I would probably have argued either from high principle – the art of fiction takes its stories where it finds them, and then moulds its characters according to its own purposes and needs – or from low practicality: it's extremely unlikely that any grandchildren or great-grandchildren of characters in the novel will pick it up. And if they do, so what? It's fiction, not biography or history.

As you can hear, there's an element of special pleading in this. There often is when you write a novel, just to get it written. You submit to the ruthlessness of the idea, and then you try to have things both ways – indeed, every way you can. For instance, I once or twice toyed with changing some of the policemen's names. If I couldn't be sure that Sergeant Upton was as coarse and bigoted as I had made him, perhaps I should call him something different. He's dead, and can't answer back (or, happily, sue). But then, if I am keeping Anson's name, he being the exemplar of high social and police prejudice, why should I not retain Upton's name, he being the exemplar of lower social and police prejudice? And otherwise, I'd have policemen with their own names talking to superiors or subordinates operating under pseudonyms. That would be peculiar, and downright unreliable.

In all my research for *Arthur & George,* I at no point had a sniff of anyone who had ever met George. After his case ended in 1907, he more or less vanished from public view, even though he lived another forty-six years. (I remember my sense of shock when first realizing that his life had overlapped with mine – and that, with thirty or so miles separating us, I might conceivably have set unknowing eyes upon him.) But a few weeks after the novel came out, I received a letter from a woman who, as a fifteen-year-old in 1939, had been evacuated to Welwyn Garden City. She and a friend had been placed for a few weeks into the household of Maud Edalji. Maud, she told me, had talked freely about her life. 'Do you know Conan Doyle?' she had asked, 'He was very kind to us.' On another occasion, she said, gnomically as it then seemed to the teenaged girl, 'My brother has not had a happy life.' One day Maud took my correspondent to a room at the back of the house which George used as an office: 'Maud opened the door to show me her brother, and he looked up and acknowledged me.'

This ordinary – but to me, wonderful – moment, recalled sixty-five years on, struck me as a parallel to what I had been trying to do in the novel. I was taking you, the reader, into my house, looking after you for a few weeks, leading you to a back room, opening the door and saying, 'Look, here is George Edalji.' And George would look up and acknowledge you, and perhaps give you the smile he never gave the camera; he would look up at you from my pages, from his life, from the life I had created for him.

This incident made me feel strangely content as a writer, possibly a little self-satisfied. A few weeks later I found myself talking about *Arthur & George* at a book festival. Afterwards a man of about my age came up and handed me a business card. It said he was a science writer, and I assumed he was going to ask about Conan Doyle's involvement in psychical research. Instead, he began, 'Inspector Campbell was my grandfather.' Uh-huh – his expression was not that of someone come to congratulate. 'He didn't come from Birmingham, he didn't have red hair and he wasn't . . . camel-headed.' Oh dear, I thought, I can quite see how that might have been taken amiss. I didn't manage an immediate reply, largely because a cheerful 'Sorry about that' didn't seem to meet the case. 'But I suppose,' he went on, his tone now striking me as more actively resentful, '*he's your character now.*'

Our uneasy exchange left me wondering if I shouldn't have changed the Inspector's name. But I would still have ascribed the same actions to someone called Roberts or Wilson, a disguise easily penetrable. Should I have advertised in the Staffordshire press for personal details, a likeness, family anecdotes? Perhaps – except that I wasn't a biographer. Did I have any definable responsibility to this long-dead policeman who, as I pointed out to his grandson, was the most sympathetic member of the force in my novel? Or for that matter, to his descendants? Faced with the grandson's displeasure, I wondered if I had shirked some duty. But this was mainly a social response to a sticky moment. Later, reflecting on the exchange, the writer's response kicked in, one you may find narrowly selfish or artistically defiant (or both), according to your point of view: yes, actually, thank you very much, he *is* my character now.

Ma Jian

A Chinese Writer in London

In the novel I have just completed, a sparrow flies into a hospital room and lands on the body of a comatose patient. It makes its nest in the young man's armpit, and although free to return to its natural habitat, it chooses not to. As the years pass, the bird slowly loses its feathers and forgets how to fly. In the end all it can do is perch on the bed and imagine the world it had once known. When I sit down at my desk every day, I feel a similar sense of dislocation and enfeeblement. I live in London, in self-imposed exile, but my thoughts continually travel back to the country I've chosen to leave.

I first left China in 1987. My life in Beijing had reached a dead end. The authorities had singled me out for persecution, criticizing me for my bohemian, 'dissident' lifestyle and accusing me of 'spiritual pollution'. I was under constant police observation, and it became impossible for me to write in peace. So, with the help of some friends, I secured a passport and escaped across the border to Hong Kong. Shortly afterwards my first book, *Stick Out Your Tongue*, was attacked by the government, and a ban was placed on the future publication of my books in mainland China.

For the next ten years I lived in Hong Kong. It felt like China, but without the police. Although the main language there is Cantonese, enough people spoke Mandarin for me to feel at home. I had a close circle of friends – artists and writers from the mainland who, like me, had sought refuge in Hong Kong. My best friend was a long-haired poet who drank too much. I would listen to his drunken ravings as he lay on the beach outside my door, and at night I'd weave them into the novel I was writing about doomed love and reincarnation. When my writing reached an impasse, I'd jump on a train to China in search of ideas. (Although my books were banned and my movements were still monitored, I was now free to come and go as I wished.) I had my toe in China, but was no longer bound by its laws. I felt a sense of freedom I'd never enjoyed before.

When Hong Kong reverted to Chinese rule in 1997, this freedom seemed to suddenly vanish. I could feel the prison walls closing in again. I knew I had to leave. After a brief stint teaching Chinese literature at a German university, I moved to London. I soon discovered, however, that I had exchanged one kind of prison for another. Although I was free from any political persecution or interference, I had suddenly lost both the source of my inspiration and the means to communicate it. I spoke barely a word of English, and nothing I saw in the clean, orderly streets outside my window could be incorporated into my books. I was a writer without a voice or a home.

Cut off from the world I knew, my only choice was to retreat into my memories. I started writing *Red Dust*, an account of three years I spent in the mid-1980s travelling through the dusty hinterlands of China. I had never considered writing about this journey before – I wrote fiction, not travel books or autobiography. But living in London gave me the distance I needed to see this journey in a new light. I realized how important it had been to me, and to my understanding of China.

First, though, I needed a desk – the flat I was living in had only a bed and an upright piano. I picked up a piece of hardboard that I found lying in the street and perched it on a small fold-up table that I'd stolen from a tip. I squeezed this makeshift desk into the corner of my small bedroom, and pasted the wall above it with maps of China and old photographs that I'd taken during the journey. Before I sat down to write, I played tapes of Deng Lijun – a Taiwanese singer who was popular twenty years ago – and leafed through the random jottings in my old, dog-eared notebooks.

To write the book, I had to close my eyes and retrace the journey step by step. Sometimes I'd lie in bed and repeat out loud the conversations I'd had with people I'd met on the road – farmers, traders, migrant workers, Buddhist monks. I had to write the book in the present tense and forget that I was now living in London. When I went to buy a pint of milk from the local corner shop on the Harrow Road, in my mind I was still crossing the Gobi Desert or clambering up Mount Taishan. By the end of this imaginary journey, I was far more exhausted than I'd been when my original journey had reached its end. I'd not only had to travel into my past, but also try to make sense of it. When the book was finally finished, a year and a half later, I was so desperate to travel with my feet rather than my mind that I jumped on a coach to Edinburgh and trekked through the Scottish Highlands for a month.

When I returned to London, I set to work on a novel that I'd started in Hong Kong – the one about the comatose patient that I mentioned at the beginning. This proved to be a much more difficult task than *Red Dust*. All the material for *Red Dust* was locked in my memories, so I didn't need to travel further than my desk to write it. But fiction is a different matter. I wouldn't enjoy writing fiction on a desert island – I like to be in the thick of things. Every day I need to see, hear, smell and touch things that fire my imagination. I need to speak with the people that I write about, and walk the same streets that they do. In London the characters that I'd created in Hong Kong became silent, black-and-white images. I could no longer hear them speak, or have a conversation with them.

By then I had moved into a flat further down the Harrow Road. The area was much rougher, but the flat was twice as large, so I now had a study to myself. I tried to create a 'Little China' inside my new room. I installed a satellite television and kept it tuned to CCTV, the only station broadcast from mainland China, so that I had a constant background noise of Mandarin Chinese. I covered my walls with bookshelves, and filled them with all the Chinese books that for years I'd had to store in boxes. I spent hours on the telephone to family and friends in China, and latched on to any new Chinese acquaintances I made in London, inviting them round to my flat as soon as I'd met them, as though we were long-lost friends. When an English friend of mine told me that a woman he'd met in Liverpool came from my hometown in China, I asked for her number, phoned her up and begged her to come and visit me next time she was in London. Whenever I passed a Chinese person on the street, I had to stop myself from running up to them, flinging my arms around them and dragging them back home with me.

One advantage of living in London was that I was able to form a clear picture of the political and social background of the book. The comatose patient in the novel is a student who was injured in the Tiananmen Massacre; his mother is a member of the outlawed Falun Gong sect. Since both the massacre and the sect are taboo subjects in China, it would have been very difficult to research these topics in Beijing. In London I had access to books and internet sites that are banned in China, and was able to speak freely with political activists who wouldn't have dared talk to me in the mainland.

After a year of hard work, I'd provided the book with a political context, but had failed to bring the characters to life. It was time for me to go back to China. I flew to Beijing and rented from a friend a small flat in a compound of red-brick buildings. It was the kind of flat that everyone in Beijing used to live in, until the concrete tower blocks started springing up everywhere a few years ago. As soon as I walked through the door, I knew that I'd found the home for my main character. It was a dark, one-bedroom flat with bare concrete floors and just a bed, a sofa and a television. The damp quilts on the bed had belonged to my friend's grandmother. The cupboard in the hallway was crammed with bottles of pills for illnesses that no one had contracted. The calendar hanging in the grimy bathroom was ten years old. When I opened the window to let in some air, I could smell the oil frying in the restaurants below and the sour pollution wafting from a nearby factory. Once I knew where my main character lived, everything else fell into place.

I walked through the dusty alleys of Beijing and felt exhilarated. There was a beauty to even the ugliest things: the cabbage leaves rotting in the gutters, the mounds of rubble outside demolition sites. Behind the stench from the public latrines, I could smell jasmine growing in a hidden courtyard. I stopped at a street corner and chatted with women who sold fried dough sticks. I lingered at a bus stop to listen to people complaining about the heat and the dust. When I finally jumped on a bus and heard a conductress shriek at the passengers in a coarse Beijing dialect, I was so happy that I laughed out loud. Like the character in my book, I felt that I too was waking from a long coma. I wrote more in my first month in Beijing than I had in a year in London.

But slowly my mood started to change again. I became frustrated at being cut off from the rest of the world. I couldn't access the BBC website, or search controversial subjects on Chinese Google. When I sent an email that contained the word 'freedom', my computer mysteriously crashed. The police visited a friend of mine and demanded that he give them my mobile phone number. Each morning, before I sat down to write, I'd lock the front door and draw the curtains. I felt I was committing a crime. So it was with relief that I boarded my plane back to London a few months later, and returned to my flat off the Harrow Road. But, inevitably, hardly a week had gone by before I was traipsing off to London's Chinatown. I'd told myself that I needed to buy some sesame-seed oil, but my real reason for going was just to see some Chinese faces.

Today the communist government is a much more sophisticated organization than it was during the time of Chairman Mao. It knows that to silence writers it disapproves of, it doesn't need to execute them or fling them in jail. All it has to do is slowly and subtly increase the pressure until they have no choice but to run away. The Party has discovered that there is no better way to punish Chinese dissident writers than to force them into exile.

Ursula Holden

(b. 1921), author of twelve novels, looks back over her life as a writer

Write at Your Peril

Writing for me is an addiction that I compare to a monkey on my back. It gives me no peace unless I feed it a daily dose of words.

I didn't begin trying to write until 1962, when I was in my early forties. Until then I had only dreamed about it. Paul Sheridan, the teacher at a local creative-writing class, encouraged me, stressing the need for daily application. 'A degree of talent is needed, but as with dancers or musicians there is no substitute for daily practice.'

He advised the class to look on ourselves as professionals from the start, however unlikely that might seem. If we didn't take our work seriously, why should anyone else?

For the next twelve years rejections from editors slithered through my letter box. My first novel went to over forty publishers without success. My second was luckier. *Endless Race* was accepted by Carcanet Press and reached the catalogue stage in the publishing process, but lack of money prevented it from going into print. I tried to sublimate my disappointment by working at my next book with a sharper edge. The late Alan Ross of *London Magazine* was then publishing a few books in hardback. He took on *Endless Race*, followed by *String Horses*. I could look on myself as a real writer at last.

I took a risk and left my part-time job at the library to write full-time. Writing for a living is at best precarious, especially for writers of literary fiction. Good reviews don't sell books. The novelist Barbara Comyns used to say that money earned from writing should be looked on as fairy gold. If you rely on it, it may melt in your hands.

In the past I had worked at many unskilled jobs. Stacking the

305

shelves, caring for the elderly, child-minding, a lot of babysitting, life-class modelling and typing. Ernest Hemingway used to say that writers should aim at working late shifts. 'Let the employer have you after you are tired from your own work.'

Sometimes I used to rise at 3 a.m. to write, away from the demands of home and family. I worked in a room where we had a cage full of gerbils. I had been feeding them when the postman brought a letter from my agent, John Johnson. 'I think you have written a good novel and I hope to get it published.'

In my euphoria I left the cage door open and our ginger cat, James, got inside. He scratched and growled, I couldn't get him out. The noise, my daughter's screams and the blood were awful. I managed at last. Our best gerbil was chewed and dead. The mother ate her babies after that. We gave the rest away. All of that could be seen as a portent of my life ahead.

If asked for advice for aspiring writers I tell them to keep their health and keep going. Remember that you are your first reader and your first critic. Be ruthless. Beware of who you ask for a comment. Friends will nearly always lie. Mockery and discouragement from friends and relatives can be hard, but there is nothing to equal the joy of an editor's acceptance of a sustained piece of work. I need to rewrite copiously and to trust my inner guide, whom I liken to a fierce old person deep in my psyche who never stops writing.

I have a tiny shed which I call 'Enigma' at the end of my yard where I work in good weather. I keep a piece of dead tree root from Ireland, shaped a bit like a fox, which is a talisman. (I am partly Irish and have always been drawn to Irish writers. I mourn the death of John McGahern, who was, I think, without equal. I admire Colm Toíbín, Bernard MacLaverty, and the recent novels of Sebastian Barry, not to mention James Joyce and others long gone.) I love looking on to a thicket of greenery, away from the telephones and doorbells. I take off watches and rings before I work, to aid my isolation from reality. One summer a blackbird used to come and feed beside me. I was sad when it died.

Interest in my novels died in the early nineties. A few short stories and some non-fiction have found favour since, and I have just finished some recollections of my wartime years. But the urge to write fiction has gone.

I think that writers need a skin like leather, while maintaining great sensitivity towards others, in order to survive the setbacks. I try not to scatter words carelessly on the page but to treat them with respect. They are our only tools. In the same way that a carpenter uses nails, each word matters. Our world is bombarded with words on paper and on screens, much of which is of scant value. 'Less is more' is a good motto for me.

I don't often attend literary gatherings. Jealousy, arrogance and waspishness can flourish in such groups, which doesn't help the work. I think it masks the extreme vulnerability that we want to conceal. I remember saying, rather pretentiously, 'We walk with the gods,' to Dermot Bolger, the Irish writer. I might have added, 'Whom the gods love they punish.'

The monkey on my back retains its grasp. You can't kill Hope, that treasure at the bottom of Pandora's box: I don't regret the life I chose.

Biographical Notes

Moniza Alvi was born in Pakistan and grew up in Hertfordshire. She has published five books of poetry, including a compendium collection, *Carrying My Wife* (Bloodaxe, 2000), and *How the Stone Found Its Voice* (Bloodaxe, 2005). She received a Cholmondeley Award for poetry in 2002.

Julian Barnes is the author of nine novels, including *Metroland, Flaubert's Parrot, A History of the World in 10½ Chapters, England, England* and *Love, etc*, and two collections of short stories, *Cross Channel* and *The Lemon Table*.

Richard Beard is the author of four novels, most recently *Dry Bones* (Secker), and two sports-travel books with Yellow Jersey Press. He lives in Strasbourg.

Wayne Burrows's first collection, *Marginalia*, was published by Peterloo Poets in 2001, and his work featured in *New Writing 12* (Picador, 2004). He recently completed *The Protein Songs*, a sequence about genetics for use in Retina Dance Company's *Eleven Stories for the Body*, which toured the UK and Europe in 2005–6. He is currently editor of *Staple* magazine and lives in Nottingham.

Jacqueline Crooks was born in Jamaica and grew up in London. She has an MA in Creative & Life Writing from Goldsmiths College. She runs creative-writing mentoring projects for young people. She has completed a collection of linked short stories and is now working on a novel.

Andrew Crumey has a PhD in theoretical physics and is the author of five novels, including *Mobius Dick* and *Mr Mee*. He is a former literary editor of *Scotland on Sunday*, and in 2006 he won the Northern Rock Foundation Writer's Award. He lives in Newcastle upon Tyne.

Selma Dabbagh is a British Palestinian writer whose work has appeared in *Qissat: Short Stories by Palestinian Women* (ed. J. Glanville, Telegram) and in the *Fish* anthologies of 2004 and 2005, which comprise the winning entries to the Irish publisher's International Short Story Competitions. She was English PEN's nominee for International PEN's David T. K. Wong Prize 2005.

Born in 1962, **Kwame Dawes** is the author of twenty-one books of poetry, fiction, theatre and criticism. His most recent collections are *Impossible Flying* (2007) and *Wisteria* (2006). His non-fiction books include *Bob Marley: Lyrical Genius* (2003) and *A Far Cry from Plymouth Rock: A Personal Narrative* (2007). He is the winner of the Forward Poetry Prize and the Pushcart Prize. He is the Distinguished Poet in Residence at the University of South Carolina. Dawes is the programmer for the Calabash International Literary Festival.

Anita Desai was born and educated in India. She is the author of several novels, of which three, *Clear Light of Day*, *In Custody* and *Fasting, Feasting,* were shortlisted for the Booker Prize. *In Custody* was filmed by Merchant Ivory Productions. She is a Fellow of the Royal Society of Literature and of the American Academy of Arts and Letters. She is an Honorary Fellow of Girton College and Clare Hall, Cambridge University, and an Emeritus Professor of the Humanities at the Massachusetts Institute of Technology.

Helen Dunmore is a poet, novelist, short-story writer and writer for children. She won the inaugural Orange Prize for Fiction for her novel *A Spell of Winter*. Her latest novel is *House of Orphans* (2006). The second volume in the 'Ingo' series of novels for children, *The Tide Knot*, was also published in 2006. A new collection of poems, *Glad of These Times*, was published in spring 2007. Helen Dunmore is a Fellow of the Royal Society of Literature.

Robert Ewing is a thirty-four-year-old GP living in Edinburgh. In the past year his fiction has appeared in *Northwords Now*, *Chapman*, *Libbon* and on BBC Radio Scotland. He is currently working on a novel set in the Scottish Highlands and London during the Victorian era.

Lucy Eyre grew up in London and currently lives in Addis Ababa, Ethiopia. Her first book, *If Minds Had Toes*, published in January 2007, is a philosophical romp. She is currently working on her second novel, about foreigners in Ethiopia.

Lisa Fugard grew up in South Africa. She is the author of *Skinner's Drift*, a novel. Her many travel articles and essays have been published in the *New York Times*.

Alasdair Gray, a Glaswegian, was born in 1934 and has written, designed and illustrated several books. His novel, *Men in Love*, will be published in 2007 by Bloomsbury.

Tod Hartman was born in 1978. He studied literature before training as an anthropologist and working in Romania. He is currently a member of the Department of Social Anthropology at Cambridge, and has carried out ethnographic studies on various different topics: shopping at Ikea, migrant labourers in the Spanish greenhouse industry, and the 'new rich' in Eastern Europe. A novel drawing on the latter theme is underway.

Ursula Holden was born in Dorset, one of five children, in 1921. She lived in Egypt until she was almost three. She didn't shine at school in Bognor Regis, except in poetry. During the war she served in the Women's Royal Naval Service. She has three children and has published twelve novels. She lives in London.

Sarah Hymas lives in Lancaster. She writes short stories as well as poems, and collaborates and performs with a musician. She also works as a publishing development manager and tutor. 'A Wise Man' is from a sequence spanning 100 years of a family and its building business.

Moses Isegawa was born in Uganda in 1963. In 1990 he left the country for the Netherlands. In 2000 he published *Abyssinian Chronicles*, which was well received and went on to be published in seventeen countries. In 2004 *Snakepit* appeared, which has been published in nine countries. At the moment he is in Uganda, where he is working on his new novel.

Ma Jian is the author of *Red Dust*, which won the Thomas Cook Travel Award, *The Noodle Maker* and *Stick Out Your Tongue*. He was born in Qingdao, China, in 1953 and moved to Hong Kong in 1986, shortly before his novels were banned in China. After the handover he moved to London, where he now lives.

Anthony Joseph is a Trinidadian-born poet, novelist and musician. He is the author of two poetry collections, *Desafinado* (1994) and *Teragaton* (1997). In 2004 he was selected by the Arts Council of England for the historic 'Great Day' photo as one of fifty Black and Asian writers who have made major contributions to British literature. His new book, *The African Origins of UFOs*, is published by Salt Publishing.

Jason Kennedy lives in the mountains of Guatemala. He is a graduate of the Performance Writing course at Dartington College of Arts, Devon, and was previously active in underground publishing, producing *Finest Mexican Engineering* and *Pinhut Enterprises*. A collection of his monologues, *Heaven is Hairless*, was performed at the Burton Taylor Theatre in Oxford in 1997. He maintains an online journal at www.bookarmor.com.

Accepting the injustice of a childhood without a Muslim School of Rock, but still bitter, **Rahat Kurd** began writing *The Zealot in the Mirror: A Memoir of Modest Appearances* in 2003. She lives in Vancouver, Canada.

Born in England, **Charles Lambert** studied English at Cambridge and now lives in Fondi, near Rome. A language teacher and freelance editor for international agencies, his academic translations, including work by Umberto Eco, have been published worldwide. His short story 'The Scent of Cinnamon' published in *One Story*, has been nominated for a 2007 O. Henry Prize in the US. His debut novel, *Fern Seed*, will be published by Picador in 2008.

Doris Lessing was born in 1919 in Persia, now Iran. She grew up in Southern Rhodesia, now Zimbabwe, and arrived in England in 1949. Her first novel, *The Grass is Singing*, was published in 1950. She is now regarded as one of the most important post-war writers in English. A Companion of Honour and a Companion of Literature, she has been awarded the David Cohen Memorial Prize for British Literature and Spain's Prince of Asturias Prize, as well as a host of other prestigious international awards. She has been short-listed for the Booker Prize three times and was nominated for the Man Booker International Prize 2005. Her most recent novel, *The Cleft*, was published by Fourth Estate in 2007. She lives in London.

Rob A. Mackenzie published a poetry pamphlet, *The Clown of Natural Sorrow*, with HappenStance Press in 2005. One of his poems was commended in the UK National Poetry Competition 2005. He is currently living in Edinburgh and he blogs at http://robmack.blogspot.com.

Adam Marek was born in 1974. His stories have appeared in *Prospect* magazine, *Parenthesis* (Comma Press), the Bridport Prize anthology, and on line at www.pulp.net. He has recently completed a collection of short stories and is working on a novel.

Karen McCarthy has presented her work at a variety of venues, including the Barbican, South Bank Centre, Bath Literature Festival and the International Festival of Women in Slovenia. Her poetry is published in books, magazines, in the London Underground and on a bottle of single-malt whisky. Spread the Word published her chapbook, *The Worshipful Company of Pomegranate Slicers*, to conclude her residency there in 2005. She is a contributing editor at the literary journal *Wasafiri* and has edited two critically acclaimed anthologies, *Bittersweet: Contemporary Black Women's Poetry* (Women's Press, 1998) and *Kin* (Serpent's Tail, 2004).

Jane McKie, originally from Sussex, now lives in Scotland with her husband and daughter. She has had poems published in *Island Magazine*, *New Writing Scotland*, *The Red Wheelbarrow*, *Other Poetry* and *Pennine Platform*, and has a first collection coming out in 2007 called *Morocco Rococo* (Cinnamon Press).

Sharmistha Mohanty is the author of *New Life*, a novel published in 2005 by India Ink/Roli Books. Her translations of Tagore, *Broken Nest and Other Stories*, will appear in 2007. She is currently at work on a new novel and a book of prose texts. Mohanty attended the graduate programme in fiction at the Iowa Writers' Workshop in the United States. She lives in Bombay and is editor of Almost Island, a forthcoming web journal of literature.

Nii Ayikwei Parkes is a writer, socio-cultural commentator and advocate for African writing. He was a 2005 Associate Writer-in-Residence on BBC Radio 3 and is the author of three poetry pamphlets and several short stories. Currently he is working on two novels and a collection of poetry.

M. R. Peacocke lives on a small farm in Cumbria and is working on a fourth collection of poetry which will be published by Peterloo Poets in 2008.

Kate Rhodes was born in London in 1964. Her first collection of poems, *Reversal*, was published by Enitharmon in 2005 and her second collection, *The Alice Trap*, will be published in 2008. She teaches English for the Open University and is currently working on her first novel.

Robin Robertson is from the north-east coast of Scotland. His most recent book is a selection of free English versions of poems by Tomas Tranströmer, *The Deleted World*. He has received numerous awards for his work, and his third book of poetry, *Swithering*, recently won the 2006 Forward Prize for Best Collection.

Sue Rullière lives in East Lothian, Scotland. One of her short stories has been read on BBC Radio 4; others have won prizes in regional competitions and have appeared in literary magazines and anthologies. Her first novel, *Cinema Blue*, will be published in 2008.

Kerri Sakamoto is a Toronto-based writer of novels, screenplays and essays on visual art. Her first novel, *The Electrical Field*, received the overall Commonwealth Prize for Best First Book and the Canada–Japan Literary Award. Her most recent book is *One Hundred Million Hearts*.

Fiona Sampson is the author of fourteen books, of which the latest are The *Distance Between Us* (Seren, 2005) and *Writing: Self and Reflexivity* (Macmillan, 2005). *Common Prayer* is forthcoming from Carcanet in 2007. Her awards include the Newdigate Prize. 'Trumpeldor Beach' was shortlisted for the 2006 Forward Prize. She is the editor of *Poetry Review*.

Sudeep Sen is the 2004 recipient of the prestigious Pleiades honour for having made a 'significant contribution to modern world poetry'. He was also awarded a Hawthornden Fellowship in the UK and nominated for a Pushcart Prize in the US for poems included in *Postmarked India: New & Selected Poems* (HarperCollins). His recent books include *Prayer Flag*, *Distracted Geographies* and *Rain*. Sen was an international poet-in-residence at the Scottish Poetry Library in Edinburgh, and a visiting scholar at Harvard University. He is the editor of *Atlas* and editorial director of AARK ARTS. www.sudeepsen.net

Henry Shukman's collection *In Dr No's Garden* was a Book of the Year in *The Times* and the *Guardian*, and won the Aldeburgh Poetry Prize in 2003. He has also won the *Daily Telegraph* Arvon Poetry Prize, and his poems have appeared in the *Guardian*, *The Times*, *Daily Telegraph*, *Independent on Sunday*, *Times Literary Supplement*, *London Review* of *Books* and *New Republic*. He has worked as a travel writer and a trombonist.

John Siddique is the author of *The Prize* (Rialto), *Poems from a Northern Soul* (Crocus Books), *Don't Wear It on Your Head* –

Poems for Young People (Peepal Tree) and the editor of *Transparency* (Crocus Books) and co-author of *Four Fathers* (ROUTE). He gives readings, mentors and teaches creative writing in the UK and abroad. www.johnsiddique.co.uk

Catherine Smith's pamphlet *The New Bride* was shortlisted for the Forward Prize Best First Collection 2001. Her first full collection, *The Butcher's Hands*, was a PBS recommendation. In 2004 she was voted both one of the top ten women poets to have emerged in the past ten years by *Mslexia* magazine and one of the top twenty 'Next Generation' poets by the PBS/Arts Council. Her latest collection, *Lip*, will be published by Smith Doorstop in 2007.

Saradha Soobrayen received an Eric Gregory Award for Poetry in 2004. She facilitates poetry workshops and mentoring for writers across London. She is the poetry editor of *Chroma: A LGBT Literary Journal*. Her poems are published in *This Little Stretch of Life* (Hearing Eye) and *I am Twenty People!* (Enitharmon).

Jean Sprackland's second book of poems, *Hard Water* (Cape, 2003), was shortlisted for both the T. S. Eliot Prize and the Whitbread Poetry Award. A new collection will be published by Cape in autumn 2007.

Zoë Strachan was born in 1975 and grew up in Kilmarnock, Scotland. Her novels *Spin Cycle* and *Negative Space*, which won a Betty Trask Award and was shortlisted for the Saltire First Book of the Year Award, are published by Picador. She has also written for radio and contributed short stories and extensive journalism to various magazines and newspapers, and is currently working on her third novel, *Play Dead*.

Boyd Tonkin is literary editor of the *Independent*. Before joining the newspaper he wrote for the *Observer*, and was literary editor of the *New Statesman* and features editor of *Community Care* magazine. He has judged the Booker Prize, the David Cohen Prize and the Commonwealth Writers' Prize, and re-founded the

Independent Foreign Fiction Prize. Books to which he has contributed range from the *Oxford Good Fiction Guide* to *Reading the Vampire Slayer*.

Fiona Ritchie Walker is from Montrose, Scotland, and now lives in north-east England. She writes poetry, short stories and plays. Her latest poetry collections are *Garibaldi's Legs* (Iron Press) and the chapbook *Angus Palette* (Sand), which is illustrated by her sister, Kirsten Ritchie Walker. www.fionaritchiewalker.co.uk

Gerard Woodward is a poet and novelist. His poetry has twice been shortlisted for the T. S. Eliot Prize, while his novels have been shortlisted for the Whitbread Award and the Booker Prize. He teaches creative writing at Bath Spa University and lives in Somerset. His third novel, *A Curious Earth*, will be published in 2007.

Robin Yassin-Kassab was born in west London to an English mother and a Syrian father. He was educated in Scotland and received a first in English from Oxford University. He has worked in journalism and taught English in Europe, South Asia and the Middle East. He currently teaches at a university in Oman. He is finishing his first novel.

Pam Zinnemann-Hope's poems have appeared in poetry magazines including *Stand* and *Poetry London*, in anthologies including *Why Does My Mum Always Iron a Crease in My Jeans?* (Puffin, 2005) and her 'Ned' books for young children were published by Walker in 1986. She is adapting *On Cigarette Papers* for the stage, with the support of industry professionals and a grant from ACESW. She founded and facilitates Poetry Dorchester.